W9-BAH-812

On Night's Shore

Also by Randall Silvis

Mysticus
Blood and Ink
Dead Man Falling
Under the Rainbow
An Occasional Hell
Excelsior
The Luckiest Man in the World

On Night's Shore

Randall Silvis

Thomas Dunne Books / St. Martin's Minotaur
New York

THOMAS DUNNE BOOKS.
An imprint of St. Martin's Press.

www.minotaurbooks.com

Production Editor: David Stanford Burr
Design by Heidi M. Eriksen
Illustration by Heidi M. Eriksen

ISBN 0-312-26201-9

First Edition: January 2001

10 9 8 7 6 5 4 3 2 1

This book,
every book,
every breath,
is for Rita and Bret and Nathan.

AUTHOR'S NOTE: *On Night's Shore* is a work of fiction. I have made every effort to remain true to the character of E. A. Poe and all other actual persons portrayed in this novel, and have striven to present an accurate picture of New York City in 1840, but I have on occasion been forced to choose between narrative unity and fidelity to chronological facts. In every case, story and drama won out over fact. The body of Mary Rogers, for example, was actually discovered in the Hudson River a year later than I have depicted here; the same holds true for the onset of Virginia Poe's tuberculosis. Also, although Poe resided in or near New York City at various times throughout his adult life, he was not to my knowledge living in New York City in the summer of 1840.

Finally, this book might never have been written were it not for the efforts of my agent, Peter Rubie, and my editor, Barry Neville. Every time I wanted to discard the idea, every time the research threatened to bury me, every time I longed to let the story die a silent death, Peter coerced, cajoled, and encouraged me to keep going. His and Barry's insightful remarks and suggestions helped in a significant way to create and shape this book. Thank you, gentlemen.

RS

On Night's Shore

1

THE BABY came sailing out of the window like a spider unwinding its silk, spinning down, slowly turning, an elegy in free fall.

It was one of those sights which, even as you watch, you do not see the horror of the madness. Otherwise you would turn away. Or maybe because the sun was in my eyes that afternoon and cast the baby as a silhouette on coral sky, no more startling at first than the black frown of a crow's wings. Or maybe because of the grace with which the infant fell, neither tumbling as you would think a baby might when thrown from thirty feet up nor undulating like a broad leaf but falling instead as a small shadow of negligible weight, a shadow drawn as we all are to the water, as if the river had been waiting there to catch the infant and carry it away, downstream and out to sea and into some vast and deep and swifter existence, a river positioned at the bottom of that moment like grief itself to swallow the child and the mother alike.

Or maybe the infant only appeared to fall so slowly because a baby tossed from a window does indeed represent the epitome of human madness, all of mankind's folly summed up in that brief descent, and so my mind to protect itself from too much recognition too soon slowed its intake of the world. I have come to believe since that day that bitter epigrams like this one are thrust before us from time to time, by whom or what I have ceased to speculate, but offered up on occasion for us to behold and consider, to remind us, warn us, prepare us for the life to come, the twisted road that lies ahead.

Or maybe I make too much of what was, simply, a flash of horror on a lugubrious day. Maybe I see the infant plummeting so slowly because this is the way an old man remembers the strike of lightning that came out of clear sky to change him as a boy.

IT WAS July 1840. I was approximately ten years old that summer. (My mother, when pestered into providing a year for my birth, might answer 1829, 1830, or 1831. When asked for a month she was even less precise, and invariably placed my birth date several months into the future. That is, if I asked in April, she said November; if I asked in November, she said March. In truth the event of my birth had left little impression on her, and her answers were calculated less to inform my curiosity than to silence it.)

But to July 1840. Another ship was easing toward the Battery, another boatload of wide-eyed immigrants, foreigners in rags or finery, exiles babbling or made mute by awe, but every last one of them an Ishmael come here to make a mark, leave some small impression on what they saw as a malleable world, a city that shone as brightly to their eyes as a new gold coin.

The immigrants were not overwhelmingly Irish yet, as they would be in less than a year, and so for a ten-year-old boy (to choose the average of the options provided) there was still some novelty in the approach of a ship, some excitement as I wondered what language I would dance to, what strange music of voice. I had picked up a few words here and there, enough to ask in pidgin German or Italian if the new arrival and his family needed a room, a place to stay, and by the accent of the answer I would know what kind of money to ask for when the cloud of confusion lifted from their eyes momentarily, to hold out my palm for lire or shillings or marks or guilders or tuppence.

"I'll run ahead and secure the room," I would say, and give a smile and a phony address before racing off with my day's wages, straight to the nearest money changer, who would then cheat me in turn.

Employment, therefore, my livelihood of fraud, was one of the reasons I was on the waterfront that afternoon. I was on the waterfront nearly every afternoon because it was my primary place of business, where the hoodwinking began, two steps off the gangplank. This was America after all and I believed the mythos too, I believed I had the sovereign right to lie and cheat in the service of self-improvement. Such was the precedent I observed in every direction; the road to greatness had been paved with dissimulation.

In those days there was more activity along the wharves and slips than there was on Wall Street and Broadway, and to a boy it seemed a more robust activity, more promising and salubrious, loud with the barked curses of stevedores climbing over and around the forest of barrels and crates and great heavy trunks—a forest that was built and dismantled and rebuilt daily. And in every trunk a treasure, or so I believed back then.

And when the activity of the docks slowed, there were other entertainments. In those days there were still lots of birds along the shore, not just the noisy gulls or boring ducks but more interesting birds as well, the slow and patient gangly bird I called a stork but found out later was a great blue heron, fascinating to me with its long snake's neck and pterodactyl wings. And the turkey buzzards that circled singly or in flocks as large as a dozen, those graceful dark vultures who gleaned the unpaved shores of every carcass left too long in the sun.

Nor was the wildlife restricted to the air. Sometimes I could hear wild turkeys gobbling from the New Jersey woods. Once, I watched the carcass of a white-tailed deer float by, a stag as bloated as the pigs' bladders some boys kicked across open fields. On occasion a yellow dog would trot past with a greasy wet rat clamped in its teeth. Or a red fox would streak about in a dither, trying to remember where it had hidden its burrow. Or a bandit-faced raccoon would squat at the water's edge and delicately rinse off some pilfered morsel.

Life came and went under the aegis of the river, was conveyed or halted at the river's discretion, was dragged under or floated into view, was nourished or destroyed. Whatever the outcome it was intriguing to me, I flinched from none of it, I took it all in precisely because I was a child and had not yet learned to fear too far into the future, still believed in the inevitability of change, the unavoidable prospect of good fortune.

The waterfront was a wild place born anew in the gray light of every dawn, and all the brighter because I was allowed to be wild in it. Like half the children in New York I seldom attended school, and then only in winter when I needed to warm myself for a few hours. And as long as I brought home a few pennies each night I could rest easy that my mother's threats to send me off to the House of Refuge would remain only that; I understood that she left the door unlatched each night in anticipation of my pennies rather than of me. There was currency then as now in both copper and flesh but less work involved in converting the former to victuals and drink. Yet there was some comfort too, albeit easily soured, usually soured, in knowing I had a dry corner to return to when too much darkness of one kind or another drove me off the streets and into the den of thieves I called my home.

It was this home that made the waterfront an Eden to me. How can I convey the scene of my residence politely, in a manner that will not offend? It was called the Old Brewery and it sat like a canker on Cross Street, midway between Pearl and Orange, the crowning insult to the squalor known as Five Points. Picture a tall and rambling building rotten in every board, and cram into it a thousand souls of every color and accent, every infirmity of body and spirit. All told, the place was too much for the senses.

Visually: the building and everything in it was layered over with a patina of shadow like a Rembrandt painting, but in this case the shadow was accumulated filth, every surface darkly reflective, but only because it was also greasy to the touch. Olfactorily: every breath drew rankness into the lungs, the sour smell of the brewery's former life ingrained in the wood, the effluvia of excrement and rum and vomitus and blood and tobacco smoke, the slaughterhouse reek of bodies that had lain in their rooms nearly to putrefaction before being buried beneath the dirt floor of the lower basement. These smells became a kind of gustatory experience as well, so that I spat a dozen times each morning on my way to the river, hawking up what I could of the night before. And finally there was the auditory assault: the wet, glutinous coughing that never ceased, the rattle of ossifying lungs, the breaking and smashing and poundings of a despair whose only release was in violence and violent fucking, the moans and sighs and curses and farts and the general bellicosity that passed in our building for polite conversation.

Here I lived in a single small room with my mother and a continuous parade of itinerant men whose names I never bothered to learn.

Small wonder then that to me the blunted tip of Manhattan was the most dynamic and potent part of the city, wide open and brightly lit. One day there might be a fire, and an entire block would vanish in a roar of flames and a mad spectacular swirling of sparks. Even a quarter of the city might disappear overnight, as in the fire of 1835, when nearly every building east of Broad Street was destroyed.

But fire was not the only agent of change. Just two years earlier the first foreign steamship, the *Sirius*, had docked in New York City. A day later the *Great Western* arrived. By 1840 most of the ships still came under sail or with auxiliary steam power but the ratio was closing daily, and that summer I could watch both kinds traversing the Hudson and East Rivers, the sailboats gliding by in full rigging, the steamships belching black smoke from their stout stacks, paddle wheels churning the water into a wide avenue of froth. This was change, the reach of civilization. The lurch of progress before my very eyes. And I, if only as spectator, penny-ante grifter, was a part of it all. How could I help but be emendatory about what I saw as a general elevation of mankind?

Even in what was typically a slow procession to port, spectacle was possible. In January the steamship *Lexington* burned and sank in Long Island Sound; one hundred and twenty lives were lost. But even those poor souls seemed less substantial to me than the cargo that washed ashore and barely had time to touch land before it was seized and rifled by scavengers. For a full month afterward I hawked copies of a print of the tragedy made by the lithographer Currier; sales were brisk, as they usually are for glimpses of disaster, and with my proceeds every afternoon I was able to buy myself a treat at Mead's Soda Water Shoppe and still have sufficient sedation in hand to quiet my mother's tongue and to keep the leather strap dangling cold from the peg beside her bed.

In calamitate, opportunitas. It wasn't the official motto of New York City in those unpredictable times, but it might as well have been. It was certainly my own.

With this hope, conceived of then in much simplified language, I awoke each morning. With luck I could rub the sleep from my eyes and grab my brogans and slip out of the room before my mother stirred. Across Little Water Street to Anthony, then north along Centre until I struck Franklin. A less than direct route to the Hudson, yes, but only by a couple of blocks. A diversion made twice daily, once going to the waterfront and once returning, in order that I might pass by the Tombs, that fortress of brick and stone and misery wherein I assumed my father resided.

I envisioned him then as a quiet man amidst the shrieks and curses, a man with powerful secrets he would someday bequeath to his son. And I intended to be there on the day he was released, on that morning or afternoon when a man with my eyes and my sidelong way of taking measure of the world would come striding out between the four front columns and down the steps to the sidewalk, perhaps blinking in the unenclosed brightness but wearing his own small smile, a knowing smile to be matched with my own. With a nod I would steer him away from the Old Brewery; he would know just by looking at me that we did not belong in that haven of vermin and vice; we had our own place to find, someplace downriver, westward, the two of us perched together on the bow of the roiling ship of progress.

And so I came daily to the waterfront, the west side this particular day, about midway between Rector Street and the Bowling Green. The Tombs to my rear, Castle Garden to my far left. There were many other people milling about along the streets at my back, I'm sure; there always were. Though not as many as you might expect, for in those days downtown was not the clamorous place it would all too soon become, not yet "one of the most rucketing cities in the world," as Washington Irving would describe it in just a few years.

On this Sunday afternoon, in fact, it, seemed to bear an air of tranquillity, of unhurried expectation. Picture a small southern port today, or a sleepy midsize town along the New England coast, and you will have the proper tone of Sunday life away from the docks. Now add, as you move farther inland, an ever stronger scent of horses, of leather and stables and those fine sweating animals pulling omnibuses and carriages and wagons along Broadway, the horses raising clouds of dust with every clopping step, or releasing their sour issues of piss and manure. And now you have the proper fragrance—which tells you, perhaps, why I preferred the squawk of gulls and the scent of moving water.

Altogether, then, this was the city of New York, soon to vie with Paris and London as the hub of the world but still overwhelmingly rural, bucolic as far north as Fourteenth Street, and beyond that not much more than swamp. A Victorian city replete with that uneasy duality of gentility and vulgarity, wealth and dire need, fine ladies daintily lifting their petticoats to step over gobs of tobacco spat upon the plank sidewalk.

But again, to the day in question. A fine July afternoon, midsummer, and as I've said a blue coral sky. A few mackerel clouds to the south but otherwise clear. I sat watching the slow progress of a double-masted ship tacking in. It was still a good ways out, not yet clear of Governor's Island; the dock workers hadn't yet appeared to stand ready at the slip.

And then, to my left, a splash. I saw the ripples only moments before they faded. Something small had broken the water just beyond the tongue of a pier but I could not see what it might have been, and there was no one standing nearby. But behind the pier, just a few yards off the water's edge, stood a brick warehouse that should have been empty. A fire a few weeks earlier had blown out the windows and blackened all the pediments; the building would soon be razed. And from an upper window somebody was leaning out, looking down to where the ripples sighed and broke and disappeared.

I put a hand over my eyes and tried to make out the figure. It was a woman, a girl not much older than me. She had tossed something small into the water. I know now that it was probably just a stone, something to test her throw, to gauge how far an object would carry. Far enough, it seemed. For within a minute she disappeared from the window, bent down, that is, and then rose into view again, but this time with a baby in her arms. It was dressed in white and pale blue, just like the sky. Its head was bare.

She hugged the infant to her shoulder, her cheek to the baby's head, and held it tight, rocking back and forth. I knew even then what she was about to do. It was as if the thing had already happened. I did not look around to see if anybody else was witnessing this, it did not seem to matter. I did not think to call out; words were of no consequence either. This thing was already done. I sat and watched.

She leaned out then, the window sash across her upper thighs. She leaned out as far as she could go without tumbling head over heels. Her arms extending down the face of the building formed a U, a cradle for the baby. She closed her eyes—though whether I was actually near enough to see this, I cannot say, but it is how I see it now—and for several seconds she did not move. And then with one smooth motion her arms swung outward, the half-arc of a pendulum's swing, and the baby sailed free and out against the coral sky, and down. In silhouette it seemed a falling crow, one wing bent, tucked, broken.

The splash had barely sounded before somebody screamed, some woman on the ground. Then voices shouting, men running hard across the pier, leaping into the river. I looked toward the warehouse again and the girl was standing on the window ledge, hands gripping the brick frame, leaning out. And then she too sprang into the sky. And what I remember now is the way her dress ballooned out around her slender legs, and how even as she fell, tilting sideways, she tried to hold the hem against her thighs, and the purling fluttering sound the fabric made, rippling like a torn kite, all the way to the water.

I remember too an odd intriguing lethargy to her descent, as if no string of time were attached to the desperate act, a slow sweet timeless fall in the form of a song I had once heard and just then remembered, a harmony of clouds and water and sky and she was the lyrics somebody had sung slightly out of tune, yet a haunting rasp of song all the same, a slave song, a prison song, this was how it affected me then and affects me still; it broke my heart and it lifted me up.

In less than two minutes they were dragged out of the water, first the girl and then the child, laid side by side atop a pier. I remember how when I stood and moved closer I saw the dark stain of water on the bleached wood and thought at first it must be blood. But it was only water. And just before they were carried away I saw the girl move; she raised a hand to shield her eyes, because she could not bear to see the sky or could not bear to be seen. The baby never stirred.

And I sat there for the longest time. The ship docked finally and its passengers disembarked but I did not go to it. What kept me still was not that I could not fathom what had made the girl decide to jump, I could, and too easily. But that her misery, whatever it was, reminded me of my own, and for a while I felt fully infected by her lethargy, I was rendered all but motionless, somehow damned by the failure of her act of absolution.

THEN CAME the early evening and the softening of light. I seemed to awake finally to recognize that the ship's passengers were gone, dispersed. So too my hope for income for the day. Until I remembered the girl's first offering to the Hudson. Again and again I replayed the simple action in my mind's eye, as if that initial toss might explain somehow what had followed.

I remembered the way the object had sparkled as it fell (or, after a dozen re-creations, I began to see it sparkling as it fell), a quick glittering tumble. It must have been a coin she threw, I told myself.

But wait—a coin? No; the more I thought about it the more I convinced myself that it had to have been some small thing of symbolic value, so that the toss became a gesture of dismissal, an act of closure, a way of saying *It's over, it's done*. The object could not have been anything as practical as a stone or as mundane as a coin. It must have been a small piece of jewelry. Maybe a ring? Of course! Wasn't that the cliché, the way all relationships ended? And wasn't I just a boy who thought all clichés new?

Ten more minutes of runaway speculation and I could have told you the size of the ring as it fell from the warehouse window, the way the gold band had spun as it fell, spinning like a tiny sun. If I stared hard enough I could see the indentation it had left in the water. If I stared even harder I could detect a dull golden glow eight feet down in the river mud. Only a fool would hesitate to retrieve it.

I kicked off my shoes and went in. The water was cool, not startling but bracing. All the stickiness of the day washed off me. I thought I knew precisely where the ring lay, and by the time I ducked my head underwater the object had blossomed in my imagination from a gold band to a diamond ring, a fortune, despite the fact that the girl's clothing had not been of Chinese silk but New Jersey gingham.

Unfortunately the current was strong and before I could reach the mud where I expected to spot the glint of sudden fortune I was pulled several yards downstream. Time after time I surfaced and dove, fighting my way north, feeling along the river bottom, kicking up silt, pulling my way past the murky pilings.

It was then I saw it, not a ring but what seemed a glow beneath a pier, something that caught the cracks of light, something wedged there, as huge, it seemed to me, as a horse, but only if horses were made of gossamer and wore ribbons of glowing light, and no horses I had ever seen had been so attired.

Imagine if you can an object six or seven feet long, its girth at the center maybe two feet around, the ends tapered but constantly changing shape, tattered and fluttering. I was four or five feet downstream of the object and it seemed to be reaching out for me from both ends, one end nearly as brown as the water and somewhat blunted but the other end tendriled and white. I thought at first of a horse because of its size, and because it would not have been uncommon for a dead horse to have been disposed of in the river, but this thing beneath the pier was more like the ghost of a horse, one end shredded, the entire object festooned with tentacles of opaque white, each one flapping at me and pulsing with the pulse of the current while my own pulse hammered in the gasp I dared not free from my chest.

Those two things conspired then—the magnifying power of water and the magnifying power of a boy's imagination and fear—to make the thing more horrific than it was. (Though there would be no shortage of horror when it was dragged into full light.) I had heard enough stories of mermaids and sea monsters, of giant squid and spectral sharks, to know that a glimpse of the thing was all I needed to want solid earth beneath my feet again. The water had become like ice, my limbs slow and thick and stiff with fear.

I splashed to the near edge of the dock, as far as I could get from the thing lodged beneath the boards. I pulled myself up, and, reluctant to even tread above the horror, I hopped across it, I snatched up my boots and leapt toward the foot of the pier and sprinted onto land. There, with warm ground beneath my feet, I shook like a dog and tried to convince myself that I shivered because the water had been cold.

I pulled on my boots and sloshed uptown. I wanted to forget about what I thought I had seen beneath the pier and so I concentrated instead on my stomach. I called its hollowness hunger, I ascribed my nausea to the water I had swallowed, a rancidness I kept trying to spit away, a revulsion I thought I could suffocate with food. A few hours remained before I could sneak safely home and into bed—plenty of time to steal a piece of fruit and a bucket of oysters for my supper.

2

WE WERE drawn to the dock like flies to a ripe carcass. By nine the next morning half of New York had come to peer up at the window from which the baby had been tossed and to peer down at the water where mother and child had landed. I was quick to spot my advantage in this, in our natural curiosity of the macabre—or does it seem now, so many years down the road, a macabre curiosity of the natural?—and I assumed the persona of a sideshow barker. In lieu of a baton I flailed my arms for emphasis.

My first tack was to crowd onto the jetty and announce myself as preeminent witness and offer to unfold the tragic events in proper chronological horror for a penny or two. But I was brushed aside by the merchants and businessmen in their handsome suits, ignored like a smelly dog with nothing to offer but his stench.

I had better luck farther inland. There, some twenty yards from the wharf, I would hasten to catch a carriage stopped along the avenue, or a pedestrian pausing for a long glance before turning toward town. "Did you come to see where the girl jumped?" I would ask, and before an answer could be received I would continue, "I was down there on the dock, the baby went sailing right over my head. You want to hear about it, I'm the one who saw it all, beginning to end. A penny's all it will cost you." By noon, when the trade waned to a trickle, I had a pocketful of pennies and a bellyful of biscuits.

The girl survived, I heard. She would be taken to the Bloomingdale Asylum north of town, on a site now occupied by Columbia College. I had seen the grand stone building myself, refuge for those tired souls who had lost all tolerance of the world, all forbearance—a flat-faced palace some sixty feet long and three stories high, surrounded by its wide yards and shade trees. It seemed to me more of an English castle than a hospital and so I had not a lot of pity to waste on the girl. If anything I envied her the luxuries she would find behind those strong walls, the walks in the fragrant garden, regular meals, an undisturbed bed. I was too young at the time to know that even the most splendid physical comfort can be rendered misery by a tiny grain of grief.

As for the baby, there was speculation on the dock that it had been dead even before its slow fall to the Hudson. No water in the lungs, I heard one man say. But then another man wanted to know why, if this were so, the mother had not held the child to her bosom as she leapt, as any loving mother, no matter how distraught, would do; an embrace, as it were, into the unknown. I could not speak to what a loving mother would do in that or any other circumstances, and said nothing. Not that I would have been listened to anyway.

In this manner then, the day waned. The business of the city boiled away behind me, fortunes being made, fortunes stolen, inventions that would change the world, inventions never to be seen, pages of fact and fabrication composed by writers and poets unheard of, never to be heard of, soon to be famous, soon to be forgotten.

As for me, I passed much of the day in dilatory contemplation, chewing alternately on a sassafras twig and on an augury of the nature of curiosity, whether the predominant effect of tragedy is to titillate or enervate, whether the desire to come gawking to a place like this suggests that the soul is folding in upon itself, or straining to come open.

Does another person's tragedy make us spectators feel somehow lucky, I wondered. Make us feel spared and therefore singled out for good fortune? This was how I felt as a naive boy. Or is tragedy meant to touch us deeper than that? Should it remind us of other forces atremble in the world, forces that lurk behind the corners, forces that might at any given moment spring out to toss any one of us off the ledge and into the abyss?

I also spent a good many moments wondering in a sidelong way, safe in the grass near the Bowling Green, about the thing beneath the dock, that which only I had seen, had dreamed of all the night, both awake and sleeping. In my childish mind I connected it to the girl who had jumped, cause and effect. This is what we do with mysteries too big or awful to embrace, what children and even grown men do—we ascribe to them a supernatural element. The thing beneath the dock had called to the girl, seduced her somehow, beguiled her to fling herself and child into the river.

On the dock men spoke of the girl's poverty, her sinful state, her numbing grief. None of these explanations satisfied me. But the thing beneath the dock . . . I sat there waiting, hour after hour, believing at any moment that it would soon call out to me too, a damp breeze, a watery hiss in the shape of my name. And I worried about my strength to resist, to not be pulled off the grass, for all I had to anchor me to land were a few last pennies in my pocket.

It was midday when he arrived, the most interesting, and it seemed to me most interested spectator. I had been dozing with my face in the sun and was awakened by a stevedore's curse, an epithet not meant for me except in the dream I had been wading through, a recurring nightmare of a stern schoolmaster chasing me around his glutinous room. The curse awoke me and I sat up blinking, wanting to keep running but my legs not yet fully composed beneath me, and I looked around for the schoolmaster and saw instead a less penumbral man, one of normal size and standing thirty yards to my left.

From a distance he appeared well dressed, the dark waistcoat and silk tie, the long loose trousers. A slight and slender man, almost dainty in his movements, he stood in the garden at the Bowling Green for a full twenty minutes, peering upriver. His hair was shiny black and hung ragged across his neck, in long lank strands over a high forehead and large eyes, which, depending upon how the light fell upon them, were either charcoal gray or Stygian black. Now and then he scribbled something in a little notebook he carried. At first I pegged him for an uptowner slumming for a story with which to shock his cronies over dinner, so imperious was his posture, chin held high, back rigidly straight. But distances can be deceiving.

After a while he came walking past where I sat. I saw then that his cuffs and sleeves were frayed, the waistcoat neatly patched in several places. And his eyes, those darkened windows I had thought imperious, they glanced my way as he passed and I saw instead a reflection of my own uncertainties.

He spent another fifteen minutes on the dock, slowly walking the boards, then standing on the edge, watching the empty water. Then ten minutes facing the warehouse, studying the window as if yet waiting for the girl to jump. Then, before he came off the pier at last, he looked my way again. And with that glance something jumped in the pit of my stomach, some sudden recognition that we were the same, this stranger and I, gawkers like all the others but different from them in our . . . what shall I call it—our affiliation with the girl? The others came quickly and just as quickly left, as if a moment's glance were sufficient to them, they needed stay only long enough for the requisite shudder, a quick fix of fear that would melt away soon as they leaned over their supper plates of steak and buttered potatoes and mumbled their *Glory to God Amen*. But this other stranger and I, we lingered. No, we were made to linger there. Compelled.

He came and sat on the grass within a yard of me. He smiled once, then wrote in his notebook for a while. When he finished writing he opened to a blank page and began a sketch of the docks, the water, and of a ship in full rigging that wasn't there.

Only after he had laid the notebook aside, after he had leaned back on his hands and gazed again toward the warehouse, did he speak. "You mustn't let it disturb you," he said without looking in my direction. His voice was soft, like slow water over rocks. With just a trickle, the slight meander of a Southern accent.

At first I assumed he was speaking to himself, trying to quiet with the reassurance of his own voice some secret trepidation. Or perhaps he was talking to a spirit only he could see, the mere shadow of an acquaintance. In any case I offered no reply. But I did keep watching him out of the corner of my eye, intrigued and yet cautious that some further strangeness might soon manifest itself in more volatile behavior.

"Sometimes a foreign discontent can catch us unawares," he said.

I felt myself leaning toward him with head cocked, ear turned. There was music in his voice, a soft dirgelike tone, and though the music for all I knew was not aimed at me, the words only half understood by me, I was drawn by the slow dark rhythms.

"It will blow across us from out of nowhere," he continued, his eyes still on the warehouse window, the scorched pediment, the empty rectangle as gray as smoke, "a murky breeze meant to stir the limbs of some other tree. But there we sit directly in its path, and we have no option but to take the chill of it."

He paused for a moment and plucked a blade of grass. He slowly split it down the center vein. "It would be a mistake, however, to let some stranger's chill become your own affliction."

I still imagined that he was speaking to his own mind. But then he turned to me and smiled.

He had such a delicate face, the small mouth and tapering chin, the high broad forehead. The gaze was what held you, though—as dark and wretched a gaze as ever I have seen, save on a wounded animal. "Will you tell me what you saw?" he asked. He was already reaching into a pocket. "A penny, if I'm not mistaken."

And now I knew, at least, what he was referring to.

"But what I require is the authentic and complete story," he said, and held a coin in the cup of his hand. "So shall we say . . . a tuppence for the truth?"

I leaned toward him and plucked the coin from his palm. He had long and slender fingers, well-cared-for hands. Not a workman's claws thickened and grimed with common labor, but neither were they weak. The thumb and forefinger were stained with ink.

What made me trust him, though, was something other than the sureness of his hands, something all the more palpable for being insubstantial. I would not be able to put a name to it until years later, until I read, long after it had been penned, the phrases composed by another unheralded writer, Melville, in his description of his first meeting with Hawthorne, and realized that I too had experienced "the shock of recognition" that strikes when two strangers suddenly behold themselves in each other's eyes.

As I fingered the coin and drew it back and slipped it quickly into a pocket, he remained entirely still, palm yet outstretched but empty now, thin mouth smiling. In that moment I knew him as well as I have ever known any man. I understood him in a way that did not require words, a way to which no words can be put until years later, when, in the stillness of loss, a remembered moment suddenly describes itself, and I felt how the rivers of his soul had flowed with sadness, and how the currents of his soul had tugged at mine.

And so I told him all that I had witnessed, I described how the girl had made a cradle of her hands, the awkward toss, the child's slow descent, the girl's modesty as she too fell. I told him all the things that no one else had wanted to hear.

"You have a writer's instincts," he told me when he finished his notes.

"Is that good or bad?"

"Every gift its curse," he said, and smiled again. "You never found what it was she threw the first time? The ring, if that indeed is what it was?"

"It's buried in the mud by now."

He nodded. "If only you had found it, though. The inconsequential details are invariably the ones of greatest consequence."

I had no idea what he was talking about, but I was flattered by his assumption that I did. I wondered whether to take a chance and tell him of what else I had seen in the river, the true source of the gravity that held me there, a pull more strong and black and strangulating than a child's graceful fall.

But then he turned my way and held out his hand to me. "I am grateful for your time, sir."

I took his hand, but awkwardly; it was the first hand I had ever shaken, the first time I had felt a grip on me so firm and yet unmenacing. "If you should remember any further details," he said, "please come see me at the *Mirror*. Ask for Poe. We might even find a few more pennies for you." He pushed himself to his feet.

I looked up into the sun. "I seen something else," I said.

A moment passed. I had the feeling he was considering the tenor of my voice, reading it for authenticity. Then he squatted down beside me again. He plucked another blade of grass. This one he did not tear apart but merely drew through his fingers in patient repetition.

I watched four times before I spoke. "Underneath the dock," I told him. "It's why she jumped, I think. It wanted her. Or the baby. I'm not sure which."

I expected him to laugh. At least to smile in that scornful way of every other smile ever bestowed on me. Instead he laid a hand on my filthy pant leg. "Why don't you show me," he said.

Despite the constriction rising in my chest, my instincts took over. "How much is it worth to you?"

"That will depend on the quality of what you show me."

He stood again, then held out a hand and pulled me up. "Perhaps it's time I knew your name," he said.

"Dubbins," I told him. "Augie. It's short for August. But don't nobody call me that."

He put a hand on my shoulder. I nearly reeled from all the contact. "Lead the way, Master Dubbins," he said.

And so I took him to the pier.

3

I WAS not confident it would still be there; I hadn't looked that day. A part of me hoped, I suppose, that it had dissolved somehow and might therefore disintegrate too from my dreams, so that I would not have to cower so tightly that night within my pillow of darkness.

Gingerly I walked the length of the pier, glimpsed nothing unusual, and felt both disappointment and relief. But the sun was angling low by now and the light was soft and even my shadow elusive. There was a trembling to the sunlight, a dizzying oscillation due to the river and my own nerves, but disconcerting whatever the source. And a dreamlike distance to the work transpiring all around us, the scraping and banging of all manner of freight, the chorus of disconnected voices, the music of the docks which now struck me as grating and discordant.

Yet I did not want to fail Poe, who waited at the foot of the dock, lips pursed in a small yet encouraging smile. I wanted both his money and his respect, yet more than that, I wanted to prove myself not a fool.

Onto my hands and knees I sank. Breathlessly I began to crawl toward the end of the pier. I could feel my heart dangling like a clapper in my chest, hammering hard. As I crawled I squinted into each crack in turn, every sliver between the planking.

And suddenly the liquid glow, as sharp as a prick in the eye. I jerked away.

"Have you found it?" Poe asked.

I stood and stepped back and thrust my chin at the boot-worn boards.

He came forward and knelt to put his eye to the crack. He turned this way and that, moving his body so that it did not block the trembling light. "Find me a twig," he said without rising.

I raced back to the Bowling Green—it was my legs that trembled now and not the light—soon to return with a long sassafras switch from which I had stripped the leaves. I whipped it through the air as I came onto the slip, the thin quick whistling sound adamant and shrill: I thrilled at handling a switch from the butt end for a change. Then I passed it to Poe, and he worked the shank between the boards and poked at whatever was snuggled there. It gave a bit, but the thing was solid; no water ghost at least. I let out a quivering breath.

He sat up after a few minutes of work and stretched his back. There was no one else besides us on that particular slip but we were being watched; any anomalous action will draw attention, and Poe's activity was certainly that—a grown man on his knees on the dirty boards, jabbing at the water with a long stick as if spear-fishing through a crack. But Poe gave not a thought to the onlookers. He paused only long enough to twist a kink from his shoulders, then he bent to the task again. I saw by his movements that he had soon hooked something and was trying to work it up through the crack.

"Can you get your fingers down there?" he asked, meaning that he wanted me to reach between the boards and pull forth the white thing he had snagged.

In answer I backed away another step. I imagined that I could smell it now, a scent unloosed, something dank and foul and best left hidden in the darkness.

Poe twisted the stick and nearly bent it flat against the dock before trying to elevate the fishing end. In this way he managed to work a tuft of gray into view. I remember seeing it in those few moments as a flap of skin, something slimy and translucent. This he seized between finger and thumb and firmly pulled. It tore away immediately. He was left holding a piece no bigger than a maple leaf.

He held it to the light. "Muslin," he said.

A few moments later he looked to me. His eyes were sparkling now. "It's a fine afternoon for a swim, don't you think?"

My body ached to move even farther away, far beyond the realm of such a crazy suggestion. But I held my ground and told him, "Would. Can't swim a lick, though."

He smiled and considered me for a moment with his chin tucked low. Finally he answered, "Fair enough. You hired on as guide and nothing more." Then he stood and took off his coat and handed it to me.

"Watch out for the current," I told him. "It's strong."

"And how would you know that, having never tested it yourself?" But he continued to smile all the same.

"You can see just by looking at it how fast it is."

"Don't worry," he said as he pried off his shoes. "I once swam seven and a half miles in a heavy tide. I think I can handle the Hudson River."

He removed his tie and collar and rolled up his sleeves and I saw then that he was more muscular than I had first assumed. In his heavy waistcoat he had even looked frail, but perhaps this was a result of the delicacy with which he always moved. In truth he was lean and sinewy, his shoulders strong.

The last thing he did was to empty his pockets and lay their contents on the dock: his notebook, two stubs of pencil, and a few coins—fewer even than in my own pocket. Then, in trousers and shirt he slipped into the water on the upriver side of the dock. Submerged to his neck, he held to the boards and looked back at me. "If I haven't emerged in four minutes," he told me, and smiled again, "you will have to come in and rescue me."

I backed away. "If that thing gets you . . . too bad. But it ain't getting me."

He winked, he took a deep breath, and he sank away.

For half a minute I listened to his movements beneath my feet, the scraping sounds as he maneuvered in close to the thing, the slap and splash of his kicking feet as he fought to hold his position against the current. Then there was a pounding sound, as like a fist on wood under water, and I thought immediately about screaming out for help, calling to a stevedore to rip up the boards and rescue Poe before he could be dragged away beyond salvation. But a life of attempted invisibility is not easy to surrender even in a moment of fear, especially when I myself was in no apparent jeopardy. And so I stood, fifty inches of cowardice, and did little more than wonder in what manner the thing down there was doing Poe in—would it strangle him or rip him apart? Or would it merely hold him under until his body went limp? Would it wrap long tentacles around his neck, or sink a pointed beak into his heart?

The only thing I knew for certain was that there was something dramatic going on underneath me, something that felt for all the world like a struggle to the death. The boards trembled, and at one point the entire pier seemed to shake. Though maybe that was just my knees. I wanted to run but kept telling myself that the thing couldn't break through the dock or it would have done so already. In any case I moved two steps closer to the street. And now and then counted the seconds. It seemed a quarter hour passed in the next two minutes.

I meanwhile kept an eye on Poe's small pile of coins; the vibration of the dock had caused one of them to slide closer to a crack. I had almost convinced myself to hurry forward, grab the coins, and be off, when Poe's head broke the surface of the water on the downriver side of the dock. The splash and his explosive exhalation nearly made me shriek out loud.

"Augie," he said, and took two more quick breaths, "come give me your hand."

I could not move.

"Up onto the deck," he said, and held out a hand to me. Long strands of black hair hung over his eyes, and his pale hand was trembling. I could see that he was exhausted. But what if he pulled me in there with him? I could not yet convince myself to trust him completely; a lifetime of experience is not so easily undone.

In the end he hauled himself out, hoisting his body up with a last great effort to lie half on the dock, feet still in the water, his face against the boards. "You were right," he said. "The current's strong."

But I had already moved past him by then, had walked by slow degrees to the very end of the pier. I no longer feared the thing beneath the boards, because it was no longer there; it was floating away, glowing more brightly than ever now that its white shape had broken the surface and I could see clearly what it was, the long torn ribbons of cloth trailing after it, undulating in the current, as pale and transparent as a snake's old skin, the body turning as gently in the water as the baby had glided through air the day before, drifting away from us, out into the darker depths.

Poe, who had been facing upriver, now drew in his legs and pushed himself onto his hands and knees. "I tried to break it loose," he said, "but I think I will need some assistance. Go find us a couple of willing stevedores, Augie."

When I did not answer or move he finally looked my way. I heard him crawl to his feet then and come to stand beside me. I pointed toward New Jersey.

Together we watched the body moving like a sleeping mermaid toward the opposite shore, no longer a monster and yet fearful all the same, the long brown hair flowing back like seaweed, the white dreamlike flutter of the woman's dress, the utter tranquillity and perfection of death, all terrifying in its beauty and mystery. I shivered, completely dry. And Poe, dripping wet, shivered beside me.

It wasn't long before the body was spotted by others as well. Men on shore began to shout at one another, gesticulating. Down on the Battery two men pushed a bumboat into the river and went in pursuit, their paddles chopping at the water as at a great blue block of ice, spraying rainbow splinters into the air.

Poe turned away from me. He bent down over his small pile of coins, picked up the only piece of silver there, the rest dull pennies, and then returned to where I stood. "For that discovery, Master Dubbins," he said, and he held the coin out to me, a thin slice of brilliance glinting in the sun, "for that you deserve a half-dime."

Whereupon we both returned our gazes to the river and to the fey but radiant flotsam being ferried to the distant shore.

4

HER NAME was Mary Rogers.

I learned this fact well after it was announced to the rest of New York, for it was not my habit in those days to use a newspaper for anything other than chinking for a leaky boot or a drafty window. Not that the printed word was burdensome to me; I could read with the same ease I could sort out the mess of foreign and American coins that passed through my hands. I had a sharp ear for accents and a keen eye for dissembling. But except for tales of derring-do or catastrophe, the incidents discussed in the news, like those discussed in schoolrooms, seemed unrelated to my existence.

(It would not be long, however, before I would uncover, thanks in no small part to Poe, an avidity for the written word, an avidity that before the dawn of adolescence would bloom into an avarice, so that now, as I sit here in the cusp of my fourth score of years, an ancient ivory-barreled pen in hand—the very one I lifted from Poe's pocket before they laid him under, after which his brief but fiery charge through life would remain as misunderstood as ever—with this pen in hand I can now gaze in any direction and see nothing but the written word, a house constructed of the written word, and furnished by it a line at a time, a large house and a long life both circumscribed by the one human compulsion that might, if any will, get the race of man onto at least the greensward of Heaven.)

But I stray from the narrative. (In my own defense, I never swore fealty to Poe's thesis regarding the unity of effect in a tale. And especially not in a tale as crenellated as this one.) Let me be returned to the path by the call of her name: Mary Rogers.

Even now it stirs me. Upon first reading that name I was struck by its simplicity. A plainness so stark as to obtain elegance. A name, I hasten to add, that scarcely seemed to fit the form Poe had dislodged from beneath the pier, a form that must surely be the human physiognomy at its most ignominious, the bloat and pallor, as if the body were attempting to regress to the shape of something antecedent and elemental, an ovum housed in a translucent membrane, an egg without a shell.

The name was better fitted to the girl who had leapt from the warehouse ledge. Or to the leap itself, unadorned and desperate, a failed embrace of a merciful end.

But it belonged to the other girl instead. The one whose body had been stuffed by Nature beneath the dock, an act devoid of all grace and poetry and simplicity of intent. She was twenty-two years old. A shop girl. Her mother's only child. All this I read in a leaf from the *Mirror* left behind when an omnibus of gawkers pulled away from the Battery the following afternoon. They had come like dozens of others all that day— the analogy of flies to carrion is again most apt—as I myself had come. To peer at the current that had carried her across. To wonder at the current of a life that had directed her demise. To squint at the far shore where she had finally been grappled and dragged. To play out some vague scenario in the mind's eye: seeing themselves transposed onto her corpse, or their daughters or wives or mistresses juxtaposed, their homesickness, fear, uncertainties, or reading into it a cautionary tale to carry back to one's own hearth, or to keep buried in the embers of one's own heart.

Poe had authored the account, of course. There was no mention of his role in freeing the body from its watery box. No mention of my own. No mention of the girl who had tossed herself and the child into the river the day before, an unrelated incident, precipitant from a personal point of view but inconsequential from a public one. Poe's story began with the two men in the bumboat. They had spotted the body turning in the current midriver, a gruesome sight to behold on such a lemony afternoon. They had rowed in pursuit of it then, rowed abreast of it finally, only to be too appalled to reach overboard and secure it. And so they had put the boat downstream of her, its hull hard to her shoulder, and in this manner maneuvered both the boat and the corpse of Mary Rogers to the New Jersey shore.

Poe had left my side the previous afternoon to gather the disparate pieces of this story, and thus had sewn up his narrative with details and statements provided not only by the men in the boat but by the police and Mary Rogers's own mother.

On the day of her discovery, Poe wrote, the girl had been missing for four days. According to the widow Rogers, who ran a boardinghouse on Nassau Street, Mary had departed their home at approximately nine on Sunday morning, meaning to spend the day with an aunt who lived some two miles distant, north along Manhattan's western shore. Before setting out, Mary had knocked at the room of one Jack Payne, a boarder in the Rogers' house, to inform him of her plans. Mr. Payne, Mary's betrothed, agreed to call at the aunt's domicile at dusk that evening so as to escort Mary home.

In late afternoon a heavy rain set in. A downpour that lasted half the hour was followed by a lighter but no less constant rain, as well as a shroud of fog that seeped in from off the river. By dusk these conditions had made the roadside all but impassable, the visibility reduced to less than a few yards. Mr. Payne assumed that under such conditions his betrothed would prefer to pass the night with her aunt, as, the widow Rogers assured him, Mary had done on previous occasions. And so he failed to keep his appointment with her.

Come Monday morning, Mary Rogers was absent from her counter at Anderson's Tobacco Shop on Wall Street, not far from its intersection with Broadway. Mr. Anderson assumed that she was ill, and he attended the counter himself in addition to his other duties. Mary's mother and fiancé, who had as yet had no contact with Mr. Anderson, assumed that Mary had gone straight to work from her aunt's house.

Not until Mary failed to return home that evening were suspicions aroused. Mr. Payne made the short walk to the tobacconist's establishment, only to find the store closed and locked for the evening. Finally, a full twenty-four hours after his appointed rendezvous with Miss Rogers, Mr. Payne arrived by carriage at the aunt's home. Only to be there informed that the aunt had not been visited by Mary on the day previous, and that she had not in fact seen her since the last visit some three weeks earlier.

Mr. Payne returned with this news to the boardinghouse. Whereupon the widow Rogers, Poe reported, was seized by an awful premonition which caused her to cry out that she would never see her daughter again. Unwilling to accept this prognostication as fact, Mr. Payne instituted a hasty search of the city, making inquiries well into the night at the homes of various of Mary's acquaintances, stirring up widespread concern for her, all to no avail.

On Tuesday morning the constabulary was apprised of Mary's disappearance, but there was little they could do. Until, Poe wrote, the afternoon of the day of her absence, when the body of Mary Rogers revealed itself in a lugubrious promenade down the Hudson.

I do not know, did not know then and do not know now, why Poe chose to lop off from his narrative what to me was the most stimulating part, mainly my discovery of the body beneath the pier and his chilly baptism to free it from the pilings. No doubt his decision had something to do with one of his literary theories—most of which I would remain ignorant of until long after his own ignominious demise.

I knew little of the man at this time, and even less of the vagaries and trials of his past. His eyes betrayed a fire and a strangeness and his voice at times conveyed a subtle drawl of disdain, but these characteristics proved insufficient, in light of the polymorphic nature of the city, to distinguish him as one of the more spectacular denizens of New York. He was a newspaperman, that was all I knew. And that he had treated me with greater equanimity than had any man before him.

I assumed he had made a pretty penny for a story that had so stirred up the populace as to transform the riverfront, for the next few days, into as beguiling an attraction as the Broadway and Bowery theaters.

It was Mr. Payne who identified the corpse as that of his betrothed. She had been lying ashore but a half hour when word of the tragedy was delivered to him by one Charles T. Andrews. Payne was little more than a mile away at the time, having embarked, with the aid of a coterie of Mary's concerned acquaintances, Charles Andrews included, upon a canvassing of all establishments south of Union Square. Andrews was the first among them to catch wind of the news that the body of a young female had been discovered.

At this point in Poe's lengthy narrative he described the appearance of the body in such detail that even a physician might have flinched. Not a physician myself, I flinched repeatedly upon reading the report. But it was the fashion of newspapers in those days not to shrink from a vivid recapitulation, nor from embellishment of known or assumed facts, nor from conveying in twenty words what might have been conveyed in five, and Poe, who had earlier theorized (I would later discover) that authenticity in narrative is best imparted through a flood of details, was an enthusiastic purveyor of this prolixity.

(Perhaps more than a little of his style has rubbed off on me.)

But to the condition of Mary's body, which I will encapsulate from memory:

Her face, wrote Poe, was a moon of palest blue, but suffused here and there with the adumbrations of dark blood, indications of blunt trauma about the forehead and cheeks. More blood was discovered in her mouth and nostrils and in the canal of her left ear. A slender chain of bruises, as might be made by a rope or the crimp of a man's hands, ringed her neck, and a bracelet of bruised skin encircled each wrist. Dangling by its slender chain from her left wrist was a small brocaded purse containing a few coins, a vial of lilac water, and a lace handkerchief. No cuts or lacerations were discerned upon her flesh, so it was quickly ascertained that she had been done in by other than mechanical means.

Likewise, though her frock was torn and much disordered, and the muslin slip also rent in no fewer than three places, and the strings of her bonnet tied about her neck not with a lady's bow but a sailor's knot, every article of clothing was more or less intact, including and especially the undergarments—all testimony, said the medical professional who, in the modest and perfunctory fashion of the day, examined her, to the fact that the young lady's virtuous character, vouched for by her mother and Mr. Payne, remained intact.

Mr. Jack Payne, though much grieved to do so, was ferried across the Hudson where he identified the body as being, beyond dispute, that of his beloved. The medical examiner classified most of her bruises as post-mortem. The exception were those that ringed her neck. The death was attributed to strangulation—exacted, perhaps, by the strings of her own bonnet.

As a matter of routine, and because Miss Rogers had been a citizen of Gotham proper, the body was then delivered to the city's morgue. Early next morning it was turned over to Mr. Payne, who, on behalf of the young girl's mother, accompanied the remains to a nonsectarian cemetery not far north from where Mary Rogers had lived, and there she was properly, if hastily, laid to rest.

In conclusion Poe presented the observation of the local gendarmes—which he, no doubt, being on the spot, had helped to formulate—that Mary Rogers had been the unfortunate victim of an unplanned assault by a gang of ruffians, packs of whom were known to frequent the woods and shaded byways along the fringes of the city. The assault would have taken place between nine and nine-thirty on the Sunday morning of her disappearance; just prior to nine she was taking her leave from her mother's boardinghouse, and after nine-thirty she would have arrived at her aunt's domicile. By ten she and her aunt would have settled together in the fourth pew from the altar of the Methodist Episcopal Church (this being the chapel closest to the aunt's house, though she was in fact a Catholic). Neither of these later chronologies was met.

In all probability, Poe reasoned, Mary's path had caused her to tread within earshot of where a gang of ruffians had passed the night. One or more of these thugs (and I shivered upon reading this passage, knowing myself to be a hair's breadth from joining their ranks), still groggy from his night of debauch in a local doggery, had happened to glance up at her passing, the flash of creamy gingham seen through the trees, a glimpse of heaven 'midst the wood's chill shadows.

In any case she was spotted. The assailant was seized, Poe wrote, "with an animal passion." The pursuit could not have lasted long. In all likelihood murder was not the thug's intention, but merely to render Mary Rogers docile for a while. When she instead expired at his hands, when the last breath of air was choked from her lungs, when she went even limper in his hands than he had hoped for, the thug panicked. He and his fellows, if indeed there were any fellows, sequestered the evidence of their misdeed until nightfall, then, without bothering to weight the corpse with rocks, had tossed the body of Mary Rogers into the river and thought themselves done with it.

In conclusion Poe chided the Common Council for their reluctance to establish a municipal police force, and pointed to Mary Rogers's murder as but one example of the city's escalating social and moral decay. Banditti, he said, were claiming as their empire more and more of Manhattan, while the numerous squads of privatized watchmen squabbled among themselves for docks to patrol, lamps to light, benches to doze upon. Savagery, he warned, was spreading like fire; without a unified professional police force to engage it, the fire would inevitably reduce our city to ashes.

I had no argument with Poe's conclusion. Why, then, could I not shake a disconcertion, an uneasiness that, the more I picked at it, finally revealed itself as two-pronged? In the first case, I was unsettled by Poe's description of the body as it lay ashore in New Jersey. For all his attention to the state of her clothing and flesh, why had he made no reference to mitigating details, what the French call the *ambiance* of her situation? Not that I had even glimpsed the body myself, save for its distorted and magnified glow when submerged beneath the dock, then as a grotesquerie freed to float along the hungry current—but I saw it many times in my imagination, a thousand times. I see it even yet, a scene unbidden and as clear in my mind's eye as if I had been standing there with Poe myself while Mr. Jack Payne bent over the body to perceive in it the countenance of his beloved. I smell the fetor of river mud, the rank odor of decay. I see the way the afternoon light slants in through the branches and is broken into thick splinters of light and how the shadows of the men closest to the river lie stretched out thin and quivering upon the mottled water. And I see the small white moths, five of them, that flutter over Mary Rogers's face, moths that alight for a moment upon her hair or atop her forehead or along the rigid length of her body. I hear the water and the muted thuds of activity from across the water. I hear a songbird from deep in the woods, the call of a crow even more distant.

They are inconsequential details, you might argue, and they do not contribute to the singularity of effect that Poe was always striving to achieve. But without them, to my eyes, Mary Rogers is diminished.

As for the second prong of dissatisfaction with Poe's narrative, a simpler point, but sharper:

I read Poe's article and laid the paper aside and then I carried his words in my head for the next hour or two. Until finally, incontrovertibly, they jelled into my own hard observation: he had gotten it wrong. The medical examiner, Poe, the consensus achieved by all those men who had bent over the body of Mary Rogers as it lay on the New Jersey shore, all those calloused and unshakable men who stood with their handkerchiefs pressed to their mouths while five white moths fluttered about her, they had gotten it wrong. No murderer was skulking through the woods of upper Manhattan. No illiterate thug cowered silent in tremulous shadows. The murderer was standing there among them.

5

THE OFFICES of the *Mirror* were shadowy and crowded and stank of onion sandwiches and old cigars, and the dim clamor of the place brought my flesh alive with an excitement of gooseflesh, my arms and neck stippled with it as if I had made my way into the caverns of Delphi where the world was not only comprehended but perhaps fashioned, perhaps kneaded and molded here in the fists of strange gods.

A dozen or more men were at work in the main room, a few of the men rushing about as if late for an appointment that would change their lives, others huddled in whispered conference, and the rest scribbling alone at scarred and cluttered desks. They were hunched and coiled and flannel-cheeked men, ruby nosed, men with darting eyes and greasy flocks of hair, one man chewing on the butt of a corncob pipe and another coughing smoke though no pipe or cigar was visible in his hand or on his desk. All told it seemed a cramped and adumbrated place, a cavern stained with smoke and ink and curses and black stories spilled from broken lives.

It looked like home to me.

I crept along toward the rear of the room, blinking like a mole in a maze, until one man raised his hand and stopped my progress and asked me what I was up to. I told him, "I'm here to see Poe."

"Pa?" he said.

"Poe."

He said without smiling, "What's a *po?*"

I showed him the leaf from the morning's paper and laid it across his desk and pointed to the story about Mary Rogers. He looked me up and down and grinned finally and jerked his head toward the door at the end of the room. Half the door was made of milk glass, and painted on it in gold letters was the name *Edmund Neely* and the words *Managing Editor.*

I was not then familiar with the civilities of polite or even journalistic society and so I did not knock on the door; I put my hand to the glass knob and twisted it and shoved the door open. With Neely's initial harpoon of a glance I knew I was about to be shouted off the premises, so I held up the newspaper and announced, "I'm here to see Poe. He wrote this story about the dead girl they pulled out the river."

Three ticks of a clock, like huge dominoes crashing into one another. He considered me a while longer. Then, "She your girlfriend or your long-lost mother?"

I almost blurted out, "I'm the one found the body," because a part of me wanted credit for it, credit for any act deserving of applause or at least a redirection of Neely's hard cynicism. But I thought better of it and told him, "I've got some more information for Mr. Poe."

"More?" Neely said. He looked at me with his broad head slightly cocked, the gaslight on the near wall flickering in the dampness of his brow.

This time I decided to keep quiet. What I sensed then and have since confirmed about the society of journalists, about all scribes and scribblers in fact, is that the successful ones are equipped not only with a keen eye and ear and an innate sense of drama but with a fair degree of rapaciousness as well, a desire to transform every story into their own, to possess it by transcribing it, setting the abstract into the concrete of words and thereby making it real, in essence creating it, and with every new composition creating a bit more of themselves.

"And what's the nature of your information?" Neely asked.

Once again I thought it best to hold my tongue. The murder of Mary Rogers was the hottest story in town. I nodded over my shoulder to the roomful of writing desks. "I didn't see him out there."

"Nor are you likely to," he said.

And now confusion. Poe's byline was there on the story, E. A. Poe. Yet he was not employed here?

I was saved by a hulking presence at my back, somebody else with business for the editor. Someone obviously more significant than me, for after a nod at the man looming over me Neely dismissed me with, "You'll find him at home, no doubt."

"And where's that?"

He had already looked away from me and now had to cut his eyes back in my direction. "Fordham," he said. Then to the man behind me, "Come on in, Frank. Kick out the cat and close the door."

As quick as a cat I slipped beneath the man's hand and made my way back through the room and observed to myself, *From mole to cat in two minutes; not bad.*

Out on Broadway again, I snagged a ride on a horse railway car. By hanging off the side I was able to duck the five-cent fare. The smaller omnibuses charged ten cents to each of their twelve passengers, and those conveyances lumbered along at a clopping pace, rattling like bloated stagecoaches over rough ground. In comparison the horse railway seemed a futuristic wonder as it glided over metal rails, and though I seldom availed myself of the upholstered benches inside, I yet found the ride invigorating and a miracle of progress.

It was an experience all the more wondrous for the scenery, past the rebuilt Trinity Church with its single tall spire groping for the magnificence of Heaven, past the sarcophagus-like splendor of Astor's Opera House, past Washington Hall and Gothic Hall and the New York Hospital, and eventually under the arched stone bridge at Canal Street and leaving all the fashionable shops behind. Before long, though, the car made its turnaround and I was forced to go clopping out of this center-of-gravity on foot again, from graded street to irregular horse path, the ground as often slimy now as it was dry.

North of Canal there was little to catch a boy's eye, and after Union Square I followed Fourth up to Fifty-first, just because I wanted to gawk at Madame Restell's Palace again. Not that I could quite yet grasp the nefarious deeds Madame Restell had perpetrated to acquire such wealth—for me at ten years old, sex was (and, sadly, has more or less become again) a fantasy of lying naked in a dark room and touching womanly parts whose function and appeal I insufficiently comprehended—but her marble mansion never failed to inspire me with the knowledge that even an uneducated drudge could rise to grandeur in this city. All success required was ambition and cleverness. Thus Caroline Ann Trace had transformed herself from a maid in Gloucester to a dressmaker in New York City, then to a pill maker, then rechristened herself as the physician Madame Restell, whose Preventive Powders, advertised in the *Sun* and the *Herald,* sold so briskly as to bring her not only notoriety as an abortionist but also great wealth.

I will not go into details here of how in the mind of a ten-year-old boy the mechanics of intercourse and procreation and abortion were convoluted into a Gordian mess, but suffice it to say that just the sight of Restell's Palace would bring a twinkle to my eye and put a bounce in my step. But if Madame Restell's example of the potential for acquiring wealth energized me, it was with an energy that contained a negative charge as well, for I could not gaze upon her mansion long without at least one grimace when I recalled what was so often said about it, that every brick represented the skull of an unborn child.

From Fifty-first I angled left my way through an area I beheld as my other possible fate. If I failed to hustle as cleverly as Madame Restell I would end up here, I told myself, here in the mud and garbage heaps of these shantytowns, here with the ragpickers and their half-feral pigs. The swampy pestilence of the area was an assault on the senses, and I mucked along as briskly as I could, imagining not for a second that this festering terrain could ever be the site of summer concerts and promenades and the fashionable turnouts of Central Park today.

Then all the way to 174th Street, a very long walk for a boy but a pleasant one, unhurried, and made even more enjoyable when I clambered atop the massive stone arches of High Bridge to cross the East River. Here the huge pipe was being laid that would eventually convey water a distance of some thirty-two miles, from the Croton River into Gotham, an undertaking so huge as to dizzy me more than did the height of the bridge above the river.

Then on to Fordham and the sweetness of true bucolia. After inquiring of a man weeding his garden—he was so thin and bent and slow that I first mistook him for a scarecrow—I found Poe's farmhouse. It was surrounded on three sides by an apple orchard, and I remember how surprised I was to discover that the newspaperman was also an apple farmer.

As I approached, a woman came out the front door, banging it open with a small washtub she carried. She was a stout woman of middle age, her hair dull black and chopped off squarely just below her ears. She did not look my way but went straight to a pump at the side of the house and worked the handle up and down until water sloshed over the brim of the tub.

By now I was less than five yards from her. I stood and waited until she had picked up the washtub to return to the house and there saw me standing. She was startled to see a boy where none was expected, but quickly recovered and greeted me with a scowl.

"There's nothing in the house," she told me. "If you're hungry, go pick a couple apples. They're green yet but it's the best I can do."

She thought I was a beggar-child looking for a handout. "Are you Mrs. Poe?" I asked.

She hunched forward and gave me a stare. "You know him, do you?"

"I help him with his newspaper work."

"Is that right?"

"I come to give him some information."

"Then you come for nothing," she said.

And now it was my turn to stare.

"They're gone," she said. "Packed up and cleared out two days back. Supposed to take the house till October at least, that's what he promised me. But no."

She sniffed once, then shook her head. Her tone was softer now. "He was walking that trip every day, can you imagine? There and back every day without a single complaint for hisself. They was good company, I'll tell you that."

She might as well have been talking Greek. "He moved?"

"Isn't that what I just now said?"

I could only stare at her and blink.

"I can't even blame him, that's the thing. What with all he's got weighing down on him. Worries like that build up on a man. Knocks the starch right out of him."

I could not help myself; I turned and looked back toward the city some thirteen miles away. She must have read the weariness of my posture, for her tone softened even more.

"If you need a drink of water, you can get it," she said.

I lacked the strength to thank her. "Did he say where he was moving to?"

"Back across the river and south a ways. Just off Bloomingdale Road is what he told me. Quarter mile or so below the reservoir."

I nodded and pushed one foot in front of the other to start myself moving, then thought better of it and turned toward the pump. The woman picked up her washtub again and headed for the house. I waited until she was inside, then put my hand to the pump and worked the handle up and down until a gush of water gurgled forth. I ducked my head under it and doused myself and then turned to gulp it down until the slender torrent died away. Then I pushed the hair out of my eyes and thought, *The hell with Poe,* and walked away from there.

I was too hungry and tired to care if Poe got his story right or not. What did any of it matter to me? Who was this Poe fellow anyway? Just another hustler, a rung or two above my own position perhaps but at least I did not go moving about the countryside at the drop of a hat. I was done with him. He wasn't worth the trouble.

The flaw in my logic was that I would have to retrace my steps to return to the city, and in doing so I would pass within a few hundred yards of Bloomingdale Road (which is what Broadway, at least the upper portion of it, was then called). And when after another two hours of sluggish marching I came to the northern shore of the reservoir, I again thought, *The hell with it,* and swiveled to my right and followed the western shore rather than the eastern. If I spotted a likely-looking house off Bloomingdale Road, maybe I would stop. Maybe I would give Poe a piece of my mind.

It was an area of fields and woods and a scarcity of houses. There was only one building visible in the area Poe had described to his former landlady. It was a small white cottage set in a clearing at the end of a long grassy lane. A ribbon of white smoke curled out of the stovepipe protruding from the roof. On a day as warm as this, the smoke could mean only one thing: somebody was cooking supper.

I trudged down the lane and came to a halt at the side of an oak tree not fifteen feet from the front steps. A narrow covered porch ran along the front of the cottage, and on the porch was a deacon's bench and a wicker chair. The front door stood open by half. Through the doorway came the scent of something delicious and stupefying, frying meat, a simmering pot. I lifted my nose to it and closed my eyes and did nothing to keep my body from dissolving into pure hunger.

When the heavy boots hit the porch floor I must have been dozing on my feet, for I jerked upright at the sound and scraped my spine against the tree trunk. The individual peering out at me from the edge of the porch was sufficiently frightening to make me consider immediate retreat. My first guess would have been of a circus strong man in a long loose dress. Of a man with thick forearms and broad shoulders and a wide round face and with a chest as broad as a beer keg, with hands as large as any stevedore's and a solid splayfooted stance to match. For some reason I envisioned this person hoisting me up like a barrel and sailing me high above the trees.

But no, she smiled. A womanly smile, with a gaze as soft as her hands were strong. "Are you looking for something to eat?" she said. I saw then that she had a dipper and tin pail in her hand and, since I saw no sign of a pump, was apparently on her way to the springhouse.

"I'm looking for Poe," I said.

"You're here to see Eddie?"

"Poe," I said again. "That's what he told me his name is."

She cocked her head and gave me a look of amused curiosity. Then she stepped back inside the cottage and I heard her muted voice. A moment later she returned to the door and came outside and down off the porch and with a lumbering gait in perfect counterpoise to her smile she went off to fetch the water.

And soon, there was Poe at the door, looking just as he had on the day previous save that his collar now hung open at the side of his neck. And instead of clutching a small pad of paper in his right hand he now held a thick book, one finger closed inside it.

"Master Dubbins," he said. "You're a long way from home."

"I've been farther out than this already."

He misunderstood my insinuation, which was delivered too wearily to convey the indignation I intended. "No doubt you have. And no doubt you've come to collect your share of the byline, am I right?"

It was my feeling then, as now, that when the drift of a conversation has missed your ken, the wisest response is silence and a sneer.

He turned sideways and waved his hand through the doorway. "Come in, come in and take a seat. Let us conduct our business as the gentlemen we are or at least pretend to be."

He winked at me then and when I came forward he stepped aside and held the door for me and with his little pat on my back I once again felt reconstituted. Light-handed as it was and as leg weary as I was it engendered in me some brotherly affection, some strangely emollient suffusion of sufferance for even the ragpickers and their pigs and for myself and all the world.

The interior of the cottage seemed as foreign to me as some distant star, though it was a place only slightly more lavish than the one I returned to each night, the scant furniture of a Boston rocker and straight-backed chairs and table and cast-iron potbellied stove, all the necessary accoutrements of domesticity but no more than the necessary ones, no gilded mirrors or marble vases or carpets from the mysterious East, nothing I had not seen before in a score of other impecunious homes. With the exception of the books. Books were everywhere. Books were stacked or lined on nearly every flat surface, even shelved standing on the floor. It was as much a library as a cottage, a clapboard athenaeum.

Yet the element most disconcerting about those three small rooms—the kitchen area flowed wall-less into a sitting room, at the rear of which stood a closed doorway, a bedroom I presumed—the element most disconcerting because it was something I had never encountered in the residences near my own, not in the tenement row houses or the slapdash shacks, was the cleanliness. In fact to refer to the condition as mere cleanliness is to soil it with understatement. Spotlessness does not do the job either. Nor even meticulousness. Let me just say that had I been aware in those days of the existence of bacteria, I might too have discerned the sudden expiration by fright of each of the myriad germs and mites and microbia to whom my body, until that moment, had been home sweet home.

There was not a single scuff of dirt upon the dull plank floor. Not a sniff of dust on any surface. No discarded bottles or tins oozing mold, no gobs of spat tobacco or hawked-up phlegm, no rags wadded into cracks or tossed about willy-nilly, no overflowing slop pots or blobs of hardened food or rat droppings or insect hulls or the stink and stain of urine from a corn-shuck mattress or coal bucket or the crackery stench of unwashed bodies. No reek upon reek. No stink of squalor, not even a hint of it. Every surface had been scrubbed and scrubbed again. The place was so clean that it took my breath away. It was so startling that upon my first contact with it, it stung my eyes. I have no other words to describe it.

Poe led me to the small square table and pulled out a chair and motioned that I should sit. Then, after marking his book with a slip of parchment, he laid the book aside and sat opposite me and placed both hands flat on the table.

"You saw the story, then," he said.

And I, still reeling from the blast of unfouled air, could only nod cross-eyed.

"And you believe that you are entitled to a larger share of the remuneration."

I understood most of the words, at least the gist of them. But it was his implication that confounded me, that I had come there to demand further payment for a transaction already completed.

He dug into one of his pockets and brought out a small leather purse and opened it. "I was paid four dollars for the story," he told me as he picked through the coins. "A paltry sum, I agree. Especially considering the hours spent gathering the requisite facts and fashioning them into a coherent tale. Even so . . . ."

By now he had laid three dimes upon the table. He paused for a moment to stare into the small mouth of the purse. Finally he extracted a fourth moon of silver and laid it with the others. He pushed all four across the table.

"Ten percent," he said. "Would you consider this a fair commission?"

It looked like a small fortune beneath my very nose. All I had to do was to put out my hand and claim it. But something kept my hands clasped together between my knees.

"You already paid me the half-dime," I told him.

"But apparently you feel slighted. And that I cannot abide." He pushed the coins a bit closer to me.

My mind spun as I considered the mountain of confections I could stuff into my cheeks as the owner of those dimes. But also, alas, my stomach churned.

"I would gladly pay more if more remained," he told me. "But it goes so quickly."

And then the sound of footfalls on the porch, a lumbering stride. He brushed his hand over the coins. "Take them, Augie, please. Hurry and put them away."

I raised my hand to cover them. But at the last moment, only one finger presented itself, and this I laid upon a single coin. "This one is plenty," I told him.

He cut a glance at the door, then back at me. "You're certain?"

"I didn't come to squeeze more money out of you," I said.

A slight smile, a tiny nod. And then he scooped up the remaining dimes and quickly returned them to his purse and returned the purse to his pocket. I detected in this sleight of hand a conspiracy between us, and it warmed me to him even more.

And then in strode the large woman with a full bucket of spring water. She smiled down at me as she waddled toward the pair of enameled basins on a raised plank adjacent to the stove. She set down the bucket and dipped out a glassful and set the glass before me and then turned away without uttering a word.

Poe watched me and kept smiling. He knew, I think, how alien her gesture was to me, this simple generosity, and how filthy I suddenly felt in my dirty skin and rags.

After a moment he nodded toward the glass. It was all I needed to reach for it with both hands. I drank it down and wiped my mouth.

"What I come here for was to tell you something," I finally said.

He sat all but motionless, waiting, and it was then I first observed how birdlike was his countenance, how hawklike or owlish, by which I mean not menacing or predatory but keen-eyed, with a patient and acute intelligence.

"I think you got it wrong about that girl," I said.

At this the woman—I had not yet determined if she was his mother or his wife, though had you pressed me at the moment I would have guessed the former—turned from her sink to regard first me and then Poe. She had been washing carrots and onions in one of the basins but now she turned at the waist with both hands still immersed.

"Eddie doesn't get things wrong," she told me. This, as with every word she said to me that day and thereafter, was delivered with a velvet firmness of intonation.

And Poe said, smiling, "Sometimes, Muddy, I sometimes do. But we mustn't let anybody else ever suspect as much."

She pursed her lips and shook her head as if she could not abide this confession.

Poe said to me, "Mrs. Clemm is my most stalwart champion and my greatest source of strength. Isn't that true, Muddy?"

Her broad cheeks blossomed like roses in bright sunlight. I had never witnessed people behaving in this manner before, such kindliness of spirit and with such unveiled affection—not unless their speech was slurred and their eyes foggy with drink.

Soon Poe regarded me once more. "In what particular was I incorrect?" he asked.

"The gang of ruffians," I answered. "I don't know whose idea that was, but it don't seem right to me, whoever thought it up."

"And why is that?"

"Because I would of heard by now. There would of been talking. Bragging. People would of been whispering all about it where I live."

"And there has been no such whispering?" he said.

"And her little purse being still there hanging around her wrist the way you said. The people I know would of took it, you can count on that. Whether there was anything in it or not. And this one still had coins in it? That's just about the unlikeliest thing I ever heard of."

He tilted his head slightly as he considered this.

"And that sailor's knot on the bonnet," I said. "That's another thing."

"Yes?"

"Anybody I know who could tie a sailor's knot wouldn't be anybody I know."

At this he laughed. "A sailor's knot is too intricate for your fraternity of acquaintances—is this your implication?"

"I'm saying why tie a bonnet back on in the first place? Why take the time to bother? If you care so little that you can strangle somebody, do you care enough that you're going to put her bonnet back on her?"

And now his eyes narrowed. "Your point is well made."

He sat very still and did not take his eyes from mine, though I suspected he was not really seeing me at that moment, he was gazing again upon the New Jersey shore, taking his bearings, readjusting his conclusions. Slowly, then, he closed his eyes and held them closed for half a minute.

Mrs. Clemm stood motionless at the sink, her shoulders hunched.

Finally he opened his eyes and said to me, "I need to rectify this immediately. Will you accompany me back into town?"

At this Mrs. Clemm spoke. "You will do no such thing. It will be nightfall in an hour and you haven't had your supper yet. And besides all that there's the scent of rain in the air."

"I think she's right about the rain," I said.

Poe's expression relaxed. "Mrs. Clemm has a wondrous tempering effect on my impetuosity."

I nodded, and decided then and there that I must remember a few of his big words and try to uncover their meanings.

"Your young friend is welcome to stay," she said. "He looks as if he could use a bowl or two of my good soup."

"And good soup it truly is," Poe said. Then, "Would you care to pass the evening with us, Master Dubbins?"

Truth was, with an extra dime in my pocket I was in no hurry to sneak back home just to have the wealth shaken out of me. I was in no hurry, in fact, to take another unnecessary step.

"I could sleep out on the porch," I told him. "And we could head back to town first thing tomorrow."

"Will your absence at home cause no consternation?"

"I won't be much missed, if that's what you're saying."

And suddenly there was Mrs. Clemm's hand on my shoulder, warm and heavy. "I'll show you where you can wash up," she said. "Afterward, Mr. Poe could read to you if you'd like."

"Dickens is always good for the appetite," he said.

"I don't need no help in that area," I told him. In fact the prospect of prolonging the warmth of Mrs. Clemm's touch, of spending an evening in a warm clean room and taking supper with her and Poe out here in the fresh-air silence of upper Manhattan, it was all so beguiling that for once in my life even the suggestion of soap and water did not revolt me.

6

I HAD no idea there was a person in the other room. For over an hour no sound had issued from behind the closed door, not so much as a squeak of bedsprings or the scuff of a footfall. But then the door opened as softly as an apology and I looked up at the sighing sound and saw her there and though but ten years old I felt the first distant stirrings of a fancy that would haunt me for the remainder of my life.

We were sitting as before at the small square table, Poe and I. He had laid a copy of his newspaper article flat in front of him and was reading through line by line and making notes to himself in the margins. From what I could ascertain, the notes were of two orders: the first, distinguished by question marks and exclamation points and by whole phrases underlined or circled, had to do with the accuracy of known or assumed facts in regard to Mary Rogers. He had his own shorthand, I suppose, and knew which of his marks indicated which facts to maintain and which to reconsider. The other notes were purely editorial—the writer's compulsion to change words and syntax even after the story had been set in hot type and was irrevocably printed.

He had given me a book with which to entertain myself—it was *The Story of a Bad Boy* by T. B. Aldrich, which Poe presented to me with the remark, "Here's a book you might find amusing. I certainly did, though it contains not a single humorous line." But I found his obsessive revision and reanalysis a far greater divertissement. I had never before witnessed a writer at work, and if invited to observe one I would have thought the spectacle dull indeed, a furrowed brow and a scribbling fist, a secret smile and a scratching pen. But with Poe there was more to it than that. A tension, as of a spring coiling ever tighter. A profound and abiding discontent. A desperate and almost fevered sense of time trickling away. Here was a man, I thought, trying to reweave the fabric of the universe, one word at a time.

We had been at this for perhaps thirty minutes—Poe writing, I watching, Mrs. Clemm stirring the soup—when the bedroom door came whispering open. We all wheeled at the sound, turning like a small flock of birds in sudden but harmonious tilt with a maverick breeze. She was not much more than a girl, certainly still in her teens, though perhaps a year or two older than she looked, and she looked to be a child, a cherub; she was plump and sleepy-eyed and not very tall and her breasts were full and round and her skin was as pale, paler than that of any of the gaslight courtesans of Broadway. She exuded both innocence and sexuality. On her eyelids and hands the pale blue veins showed through, and on each of her cheeks a small scarlet blush that seldom faded, a tiny crimson carnation of blood beneath her skin.

Poe was at her side in an instant. An arm around her shoulder, a hand smoothing back her hair, his voice murmuring. She looked up at him with adoring eyes. His daughter, I told myself. Poe and Mrs. Clemm have a daughter. And with that observation, a part of me claimed her for myself.

But then the jolt. He led her closer to the table. A scent of musty sweetness rose off her pallid skin.

"Sissie," he said, which caused me to revise my observation, transform her from his daughter to his sister, "this is the resourceful young man I told you about last night. The one I met on the waterfront."

"Master Dubbins," she said, and held out her hand to me. I did not know what to do with it. But I took it just the same, seeing as my own hand was anomalously clean and would in all probability not long remain in that condition. Her hand was warm and plump and damp. I felt it reaching all the way inside me.

"Augie," Poe continued, "this is my wife, Virginia. My angel."

I could not help myself; I pivoted to shoot a look at Mrs. Clemm to see how she was taking this news, but she stood grinning ear to ear, beaming with such adoration for both of them that even her broad homely countenance seemed beatified.

Poe, no doubt no stranger to shock such as mine, explained, "Mrs. Clemm is Sissie's mother."

"I thought you two was married," I blurted out, and wagged a finger between the two adults.

Mrs. Clemm gasped and turned her face but Poe never flinched. "In a sense we are," he said. "In the deepest and purest sense, all three of us are married. Together we form a complete and single One."

For the next several minutes, then, both Poe and Mrs. Clemm fussed over Virginia. They made her comfortable at the table with a shawl across her lap and a pillow beneath her stockinged feet. When she spoke, which was not often, it was to thank Poe or her mother, to assure them that she was fine, they should go back to what they were doing, her voice as musical as a meadowlark's but muted, as if the lark were singing not to the sky but to the ground. She did not seem so much weak as fragile, made of some rare and delicate stuff that her husband and mother were ever careful not to jar.

I knew nothing then of her illness, of the white plague that had tattooed the crimson bloom of death to her cheeks. I thought the lassitude with which she moved, the dreaminess, a kind of sultry affectation, the little girl as actor, child pretending to be seductress.

And finally supper, and none too soon. How to describe my first dinner with the Poes? Mere soup and bread, yes, except that there was nothing mere about it, the bread sliced thick and warm and as dense as soft wood, as fecund and filling as manna. And the soup, my bowl overflowing, filled twice to the brim from Mrs. Clemm's generous ladle, the thick white floury broth in which floated islands of potatoes and carrot and wild onion and soft buttery chunks of seared rabbit meat. And to top it all off, my hands were clean. It was as near to a religious experience as I had yet enjoyed.

After supper Poe and Mrs. Clemm cleared the table. I had never before witnessed a man helping to wash the dishes—had seldom enough seen my own mother bother with it—and so I sat there awkwardly at the table, trying not to blush or fidget or pick at myself while Virginia smiled at me.

"Please tell me what it's like where you live," she asked out of nowhere.

When I failed to answer, tongue-tied, wishing suddenly that my clothes could be as clean as my hands, she asked, "Do you live with your mother and father?"

"Well, most times," I answered finally, "it's just my mother more or less. Plus whoever she has with her that night. From what I can guess my pap's in the Tombs."

At this Mrs. Clemm released a tiny moan. I could not look at her or at anyone else for the moment, I looked only at the tablecloth, the stain on white cotton where I had slopped my soup.

"There was a man used to live next door to us," I continued, unable to stop the river of words now that the sluice gate had been opened, "but he was always coming into the house whenever my pap wasn't there. They had more than one go-round over it from what I can remember. Still the man wouldn't stop coming round. Finally my pap come in one night and the man was there on the bed with her and my pap picked up a board lying in with the coal and he went after the man and didn't let up until he had bashed his head to a pulp. They got my pap down on the bottom floor of the Tombs now is what she told me once, that time she said it was where I was going to end up myself sooner or later. Sometimes I ask her about him but she just waves her hand away at me, so I don't know what's true and what's not. I guess he's in there though. They say they put the bad ones on the bottom floor where it's damp and you don't get much light because they die quicker there. This was maybe five or six years ago when he went in. I imagine he's hanging on all right though. I imagine it don't bother him much."

When I finally lifted my eyes off the table it was to find all three of them staring at me as if I were some alien thing. Which is exactly how I felt. Something hawked up and spat out. Virginia sat with a cream-colored handkerchief pressed to her mouth, Mrs. Clemm with both hands clasped beneath her neck, and Poe with one hand pressed to his cheek. But their eyes all said that they saw me differently than I saw myself; they could gaze upon something as ill favored as me and not be revolted, but filled instead with a warm and illuminating pity, an emotion I did not yet know.

I was ashamed of myself for talking so much and would have preferred to bury my head or at least turn away, yet I could not keep my gaze from returning to Virginia's bosom, her round breasts heaving. It gave me a perverse kind of pleasure to suppose that something I had said could make her breasts heave so.

Half a minute later Poe went to a cupboard and took out a small tin pail. With this in hand he crossed toward the door. "My evening stroll," he said, "while yet the gloaming lingers." There was more than a bit of the actor in him, in both him and his wife, I suppose, he with his histrionic flourishes of language, she with her swoonish demeanor. Mrs. Clemm, in size and temperament, was the rock to which both of them were anchored.

"Augie," Poe said at the door, "come stretch your legs with me."

We walked together out the lane and at the main thoroughfare turned east. Poe fiddled with a pipe, scraping out the bowl with a small knife, but he did not fill the pipe and after ten minutes or so he slipped it into a pocket. As we were approaching a roadhouse he finally spoke.

"Perhaps two or three ruffians," he said, as if the subject of Mary Rogers had been on our lips all along, "who then swore an oath of silence. Knowing, of course, the dire consequences of careless talk."

I shook my head. "Careless talk where I come from is what makes you who you are. You do something, you make good and sure everybody knows about it. You put your name on the deed before anybody else can lay claim to it."

"And nobody has laid claim to Mary Rogers," he said.

"She was in too good of shape for the people I know. She'd of been stripped to the skin, and maybe even below that."

He nodded to himself but said nothing more. At the roadhouse he went inside and purchased a bucket of the local brew, and when he stepped back outside and my gaze went to the bucket, he made the only remark ever offered me about his wife's condition. "A glass or two helps Sissie to rest," he said.

"So what is it that's wrong with her?"

He closed his eyes briefly, walked blind for two steps. I fell in beside him and asked nothing more.

On our return to the cottage I silently formulated a dozen questions about this man who, by all indications, had opened a doorway in my life, questions I would be ill equipped to answer for a while. In time I grew to understand him better, I think, to piece together from his writings and from conversations with Mrs. Clemm the tragedies of his past, his parents' lives as itinerant actors, his mother's early death from tuberculosis and his father's disappearance, the estrangement from and finally abandonment by his foster father, the self-destructive moods that seized him from time to time and regularly cast him in dishonor, the death by brain tumor, when he was fourteen, of the first woman he loved, the way he clung as if for salvation to his remaining family, his aunt Martha Clemm, his cousin and adolescent wife Virginia, both of whom were unabashedly devoted to him. And also the desperation of poverty, the destitution, the sense of hanging by his fingernails over the black abyss.

All this, known only in hindsight, helps to explain how, in the face of Mary Rogers's drifting corpse, he had remained so calm. And why the subjects most treated in his writings, the investigations he never finished probing, were of death and loss and madness. At thirty-one years of age he had already deduced from too much firsthand evidence that death was arbitrary and capricious and ubiquitous, that all sources of pleasure were as dandelion fluff in the sweep of an unseen hand, and that every human mind was capable of disintegrating into lunacy, that most in fact were already halfway there.

I always wondered back then, but no longer, why he, a learned man, a Southern gentleman of grace and erudition, would deign to pass his time with a dirty-necked street rat such as myself. A clue to this mystery can be found in his own writings. Much of his life can be studied in his fictions. Take, for example, "A Man in the Crowd." In this tale the narrator relates, in a voice remarkably like Poe's own, how he frequently sat at a coffee shop and watched the pedestrian traffic pass by on a busy street. The narrator doesn't express but the reader can certainly intuit an atmosphere of alienation in the tale, the narrator's sense that he does not fit with society, that he cannot participate but as an observer on the fringe. There is too a sense of superiority, of being more insightful, more intellectually alive than the clerks and gamblers and gentry and ruffians who pass the narrator's table.

But then the narrator's gaze is arrested by the appearance of an old man, an old man dressed in rags that were once fine linen, who carries both a diamond and a dagger, a man whose gnarled visage suggests "the ideas of vast mental power, of caution, of penuriousness, of avarice, of coolness, of malice, of blood-thirstiness, of triumph, of merriment, of excessive terror, of intense—of extreme despair." The narrator is so intrigued by this countenance that he leaps from his chair and follows the old man throughout the city, through the dark rain of night and into the gray of dawn, always where crowds are thickest and most boisterous, the old man milling about but never pausing, never coming to a halt. Finally the narrator is too weary to follow any longer. The narrator's conclusion? That the old man is so driven to keep moving, even unto death, because he cannot stand to be alone for even a few minutes.

The reader of this tale never knows who the old man is, but I think I know. The narrator of the story is Poe himself, of course, and the old man he chases is the person Poe fears he will become, the person he has every capacity to become. Poe, in the story, was following his own future, hoping to see where it might lead. And what he saw was terrifying: a wholly empty existence, the ceaseless peregrination of a man who though estranged from all humanity is yet compelled to a desperate if insubstantial intercourse with it, a man who, like Poe, cannot endure the hideous knowledge that he is utterly and irremediably alone.

And so the night was ushered in. An aubergine night, smelling sweetly of a rain that did not come until the last hours of darkness, and then as softly as a mist. When Poe and I returned with the bucket of beer we all retired for a while to the front porch and the coolness of descending night. And I, who knew little then of Poe's misery or the nature of Virginia's delicate coughs, I never felt sweeter than I did sitting there belly full on the porch steps, Poe with his pipe filled finally and the vague cherry scent of it, the fireflies winking through the trees, the gossamer stars; it was the truest moment I had ever lived, the most safe and painless even though precipitated by the corpse of a strangled woman, and I lived that night all the way through my body, from matted mop of hair right down to unwashed toes.

Poe and Virginia sharing a deacon's bench, Mrs. Clemm filling a straight-back chair close to her daughter's side, and me content to claim the bottom step, legs stretched out toward the flower bed. Poe took his wife's hand into his lap and held it there and sometimes stroked it, and more than once I saw out of the corner of my eye—wanting to watch them head-on but not wanting anybody to know how desperately I craved such tranquil scenes—I watched how he would lean close to her and with an open palm fan air into her face, she with mouth open slightly as she breathed the breeze in, pale lips making a small O to take in the shallow drafts, a low and susurrous flutter in the back of her throat. I thought the sound amusing then, a kitten's purr. Such a softness emanated from her, in voice and flesh and temperament and bearing, the gaze from her eyes the very soul of softness, that it would have been difficult for me to imagine any part of her as hard. But her lungs were hardening day by day, brittling, ossifying, and in due course she would cough them out a shard at a time.

Most times she sat there with her head against Poe's shoulder, or leaned forward momentarily to sip from her glass of warm beer. I was fascinated by her and stole a lingering glance whenever I could. And it was more than the first flickers of a prepubescent fire she aroused in me, it was something I had hitherto not known, had until that night small occasion for, too wrapped up in my own survival, too desperate for myself to allow any true compassion for another human being. But Virginia brought out in me those feelings for all three of them, and at times that night I trembled in wonder and fear of this new deep stream that flowed through me.

I imagined that Poe and I might continue our discussion of Mary Rogers that night, but he did not return to the subject, and I, after immersing myself in their rural serenity, was content to hold my tongue until morning. Certainly Virginia and Mrs. Clemm would have been well apprised of the murder by then, his investigation and consequent newspaper story, yet this was not the time or place to advance the discussion. From time to time Poe flashed me a small smile, a wink of complicity. We were the men here, this was what his wink told me. It took me in and made me a part of their tableau. It was our duty, his wink implied, to sit strong and silent in watchful protection of the women.

I had no idea how much protection Poe himself would require in the days ahead.

Early on in our evening a red tabby came strutting around the corner of the house and leapt onto the porch. I drew back with a start, as surprised as if it were a mountain lion. In the next instant the cat was atop Poe's lap and pushing its head under his hand.

"Well, well," Poe said, "the General has returned, home from his wanderings."

He stroked the cat's head a few times. "Augie," he said, "this old soldier on my lap is General Tom. An infrequent boarder in our home. Recently returned, if these nicks on his ear are any indication, from the conflict in Cuba."

"And where are your comrades in arms tonight?" he asked the cat. General Tom arched his neck and pushed his head against Poe's hand.

Then, to me, "Now that Tom is here, his two scouts will no doubt wander in as well. Aristotle is a blue Parisian; he will typically announce his presence by singing from beneath the big lilac bush out there. But Asmodaios—" He paused to flash me a look of dark foreboding.

Virginia raised the handkerchief to her mouth and giggled softly.

"You will not see our black Asmodaios," Poe said, "until he has wrapped himself around your face. By then his mouth will be pressed to yours, and you will feel your life force being sucked away. . . ."

Even in the faltering light I could see how wide were Poe's eyes, how riveting. I sat paralyzed. Then Mrs. Clemm broke the spell with a loud pshaw.

"Now, Eddie," she scolded, "you will give the boy night tremors."

I turned to her. "Is he talking about another cat or something worse?"

"He's just a stringy old tomcat, don't you worry. But he does like to sneak up on a person sleeping and curl up underneath your chin. Which wouldn't be so bad if he wasn't so black and invisible in the night, and if his breath didn't reek of bird eggs and fetor."

Virginia said with a devilish smile, "You had better sleep with a blanket over your head tonight, Augie."

It was how I always slept in any case, with just a tiny opening for my mouth to take in air. That night, however, I resolved to try sleeping without access to fresh oxygen.

Soon dusk relented to full twilight, and it was then a raucous and wild sound came shooting like arrows from the woods behind the house.

"Our local murder has returned," Poe announced.

Mrs. Clemm tsk-tsked him again. "A *murder* is the term for a flock of crows," she told me. "They come in this time every evening to take roost in the high branches. You will hear them again at sunrise."

"I dreamed of crows," Virginia said. "This afternoon when I was napping. I just now remembered it."

"Did you, beloved?" Poe said. He kept one hand atop the cat's head, the other covering his wife's small hand.

"They were sitting at my window," she told him. "That's all there was to the dream. A half-dozen of them all lined up on the casement, their beaks pressed hard against the glass."

"It's because of the bread and seed you lay on the windowsill," he said.

"I feed the finches and chickadees. I have no desire to attract the lank one to my window. He will come soon enough without invitation."

Poe made a sound at this, a kind of *shhshhshhshhshh* with his teeth tightly clenched.

"What's the line from *Macbeth*?" Virginia asked. " 'The raven himself is hoarse that croaks the fatal entrance.' "

"Of Duncan," Poe said. "Of Duncan. 'Of Duncan under my battlements.' "

Even I, too illiterate to know who were the Macbeth and Duncan of whom they spoke, could not miss the trembling shadows in Virginia's voice. Nor could I miss the pall that descended on the porch in the aftermath, all three of them silent, all motionless but for Poe who with eyes closed tightly now shook his head back and forth as if negating the image of something cruel that had raced before his eyes.

And I felt something more tangible as well, a shudder through my company as real as a Canadian gust. As was his way, Poe attempted to sweep the chill aside with his wide broom of erudition.

"In fact *Corvus* is a most admirable bird," he said. "It inhabits arctic ice floes and the kiln of the deserts and everywhere in between. Its plumage shines like ink," he said, "and helps it to fly with liquid strokes. It writes an ancient mystery across the sky. The variety of its language finds equal only with our own.

"William the Conqueror carried a standard emblazoned with the *Corvus corax*," he said. He leaned slightly forward in his seat now and gazed into the distance down the hallway of deep night. "Lord Odian learned the secrets of the world from a pair of birds—Thought and Memory—that rode upon his shoulders. The prophet Elijah was fed by ravens sent by God."

He paused for a moment, and when he continued his voice dropped in pitch, as if he were reluctant to acknowledge the rest, to utter it, yet could not but yield to the compulsion to view both sides. "But it's true," he said, "that the dark-coated one is also an outlaw. It repeatedly ignored the ban on lovemaking levied against all inhabitants of the Ark. And when Noah sent a raven forth to search for land, the bird did not return."

"Because the world was filled with bodies," Mrs. Clemm observed. "A feast for the raven. Only Noah and his eight were saved."

"Only those nine were chosen to be saved," Poe corrected her. "A few of the Nephilim survived as well. The godforsaken giants."

She sniffed at this, and shook her head once. I could not tell if she agreed with him or not. As for me, I believed every word he uttered. With every remark he stretched my universe and made it larger, more wondrous and mysterious.

"In any case," Poe said, "the *Corvus* has been revered the world over. The Chinese, the Greeks, the Vikings, even our own mysterious Indians—all revered the *Corvus* as both a god and a rogue, as keeper and disseminator of other-worldly wisdom."

"So perhaps my dream was more than merely that," Virginia said with a small but satisfied smile.

Poe caressed her hand. "It is the waking dreams from which true edification comes. Only then do one's physical senses cease to impinge, which allows for a truer if fleeting glimpse of a world superior to the corporeal. A glimpse of the outer world of Eternity."

And here suddenly was another world I had never paused to imagine, the world of Poe's small porch whereon all things were alien to me, the words and phrases never before heard and so poorly understood by me that they acted on my brain as an intoxicant. But not giddy-making or vertiginous. All their talk of crows and dreams and invisible Eternity; the cat purring in Poe's lap and the glutinous purr from the back of Virginia's throat; Poe's stillness juxtaposed upon his all but throbbing discontent; Mrs. Clemm's huge and mighty gentleness; and not least of all my own place in this tableau, invited guest, half-informed outsider drawn close in the wake of a floating corpse—it all conspired now, all elements combined, the deepening night and the amorous fireflies and the last harsh cawing cries, it all synthesized into a bleak intimation, a whispered but unwavering voice disclosing that I had blundered into something beautiful but awful here, something beguiling, a bog of tragedy that would inevitably entomb us all.

7

I SLEPT deeply for the first half of the night, as if drugged by the company of three sober and unarmed individuals. But as always I awoke with a start in the darkest hour and sat up quickly, arms wrapped about my head to ward off the blow that this time did not come. Gradually I became aware of the glow through the metal plates of the kitchen stove, the red moon rings and scimitars of ember light, and I recollected then just where I was—on a pallet not far from the stove, though far enough that I would not roll over and against it, Mrs. Clemm's usual space, I think—and by degrees the hoary fear sifted out of me. I could hear Mrs. Clemm's heavy snores, a rumble as calming to me as a lullaby.

Before giving myself over to sleep again I rolled toward the bedroom door, saw it closed tight, and imagined, erroneously, Poe and Virginia lying side by side on the soft mattress, in a posture both affectionate and decorous, not in the kind of vulgar tangle my mother and her visitors seemed to prefer, a knot of naked flesh and stink and clotted clothing. This too I found soothing, this idealized image of connubial repose, and so I was able to close my eyes a while longer, awaking just before dawn to see Poe wrapped in a dun-colored damask banyan, a faded old overcoat with flared skirts, seated at the table and bent over a manuscript. A candle illuminated the right side of his face as he scribbled down his thoughts.

When I awoke the final time it was to the vibration of Mrs. Clemm's movements as she built up the fire in the stove. The room was pink with morning, redolent with the tannic perfume of a pot of boiling tea, and as humid as a Turkish bath. Besides the tea there were two large kettles of water bubbling and hissing on the stove.

Mrs. Clemm spotted me wiggling deeper into the pocket of blankets.

She was on me in a flash, stripping the blanket away and spilling me out of my cocoon.

"Smelled it coming, didn't you?" she said with a grin.

"I figured it was just a matter of time."

She held out a hand to me. "Cleanliness is next to godliness."

"Neither of which I ever claimed to be."

"Dirt is the devil's playground."

"What's wrong with a little fun now and then?"

She laughed at this but hauled me to my feet all the same. "You'll find it waiting for you out on the porch," she said. "You better hurry if you don't want the rest of New York waking up to see you naked as a baby. And do it right, young man, or I will do it right myself."

I could easily have kept on going when I walked out her door, could have raced down the lane and avoided that steaming washtub altogether, but that I had spotted a block of salt pork waiting near the stove, poised beside the bag of cornmeal and the crock of apple butter already fetched from the springhouse, and at that moment I would have leapt into an icy stream were that the ultimatum.

"There's some clean clothes out there too," she told me. "Leave your old ones on the porch. They'll be good for keeping the weevils out of the cabbage."

The moment I was outside she probably flew to my blankets to pick through them for fleas and lice, but I could never resent her fastidiousness; she was as generous with goodness as she was stingy with dirt. Besides, my brains were in my stomach, and this, coupled with the crust of dirt I wore everywhere except on my hands, rendered her zealotry nothing short of practical.

Never before had I faced water so early in the day, but face it I did, squeamishly at first, then gluttonously, chortling and splashing until the porch boards were as slick as my carcass. Mrs. Clemm came out midway to pour another blistering kettle of water over my head—a warning to the lice, I imagine, before she applied the bar of lye soap. I squirmed and complained, of course, but I loved every abrasive thrust and pull of her fingers through my hair.

"Breakfast in ten minutes," she finally said. "And don't you come waltzing in buck naked either."

The trousers she left for me had once been Poe's, mended and patched so many times that less than half the material was original cloth. She must have risen early to cut and hem the cuffs and take in the waistline. The blouse was of white poplin and carried the vague scent of lilacs. I was both thrilled and chagrined to imagine this same blouse once distended by Virginia's bosom. The undergarments too—I preferred not to think about who else might have worn them previous to my pulling them on.

Virginia slept late and did not join us for breakfast. Poe came to the table in his banyan and saw me freshly scrubbed and said, "Who's this?"

"That's Master Dubbins," said Mrs. Clemm.

"I believe you are mistaken, Muddy. Master Dubbins is a colored boy and at least two inches taller than this pink fellow."

"Then I don't know who this one is," she said. "Except that he smells a whole lot sweeter than the last one that was here."

Later, when Poe returned to his bedroom to dress for the day, she pushed a broom into my hands. "Watch you don't miss the corners," she said. "And do both rooms, please."

I went to work happily, almost moronically content. If half my little soul, as Tennyson said, was dirt, that half had long evaporated off the floorboards on the porch. What remained had been swollen to twice its normal size by cracklin' bread, salt pork, oatmeal with apple butter, and a beneficence I had never dared to imagine for myself.

Meanwhile I swept to the noises that soon issued from the bedroom, Virginia's fit of coughing upon awakening, Poe's gentle inquiry in response to it. I did not then know that she would cough like this every morning, as well as once or twice during the day, and just as vociferously again at night, and so my thoughts were on Poe instead and on the alchemy he practiced, this prestidigitation called writing.

"He always get up in the middle of the night to write?" I asked.

"It's not unusual," said Mrs. Clemm.

"He's working on the newspaper story, you think?"

She shook her head. "Mr. Poe is a very great writer. A critic of literature. A poet as well."

"Is that for true?"

"His work has been published in numerous periodicals. Before moving here he was the editor of a highly esteemed journal in Richmond, *The Southern Literary Messenger*."

"Well I'll be damned."

She cast a cocked eye in my direction. "I hope and expect that you will subdue your colorful language while in my presence, Augie."

"I thought I did."

"You must try a little harder, please."

"What if I say danged instead?"

She shook her head.

"How about blasted?"

Another chiding look.

"I guess I can't think of no other way to say it then."

"You could say 'My my, isn't that interesting!' "

I giggled so hard I had to steady myself with the broom.

Mrs. Clemm pretended to be in a pucker but I caught the corner of her mouth twitching.

"So if he's so all important," I asked, "why ain't he rich?"

At this she flinched. Her smile evaporated.

A moment later Poe surprised me from the bedroom doorway. *"Felix qui potuit rerum cognoscere causas,"* he said.

"Which means something, I suppose, though I don't know what." I said this fairly quickly and without much interest in pursuing the conversation, for I was straining then for a fuller glimpse of Virginia still supine on her bed. I glimpsed too a Hitchcock chair on the window side of the bed, the chair pulled close to the bed, and slung over the chair a patchwork quilt and Poe's banyan, and only one bolster on the bed and this under Virginia's head, and somehow I knew with a glance that this marriage was in yet another way unlike those I had witnessed before.

Poe must have asked me a question to which I failed to respond, for he then eased shut the bedroom door and told me, "No matter. Latin is a dead language anyway. Good for nothing but a bit of ostentation from time to time."

He winked at Mrs. Clemm then and she crossed quickly to brush a speck of lint off his shoulder. "Fortune awaits," she told him, and kissed his cheek.

He held her close and patted the small of her back. "On the wings of your faith, sweet Muddy."

I thought for a moment they might embrace and kiss, their posture was that intimate. But then he turned, and striding toward the door, announced, "To work, Master Dubbins?"

"I'm ready."

"Might I suggest you leave the broom behind?"

He retrieved a slender satchel of cracked brown cowhide from behind a chair and was soon out the door. I followed at a gallop.

The morning smelled of dew and apples and I swelled myself with the scent. The crows' aubade, the sweep of the sky, the chit and buzz of insects—it all struck me as remarkable in its newness, the incunabula of an unexpected grace. One of Poe's cats watched us from the tall grass; its green eyes glinting from the shadows made my smile even wider.

But we were barely down the lane before Poe's stride faltered. A weariness came into his limbs and into his eyes—as if he had only been feigning jauntiness.

We walked awhile longer before I spoke. "You got up too early, I think."

He offered me a sidelong smile.

"What was it you were writing on?"

"A poem," he said. "A villanelle."

"What's it about?"

"There are but two fit subjects for poetry. Love and death."

"Must be a good one whatever it is. Mrs. Clemm says you're a genius at poem writing."

Another wistful and broken smile. "Some days you wake with honey in your mouth. Some days bile."

Even to a boy it was clear he was not happy with himself, more inclined that morning to see the shadows than the sunlight. In time I would realize that this was his gift as much as it was the burden that would destroy him. He heard the groan of life in common things that other men scarcely noticed—a tree bent in the wind, a floorboard creaking, a trodden stair, a door eased shut, a bedspring, a house at night. He heard the sigh of life in leaf rustle, wing flutter, the flicker of gaslights, in pulling on his trousers, dragging a brush through his hair. There were times too when a trickle of stream spoke to him, the rain tumbling off roof shingles, a trill of laughter, steam from a teakettle, the way Virginia sipped her soup.

In all this and more he also found the pleasures of life, small pleasures, strophes, moments when the ubiquitous groans and sighs became almost comic to him, a cosmic joke. But this surcease never prevailed and scarcely lingered. He heard the darkness of approaching night, the rasp of Virginia's breath, and soon he was attuned once more to life's chorus of protest, its murmured song of misery.

Not until the palaces of Broadway rose into view did he break our silence. He thrust his chin down the avenue. "There are men in this city doing masterful work," he told me, apropos of nothing but his own hoarded thoughts. "Men who at this very minute are alone in their rooms and composing words that will ring through the ages. The poems and tales and philosophies that will lend sustenance and elucidation to the souls of humankind."

I noticed that his pace had quickened again, lengthened, as if he were being drawn by some force, a compulsion I would only later come to recognize as his hunger.

"Like you," I answered.

"Do I count myself among them? Is this what you ask?"

I was about to reply that it hadn't been a question, but he continued. "One day," he said.

And I, because I was just a boy, responded, "Why not now?"

By this time our feet were striking harder ground, cobblestone. There was a bit of carriage traffic about, the growing bustle. "Were you ever alone in a large house?" he asked. "A large and unfamiliar house? The house of a stranger?"

"Once or twice," I answered, though in truth I had been in as many as a roving chambermaid, albeit not to tidy up the beds.

"In such a house," Poe said, "if you sit very quietly, if you do not stir, it is possible at times to sense a presence other than your own. You can never quite locate the room it occupies, yet you know nonetheless that the presence exists. As surely as your breath it exists. This is the way it is with my own greatness, Augie. It sits in one of my rooms, waiting. But I have yet to find the door."

He seemed done in by this revelation, exhausted. He came to a halt on the corner and stood gazing blankly across the street. My own face was flushed and my body warmed from the pace of our walk. I thought it a mistake to let either of us stand in one place too long.

"Where to now?" I finally asked.

He blinked twice, then turned to me.

"We going to talk to somebody about that girl?" I asked. "That Mary Rogers?"

"Soon," he said, and then he was off again, striding so briskly that I had to run to keep up.

FOR THE next two hours I followed Poe from doorway to dark doorway. Before we could take up the business of Mary Rogers he first needed to attend to the business of making a living, and so attempted to peddle his latest composition from editor to editor. This he had in his cowhide satchel, along with several other pieces yet to see print.

"What I most desire in life," he had explained to me before entering the first building, "is the freedom to immerse myself in thought. A life of unfettered contemplation. Unfortunately, the stomach and the landlord demand their due."

He gave me license to wander off where I wished, to conduct whatever business of my own I might devise. But I found this activity of peddling words intriguing, and I was keen to see how the strange process worked.

For Poe's part, it worked that morning like a movable flogging. While I stationed myself outside an office building, flush in my new clothes and refurbished skin and still tasting the morning's breakfast grease on my lips, Poe ventured inside to beg an audience. Only to emerge twenty or so minutes later looking more hangdog than when he had entered.

"What about the *Mirror*?" I finally hazarded, after Poe's seventh or eighth turndown of the morning.

"I have been holding that card to be played last."

He peered across the street as if squinting into a fog.

"Your ace of diamonds," I said.

"Five of spades, I'm afraid."

And to my eyes Neely beat up on him worse than had all the others. When Poe emerged from the *Mirror* building he was listing to one side, as if his satchel contained not paper but the rock of Sisyphus.

"The bastard," I hissed before Poe had uttered a word.

"Oh, he will be happy to publish it," Poe said. "He will be delighted. If only I will make a minor adjustment to the text and trim it by two-thirds."

"And will you?"

In lieu of answering he stared at the cobblestones and pinched the bridge of his nose. "A dollar for a week's cerebration," he muttered.

It seemed a punishing way to make a go of things. Especially when I, in a single afternoon on the waterfront, could pocket a dollar with scarcely having to think at all.

"If it's so hard on you, why do you bother doing it?"

"Why does the river seek the ocean? Why does a star send forth its feeble light?"

I understood this to mean that he had no choice in the matter; the urge to create and to see the creation recognized was a force of nature too compelling to be resisted.

He stood as if in trance for another twenty seconds or so. Then he shook himself out of it. "But it is another matter that puzzles me now."

"And what's that?"

"You will be pleased to know," he said, "that your intuitions concerning Miss Rogers were on target."

"They was?"

"While mine, according to the latest bit of evidence, missed the mark entirely."

"I wish I could say I know what you're talking about."

"This morning's paper. Shown to me—almost gleefully, I might add—by Mr. Neely. Wherein appeared a short article in refutation of my premise concerning the manner of Miss Rogers's demise. The medical examiner now claims that prior to relinquishing the body for interment, he discerned evidence of a recent abortion. Her demise is now attributed to the failure of that procedure."

In answer to this I cocked an eyebrow.

"Are you familiar with the operation?" he asked.

"I know it don't leave finger marks on the neck."

"It is yet another abomination of this city."

"Better an abortion than a foundling," I muttered.

He gave me a long look then, at first squint-eyed, as if he were trying to peer into the wrinkles of my brain. By degrees his visage relaxed, and he warmed me with a small smile.

"Even so," he said, "I should very much like to speak with the official who arrived at this conclusion."

The prospect of a visit to the morgue set me to quivering with a strange excitement. Romantics and children—Poe and I made a full set—harbor a fascination with death, and, whether the roots of this fascination lie in fecund or sour soil, death seems to us a kind of treasure to be, pardon the pun, unearthed.

"How much is Neely paying this time?" I asked.

"Mr. Neely regards the story as having reached its terminus. I believe his words were 'just another countergirl dead of a botched abortion.' "

"And he don't find that interesting?"

"Not interesting nor unusual enough, no."

"Whether it's the truth or not."

"Mr. Neely's first job is to sell papers. The truth notwithstanding."

"So you're off the story now?"

"He offered me instead the opportunity to investigate a second mystery—the disappearance of a man named Fordyce. One whose social status renders him more deserving of the ink."

"He's a muckety-muck, is he?"

"A member of the municipal council."

"Probably holed up somewhere with his Quakeress."

Poe laughed. "Precisely. And I have no inclination to go canvasing the city's brothels, even those better ones, for a wayward councilman."

"Myself, I vote for the morgue."

"Motion carried," he said.

North by northeast we went then, all the way up to the wide-open spaces around Twenty-second Street. This area, while still smelling of orchards and pastures, was home to a few notable establishments. Most prominent in my mind was the walled enclosure of the old federal arsenal, for inside it sat the stolid building with which I had been so frequently threatened by my mother, the House of Refuge. Here criminals under the age of sixteen were sent—pickpockets, prostitutes, thieves, vandals, brawlers; in other words, my peers—sent here to be redeemed through a generous application of hard work, leg irons, brickbats, the cat-o'-nine-tails, and the rule of absolute silence enforced through long nights in a windowless cell.

I glanced at the place, but furtively. I did not really want to get a full look at the establishment, or allow it a look at me.

East of the House of Refuge, on a couple dozen acres overlooking the East River, was another walled complex of buildings, our destination. This was the Bellevue Institution, comprising not only a hospital and morgue but also an icehouse, an almshouse, a greenhouse, a penitentiary, a soap factory, a bakery, a school, and a washhouse. The blue stone poorhouse, at three stories high and over three hundred feet long, was the largest building in the city. It was a small town unto itself, crammed to the gills with sixteen hundred or so wretches at a time. This was where most of the patients from the Bellevue Hospital ended up if they were unlucky enough to survive their treatment, having been earlier turned away from the hospital downtown because their diseases were too contagious or their poverty insufficiently decorous.

But the complex was not without its entertaining side as well, for here inside its walls was the city's main execution ground. Criminals from the various prisons were brought here to meet their Maker at the end of a rope. The audience for these spectacles was not what it had once been, however; in fact the gallows had been moved to the Bellevue for precisely that reason, so that the long commute might deter the picnicking and generally frolicsome spirit, not to mention the inflammation of animal passions, that had accompanied the hangings downtown.

There was little frolic to my spirit, though, or to Poe's, as we passed solemnly through the complex's main gate. The guard who pointed us toward the morgue was a cheerless fellow, yet sufficiently impressed by Poe's introduction of himself, ingenuous as it was—"I am E. A. Poe, sir. On assignment for the *Mirror*"—to wave us through unmolested.

The guard stationed outside the morgue, on the other hand, was downright baleful. There was more than a little of the wolverine in him, I think: squat and heavy-jawed, odoriferous, dark eyes sneaky and seething. The moment he saw us coming he leaned back in his chair propped against the fieldstone wall and threw his legs across the threshold.

Poe introduced himself as usual, then moved to step over the outstretched legs. The guard held up a hand.

"What's your business here?" he said.

"I am here to interview the medical examiner."

"Which one?"

"Dr. Spirnock," said Poe.

The guard nodded and sat there rubbing both sets of fingers and thumbs together. His hands were stained yellow from nicotine, as were his teeth. The crease that ran from the right corner of his mouth was permanently darkened from tobacco juice.

"About what in particular?" the guard asked.

At this Poe's eyes narrowed. He must have sensed as I did that this questioning was being conducted for its own sake, that the guard was determined in his own morbid way to wring as much interaction as possible from the only ambulatory visitors he would have all week.

"I am here," Poe said evenly, "on assignment for the *Mirror*, to complete an interview with Dr. Spirnock in regards to a matter that is not your concern. Now then. Do you intend to withdraw your feet or shall I step over them?"

Cowed by Poe, the guard turned his eyes on me. "That ain't no place for a boy inside."

"The young man is my apprentice. He will accompany me."

Still the guard did not withdraw his feet.

Poe patted his jacket pocket, as if searching for paper and pen. "What is your name, sir?"

The guard glared at him.

Poe glared in return.

And finally the guard dragged his feet back to his chair. He leaned toward the door, turned the knob, and shoved the door open.

Poe leaned forward and peered inside. Beyond the small foyer, unlighted, was a hallway leading deeper into the building. And beside the entrance to this corridor an open archway with a set of narrow steps leading downward.

Poe cocked an eyebrow at the guard.

"Examination rooms in the basement," the guard mumbled.

"As to be expected," said Poe. "I thank you, sir." And inside we went.

Down the crooked steps then, Poe in the lead. Almost immediately the air grew cooler, though stuffy, dense, not clean like a forest shade but stagnant and thick. The way was lighted, though poorly, by a sputtering lamp near the top turn and another at the bottom landing, the steps narrow and uneven, tilting one way and then the other but always leading steeply down, down into that sour smell that is like no living odor, acrid and vile, so that the throat and nose and eyes want to close up against it. Even Poe flinched at the first draft of charnel air. Then he set his mouth grimly and marched on down the narrow hallway, pausing moment to moment to glance into the rooms right and left until we came to the wide dim room wherein bodies were briefly stored and examined.

Poe opened this door and stood on the threshold looking in. By peeking around his side I could see one body lying naked and exposed on a long wooden table. It was a male, corpulent and grossly white. If taller I might have seen more of this individual than my eyes could handle, for as it was I saw more than I wished to see, that he had been sliced open down the middle and the flaps of his flesh laid over like those of an unbuttoned vest. A tub on a stand beside this table contained a pile of brown something, viscous and obscene, quivering in the lamplight. On both sides of the table, having slopped out over its gutters and onto the dirt floor, were wide dark stains old and new, some still shiny and slick, ominous shadows of life that had melted into the packed soil.

"There," Poe said to himself, and turned to his right. Keeping near the wall, we walked six paces to the door of a smaller adjoining room, the office of the medical examiner, a Dr. Spirnock. The door was ajar and we could see him at his desk, a smallish man in a frock stained brown and yellow.

Poe rapped his knuckles against the frame and pushed the door open. The doctor was slow to look up at him.

"A moment of your time, sir?"

Spirnock answered with an arch of his eyebrows. He was no doubt unused to being spoken to by the people he encountered in these rooms.

"My name is E. A. Poe, with the *Mirror*, sir."

"And?"

"About the girl taken from the river."

"Miss Rogers."

"The very one. A follow-up question or two, if you would be so kind."

Spirnock sighed and looked at the ceiling. He then waved his hand as if to motion Poe inside, but there were no chairs in the room other than the doctor's, and we ventured no farther in.

Poe said, "The evidence that led you to conclude the nature of Miss Rogers's demise. Could you describe it, please?"

"Could," the doctor said, "but will not. We must allow the dead their dignity."

"To be sure, yes." He paused. "Could you tell me, then, was she . . . mutilated in some way?"

"Certainly not."

"Her appearance was otherwise normal, considering the circumstances."

"It was."

"The evidence, therefore, was precisely what one would expect from an unsuccessful abortion. The presence of blood and amniotic fluids."

"Exactly."

"To such degree as to render an internal examination unnecessary."

"Correct."

The doctor struck me as a very tired rodent of a man, on the very brink of exhaustion. His lips barely moved when he spoke, and he spoke as little as possible.

"And yet . . . ," Poe said.

The doctor said nothing.

"She had been in the water for quite some time."

Still the doctor remained silent.

"And the current is strong, I can vouch for that myself."

The doctor's gaze drifted slightly to his left, to a blankness of gray wall.

"Would not these elements," Poe asked, "meaning the duration of her immersion, coupled with the erosive force of the water, tend to wash away or otherwise obliterate all evidence of a soluble nature?"

"Superficially," the doctor said. "Not in the cervix."

"It was my understanding that you performed no internal examination."

The doctor did not speak for a moment, and then he smiled. It is the anomalous gesture, not the typical one, that belies the truth. "Perhaps you misunderstood," he said.

"Yes. Perhaps." Now Poe smiled too, but pointedly. "As to the finger-marks around the young lady's neck, these raised no suspicions on your part?"

"Postmortem," he said.

"She was strangled after she passed away?"

The doctor closed his eyes for a few moments. He sat not quite huddled forward and brought his arms around his stomach as if to hold himself upright.

Finally he opened his eyes and stared at the wall and spoke. "The marks had the appearance of being made by a human hand, but this appearance was illusory. In my view they were more likely the result of incidental trauma following her immersion in the river." If he was not exhausted prior to this speech, he was wholly done in by the end of it. He appeared on the verge of slumping forward with his head on the desk. His eyes could not hold a gaze.

"Ah, well then," Poe said after a long and awkward pause. He nodded to himself. Finally he ended with, "I thank you, sir."

The doctor had no strength for reply. He lifted his hand a few inches into the air, then let it fall.

I slid to the side so as to allow Poe's exit from the doorway. I watched him moving out into the larger room and then into the hall. I turned to face the door into the doctor's office once more. "What's wrong with that fella out there on the table?" I asked.

And Spirnock answered in a voice like night wind, "Dead."

"I'd sort of figured that out already. What I'm saying is, you don't cut everybody open like that, do you?"

"Only those who ingest their employer's diamonds."

"Jesus. Is that what killed him?"

"Toxemia. Obstruction of his bowels."

"So you're saying he died because his arse was plugged up?"

"Let that be a lesson to you."

If this was the extent of wisdom to be gleaned from an intimacy with death, it suggested to me that there was not much wisdom to be had from dying. It was at that moment, no doubt, that my fascination with death began its wane. In any case I exited, took one last sidelong glance at the riven man, and made for the stairs, plunging upward through the darkness two steps at a time.

Poe stood waiting for me outside the morgue, ten yards beyond the glowering guard. The moment the sunshine hit my face I gasped for air.

Poe's first words to me were, "And what did you think of him?"

"I think he should of stuck to meat and potatoes."

Poe crinkled his brow and cocked his head at me.

"Oh, you mean the doctor. Well, as for him, he wasn't much of a talker, was he?"

"He was not. But as to the little he did have to say, how did it strike you?"

I knew enough of Poe's methods by now to guess that he was trying to coax from me what he had already surmised. I hazarded a response. "Like he knew more than he was saying?"

"It was more than a mere omission of facts, I think. A deliberate misdirection."

"Like he was maybe . . . lying through his teeth?"

His nod signaled approval of my conclusion. "Less clear is the man's motivation for deceit. Have you any thoughts on that matter?"

"Well, from the looks of him he's either worn to the bone, or he's got dropsy, or else—"

"You've seen that look before. As have I. The gaze of Morpheus."

"I was thinking he's an opium fiend."

"In which case," Poe said, "our thoughts agree. Yet that alone does not explain a deliberate misdiagnosis."

"Somebody must of put him up to it, don't you think?"

"What I think, Master Dubbins, is that we must retrace our steps a bit. I have an insistence to make."

Back we went then to the heart of the city. Back to the newspaper building and upstairs to Neely's office. All along the way Poe kept muttering to himself, trying out the adjurations with which he intended to persuade the hard-nosed editor that the case of Mary Rogers warranted further investigation.

On our way through the larger room, we passed another man on his way out, a man who looked for all the world like he was holding his breath and everything else he owned so close to his body that none of it might touch the desks or the rough and unkempt men or even the tobacco-heavy air. His manner was not so much effeminate as it was aristocratic, the ramrod carriage and imperious tilt of his chin, not to mention the flawless crease and hang of his linen suit and the near-radiant whiteness of his gloves.

I noticed that a few of the newspapermen in watching him pass suppressed a snicker or tossed a smirk to one of their fellows. But Poe, as the man in white approached down the narrow aisle between desks, drew himself up straight and came abruptly to a halt. By the time the man in white was three paces from us, Poe already had his hand extended.

"Sir, my name is Poe, and I consider it extremely fortunate that I should have the opportunity to meet you here."

The man's reluctance to shake Poe's hand was conspicuous. The handshake was brief and, it seemed to me, lacking actual contact. But if the man in white was repulsed by physical contact, it was not, apparently, specific to Poe. "I know your work," he said. "I admire it."

"Ah, well, I am grateful for the compliment. And perhaps someday we might meet to pursue the subject of belles-lettres, nothing would delight me more. In the meantime, sir, if you would not mind my calling on you in the not too distant future, there is another matter I should like to discuss. Concerning your *pensionnat pour les garçons*."

If Poe was attempting to obfuscate his meaning to me, the words, at least, were successful. But not the slight nod of his head in my direction, nor the quick glance leveled at me then by the man in white.

"Certainly," was all the man said. They nodded again and then the man swept past us and was gone.

Poe strode forward to Neely's door and rapped once and stepped inside. I barely had time to find a vacant corner from which to survey the newspapermen at work, when Neely's door reopened and out came Poe. I all but raced after him as he strode out of the room.

"No luck?" I asked when I had caught up with him on the staircase.

"On the contrary." His eyes were jubilant. "It seems that my earlier remarks had their effect after all. For between that meeting and this one Mr. Neely experienced a complete change of heart. I am charged once again with probing the mystery of our young lady's demise."

"Ain't that something," I said.

"Ain't it indeed."

"And that other fella up there, the one all done up in white. What was he all about?"

"He was about the future," Poe said. His tone was so optimistic, even reverent with hope, that I dared not ask him more.

9

OUR NEXT stop was but a lively stroll away—the emporium where, until her disappearance, Mary Rogers had been employed. At first glance Anderson's Tobacco Shop struck me as a haven of sorts, a room where bonhomie and the languid pleasures of a good cigar might be enjoyed unhurried by the clamor of greed and crapulence outside. Often I had watched gentlemen coming and going from such establishments, and always there was about these men, especially in the going, an air of fulfillment and satiation. (I would not then have thought the satisfaction sexual, but that was then. Now, a connoisseur myself of a fine Havana Imperial once a day, and at a time in my life when few other satisfactions abide, I might beg to differ.)

But of the tobacconist's shop there was a headiness encountered immediately inside the door, which is where I stationed myself. This headiness owed itself perhaps to the undulating haze of azure smoke, the thick scents that entwined all about me like vaporous serpents in a coupling frenzy. But more than the smoke it was the company of men, the ambiance of a secret society, fraternity, the scoffing at solitude.

It was not a large shop but nearly square, at least sixteen feet on every side. The eastern wall and half of the northern I remember as being paralleled by a wooden display case topped with a heavy oaken counter. Behind the glass panels of the case were crock after crock of tobaccos for Gotham's chewing and sniffing and smoking indulgence, chopped leaves of every flavor and blend imaginable, each crock tightly stoppered against the leeching air. There were lovely wooden humidors holding neatly coffined cigars that ranged in circumference from that of my thumb to that of my wrist, and in length from my little finger to my forearm. And finally there were a few small boxes of the *cigarritos* then coming into fashion, the Opera Puffs and Three Kings. To a child who more than once had snatched a smoldering butt-end from the street so as to cram it in the corner of his mouth, the place held at least as much appeal as a confectioner's shop.

The full western half of the room was given over to easy chairs, spittoons, and ashtrays. The seats were mostly wing chairs, as I recall, a half dozen of those perhaps, brocaded greens and blues of sturdy smoke-dulled fabrics. The chairs could be turned and moved about the room in various configurations conducive to discourse, for the tobacconist's shop was as much a men's social club as it was a sales outlet for the calming brown leaf.

As to the denizens therein, I spotted a conversation group of three, all smoking cigars, and another of two sucking pipes, but I quickly looked away from all five pairs of eyes because half the excitement of being there was in knowing I did not belong. I assumed a posture that I hoped conveyed both nonchalance and defiance, then watched Poe approach the counter.

Anderson, seated behind the counter, was quick to leave the table where he had been measuring out tobaccos into individual pouches. He was more than a little portly and none too tall; only his head and shoulders were visible above the countertop.

"Good day, good sir," he said to Poe. He had a pale and bulbous head whose skull was fringed with bright red hair and bristly mutton-chops. The bulb of his nose was as red as his hair, his mouth wide and lips pale.

"Good morning," Poe offered in return. He moved leisurely along the length of the display, perusing the tobaccos, his fingertips sliding along the counter's rounded edge.

"And what would your pleasure be today, sir?"

"The Sumatra blend—how does it draw?"

"It draws, sir, if you don't mind my honest opinion, like the breath of Old Joe himself. Allow me to recommend instead the Pocahontas blend. The sweetest Roanoke leaves delicately mixed by yours truly with the rum-cured leaves of the Tortuga Islands. The result is a balm to the nose and throat."

"At four times the price of the Sumatra."

"For tenfold the pleasure, sir."

Poe withdrew his purse. "I will try a pipeful or two," he said, and turned slightly from the counter so that none could see the bareness of his purse.

Anderson scooped out the tobacco and dipped it into a small cloth pouch and snapped the drawstrings shut. Poe laid a coin in the man's hand. I almost winced to see him giving up what little he had so as to avoid the appearance of brusqueness. Like every Southern gentleman or lady I have ever encountered, Poe considered it indecorous to come too quickly to the point.

"And what else for you this fine morning?" Anderson asked.

Poe raised the tobacco pouch to his nose and inhaled through the cloth. "A lovely fragrance, I agree."

"Exactly as I promised."

"You did, sir, you did. And perhaps, if you would be so kind, you might tell me something else as well."

"At your service," Anderson said.

"My name, sir, is Poe. E. A. Poe, who authored the chronicle of your former employee, as it appeared in the *Mirror*."

At the mention of his name, the pair of gentlemen smoking pipes turned to look in his direction as if simultaneously prodded. One of the men moved so abruptly that the feet of his chair squeaked across the floor. I felt a sudden swell of pride that I had been befriended by a man so illustrious that the very utterance of his name could make heads turn.

"I read the very same," Anderson told him. "Well done, sir. Well done indeed."

"Well intentioned, perhaps. Though I now suspect there remains more to the story than I was first able to ascertain."

"How so?"

"What I wonder," Poe said, "is how you found Miss Rogers as an employee. By which I mean, was she prompt to work of a morning? Was she reliable and honest?"

"To each of those particulars, yes. Otherwise I would not have grown so fond of her."

"She had worked for you for some considerable time?"

"Two years all told, short of a month."

"And she was not, to your knowledge, prone to association with . . . the rougher elements of our city?"

"That, sir, is an indelicate inquiry. To which the answer is a resounding no."

"What were her associations, then, as you were able to observe them?"

"As I observed them, none. I observed Miss Rogers only during the hours of her employ."

"She never spoke of other interests?"

"She attended the theater on occasion. She enjoyed dining out with her fiancé, whose name, as I recall, you are familiar with already. She assisted her mother with the business of the boardinghouse. She visited frequently with an aunt who lives in the country."

"All of which," Poe said, "would leave her little time for other associations."

"My point precisely, sir."

Poe looked to the floor and again pinched the bridge of his nose, as if trying to shape a thought between his finger and thumb. He stood motionless for so long that the tobacconist leaned toward him over the counter. The two pipe smokers watched with unabating interest.

"Sir?" the tobacconist said. "Are you in need of assistance?"

Poe looked up and blinked. He inhaled sharply. "A passing dizziness. No need to worry."

"The tobacco-freshened air. It sometimes overinvigorates the lungs."

"Indeed," Poe said. He smiled as he wiped a bit of dryness from the corner of his mouth.

"In regards to what you may have had occasion to observe," he continued, "concerning Miss Rogers and her acquaintances. I am sure that, from time to time, you can count a seaman or two among your customers?"

"Frequently," Anderson said.

"And of these seamen, would you say that Miss Rogers was personally acquainted with any one of them?"

"If you are insinuating, sir—"

"I am asking only if she appeared to know one or more of these seamen as a friend rather than as a customer."

"My answer, then, is no. It did not so appear to me."

"Did she to your knowledge have friends who lived upriver of, say, Cortlandt Street?"

"We attended to our business, Mr. Poe. We made no attempt to pry into one another's personal life."

"Nor am I suggesting as much. But when she was absent from her counter for a full day, having offered, I take it, no preliminary reason for her absence, you were concerned for her welfare, were you not?"

"If by that you mean for her health, yes, surely. I hoped she did not suffer from a serious illness. Though I assumed it was a recurrence of the catarrh that had caused her absence once before."

"And when would that have been?"

"Eight, nine months ago more or less. It was shortly after Thanksgiving, as I recall."

"And how long was she absent on that occasion?"

"A Monday and a Tuesday. I recall because on Mondays, first thing, she restocks the humidors, but on that occasion I attended to the chore myself."

"She returned to work on Wednesday?"

"She did."

"And offered as excuse an incidence of catarrh."

"She did just that."

"And you, of course, had no cause to doubt her word on it."

"Nor do I now."

A pause then. Poe stroked his chin.

"At any time during her tenure in your establishment," he finally said, "did you perhaps take notice of any of your customers who displayed an untoward interest in the young lady?"

"My customers? Never! Each and every one of my customers is, like the fine gentlemen here this morning, of the highest character and demeanor. High Constable Hays patronizes my shop, sir, as do the likes of Samuel Ruggles, Philip Hone, Johnston Hobbs, the Reverend Isaiah Green. Are you familiar with the names of Aspinwall, Grinnell, Roosevelt, Verplanck, for example? Each and every day, sir, it is men such as these who pass through my door!"

We were all startled, I think, by the explosiveness of Anderson's response. The hue of his cheeks now matched that of his nose.

And then, out of the reverberating silence, came a voice from the other half of the room. "The only untoward interest in the girl appears to be coming from none other than yourself, Poe."

Of the two pipe-smoking gentlemen, the one who had spoken was the younger by several years. The older man's face was squarish and open, with wide-set eyes whose smoky blue appeared not at all cold but soft and forgiving, avuncular, his thin mouth slightly crooked as if wanting to smile. The speaker's face suggested much less innate beneficence, his face long and thin, pointed at the chin and nose, his mouth upturned in a smile that did little to conceal the underlying sneer. There was something of the lupine to the man's countenance, an autocratic rigidity.

Poe only half turned to face them. He cocked an eyebrow.

"No doubt you intend to denounce the girl as you have denounced the rest of us," the man said.

"If I have denounced anyone, sir, it was with the purest of intentions."

The man laughed derisively. "Mr. Bryant will be glad to hear it," he said, "having been labeled by you as a fool. As would Mr. Longfellow, the thief. And Mr. Keskie, the master of inestimable balderdash."

"Ah, I see. But that is not denunciation, sir. Is it not the duty of the literary critic to call attention to an author's weakness as well as to praise his strength?"

"And were you praising my strengths or pointing out my weaknesses, I wonder, when you referred to my work as 'a flashy succession of ill-conceived and,' let's see, what was that lovely phrase you employed, 'and miserably executed literary productions, each more silly than its predecessor'?"

By now Poe had gone pale. He blinked several times. "Mr. Cooper," he said. "It is a pleasure to make your acquaintance."

"If so, the pleasure is yours alone."

I would not have thought it possible to smile while at the same time puckering up as if to spit, until I saw the simper of Mr. James Fenimore Cooper (whose *Leatherstocking Tales* I would later read with a guilty pleasure, thrilling to their wildness and adventure while recalling Poe's discomfort at this meeting).

Poe smiled wanly and seemed on the verge of bowing, a gesture of humility, penitence; but at the last moment he stopped himself.

"And when," Cooper now said, trying hard not to sputter with rage, "when you referred to my friend here, whom I am sure you must recognize as the most beloved storyteller in America, when you referred to his work as wandering and aimless, are we to assume that you were praising his strengths?"

Again Poe flinched. "Mr. Irving," he said, and nodded toward the older gentleman.

Washington Irving smiled in return. "Mr. Poe."

"Perhaps you would like to praise his strengths now," Cooper challenged. "Face-to-face."

"Please," Irving said, "let us not descend into hostility. Perhaps Mr. Poe would care to join us for a while. A friendly discussion between fellow laborers in the vineyard."

Poe was too quick, I think, to take a step forward. Cooper held up a hand. "Hold off. I would first like to hear his response. How is it, Mr. Poe, that you alone, in all of America and abroad, fail to be charmed by my friend's tales?"

"I have a great deal of admiration for the narratives," Poe argued. "I find them in part quite good."

"In part?" said Cooper. "You cannot commend them as a whole?"

Mr. Irving said, "He is an honest man. In what narrative can every word be praised?"

"Some are especially graceful," Poe said.

"Some," said Cooper. "In part. Please, sir, for the sake of the poor man's art, and for the sake of his illiterate readers and publishers, edify us. Where in particular do his powers fail?"

"James, please. Enough of this. I take no pleasure in inciting a riot."

"This is not riot, Wash; we are conducting a literary salon. Though perhaps Mr. Poe's legendary frankness is not so easily summoned when the subject of his attack sits but an arm's length away."

At this Cooper jabbed his pointed chin even higher and glared down the sheer slope of his nose. I, for one, was standing with fists clenched.

But Poe's hands remained loose, his left hooked limply over the fly of his coat, the right fingering the tobacco pouch. By the time he spoke, the color had returned to his cheeks.

"In many of your narratives," he said, and delivered his remarks with a smile to Washington Irving alone, "in many, the thrust seems to come apart in the end. The interest, though honestly achieved in the beginning, is frittered away. Because the conclusion of the tale is insufficiently climactic."

Irving's only response to this was a slow closing of his eyelids, as if he were falling asleep. Two seconds later his eyes half opened and he looked at Poe and offered his own wistful smile.

Cooper sneered. "You would not place him, then, along with myself as a 'merely popular' writer?"

"By which I meant a writer whose work can be read with pleasure by the masses."

"But not admired!" Cooper thundered. "Do not forget the caveat, Poe. To be read with pleasure but not with admiration!"

If the glare of heat emanating from Cooper's eyes were meant to blanch Poe, it did not succeed. Instead, he drew himself up taller. "If only the sharpness of your memory for criticism could be transferred to your memory of historical facts," he said.

Cooper's head snapped forward. "Perhaps my many *thousands* of readers have a better grasp of my work than you do, sir."

"Perhaps. Or perhaps Monsieur de Tocqueville's assertion of our country's enthusiastic embrace of mediocrity can account for those numbers."

By this time Mr. Irving had a hand on Mr. Cooper's arm. Cooper, simmering, seemed about to leap up from his chair. "How is it," he asked, "that a man so singularly gifted now finds himself doing hackwork for the *Mirror?*"

It was Poe's turn now to react as if slapped. "I am employed in the gathering of honest facts," he answered, "that will lead me to an accurate and logical observation. Unlike others present—yourself excluded, Mr. Irving—I have a high regard for these elements in my writing."

"You are fortunate, sir, that the duel has been banned in this city."

"Seeing as how I can shoot off the tip of a sulphur match at forty paces, I would say that I am not so fortunate as others might be. Good day, gentlemen."

With that, Poe turned toward the exit. I unclenched a fist and yanked upon the door and nearly climbed onto Poe's heels as we made for the unfiltered sunlight.

10

WE WERE several yards down the street from the tobacconist's shop when I, nearly breathless from trying to equal Poe's sharp pace, said, "How about teaching me to do that too?"

He did not answer.

"Shooting the head off a match at forty paces," I said. "Can you teach me how?"

Without breaking his stride he held out his right hand, palm down. He had the worst case of sudden palsy I had ever seen. "With this hand," he said, "I would be fortunate to merely maintain my grip on a pistol."

"But if you wasn't shaking so."

At last he began to slow his lightning pace. We turned the corner, and here he stopped. "When not shivering like a hairless puppy in an icy rain," he told me, "then yes, I am a fair enough marksman. At forty paces I could in all likelihood strike, for example, the Astor house. As for the head of a match . . ."

I could not believe my ears. Could not believe, *in primis,* that my new hero was incompetent in any regard, and could not believe, *in secundis,* that he was admitting to it. "What if he had called your bluff?" I asked.

"Then, sir, you would be hurrying off on your own to relate to my loving family the sad news of my untimely demise."

I stood there staring up at him with my mouth agape.

"It is the imp of the perverse," he said. "My father was so possessed, and I am likewise." He chuckled to himself, then looked down at me. He laid a hand on my shoulder.

"There is one thing, Augie, that you can always count on me to do."

"And what's that?"

"To say the wrong thing at the worst possible time."

"It's almost like you're asking somebody to take a shot at you."

"It is a strange thing indeed. To love life so. While so vigorously baiting death."

I was too young then to explore the condition further, to probe the gray overlappings and ambivalence of existence. And so I returned the discussion to Mary Rogers and asked if he had learned anything useful from the tobacconist. Poe was most intrigued by the revelation that her recent absence from her workplace was not an exception. He suggested a leisurely stroll to Mrs. Rogers's boardinghouse. I suggested that we first fortify ourselves.

"I'm afraid that I expended the day's allotment on a pouch of Mr. Anderson's goodwill. I've nothing left for food."

"Meet me in front of the Tontine in three minutes," I told him.

"And where are you off to, Mr. Dubbins?"

"You want to eat, don't you?" Before he could answer I had hightailed it back around the corner.

Three minutes later I met up with Poe in front of the coffee house. From inside my baggy shirt I produced a small loaf of dark bread and a warm apple dumpling.

He eyed them critically for a moment. He then gazed up the street in the direction from which I had arrived. "May I assume that these savories were acquired by legal means?"

"As legal as the wind," I told him. "And as far as I know, there ain't no law against the wind blowing, is there?"

The melted sugar on the crust of the dumpling had smeared across my stomach. I scoured at the sticky spot with my shirt front.

"I will perhaps sample the loaf," Poe said.

And thus we strolled to Mrs. Rogers's rambling clapboard boardinghouse, myself quite happy that I had done my bit for American journalism.

Poe had made Mrs. Rogers's acquaintance days earlier, but he nonetheless began to reintroduce himself after she responded to his knock at the front door. She cut off his introduction with a wave of her hand and a rush of words, most of which amounted to an insistence that we come inside for tea. I offered no resistance and ducked under her arm and headed for the scent of the kitchen, thereby rendering Poe's protest moot.

She led us down a darkened hallway to a sun-bright kitchen. There she bade us sit at the table. She set a kettle on the stove and tossed a stick of wood onto the coals. Then she filled the table with a block of hard cheese, a crock of pickled eggs, another of sauerkraut, and a shank of cold roast beef. I wondered if this frenetic little woman was perhaps Mrs. Clemm's long-lost sister, so similar was their hospitality.

But whereas Mrs. Clemm was large and cumbersome, this aging cherub of a woman stood only an inch or two taller than me, but thrice my girth. She moved from place to place with the alacrity of a water bug, now here, now there, and produced a soft shuddering inside the cupboards with every footfall. In no time at all, her nervous energy had me tapping my toe against the chair leg.

"Nothing's more beautiful than a woman working, isn't that right, Mr. Poe?"

"It is indeed," he said.

"That's an old Dutch proverb, you know. Learned it from my husband, I did, may he rest in peace. Who wasn't much for work himself but took no end of pleasure in seeing that I kept busy. And I've been working ever since. What else would please you gentlemen, some biscuits maybe? I have some sourdough biscuits left over from breakfast, I think."

I started to nod my head yes, but Poe, who had not yet seated himself, pulled out a chair for her. "But the proverb continues, does it not?" he asked. "Nothing's more beautiful than a woman working unless it is a woman at rest."

"He never told me that part," she said. "My guess is it never existed until this very instant."

"Please," said Poe, and drew the chair back for her.

"In a minute, in a minute." She went first to the bread box, then the washstand, then busied herself with rearranging the cutlery in a drawer. "It helps to keep busy, always did. Keeps my mind off things, you know. It's even worse now with my darling sweetheart gone." She stood still momentarily and shook her head. "What those beasts done to her, I can't stand to think about it. I can't sit still for a minute now, never could before either but now it's even worse."

Hearing this Poe gave up on her and settled in the chair himself. "I have just a question or two, if you wouldn't mind."

"It's a good thing I've a houseful," she continued. "There's no end of work when you've got a houseful. Though they say no woman can be happy with less than seven to cook for and I've never had more than six. Never more than six and only five now counting myself. But it's true, I suppose, for I haven't eaten a bite since my darling beauty was taken from me. I hope that beef isn't too fatty for you, Mr. Poe. Your young lad there seems to find it to his liking."

I grinned and nodded, my mouth stuffed full.

"What I hope to ascertain," Poe said, "if you would indulge me in your grief, is something of your daughter's habits. Any one of which might shed a bit of light on the particulars of her tragedy."

Over the next half hour he was able to put to her the same questions he had to Mr. Anderson. She answered, in a fashion, between homilies:

"A woman can throw out with a spoon more than a man can bring in with a shovel, isn't that right, Mr. Poe? Upriver, did you say? From the waterfront? I once had a boarder from that area, a drummer he said he was. But that was four, five years ago now. Haven't had a sniff of him since.

"Other people's bread always tastes better, doesn't it, lad? And then you get used to it and you want your own bread back; it works that way too. But as to my darling's absence from work, Mr. Poe, the earlier one, not this last, yes, she was ill, she was ill indeed. But it wasn't with the catarrh, as I recall. She sent word from her Auntie Sarah's; she had gone there of a Sunday morning, then was taken ill that afternoon, a stomach ailment I was told, a case of the gripes, and she ended up spending all of Monday and half of Tuesday in the care of her aunt, my late husband's older sister, may he rest in peace."

"And who was it brought you word that she would be staying over with her aunt?"

"Who was it? Well I scarcely remember. Except that now I do, yes, it was Mr. Andrews of course. He had run across her returning from church, as I recall. Out riding, he was. It was he, he said, advised her to take to bed immediately and not bother making the long walk home."

"The same Mr. Andrews who is a boarder here?"

"He is, he is. For more than two years now, I might add. Far longer than most, who come a fortnight or two and then disappear never to be seen nor heard from again. But not our Mr. Andrews. As neat and proper a man as you would care to meet. The military does that to a man, you know. You have something of the bearing about you yourself, Mr. Poe, if I am not mistaken."

"I spent some time at West Point when I was young."

"It shows, it shows indeed. The lad there needs more tea, don't he? Yes, it shows, your military bearing, there's no concealing where a man has been in his life. He wears it in his eyes and in the way he carries himself."

"As to Mr. Andrews," Poe said, his eyes suddenly alert, his posture very straight, "he is with the navy, I assume."

"He's every bit a navy man, our Charles is. An officer of the first rank. A lieutenant is what he is. Junior grade."

Poe nodded to himself. He picked up the cheese knife and sliced a sliver off the block. "And is Mr. Andrews well acquainted with Mr. Payne?"

"How could they not be well acquainted, let me ask you that. When right out there at that table they share their dinner every night."

"Is either of the gentlemen presently to home?"

"At this hour of the day? My boarders are every one of them honest and hardworking gentlemen, I assure you. Just like yourself, Mr. Poe. But dinner is at seven and Mr. Andrews for one will be here promptly."

"But not Mr. Payne?"

"I think he can not bear the change," she said, and now she looked into the distance and she wobbled like a great heavy top that has spun itself out. "Without her there to serve his soup and to take her seat beside him," she said. "He feels the pain as surely as her mother does. He would rather die now than to take his dinner without her."

And suddenly I felt piggish and small, stuffing myself while this woman's terrible grief wrung every drop of joy from her soul. Her round hot cheeks were slick with tears now, her mouth stretched wide in a down-turning line. She stood there by the table with her eyes squeezed shut, fists clamped hard to her breasts, knuckles white.

"Kissing wears out, I always told her, but cooking don't. That's what I always told my lovely sweetheart, Mr. Poe. I always told them both. But what with her looking the way she did, my dear sweet beauty. How could any man ever think a thought about her without wanting to take her in his arms."

She turned slightly and gazed through the open archway and into the dining room. "Every day I see her sitting out there, Mr. Poe. Every day I see her there."

Empty of words finally, hollow of all but despair, she began to sob now and to sway forward and back. Poe gave me a quick nod as he rose and went to her. I scrambled to my feet and retreated down the hallway and outside I went. I waited at the gate with my back to the boarding-house. I expected to hear at any moment a great crashing sound as she collapsed in grief, but heard only the clip-clop of hooves on stone, the droning clack of wheels, the shouts and discourse of other lives passing in public view, where private miseries are seldom seen.

Poe joined me there a few minutes later. He had the look of a man fresh from a funeral, dazed by the proximity of death, half blinded by the sunlight. He laid a hand on my shoulder, then stood there motionless, squinting at the traffic.

"The things we do to each other," he softly said. "The evil we do. It is beyond my ability to comprehend."

11

FROM MRS. Rogers's home we walked, if more heavily now, the short distance to Wall Street. In the bank where Mr. Payne was employed as a clerk Poe was informed that another investigator had bested us by an hour. Mr. Payne, in other words, had been taken off to the Tombs for questioning by one of High Constable Hays's leatherheads. These leatherheads, or watchmen as they were sometimes called, were all we had in those days as a police force, other than the private squads of head-busters employed by various big bugs throughout the city.

But it was the high constable's force that ruled the Tombs, and Poe considered it imperative that he interview not only Mr. Payne but Mr. Payne's interrogator as well. He suggested, however, that the Tombs was no place for a boy.

"Ain't no way I ain't going with you," I told him. "I've been wanting to see inside that place long as I can remember."

"The building has existed for only two years, Augie."

"So I have a short memory. That don't change the fact that I'm going with you. Even if I have to go alone."

He laughed to himself but did not send me away. And now it was I who set the pace, as quick as a dogtrot, so eager was I to get my first look inside those forbidding granite walls.

It was not long before the main entrance on Centre Street loomed before us like the jaws of Hell itself. Up the broad flight of steps we went, the stones as dark as despair, my knees suddenly atremble, heartbeat ticking in my throat. Between the four huge Egyptian columns we went, over the portico, through the heavy door, and there we were inside it, just like that, into the place I would never have dared venture if not bolstered by Poe's own boldness.

Inside a cavernous entrance hallway we blinked and stood quiet for a moment while our eyes adjusted to the dimness. The place was as full of muted conversations as a nightmare, with sudden sharp noises as of a door banging, a mysterious metal clank. At any one time a dozen people could be counted hurrying from one side of the hall to the other. Every footstep echoed like a dull blow. Every breath sucked in the smell of rot. There were shallow pools of water everywhere one looked, as well as dark trickles of water sliding down the stone walls. The place stank of disease and mold and awful mystery.

Because the Tombs had been built on the site of the Collect Pond, a veritable marsh, the building had been sinking and shifting since the first days of construction. The floor and walls were warped, and even in the uneven lamplight I could make out wide cracks in the mortar. I almost expected to see a sulphurous glow oozing up from those cracks.

The walls were gray granite and the floor also but much darker and smoother, polished I suppose by boots and dirt and spit and in all likelihood a fair measure of blood. Many of those stones had come from the Bridewell and so had already witnessed a generation of agonies. Light pushed in dirty through the few windows and lay like dirty water on the floor. Where sunlight fell on actual water the effect was kinder and sometimes there was even a rainbow sheen to the pool. The shafts of light themselves appeared nearly solid with dust and smoke, like solid bars whose insides were alive and wild, squirming every which way to escape the confines of the shaft, not knowing that to be outside of the light meant being invisible and forgotten.

On all sides of the entrance hall were rooms and offices, the residence of various officials, the Police Court, and the Court of Special Sessions. While I stood in the center of this hall and gawked, my heart thrumming with desires too dark for words, Poe set about discovering the whereabouts of Mr. Payne. He spoke to a half-dozen men before ascertaining the room in which Payne was being questioned. I followed him then to a room at the rear of the entrance hall, from which point I could gaze out an open rear door to a wide expanse of sunlight, a courtyard.

If any one place in the Tombs was my objective, this courtyard was it, for it was possible from here to view the two prison buildings, one for females and one for males, the latter connected to the main building by a span of stone, a walkway known as the Bridge of Sighs, the condemned man's last stroll between his cell and his grave.

I left Poe standing close to the closed door of the interrogation room while I was drawn to the courtyard. I assumed that he would knock politely, introduce himself to all inside, and ask his questions. Meantime I exited the building's rear door and stood in the sunlight as if in the gaping wound of that vile place, and there tried my best to see through the walls of the men's prison.

My father would not be housed on the fourth and highest floor of cells, I knew this much from talk overheard at the Brewery. The fourth floor was reserved for men serving short sentences or for those few muckety-mucks who had been unable to bribe their way out from under a felonious charge. The next floor down held burglars and larcenists and other middling criminals. The second floor, a general assortment of firebugs, thugs, shanghai artists, and murderers who had perpetrated their acts with sufficient class to warrant mercy. The first floor, damp and foul, sinking ever closer to the bottomless pit, was the purview of men whose only future lay either in gradual decay or in a short drop at the end of a rope. Here my father would be passing his days, if indeed he still existed. I had no choice but to believe that he did, and to believe too that his fate would one day be overturned, that he would be sprung by an angel or demon, I did not care which, but that he would walk free, stroll outside and find me waiting, and off we would walk together, allied forever against all mankind.

I must have stared at those stone walls for a quarter of an hour before something clicked in the back of my head, some turn of recognition, a realistic thought, and I lowered my eyes. The gloomy reality of the place sank into me, I suppose, and extinguished my small flame of hope. How could I look upon the thickness of those stones, their imperturbability, and fail to see the truth? And the truth was this: I could not stare through granite and I could not drive my fist or my heart through it either. Today would not be the day of my father's freedom. And if I continued to pin my own independence on his, I might never be free.

And so I turned back toward Poe. He saw me coming and put a finger to his lips. Only then did I observe that he held the door to the interrogation room open by a few inches, and was standing off to the side so that he could peer into the room unseen. I eased past him like a shadow, then had a peek myself.

A gentleman in a dark suit, Mr. Payne, sat weeping in a straight-back chair. He had his head down and his hat lay several feet away on the floor. His hair was mussed in a way that could not have been accomplished by a stray breeze. Standing behind him was a leatherhead in a rough black suit, a horse-jawed brute who stood there breathing heavily, massaging his right hand with his left.

A moment later Poe eased shut the door and stepped away and motioned for me to follow him to the exit. I did not speak until outside the heavy door, where, as soon as my face hit the air, I gasped as if suddenly remembering how to breathe again. The weight that had been pressing on my chest, squeezing my lungs the whole time I had been inside, now began to relent.

Finally I asked, "So what did you see in there?"

"Enough to know that there is no need to trouble Mr. Payne further."

"That leatherhead work him over?"

Poe held his tongue as we came down off the wide entrance steps and stood again on Centre Street. His brow was knit in that curious way of his, one corner of his mouth curled up in what others often thought a sneer, but which was, to my reckoning, a grimace—a reaction to some inner discomfort.

Again it was necessary for me to prompt him. "So what did Payne have to say?"

"Hmm? Ah yes, well; his responses revealed little of interest. What intrigues me more was the line of questioning pursued by the constable."

"Looked to me like he was doing most of the questioning with his fist."

"There was a fair share of that, yes. At all other times, however, he seemed most concerned about how Miss Rogers spent her leisure time."

"Come again?"

"One question he repeatedly asked. When Miss Rogers was neither at work nor at home nor in the company of Mr. Payne, where was she? What, he wanted to know, did Mr. Payne know about that?"

"And what did he know?"

"Only that she visited her aunt on occasion and that she maintained the usual feminine interests. Otherwise he appeared confused by the implication."

"No kidding? And what's a implication?"

"In this case it seemed a suggestion that the constable knows a bit more about the young lady's activities than does her fiancé."

"How could that be?"

"Again and again the constable inquired as to Miss Rogers's relationship with the other boarders. Was there anyone among them of whom she seemed most fond. His emphasis upon the last word fairly dripped of innuendo."

The matter of what *in-you-endo* might mean, and how it might be made to drip, was too unpleasant to contemplate. I responded only with a questioning look.

"The query was so pointedly made, and so relentlessly, that finally Mr. Payne uttered an answer, albeit with great reluctance."

"The lieutenant, I'll bet."

"In Mr. Payne's words,'Charlie. Charlie Andrews.' And with the next breath sprang to the lieutenant's defense, vouchsafing him as a brother in spirit."

"And you think the leatherhead knew what the answer was going to be before he even heard it?"

"He was fishing for one trout in particular, yes."

"Maybe you should have a talk with the leatherhead then. Find out what he knows."

"Unfortunately I failed to sense in the man a forthcoming nature. Circumspection, dear Augie. That, in the end, shall win us the day."

We then walked a bit, though it was clear to me that Poe had no particular destination in mind—none of geography, in any case. He moved because he could not stand still, that was the gist of it. And with every passing minute Poe's manner informed me that he now wished to be alone. He increasingly drew in upon himself, every nod and gesture small, every word a shadow. So that when he suggested that perhaps I wished to be free of him awhile, I did not protest, though some pale premonition whispered that I should.

My mother would be worried about me, he said. No matter how harsh I thought her, he said, a mother's love abideth strong. Also he suspected himself of some vague impropriety in involving a child in matters such as these. The morgue, the Tombs—where would he be dragging me next, he wondered aloud. Go off and play awhile, he said. Find your cronies, have yourself a swim. Wash what I could of this nastiness away.

I did not tell him that my cronies were thieves and muggers and filth-stained boys who would as soon drown me for my new livery as swim with me. I merely nodded my assent. As for himself, he would now pay a visit to the aunt. Then return to the widow's boardinghouse of the evening to interview Messrs. Payne and Andrews in a setting more conducive to candor. The latter's affiliation with the navy he found most intriguing, even culpatory. Thanks, he said, to my own perspicacity.

Of course I did not know the word but I enjoyed the sound of it, the way he bestowed it upon me with softened eyes and a melancholy smile.

If I wished, he said, I could meet him at the noon hour tomorrow on the Bowling Green. If all went well he would treat me to my midday meal.

He patted me once on the shoulder and then trudged off. His stride was foreshortened now, and I, only beginning to experience the enervation attendant to a clairvoyance of doom, could merely think to myself how tired he appeared, how wan, how overly weary for the middle of the day.

12

THE REMAINDER of the day passed uneventfully for me. In my clean clothes and with a dime in one pocket, a half-dime in the other, I strode like a princekin from Broadway to the Bowery. I considered splurging a few pennies on a pastry dripping with white icing, but my belly was still full, fuller than it had ever been, and the sweet hardness of the coins when I wrapped a fist around them gave me a satiation no mere pastry could equal. Once spent, the money would forever be gone. Hoarded, its potential would not fade.

And so I did without the pastry. Without the lively Bowery show as well, whose raucous music enticed when I ventured near the theater's doorway. I did without a carriage ride too—another indulgence long promised myself—and without the wooden locomotive painted red and black and all but crying out to me from behind a shop window.

I did without all the things I craved and could now afford—could afford not because I had a couple of coins in my pocket, which was nothing new, but because I had begun to view myself as transformed, remade in the eyes of Poe and Mrs. Clemm and Virginia from a clod of street dirt to a boy with true potential, with a future higher than the gutter. In some, this transformation would have engendered impulses of munificence, but not in me, so long used to deprivation. I did without the reward of buying anything for myself, a wooden stylus for Poe, a lace handkerchief for Virginia, a bag of gumdrops for Mrs. Clemm. I suppressed all impulses, hedonistic as well as altruistic, in favor of the miserly.

By nightfall I found myself within view of the hulk I called home. What inclination dragged me back to the Old Brewery, I wish I knew. Some desire to gloat, perhaps. To flaunt myself, my elevation to a world of less despicable beasts. Or perhaps a need to display myself as not so contemptible as my mother routinely announced me to be. Was I so naive to imagine that Poe (who for all his youthful losses never suffered from a lack of at least a surrogate mother's adoration) was correct about my own mother's love, that my face scrubbed and pink would sweeten her tongue and decalcify her heart?

Here is another mystery: the more you beat a dog, the more it grovels at your feet.

I strolled into the rancid building and up its foul stairways and through its despoiled halls. I moved quickly, purposefully, so as not to provoke more than stares and a few coarse insults from those wasted spirits I passed. Then into the oblong room which, in the thirty-six hours since last I had been there, had taken on an insufferably squalid air, was suddenly rank to each and every of my senses, so that my first thought was to turn and flee.

But I did not. The room was dark as always, with but a stub of candle burning on the table, emitting a greasy light. A man I did not recognize sat in our only chair and slumped over the table, sleeping or passed out with his cheek stuck to the wood.

My mother lay on her pile of rags in the far corner, legs splayed out, bodice drooping to her waist. She was not quick to react to my entry. She turned a lazy head my way and halfheartedly covered herself.

"What'd you bring?" she said.

No mention of my absence of the night previous, no recognition of the passage of time. Had she displayed but the least concern over what might have befallen me while we were apart, had she asked "How are you, child?" or even "Where you been?" I would have emptied my pockets for her.

Instead I chilled at the gravel of her voice. And answered icily, "Not a fip."

This, at least, roused her into a sitting position. Her feet smacked the floor with an outhouse sound. "I know your filthy tricks," she said.

"Not a Bungtown copper," I told her, and was struck again with the realization of my error in coming here, and turned to look back at the door.

"You're a lying little rat bastard is what you are." She heaved herself up. She groaned once as if she wanted to vomit, then made a gurgling sound in the back of her throat. She took two quick steps and had me by the collar.

"What's this you have on?" she demanded. "Whose clothes is these?"

"I pulled them off a wash line."

She dragged me nearer the candle. In so doing she banged me into the man asleep at the table. He mumbled a curse and turned his head the other way.

"Every word comes out of you is a dirty lie," my mother said.

Her scent sickened me, the sourness of her breath, her rank body. Two days earlier it would not have registered on me.

"Can't you ever even wash yourself?" I said.

She drew back and blinked as if she had not heard me right. Then came the sting of her hand across my mouth, knuckles cracking my lip, and my legs went out from under me and I landed hard, tasting blood. She shoved me flat to the sticky floor and knelt with one knee in the middle of my back and ran her thorny hands over my clothing, searching for booty. The shirt tore. The sound of buttons popping and plinking to the floor was more painful to me than my split lip.

Then she shoved both hands into my trouser pockets. She touched the coins and froze.

"You deceitful little rat bastard," she hissed, and yanked her hands free, my pockets pulled inside out. She stood and thrust both hands out to the candle and examined her find.

She did not look at me again, not immediately, but turned back toward her bed and grabbed the rotting leather strop she kept there and came back to me and stood over me and swung until she grew tired of it. She sprayed me with spittle and curses and damned me as a vermin and cursed me as my father's son.

I felt the spittle flying from her mouth, heard her farting from the violence of her strokes. All the while I lay curled into a ball, arms wrapped about my head. I said not a word. Only silently blasted myself for being such a fool.

Within a minute or two her stroke weakened. She paused, summoned enough energy for one more lash across my shoulders. Then she staggered away. She fell onto her bed and lay there breathing heavily, wheezing. For a while afterward she continued to curse me with mumbles.

Not until she was snoring did I begin to unwind myself. By degrees I lifted my head, eased my legs out across the floor. From arse to skull I felt scalded, still burning. Every movement provoked another stab of pain.

I tried for the longest while to make not a sound, to give her no indication that she had in any way touched me. In the end I failed, for despite myself I began to sob. I sobbed until breathless and gut sore, and then I whimpered until worn out utterly. All the joys I could have bought with my money, all the pleasure, now gone. At long last a kind of sleep came to me, sweet annihilator, and I lay with my cheek stuck to the piss- and tear-slimed floor.

DEEP IN the night I awoke. The candle had burned out. The old building was alive from ground to rooftop with snores and grunts and nightmarish moans. My first waking thought, complete and resolute and as cold as the lash wounds still stinging my skin, was this: you are done with this place.

I arose on tiptoe and crept to my mother's side. She lay on her belly, one arm stretched out across the floor, the other impossibly trapped beneath her body. I sank to my knees and squinted close at the exposed hand, but it was knotted in a fist, my sliver of silver clutched tight. I tried inserting a finger in her fist, but all I accomplished was to provoke her to drag that hand too to be buried beneath her belly.

Just go, I told myself then. Fifteen cents—it's a small price for freedom.

I looked once at the leather strop lying like a shadow snake where she had dropped it, and I envisioned what I might do with it as a way of bidding farewell. In my mind I watched it whipping down on her, laying open the flesh between her shoulderblades. I envisioned it cinching around her neck, her face going red, eyes huge.

This was my only revenge available, a fiction of the mind, but a composition all the more satisfying than the real because it prompted no recriminations or rebuttal. By the time I made the door my eyes were hot with tears, but I was at the same instant smiling.

Down the stairs and out then, through the greasy warren of wasted lives, the labyrinth of squalor. In my mind I was shedding it all with every step, the stink and violence, the suffocating vulgarity of noise, the obscene smells that clotted like phlegm in the throat. I was quitting it all, peeling it off a layer at a time so as to stand like a shorn lamb in the cool stillness of open night.

I felt as tender as a shorn lamb, I can tell you that. The air stung fiercely on my welts and lacerations. But did I feel cast out or alone? Abandoned? Bereft? Just the opposite. I felt strangely reconnected to the world at large.

I knew there were gangs out in the shadows who would take me in, make me one of their own. Any number of pimps and ponces and thief masters willing to grant me a shilling of succor in exchange for a pound of my devotion. But first I would try it on my own, that was what I told myself. And started walking uptown with no destination in mind.

Along the way I alternately convinced myself that I was the long-lost son of an Astor or Vanderbilt, destined any moment for rediscovery and re-eminence. Or I was the long-lost son of a gypsy king, a virtuoso of song and brilliant mischief. Or the long-lost son of the vilest man on the planet and destined myself to soon usurp my father's throne.

In truth I had only the common modifier correct: *long-lost*. I had been lost since birth, and was even yet.

And so I walked. Onto Broadway, through the sputter and glow of gaslights. Over cobblestones, past palatial silhouettes, around horse reek and tobacco splatter, a soft-footed boy in transit beneath the stars. I was not then and never have been afraid of the dark; the blacker the night, the surer the sanctuary—that was how I have always viewed it.

I circled the Tombs twice that night, as if in a wide elliptical orbit around some larger mass, some gravity that called to me. But on the second pass I broke free. How to explain it? In my mind's eye I saw the Bridge of Sighs arched over the inner courtyard, I saw a shadow man moving across that bridge, chained at the wrists and ankles, shambling toward the gallows. He paused at the arch's peak and lifted his head and looked my way, and for just an instant his dulled eyes flared with light, a strange white fire, and I felt—I know of no other word to describe this jolt—liberated.

I turned away from the Tombs and, without a conscious thought, as if thrust away centrifugally, moved toward the north. I walked a few more minutes before admitting to myself that I was returning to Poe.

With this acknowledgment I ceased cajoling myself with fantasies of wealth and notoriety and turned my thoughts to the subject that Mr. Poe and I shared, the one thing that bound us—Mary Rogers. I thrilled myself now with the boyish notion that I was being led back to Poe for a mighty reason, that somewhere along the way I was bound to trip across a treasure of evidence to carry back to him, a drunken confession overheard, the complete and total solution to the conundrum dropped plop into my hands like a bowl of birthday pudding.

Thanks to my perspicacity, he had said. It was a term of praise, that was all I understood or needed to. The sweet lilt and ululations were comprehension enough.

How I sucked every nutrient from the marrow of that word. But I had never been offered a birthday pudding, and I discovered no treasure of evidence in the dark of the night. Only the treasure of darkness itself, the blessing of invisibility.

It must have been two or three in the morning when I trudged within view of Poe's cottage. An oil lamp shone in the window that faced the lane. At first I thought this strange, a light burning so late at night, but soon I reminded myself of Poe's nocturnal habits. He was at work on another manuscript, turning sentences on the lathe of cogitation, putting rhyme to philosophy, transforming misery to poetry.

Not wishing to disturb his thoughts, I crept like a phantom onto the porch, and there sequestered myself in a leeward corner and curled myself up to await the morning. Within minutes I was joined by both General Tom and Aristotle. A while later the stealthy Asmodaios slunk onto the porch. Tom snuggled into the crook of my knees while Aristotle curled at my ankles. So as to keep black Asmodaios from crawling onto my face and suffocating me in my sleep, I held him cradled to my heart.

13

A HEAVY hand jostled me awake. I reacted with a start, arms around my head, until I recognized her voice.

"Augie, please, sit up," said Mrs. Clemm. "Where is Mr. Poe?"

I uncurled and looked up at her. She was there before me on one knee, her broad face gray with concern, eyes weary. Behind her the yard was still in mist, the trees backlit with the soft pink of dawn.

"Is he out already?" I asked.

"When did you arrive?"

I sat up and rubbed my face. "Middle of the night."

"And Mr. Poe? He left you here and came inside?"

We were making no sense to each other. Something tickled at my nose and mouth. Cat hair. I swiped at it with both hands. "Last time I sleep with cats," I said.

She leaned even closer. "Augie, listen. I need to know this. Did Mr. Poe say anything after he left you here? Anything about where he was off to next?"

I finally understood what she was getting at. "There was a lamp lit. I thought he was already inside."

"He didn't return here with you last night?"

"I came back late. I thought he was home already."

She leaned away and drew in a wearisome breath. "When did you last see him?"

"Midday. At Mrs. Rogers's boardinghouse."

"And what were his plans—did he say?"

"To interview the girl's aunt. Then back to the boardinghouse to talk with the other two. The lieutenant and the boyfriend."

She leaned even farther back on folded knee, head laid back and eyes on the porch ceiling. With an open palm she patted her chest as if patting air into her lungs. "Sissie will sleep another hour or so," she said. "Will you stay with her awhile?"

I rolled onto hands and knees and stood and stepped out of the shadowed corner. "I'll find him for you."

I thought she was about to embrace me, such was the gratitude that came into her eyes. Perhaps I even leaned toward her a bit. But she had scarcely touched my shoulder before she became suddenly still.

"Your cheek," she said. "Your lip . . ."

I flinched, remembering.

"Your shirt is torn. The buttons—one, two . . . three buttons missing."

"I tripped coming back in the dark. Fell into a bush," I said.

She laid a healing finger against my cheek. "This was done by no bush, boy."

To stop the inquiry I moved away from her. "Don't you worry, I'll find him and bring him home again. I know just where to look."

But she was soon on her feet and had a hand around my wrist. "You'll need some breakfast first. And a change of shirt. And a washrag."

She paused to gaze out through the trees. "I'm sure he's fine," she said, though her eyes betrayed her words.

"I'll take a piece of johnnycake if there's any to be had. That's all I need."

Ten minutes later I was galloping down the lane, chewing on a brick of corn bread as I trotted into the mist.

AT MRS. Rogers's place I was importuned to join the house for breakfast, but though the corn bread had done little more than whet my appetite, I declined. I remained on the porch and there asked the kindly widow what time Mr. Poe had left the premises the night before.

She had seen him but the one time early in the day, she said.

He had not returned to speak with the gentlemen?

He had not.

I then obtained directions to the home of the aunt, the spinster Sarah Rogers, and was on the move once more.

Mid-distance between the boardinghouse and the spinster's cottage I came to a copse of hardwood trees, and through this copse a footpath ran. Not much wider than a deer trail, it twisted and turned through dark woods into which the light came broken and soft, slender yellow shafts aquiver with dust and insects. It seemed to me a spooky place, haunted even in full morning. Tired as I was, every creak of limb and snap of twig pushed me that much faster.

As it was I made the spinster's cottage in fair time and found her hoeing in a garden at the side of the house. She was startled to see a breathless boy come running up to her low gate, so I wasted no time in informing her of my mission.

"St. Joseph and Jude," she said. "Sure he's not been lost out in the woods all night?"

She was a slender and bent old woman, even exceedingly so. The wide bonnet cast her face in shadow, but not so darkly I could fail to notice the prominence of her nose and chin. But if she bore a brittle and witchlike countenance it was all but compensated for by the melody of her voice, soft and almost whispered but resonant with Irish lilt.

"What time was it," I asked, "when he took his leave of you?"

"It was well before supper," she said. "I came outdoors for a bit of hoeing afterward and saw by that it was not yet four." On the word *that* she had aimed her hoe at a sundial mounted on a small stone pedestal.

"Did you notice which direction he went off toward?"

"I did not," she said. "I left him at the door and then went straight to the washstand. I can't have dirty glasses sitting around unwashed, that's the way I am and always have been."

"You had something to drink before he left?"

"I always take a glass of sherry an hour before my supper. It's good for the blood, you know. A glass before supper and a glass before bed. That and three green onions a day and you'll never have need of a doctor, young man."

"And Mr. Poe—he had a glass too?"

"He did, he did. Not that he finished it, though; I had to pour it back into the bottle. Got distracted, he did. And there he was recitin' for me a poem of of his own devisin', a lovely piece of a thing, he called it 'Romance.' He was right in the middle of it, it seemed to me, when he up and all of a sudden remembered what he was about. He set down his glass then and thanked me for my time, like as if there was any value to it a'tall."

She looked at me awhile longer, smiling, then turned to her garden and bent over a mound of vines and whacked at the dirt with her hoe blade.

"And then?" I asked. "What then?"

She continued hoeing. "Oh he has a mighty waterfall of words, that one, doesn't he now? All of it fairly gushin' off his tongue, it was a wonder to behold. More's the pity to have it wasted on an ignorant old woman who couldn't make heads nor tails of it, isn't that so?"

"And afterward?" I asked again. "What did he say or do before he left?"

"Nothin' a'tall," she said. "He was up and out the door just like his clothes was on fire. Said he had too much to do as yet to be enjoyin' himself so completely with my company."

At this a rosy blush came into the old leather of her cheeks. " 'Tis no wonder everybody wants to find the man and comes here lookin' for him," she said, "such a scoundrel with words as he is. I swear your Mr. Poe could charm the hee-haw right out of a donkey if he'd a mind to."

At the moment I was little concerned with Poe's charm. "Who's this everybody you're talking about?"

"Why, that other fella who was here not an hour before you."

"What other fella?"

"The one come looking for him, same as you."

"Somebody came here? Asking after Poe?"

"As dignified a gentleman as you would ever want to meet. Ma'am this and ma'am that. Quiet as a deacon and handsome as a viceroy."

"Did he tell you his name?"

"And took off his hat when he did it. Glendinning, he said. A Mr. Glendinning. Now isn't that a lovely name for a man? Reminds me of church bells ringin', don't it you?"

I did not know what to make of this but felt certain it would be a waste of time to attempt to wring more information from her. By my reckoning she had been into the sherry already that day. What mattered now was the chill prick of foreboding that was inching up my spine. The name Glendinning, though one I had never heard before, sounded not half as lovely to my ears as it did to the old lady's.

Seconds later I left her to wreak havoc upon the weeds. I returned to the woods, retracing my steps, but this time at a blind gallop, for I was tired and hungry and my mind a confusion of possibilities. If this Glendinning had been in search of Poe only an hour or so earlier, then who was responsible for Poe's disappearance? Was Poe himself the cause of our worry—could his taste of sherry have been all he needed to send him scurrying toward town and a grogshop?

I scoured every field and vista on the long jaunt back to town, surveyed every barn lot and cow pasture for the figure of a man in black coat and trousers. I gazed up and down every avenue and lane. I poked my head into every grocer's shop and bakery, every tavern and roadhouse.

"Poe, are you in here?" I would call. "Mr. Poe? Anybody here seen Mr. Poe?" Even as I did so a dark presentiment grew in the pit of my stomach, a cold hard lump of certainty that my actions would prove fruitless.

I was making my way down Broadway, nearly to Canal, when my fortune changed. I stepped out in front of the Cockscomb Saloon, nearly dizzy with frustration, hunger, and fatigue; made a weary left turn; and ran smack into a man positioned there by the side of the building.

"You're looking for Poe?" he said. His voice was deep but not much softer than a whisper. And there was little breath behind the words, as if he had been piling up as many miles as I in the past few hours and had all but reached the limits of his endurance. He was a man of average height and girth but was dressed in a crisp black suit and wearing a bowler hat. The side of his face, all that I could see of it, was shiny with perspiration.

"You might try the Velsor Club," he said. He did not look at me when he said this, nor ever grant me more than a partial view of his features.

I spoke in his presence for the first time. "Not the one on Centre Street." It was a notorious hovel in the darkest heart of Five Points, only spitting distance from the Old Brewery but so nefarious a den of thieves and cutthroats that I, who prided myself on my boldness, had never once dared to peek inside its door.

"Were I you," he said, "I would not tarry." The man put a hand to the brim of his bowler and gave it a little tip. Then he turned fully away from me and started off.

"You're Glendinning, ain't you?" I called.

His only answer was a slight hitch in his stride.

"What is it you want with Mr. Poe?"

His pace quickened at this and he hurried away from me.

I could have chased after the man, and wanted to, except that his identity was the less urgent of my two mysteries. The first was this: what had Poe gotten himself into now, and was it too late to get him out of it? And so I bolted back toward that neighborhood I had vowed never again to set foot inside. The very thought of the place filled me with dread.

Vows, I have learned, should only be made with one's final breath.

14

————

AT ANTHONY I veered due east off Centre Street. Within a block the very air seemed dimmer, as if not even sunlight wished to soil itself here. The streets throughout Five Points were little more than a greasy maze, and increasingly so the closer one came to the Old Brewery. Slapdash shacks, thrown together from boards scavenged from stabler buildings, often sprang up overnight to block what a day earlier had been a narrow lane.

Legitimate businesses were not absent from the neighborhood, but they were businesses catering to the transient and poor—butchers who sold more pigs' knuckles and tripe than filet of beef; taverns where after a mug of rum you could have a leech applied, get a tooth yanked, a boil lanced; plus a wide assortment of hucksters' shops where on Monday you might buy clams freshly dug from the beach, on Tuesday a bundle of rags begged from the rich, on Wednesday herbs and damp roots gathered from an empty lot, on Thursday a silver teapot that had somehow found its way off Fifth Avenue and was available for quick sale at a fraction of its value.

The citizens who worked these shops and who frequented them were, quite literally, of a different hue than those just a few blocks south. Here one could find Chinese tars mixing with Irish sailors, black sawyers, cockney chimney sweeps, and stout Polish prostitutes. All shared the same amenities, the same vices and diseases. If the rest of Gotham was Protestant capitalism in full swing, Five Points was the essence of democracy—which is to say that a citizen was just as free here to butcher a pig as he was to steal, cheat, beat, rape, or butcher a neighbor. Hays's troop of brutal leatherheads would not dare set foot in Five Points.

Nowhere was the community's virulence more consolidated than at the Velsor Club. It stood on Cross Street, just west of Orange, a squat, dark, slanting building that still stank of the abattoir it once had housed. There were two broad windows on the front face but they had long since been broken out and replaced with wood and sheets of tin. From the half-open door came a wheeze of accordion music and a garbled strain of voices.

The door was being held open by a slattern who had come to the light to better pick at a pimple on her left breast. She saw me watching her and cupped her breast with one hand and motioned me closer with the other. I took a step back. She laughed, then turned away and slunk back into the interior and let the door fall shut.

After a while I went to the door and squeaked it open. "Mr. Poe?" I called inside. A few of the voices fell silent but the accordion music continued as before, a sluggish kind of melody, almost funereal, pulled almost wholly out of bass notes.

I called him twice more but received no reply. No one came to the door to inquire of my mission. No one offered assistance. I had no choice but to venture inside.

At first I could make out nothing in the darkness but for the oily glow of a half-dozen lamps placed here and there. As far as I could tell the building consisted of a single room. The floor felt no different beneath my feet than that of the trammeled lane outside. The difference was in the odors, the crackery stench of unwashed bodies, the acrid stink of old meat and spilled beer, the effluvia of farts and cigar smoke, and the mingled spices from the breath of five or six of the world's beleaguered races.

Within a minute or two my eyes adjusted to the outline of dark bodies, most seated at low tables scattered here and there. I saw now that the oil lamps were hung on the wall or dangled from the ceiling. There were men and women alike in here, some whose eyes glowed like small white moons, and others as yellow as a possum's. Around a few of the oil lamps hung a blue cloud of smoke, opium sweet. I felt as excited as I was terrified.

I tried to make not a sound as I came into the room and slowly walked about. I tried to appear nonchalant as I made my way from table to table and peered into the vacant faces. It seemed that the farther into the room I went, the quieter it grew. Even the accordion died out. Soon there was no mistaking that I was the center of attention, an anomaly and therefore worthy of their dulled curiosity. From most of the patrons I detected no malevolence, yet the foreboding remained, the prick of something sharp at the top of my spine.

And then I heard him. The room was quiet enough finally to permit the sound to reach me, the steady, even rhythmic scrape of footsteps, the slow drag as regular as a narcotized heart. Contrapuntal to this dirge was a higher-pitched and irregular sound, not exactly a whimper but very whimperlike, the way a drunk will protest in his sleep, the way a madman will argue with himself.

I stood stock-still in the middle of the room. Cocked my ear. Turned slightly this way and that, zeroed in on the sound. And then squinted into the shadows and past the hazy orbs of light. And saw, near the deepest corner of the room, the shadow figure of a man who seemed to be blinking on and off, exactly as a figure might appear in a slowly revolving diorama.

Poe was walking round and round a pillar of wood, a support beam, trudging in and out of the dull illumination provided by the nearest lamp. He walked with his left hand outstretched so that his fingers rode in pivot around the pillar.

All the while he continued a litany of mumbles. I went to within three feet of him and saw then how soiled were his clothes, how bits of filth clung to him from boot to tousled hair, as if he had been rolling on the ground. He wore no coat and his shirt was torn halfway down his chest. The pockets of his trousers hung out like hounds' ears, empty.

He walked with his head down, drooping, limp. "Too wild for song," he mumbled, his voice almost shrill, desperate but too weak for volume. His right hand lifted at his side and floated for a moment as if trying to gain altitude, hip level and no higher, then slid outward from his body, transecting some invisible meridian. "Then rolled like tropic storms along."

A moment later his hand fell to his side. I moved closer. "Mr. Poe," I whispered.

He paid me no mind, but continued his dirgelike revolution.

I said it again, and again, each time louder. On the fifth "Mr. Poe!" his mumbling ceased. On the next turn I spoke again, and this time put a hand to his shoulder. "Mr. Poe."

He stopped walking and stood abreast of me, but kept his hand outstretched in contact with the pillar.

I positioned myself in front of him, so close that his down-turned eyes could not help but see me.

"Mr. Poe, it's just me. It's Augie Dubbins. I've come to fetch you home."

At this he began to mumble again but I did not recognize a single word of it; it must have been French or Latin or a language only he could comprehend. I saw that the fingers of his right hand were fluttering against his leg, twitching as if with palsy. As much to stop this movement as to calm myself, I slipped my hand into his.

He became very still for a moment and squeezed shut his eyes. In this position he muttered, "I could not love. Could not love. Not love except where death was mingling his with beauty's breath."

A chill shot through me. I squeezed his hand in mine. "It's time to get back now," I said.

He made no answer, but neither did he resist when I pulled on his hand and set us in motion away from the post. The room was now as still as death. I had dragged Poe forward only a yard or so when the man at the nearest table spoke, or rather snarled at me.

"Mind you take him straight home, boy."

I cut him a look but no lamp was close enough to illuminate him and he sat hunched forward, head turned away from me. I might have asked who he was and how he knew Mr. Poe but for the field of menace that surrounded him, that enclosed him like a deep pool, its black and sinister ripples radiating outward.

And so without a word I led Poe slowly out of the Velsor Club, back onto the narrow lane, and by degrees homeward. We skirted the busier streets as best we could, with me manufacturing a smile each time a curious glance was turned our way, my smile trying for all the world to paint a happy picture, a father and son out for a stroll, a jaunt, my soiled hero muttering of death and stumbling along as docile as a beaten plow horse on a lead.

15

———

POE SPENT the rest of that day and until darkness the next abed. By which I mean he slept in the chair beside Virginia's bed, feet propped up on a footstool, a quilted blanket tucked around his chest and shoulders. Twice during these hours I carried a bowl of broth to Virginia so that she could spoon it to him. His face was gray and his hands too shaky to guide the spoon himself. He seemed barely able to keep his eyes open and had not a word for any of us the entire first day.

In the meantime Mrs. Clemm insisted on mending my shirt and washing my clothes again. She slathered a slippery ointment on the welt down my cheek and rubbed a handful of it into my back. Not once did she ask me how I had come by my marks, and I volunteered no information.

She kept me busy in the garden and at the woodpile, sent me off once to fill a basket with huckleberries, though the season was past, and another time sent me up the road with a burlap sack to be filled with plums from an abandoned orchard.

Nor did she speak of the incidents surrounding Poe's disappearance and return until, after supper of the second day, as Virginia sat with Poe behind the closed bedroom door, I assisted Mrs. Clemm as a scullery maid, wiping each plate or bowl dry after she had scoured it clean.

She made a small wet sound then, a kind of sniffling moan, which made me look up at her. A tear track shone on each broad cheek.

A sense of helplessness washed through me at this sight, a feeling of insignificance as enervating as a midnight wind. I did a strange thing then, strange for me, awkward and alien—I reached out and patted her arm.

She nodded, acknowledging the touch. She sniffed loud and long, then composed herself. "If you are going to be his friend, Augie, you must learn to take better care of him."

I did not remind her that it was Poe who had sent me away from him at the boardinghouse, or that not until a day later, in the Velsor Club, did it become apparent to me that he required any caretaking.

In response I said, "The old lady claims he only had a glass of sherry with her. He must've gotten hold of a lot more back in town."

"He cannot have a single glass, not even one. It acts so strangely upon him and is in every way unpredictable."

"He'll go off like that after just the one? I never heard of such a thing."

"And how many men of genius have you known?" she asked.

It struck me as a terrible affliction, to be so blessed with intelligence. To be so sensitive to life, yet so tortured by it. It made me wonder if perhaps I was better off as the dolt my mother identified me as being.

It wasn't long before the bedroom door came open and out came Virginia with the half-empty soup bowl. She came directly to my side. "Mr. Poe would be grateful for your company now," she said.

"He wants to see me?"

She smiled.

I did not know how to approach him. I felt I should crawl on my hands and knees, nose scraping the floor. Because despite my weak protestation to Mrs. Clemm, I did indeed consider myself responsible for his troubles. If he had tumbled from the grace of perfection in my eyes, it was I who had pushed him.

"Come in, Augie, please." It was little more than a whisper. I stepped over the threshold and into the dark, into a room where but a sliver of evening light sneaked through the drawn curtains.

"Come sit on the bed," he told me.

Virginia's fragrance filled the room, the scent of lilacs, yes, but also the warmer body smell, deep and rich and tragic; it made my heart feel doubly bruised.

I perched on the edge of the bed, hands clasped between my knees.

"I want only to ask your forgiveness," Poe said.

I cocked my head at him.

"I should never have sent you back to that place."

"You mean to see the aunt? Why, there wasn't nothing wrong with—"

He raised a finger to silence me. "The Old Brewery." His hand turned palm upward then and came toward me another inch, a subtle gesture but clear enough. He was pointing at me, showing me myself as explanation.

I knew then that although Mrs. Clemm had said nothing to me about my beating she had said plenty about it to Poe. No wonder he sat gazing at the side of my face with such a mournful look. No wonder each time Virginia turned her eyes on me she was barely able to suppress a grimace.

"This ain't nothing," I told him. "You don't need to worry about something like this."

"It will be rectified," he said.

"It really ain't nothing."

He did not speak or move for a moment, then gave me a little nod. "In the meantime," he said, "you might be interested to know that I am in possession of an intriguing fact. Did Mr. Anderson not inform us that, on one previous occasion nearly a year past, Miss Rogers was absent from her duties because of the catarrh?"

"That's what he told us anyway."

"And did not Mrs. Rogers inform us that her daughter came down with the illness, diagnosed by her as a stomach ailment, while visiting the aunt, and thus spent her convalescence in the aunt's domicile?"

I was comforted to hear that his expedition to Gotham's Gehenna had done nothing to dilute his funny way with words. "I remember that too, sure enough."

"What would you make, then, of the spinster's claim that, to her recollection, Miss Rogers was never ill in her presence, and that the niece at no time passed as much as a single night in the cottage?"

I raised my eyebrows. "Not this last time and not the earlier time neither?"

"Precisely."

"And you don't think maybe the aunt's just playing fast and loose with the truth?"

"I do not. Do you?"

"Don't see why she would," I said. "Or maybe has a habit of forgetting the facts?"

"Did she strike you thusly?"

"She seemed a little distractable maybe, though her memory weren't the problem as much as the sherry was. But she remembered you fine enough, and every word you said to her. Same as with that Glendinning fellow."

"Glendinning, yes. According to Virginia, this is the gentleman who directed you to the Velsor Club."

"Though what I don't understand is why he didn't just fetch you out himself. What kind of a friend would take you to a place like that and then just leave you there?"

"I know of no one named Glendinning. This morning was the first I heard of him."

"He come looking for you at the aunt's, she said. And then he must of tracked you down somehow, since it was him told me where to find you. So I guess it couldn't of been him took you to the Velsor in the first place."

"As Virginia related your description of him, it was not. The man who intercepted me at the boardinghouse gate was by all appearances a scoundrel."

"So why'd you go with him into Five Points then?"

"Because he promised me information. All I needed to know, he said—in exchange for a mug of rum. And I . . . I am ashamed to admit that I was predisposed to accept his invitation."

"And did he have the information he promised?"

"He did. He did indeed."

I waited with eyebrows raised. But Poe was apparently reluctant to satisfy my curiosity.

"This Velsor Club," he said. "I could never have conceived of such a . . . a maelstrom of depravity. It was at once repulsive and intoxicating. Such a wealth of perniciousness."

He leaned closer now and whispered so that the women would not hear. "Were I to write of what I witnessed in that place, I would be labeled a madman."

"It's a pit, all right. They don't come much worse."

And suddenly the dark gleam left his eye. "Would I be wrong in thinking it indicative of the milieu in which you have lived?"

"Depends. What's a *mill-you*?"

His smile was pale and miserable. "You are as strong as I am weak," he said.

I took no pleasure in hearing him speak that way. I wanted him strong and confident, I wanted him bold and unassailable.

Moments later Poe nodded to himself and drew in a slow breath. "We will continue our work in the morning," he said. "If, that is, you are so inclined."

"I'm with you all the way. Just so long as I can be of some use to you."

"You have proven your worth a dozen times over." And now he reached out a hand to pat my knee. "My fidus Achates."

"Someday you're going to have to teach me what all those fancy words mean."

"A duty and a privilege, sir." His eyes became heavy then and it seemed to me that he was falling asleep. I leaned a bit closer and saw that he had not closed his eyes but had only averted them.

"My problem, young friend, is that I cannot think and feel at the same time. This work requires both facilities. Therefore, if, when I am doing the one, you will do the other, we shall perhaps achieve our goal."

"How will I know which one I'm supposed to be doing—the thinking or the feeling?"

"You will know. A whole person always knows."

At the time, I thought he had called me a hole person. But such was the power of his presence that even that odd phrase struck me as complimentary. I did not know if he meant that I was adept at seeing into holes or in filling or exploring holes or that I had managed to crawl out of a hole; I only knew that he had praised me somehow. He had with his praise and wan smile transmogrified a Brewery rat into a valued companion. He had made me, in a word, significant.

I knew too that he needed to rest. I rose and went to the doorway and saw that Virginia was waiting just off the threshold, a cup of tea in her hand. She looked as weak as Poe. Beyond her sat Mrs. Clemm with her broad silent back to the bedroom.

"And Augie," Poe said. "You must rest assured. Remedies will be made."

I nodded, knowing not what to answer, and stepped out of the bedroom. Virginia slipped inside and eased the door shut behind herself. I went to sit beside Mrs. Clemm, who was busy as always, this time darning a black sock.

"I don't know what he meant by that last remark," I told her.

"Whatever he meant, he meant it absolutely. He will not fail you."

I cannot adequately describe for you the vertiginous effect of such attention. To be regarded in that house with such tenderness, such solicitude, I was made mute by it. Tenderness was then as alien to me as moon water. Neither, to my knowledge, existed in fact. But Poe's promise, though I knew not yet what to make of it, touched me in a way I could not assimilate. I could ascribe no metaphor to it until years later as a fully grown man, when I first held in my hands the bare wires attached to a parlor novelty, a small hand-cranked electrical generator. As I held those wires, just as years earlier I had sat and watched Mrs. Clemm's patient hands, I felt a rippling of force so exotic that it made me want to cry out in pain. Yet the pain was so exquisite that I wanted never to release those naked wires from my grip.

16

THE WIDOW Rogers was no less happy to see us this time than on the previous occasion. She was of the opinion that Poe and Poe alone would identify the ruffians who had assaulted her daughter, and that he, with the stroke of his Olympian pen, would bring down justice. As witness to her desperate faith I was struck by the disparity of opinions in which Poe, the writer, was viewed: by Mrs. Rogers and Mrs. Clemm as godlike; by Messrs. Cooper and Irving as more a Pluto than a Zeus; by his readers as the font of all knowledge and wisdom; and by his editors as a nuisance.

In any case it was Mrs. Rogers's opinion holding sway at the moment. We arrived at her boardinghouse at approximately 10 A.M., the establishment empty of boarders. She insisted on setting out a plateful of small ginger cakes and in brewing up a fresh pot of tea.

Hays's watchmen, she told Poe, claimed to be hard at work on the case when in fact they were doing nothing at all. They claimed to be amassing evidence when in fact they were waiting for it to be dropped into their laps. One leatherhead had in fact told her as much: they were too busy unsnarling traffic on lower Broadway to be questioning every b'hoy and street arab in Gotham. Besides, their methods of questioning typically resulted not in cooperation but in mutually exchanged curses and no small amount of hemorrhaging.

"While we await the tea," Poe said, "perhaps I could make of you a rather indelicate request."

"You may ask me anything," she said.

"It is not my intention to appear indecorous. But this is a necessary matter, I think."

"If it is necessary it can hardly be indecorous."

"I should like to visit your daughter's quarters."

"You want to see her bedroom?"

"By observing your daughter's milieu, as it were, of which her boudoir is a significant component, it is possible that certain insights might be attained."

"It only matters to me that those ruffians be caught and hanged."

"If truth is justice, madam, our objective is one and the same."

With that she practically pulled him up the stairs. I followed along behind, one ginger cake stuffed in my mouth and another in my pocket.

Mary Rogers's room was on the second floor, a small but sunny room that faced the street. A rather tiny bed, I thought; a single oil lamp; a bureau on which were a hand mirror and hairbrush, a wooden jewelry box, and a porcelain statuette perhaps four inches high, painted white and pink, in the form of a robed and winged woman, an angel.

I stood on the threshold and watched as Poe examined each of these objects. I could not bring myself to step inside. It was a girl's room after all, which is to say sufficiently titillating to freeze me in my tracks. On top of that, the girl was dead. I could all but see her swollen gossamer corpse in the way the lace curtains fluttered at the windows.

"It strikes me as somewhat curious," Poe said.

"And what is that, Mr. Poe?" The widow stood with a hand on her daughter's pillow, another hand flattened to her bosom, eyes bright with grief.

"Is there not a bedroom or two on the first floor where she would have been more comfortable? Something more spacious?"

Before she could answer he turned to her and smiled. "My mother-in-law once ran a boardinghouse in Virginia. On the first floor of that house there were two sleeping rooms—one for Mrs. Clemm, another for Mrs. Poe and myself. But perhaps I draw the wrong conclusion. All houses are not the same."

"The master bedroom is downstairs, yes. Mary shared it with me until she moved up here."

"And when was that?"

She thought for a moment. "Not yet two years. And how I have missed her company, Mr. Poe. She was such a comfort to me in the darker hours."

Poe nodded and stroked his chin. "She had reached that age, I suppose, where she required a certain degree of privacy with her own thoughts."

"She liked to read at night, my girl did. And worried that the lamp would keep me awake."

Poe did not speak for a while then. He went to the window and looked out. Half a minute later he said, as if to himself, "I wonder if the tea is ready yet."

"Oh my yes," said Mrs. Rogers, and came hurrying toward the door.

"Might I remain here for just a moment longer?"

"Indeed, yes. You mustn't hurry your observations."

"We will join you shortly," he said.

Once she was on her way down the stairs he stepped straightaway to the bureau. He raised the lid on the jewelry box and peered inside. He lifted out a string of beads, a tortoiseshell comb, a red hair ribbon. Each of these he held to the light from the window and studied briefly before returning it to the box. But the last item he examined, a brooch in the shape of an angel and as yellow as sunlight, this he held longer than the others before finally returning it to the box.

Finally he withdrew his hand and closed the jewelry box lid. He came out into the hallway and stood there for a full minute, staring at the faces of the three closed doors.

Then he asked, "Did you save room for a cup of tea, Augie?"

I swallowed the last of my second ginger cake and grinned sheepishly. "Half a cup maybe."

With that we returned to the kitchen. Poe sipped politely from his tea while engaging the widow in considerations of the weather and in what he called "the execrable din" of city life. He did not speak of Mary Rogers until his cup was nearly empty. Then he cleared his throat softly and turned his eyes to the ceiling.

"Would you say that your daughter was intuitive?" he asked.

"In what way, Mr. Poe?"

"As I recall," he said, "when first we spoke you told me of your premonition, your sense, upon learning of your daughter's disappearance, that you would never see her again."

"It's true," she said "A shiver like none I'd ever felt raced through me from head to toe."

"And sadly, proved correct."

"It did. Sweet mother of Jesus, it did."

"And your daughter," Poe asked. "I wonder if she too possessed the gift."

"For seeing the future? Is this what you mean?"

"I only ask because of her apparent fondness for seraphim."

"The figurine on her dresser."

"And the brooch as well."

"They were gifts from Mr. Anderson," she said. "The brooch last Christmas. The figurine the Christmas before."

"Lovely, lovely gifts indeed. The figurine, if I'm not mistaken, is Delft."

"And the pin is purest gold. The angel's eyes are tiny sapphire stones."

"It is obvious that Mr. Anderson had a very high regard for your daughter."

"His success depended on her, that's what he always said. An attractive young woman behind the counter, in a business that caters to gentlemen . . ."

"She was his angel. Indeed." Poe turned his tea cup a half circle. He turned it back. "And how it must have warmed your heart to hear these sentiments from Mr. Anderson's own lips."

"It was what Mary told me he said of her. Having never met the fine man myself."

"Of course. You are kept too busy here to make day trips into town."

"It was Mary did all the shopping for us. Every night she would bring home whatever was needed for the next day. Whatever few things I couldn't get from the mongers passing by."

"And this would have brought her home each night, even with a bit of shopping, at what hour?"

"Half past six at the latest," she said. "Except on Saturdays of course. When she remained an hour later so as to restock the inventory for the week to come."

Poe nodded and smiled to himself but said nothing more. He drank off the last of his tea, set the empty cup on the table but kept both hands wrapped around it. "Your hospitality is more than generous," he told her. "I apologize for troubling you again."

"You're a welcome distraction from my other thoughts. Once all my boarders are gone for the day, if not for the work to be done I think I would take to my bed and never rise out of it again."

"And how many boarders have you in all?"

"At the moment there are four."

"All of whom have rooms on the second floor?"

"Mr. Andrews, Mr. Graybill, and Mr. Palmer do. Fine gentlemen every one."

"And Mr. Payne?"

"He has one of the rooms on the upper floor."

"And how many rooms does that floor comprise?"

"Two," she said. "Just the two."

"I wonder," said Poe.

"Yes?"

"It would be interesting to know the term of each of your boarder's residency here."

"Mr. Payne is my oldest resident. He's lived with us going on four years now. Unusual to keep a tenant so long, but he had his reasons to linger, you might say. Right from the beginning he was exceedingly fond of her. It took him a good while to win her over, but he kept at it. Only to end in such despair, poor man."

"And the others?"

"Let me think now. Mr. Palmer is the newest, he's been here just over a month. Mr. Graybill, he came here in the winter. This past January. Mid-January to be exact. And Mr. Andrews . . . two years and several months."

I could tell by the distant look in Poe's eyes that some puzzle was piecing itself together in his mind.

"So when Mary moved out of the room she shared with you," he said, "of your present boarders, only Mr. Andrews and Mr. Payne were then in residence?"

"That's right, yes."

"And in their present rooms?"

"The very ones. Plus one other gentleman at the time, a Mr. Jackson it was. From Ohio. Come here looking for work as a printer. Stayed just two weeks and then struck out for Albany."

"You have an estimable memory, madam."

"Most all of them have been like family to me. You don't forget family," she said. "Gather all the gold and silver you want, young man, make yourself as rich as a king and you'll see, you mark my words, it will all be as nothing when stacked up against the gentle sweet love of your family. Now isn't that right, Mr. Poe?"

"Nothing could be more right, madam."

It wasn't long then before Poe was making our good-byes. She walked us to the gate and seemed likely to follow us farther had Poe not promised to call on her again soon.

We were half a block from the boardinghouse when Poe laid a hand on my shoulder. I paused beside him. He asked, "Your insights, sir?"

"Her cakes were good."

He laughed softly. Then, "The seaman," he said. "The seaman is the fulcrum about which we now turn. Because of the sailor's knot in the strings of Miss Rogers's bonnet. Did you hear nothing of interest concerning the seaman?"

I tried to remember.

"Perhaps your youth precludes observations that smack of the prurient."

"I seen that you was thinking up a storm," I answered, "so I concentrated on feeling. Like you told me to do last night."

"And what did you feel?"

"Her cakes were good."

Again he responded with a smile. But he had his hands on something now and would not let go. "Miss Rogers's decision to vacate the bedroom she shared with her mother," he told me, "is roughly synchronous with the date upon which Mr. Andrews assumed his tenancy there. And on which floor did Miss Rogers choose to sleep?"

"Second, wasn't it? Same as the lieutenant's."

"When in fact the bedroom on the third floor, adjacent to the one in which then as now her fiancé resides, was also available."

"Interesting," I said.

"And of Miss Rogers's hours of employment. Were you struck by an inconsistency of information in that regard?"

This one I knew. "She said that Mary stayed late every Saturday night to restock for Monday. But didn't Mr. Anderson already tell us that restocking was done first thing every Monday morning?"

He smiled and patted my shoulder. Then suddenly his hand fell flat upon me and lay there heavily. I followed his gaze down the street and soon discerned the object of his attention, a man among the pedestrians who distinguished himself by his curious gait. Unlike the others on the street this man was neither sauntering nor striding, not pausing to gaze in the shop windows or to mutter a greeting to any he passed. He was coming toward us, in a fashion, but oblivious to everything but the ground before his feet. He would shuffle forward a few steps, pause, gaze downward, sigh, wobble a bit, move forward a few more steps. It took him three full minutes to cover the thirty yards between us.

We did not move until the man was a stride away. Then Poe said, clearly but not loudly, "Mr. Payne. Good morning."

Miss Rogers's former fiancé stopped as if he had run into an invisible wall, but because of his slow pace there was nothing abrupt in his movements, no strength or vigor as he lifted his head a bit to see who had hailed him. His eyes were dull, the skin around the sockets gray.

"Edgar Poe, sir. Do you remember? We spoke briefly not long ago. At the boardinghouse?"

"Poe. Yes." It seemed all he could manage to part his lips enough to push a few words out.

"How are you faring, sir?"

"Sent home," Payne said.

"I beg your pardon?"

"The bank," he said. "Sent home from work."

Poe nodded. If there was one thing he understood, it was grief. He put a hand on the man's arm. "We've just now come from the boardinghouse ourselves. Would you like us to walk back with you?"

"They said I look ill. But I am no risk, I have no fever. What I have is not contagious, you could tell them that for me."

"I think it might be wise, however, for you to rest."

"A man needs his work. His work is his dignity." His face screwed up, his eyes pooled, he seemed three seconds from collapsing in pieces before our very eyes.

And there in the middle of the street Poe stepped up square and close to him, seized him by both arms just below the shoulders, gave him one firm shake and said, "His love is his dignity, sir. The truth and loyalty with which he loves."

Payne closed his eyes and inhaled slowly, deeply. As his lungs filled, the muscles of his face gradually relaxed, as if he breathed in not city air but the opium smoke of memory, the lightness of a pleasure remembered. When he opened his eyes he seemed to be standing slightly taller.

Poe told him, "There is no indignity in a day or two of rest."

Finally a corner of Payne's thin, drawn mouth canted upward.

Poe's hands on the man's arms tightened briefly, a kind of embrace. Then Poe released him and stepped back. Payne squared himself, nodded once, and strode on.

We watched him for a moment. Then Poe, now more energized himself, turned me sharply to the right and set us walking at a brisk pace.

"Just so I know," I said. "Where are we off to now?"

"We are off," he answered, "to inquire after angels."

17

WE PASSED the tobacconist's shop three times before it emptied of customers. This opportunity, Poe explained, would allow us to enter at a time when Mr. Anderson would least resent our intrusion.

Perhaps it is an unfair speculation on my part that Poe did not wish a reprise of his previous encounter in that establishment, and that is why he was so careful to enter when no clientele were in sight.

In any case, customers or no, Mr. Anderson was noticeably cooler to our presence this time. And Poe, whose pockets were no doubt now as empty as Anderson's wing chairs, made no pretense of considering the wares.

"I have come just now from a visit with the widow Rogers," Poe said. "There are two matters of concern to her at the moment, and it is her wish that you might be of some assistance."

"Matters of what nature?" Anderson asked.

"The first of a practical nature. Her daughter's wages were not an insignificant portion of the household income."

At this the shopkeeper's eyebrows went up and his cheeks reddened. "My goodness, I owe her a week's wages. I had forgotten it entirely."

"As had Mrs. Rogers in her grief."

"I assure you, sir, it was an oversight owing to my own confusion and sadness over the matter. I meant nothing intentional."

"Nor would anyone ever suspect as much."

"I will have the packet delivered to Mrs. Rogers within the hour."

"She will be exceedingly grateful for your kindness. To the mistress of a lodging house, the wages of fifty-five hours' labor is, especially at a time such as this, a godsend."

"Of course, of course. And I must send her a note as well, my profoundest sympathies and apologies. . . ." He was searching about for a clean sheet of parchment, opening this drawer and that, when he added, "Though it is only fifty-three hours, as a point in fact."

"No doubt I am mistaken, sir. But did the girl not serve you from nine to six each day, with an hour additional on Saturday?"

"One hour less on Saturday," Anderson said.

"I apologize. I misheard."

Anderson dismissed this with a flick of his hand. Just then a customer entered; Poe, I couldn't help but notice, went slightly stiffer in his posture, but he did not turn to consider the interloper, whom I recognized all too clearly as the greengrocer from Canal Street. Fortunately, owing to my relative good grooming, he failed to recognize me.

Anderson offered him a smile. "One moment, sir, if you would be so kind."

The greengrocer went to one of the wing chairs and made himself comfortable. I turned to consider the fly specks on the window glass.

"The second matter," Poe said, now sotto voce, "and I will waste no more of your time. It is a mother's method, I suppose, of assuaging her grief. She asked only that I extend to you her heartfelt thanks. For the kindness you showed her daughter these past and precious years."

I could not resist a peek at the tobacconist now. He stood there blinking, cheeks and forehead florid, a man on the verge of blubbering.

"And to thank you as well," Poe continued, "for the angels. They will become cherished keepsakes and an enduring comfort throughout the days ahead."

Mr. Anderson blinked once more and then steadied himself. "Your meaning, sir, is not clear to me. Of what angels do you speak?"

"The pin and the figurine, of course. Your Christmas gifts to the girl."

Anderson stood there blinking and moving his head back and forth, small quick shakes that gave him the appearance of a man with tremors.

"Forgive me, forgive me," Poe said. "Apparently I have misspoken once again. We talked about so much, so many names—I was certain Mrs. Rogers said the angels came from you."

"It troubles me now that I was not more generous with the young lady. That I might have shown her greater magnanimity. And would have, certainly, had I ever suspected that something like this . . . ."

"It is impossible to know these things," Poe said.

"I imagined that she would one day be married, yes, and I would be left to find another countergirl. But this. Something like this."

"It is an imperative of life. Yet one that takes us always by surprise."

"Especially in one so young and full of life."

"Especially then," Poe said. The softness with which he uttered this line, the way his gaze drifted away from the tobacconist—I knew at once that he was thinking now of more than just Mary Rogers, thinking instead about the whole inscrutable mechanism, what he once referred to as "the fever called Living."

It was a contagious contemplation, this matter of mortality, and I turned away to ponder my own by gazing out across the street. What I saw instead shot me full of life.

"Glendinning!" I shouted. "He's there across the street!"

"Thank you, sir," Poe said to the tobacconist while hastening toward the door. "I am most grateful for your time."

"The packet will be dispatched to Mrs. Rogers within the hour!"

Poe did not respond to this but went bursting out into the sunlight. "He was standing right over there," I said, "looking straight at me."

"He must have gone down Wall Street."

An instant later Poe was sprinting through the traffic with me hard on his heels. He came onto Wall Street and abruptly stopped and while surveying the crowd of pedestrians asked me, "Just what am I looking for, Augie? How will I know the man?"

"There!" I said, because I had spotted him now; he had removed his bowler but he was leaning out slightly from the doorway of the Merchants' Exchange. He could no doubt see Poe through the crowd but he could not see me.

"Is he looking our way?"

"You bet he is."

"Then let us retreat."

"Do what?"

"Follow me," Poe said. "Back around the corner."

We retraced our steps until we had turned the nearest corner. We found our own doorway and concealed ourselves therein. "You think he'll come looking for us?" I whispered.

"Hush now. But alert me when he passes."

"Don't you worry about that," I said.

We waited barely a minute before Glendinning came striding past the doorway. I leapt out behind him and seized the tail of his coat and yelped, redundantly perhaps, "Glendinning!"

The man spun on me but Poe was already there. With an outstretched arm he moved me back a step and interceded between us.

Poe was smiling. "Mr. Glendinning," he said. "What a pleasure that at last we meet."

The man licked his lips but did not speak. His eyes darted from Poe to me to some distant point in the city. And finally back to Poe. "Sir?" he said.

"I understand I have you to thank," Poe said.

The man steadied himself. "Pardon my confusion, sir. Do I know you?"

"Do you?"

"If the question is mine to answer, then I would have to answer no. Though perhaps if you will remind me where we met . . ."

Poe's gaze never faltered, his smile never cracked. "Is this the man, Augie?"

"If he ain't I'm a blind baboon."

"My young friend here feels certain that he knows you as Glendinning."

"Your young friend is mistaken. My name is Nostrand."

"You are not the gentleman who went asking after me at the home of Sarah Rogers?"

"That name is as unknown to me as yours."

"Nor are you the man who later directed my young friend to my whereabouts?"

"Again, sir, I can only repeat that you are mistaken."

"And you're a horse's ass," I said.

Poe held up a hand to silence me. "In that case, Mr. Nostrand, my apologies. I trust that we will not be meeting again."

"I see no reason why we should."

"Good day, sir."

"And to you."

Nostrand touched the brim of his bowler, then turned sharply and strode away. Neither Poe nor I moved until Nostrand had disappeared around a corner.

"You know he's lying, don't you?" I asked.

Poe said, "It is the only thing I know."

18

WHETHER IN good spirits or gloom, Poe was a man who enjoyed walking, who adored walking, who regularly walked long and hard whether there was a place to go or not, who walked often for the mere freedom of movement and the easier flow of thoughts that walking engendered.

As for me, I was too young to appreciate the cogitative advantages of peripatetics. Get there and get on with it, that was my philosophy. I indulged Poe in his bipedalism without too much complaint as far as the foot of Fulton Street, but there I looked out across the white-stippled water and grumbled, "Now what? I suppose we're going to turn around and go back the other direction?"

He surprised me by digging deep into his purse and coming up with the coins for our round-trip fare to Brooklyn, and only then did I suspect our destination. Soon after boarding the steam ferry I left Poe at the rail while I perambulated among the other pedestrians and the carriages and wagons and eavesdropped on sundry conversations, hoping to overhear of an itinerary that matched our own; in other words, I was searching for a means to keep me off my feet the remainder of the journey.

In the end it was Poe who provided the means to our conveyance. I had been gone from him less than three minutes, half the trip across the East River, when I spotted him in conversation with an earnest young man who could have been his brother—a lean and melancholy fellow who stood with a slight stoop, though one more temperamental than congenital.

I eased my way back to them and learned that they were discussing a writer named Hawthorne, whose personal peculiarity Poe admired, because, as he said, "to be peculiar is to be original, and there is no higher literary virtue than true originality."

The young man nodded at this as a puppy will nod at its mother, as if to say *Yes, yes, I've had my turn at the teat but can't I have more, I want more, please, more!*

It was yet another reaction to Poe, the first of its kind I had witnessed, that of the fawner, the sycophant, the Grand Obsequier. Apparently he had recognized Poe from a poetry reading in the city, and here on the confines of the ferry had mustered the nerve to approach the man himself, that wonder of wonders, a published writer. And Poe, never quick to turn away from flattery, now had the young man all but intoxicated on Poe's own peculiarity.

In any case I recognized the young man as salvation for my feet. And off the bow loomed Brooklyn, less than one minute away. I walked straight to Poe's side and tugged at his sleeve and whined, "Why do we have to walk all the way to Vinegar Hill?"

Poe's look gave me to know that I would later pay for this breach of civility. He then introduced me to the young man as his good friend and colleague, Master August Dubbins. I flinched at the public utterance of my Christian name, but only for an instant. The young man seemed delighted by it.

"Just like in Pym!" he said. "Augustus being the great friend of Arthur Pym, A. P., whereas your own initials are E. A. P., and this young man's name is August!"

"True, true," Poe said, more amused, I think, by the fellow's hysterical enthusiasm than impressed with the synchronicity of names and initials.

The short of it is that over the course of the next hour Poe was to receive his fill of idolatry. For when the sycophant learned that we were on our way to the Navy Yard on Wallabout Bay, he insisted on the honor of conveying us there in his phaeton. True, he was headed himself for the Heights, and he pointed out his family's estate from the rail. But it would be the high point of his week, he said—no, make that his life . . .

We rode in comfort to Wallabout Bay. I, at least, was comfortable. Poe for some reason felt compelled to roll his dark eyes at me on more than one occasion while our chauffeur peppered him with questions, then responded to each of Poe's answers with a reverent "Yes! Quite so! How absolutely trenchant!"

Suffice it to say that we attained the Navy Yard none too quickly for Poe. I too was pleased to view it up close for the first time, then but a hamlet of shacks and piers and shops, more a village of boats than of buildings, and therein its appeal to me, the appeal of far-flung adventures in places I could not yet even imagine. It was the very place where twenty years hence the ironclad *Monitor* would be assembled stern to bow in a mere one hundred and one desperate days, the Union's vanquishing weapon.

For now, the sight of so many traditional vessels lined up at the slips, plus the chorus of hammers and saws and rasps and chisels that floated from every shack, was enough to unhinge my jaw.

"Don't that beat the Dutch," I said. "Look at that boat there, now that's a beauty for sure."

"It is," Poe said, "though it is not a boat. It is a ketch. A fast and supple ship, much favored by the privateers of the Caribbean."

"What's that one there?" I asked.

"The one with three masts? A bark. And the larger one farther out, also square-rigged, that's a brig. Now look over here—you see the single-masted craft? That one is a sloop."

"I'd like to have me one of those. I'd sail away to some strange land and never look back."

Poe smiled, remembering perhaps his own flirtations with the exotic. "And that one anchored just off the slip, Augie. What kind of ship is that?"

"Another sloop?" I said.

"Look closely now."

"The only thing different is where the masts are set. That second one's farther back."

"Farther astern," Poe said. "Which makes it not a sloop but a cutter."

He went on like this for several minutes, naming and elucidating upon every ship within view. My days on the waterfront had, of course, educated me in the various configurations of sailing vessels, but until Poe came along I had had no tutor and therefore recognized more configurations than I had names for.

"How is it that you know so much about the navy and about ships in general?" I asked.

"It is a writer's duty to know as much as he is capable of knowing. As to the genesis of this knowledge, I acquired it principally at the West Point Academy."

"Why is it you ain't in the navy yourself?"

"My talents," he said, "do not include a receptivity to the regimented life." A master of omission, he failed to add that he had been court-martialed at West Point. So I knew nothing then of his earlier disgrace or of his lingering fascination with the sea, or of his long narrative of the Pym who shared his two initials and my first name, or of how remarkably that tale would prefigure Melville's definitive novel of men at sea, of Poe's strongly physiqued and dangerous Dirk, Melville's Queequeg, Poe's vast and annihilating and God-concealing whiteness of Antarctica, Melville's God-as-white-whale.

How immensely those insights might have filled that casual moment between us! But what I knew then was pathetically little. What any of us knows at any moment in time is pathetically little. The irony of life is that when we have finally learned enough to live passably well, to live deliberately and with a finely focused purpose, with all the spindrift blown away (and most of life is spindrift), it is time for us to die.

"There it is," Poe said, and pointed to a ship anchored near the end of a long pier.

"Andrews is aboard?"

"We shall soon discover."

It was the American brig *Somers,* a school ship on which Lieutenant Andrews gave instruction to young men interested in a naval career. Had I been a few years older and from a more respectable address I might have spent my own days there in preparation for a life at sea. In which case I too might have been aboard the *Somers* in 1842 when it set sail on its first training mission in open waters, and I too, given my bent toward insubordination, my own lack of receptivity to the regimented life, might have swung from the yardarm with the three other boys who were hanged for inciting mutiny.

But forgive me. This stirring up of time and incident is a hazard of old age. If only this, if only that. I have come to a point in my life where nothing exists but the past, and as I gaze back on it the demarcations of place and chronology seem of far less significance than they did when first encountered. What matters most, what resonates throughout our lives like a struck gong, the tone not even audible after a while but still sending forth its rippled waves, is the effect of the moment. Every moment. What Poe might have referred to as its totality.

As for the *Somers,* I was, to my continuing relief, not destined to dangle from its yardarm like a fly from a spider's thread. Poe, as it would soon turn out, had other plans for me.

In the meantime he hailed a seaman aboard the brig and inquired if Lieutenant Andrews was at the moment aboard ship. When answered in the affirmative, Poe requested that word be delivered to Andrews that the journalist Edgar Poe would be grateful for a moment of his time.

Minutes later the lieutenant appeared at the ship's rail. He struck me immediately as a tall and elegant man, his face thin and angular but not in the least thorny or severe. A very good-looking man, so neat in his starched blue uniform that I felt suddenly ragged in my cut-down clothes.

But there was as he looked down on us, as he stood with both hands as still as roots around the polished rail, a tightness in his eyes, a woodenness I could only later attribute not to their depth of oaken color but to the grain and brittleness of his fear.

"Mr. Andrews," Poe called up to him from across the stretch of water. "I apologize for the intrusion. My name is E. A. Poe; I am a journalist affiliated with—"

"I know your work, sir," the lieutenant said.

There was a beat then, a shuddering pause, as each man regarded the other.

"You have come, I hope, to inform me that the arabs responsible for Miss Rogers's demise have been apprehended?"

"I wish it were so. But no, the investigation continues. To which end, perhaps, you might now assist me?"

"How so?"

"A few questions, sir. After which we will leave you to your duties."

"I have only a minute to spare."

"Then I apologize in advance if I strike you as brusque. But to the point. How was it, sir, that you happened to be so near the site where Miss Rogers's body was discovered?"

"I was participating in a search at the behest of my friend Mr. Payne. Who as you know was the young lady's betrothed."

"Indeed," said Poe. He put a hand to his chin. "I daresay you know the currents of the Hudson quite well."

The lieutenant blinked once, but otherwise did not move. "Your implication, sir?"

"None whatsoever. An observation, nothing more."

"Then if we are finished here . . ."

"I wonder," said Poe. "Do you recall your whereabouts on that Sunday morning two weeks past?"

If my eyes did not deceive me I witnessed Andrews's stillness crack at that moment, a scarcely perceptible movement of his head, a stiff and tiny twitch.

"And on the date of Miss Rogers's attack of catarrh two years previous," Poe said, "when according to her mother she was abed at the home of an aunt, though according to the aunt she was not? Do you recall your whereabouts on that date as well?"

And now the crack widened, became a fissure in the lieutenant's composure. He cocked his head slightly and lowered his gaze.

Poe said, "Though perhaps this last is too much to ask of one's memory. I only bring it up because it was you who informed the young lady's mother of her daughter's illness. Or have I been misinformed?"

The lieutenant nodded as if to himself. Thirty seconds later he lifted his eyes to Poe once again. "My apologies, Mr. Poe. I have left my charges unattended too long. They are after all only boys."

With that he turned his back to us and walked away.

I looked up at Poe. "Now what?"

"Now," he said, "we know."

"We do?"

He nodded, lips pursed, and squinted long and hard at the empty rail where Andrews had been standing. "The sailor's knot," he said. "The lieutenant's coincidental proximity to the body when it was discovered. The lieutenant's role as messenger of the girl's sickness, when in fact she was not ill. Lastly, the testimony of the witness."

"What witness?"

"The man who escorted me to the Velsor Club. Despite the condition in which he left me there, he left me also with a sworn declaration of having seen the lieutenant in the company of the deceased on the very day of her disappearance."

"Well don't that fix the flint."

"Precisely."

Finally he turned to me. He blinked once, as if to change the picture before his eyes. "And now, Master Dubbins, we attend to the second rectification of the day."

"Meaning what?"

And he said, "Meaning you."

19

OUR FIRST stop upon returning to Manhattan was the lion's den of editor Neely, a man who was both Poe's nemesis and his lifeline. I waited in the warren of outer offices, keeping one eye on the editor's closed door, the other on the scriveners smoking and scribbling, men weaving as if from the threads and skeins of tobacco haze a fabric of words, a patchwork of pages that would become a newspaper, that flimsy compilation of ink and pulp that in turn wove together the fabric of the city, even the world.

It was a moment of revelation for me, not a lightning-bolt revelation but a slow seeping in of wonder, that out of this craft of common men, out of this alchemy in which bits of observation were mixed with pieces of fact, then spun into sentences, headlines, sketches, would come a singular voice from a chorus of voices, a voice to become an identity for the whole, to create a sense of community, a personality pieced together from a scattering of disconnected lives. Feeling as I did the least connected creature of any on the earth, the vaporous possibilities of that room filled me, at that particular moment, with a quivering awareness I can only describe as magical.

And then here came Poe striding toward me. His smile—never wide, never more than a slight ascendancy at one corner of an otherwise grim mouth—was augmented by the merriment of his eyes. As he came abreast of me he even winked, a gesture of complicity so thrilling that I all but bounded after him as he headed for the street.

"You look like you had some good news," I said.

Out the door he headed north up Nassau. "Would you call six dollars good news?"

"He gave you six dollars for the story?"

"I am to be paid six dollars, yes. And one of those dollars is to be yours."

I would say that this news struck me like a blow except that the connotation carries a negative, even punitive weight. And I felt no punishment from this blow—paralysis, yes, but the paralysis of glee. I stood as if nailed to the sidewalk, mouth hanging open as Poe continued on, his head thrown back like that of a long-distance runner on his victory lap.

It is not possible now to look back on that afternoon, to remember the buoyancy with which Poe strode on, the gait so jaunty with triumph as to give the impression of levitation, without juxtaposing upon it another perambulation, weightier, and another Poe, spectral, adjoined to the first like a reflection from a candlelit mirror. This second Poe is in Baltimore, 1849. His life on that day too had seemed to be coming together finally, and in celebration of this turnaround he has spent the previous night carousing, or so one can only assume in consideration of his appearance now, wan and haggard, hands atremble. He, like us, does not know precisely where he spent the previous night, he has only a vague understanding of where he is now headed, though eventually to New York to compose his affairs, then to Richmond to wed the woman to whom he was engaged at the age of eighteen, all this eventual, somewhere out there in the fog, while now he wanders through the crepuscular light from one lamppost to the next, one flickering glow to another, as he mumbles bits of poetry, fragmented memories, until he stumbles and falls and this time does not get up; I am not there to guide him home. I have wondered ever since how long he lay conscious in that gutter before the blessing of darkness was bestowed on him.

Of course that is how I *now* envisage one momentous afternoon of 1840 as juxtaposed upon his final one nine years later. At the time I noticed not a single one of the hundred shadows lurking in our futures, tugging at our sleeves. I felt a millionaire already, though the vouchsafed dollar was not yet even in my pocket.

We continued up Nassau to Barclay Street, and from there to the public garden below Tammany Hall. There on the greensward we sat facing the Hudson. Quite a while passed before he spoke, and then with deliberation, hushed, his gaze going out long and wistful down Park Row.

"Let me begin," he finally said, "by stating that I observe in you a high intelligence. A capacity for acute observation. A resourcefulness that on its present course—were you and I to now part company, that is—

would likely lead you to great heights of criminal behavior. I say heights rather than depths because I have every confidence that you would excel at your craft. And excellence of any type, in view of humanity's proclivity for mediocrity, is to be admired."

His import was not all clear to me, but I got the gist of it.

"I am prepared, however, to offer you an alternative to your present path." He now turned to look at me. He held my gaze a moment, gave me one of those quiet smiles of his, then looked toward the distant river again.

"What if I told you," he said, "that you have in your possession the capacity for great things. That through a diligent application of your talents you might someday wear fine clothes and live in a fine house. As a man whom others respect and even admire."

I grappled with that notion.

"It is not beyond your reach, Augie."

There was a pause then, a stillness from each of us. "My own youth," he said, "was, through no efforts but my own, a frittering away of similar possibilities. I was too attached to an idealization of life to avail myself of the more practical approaches laid before me."

I watched an elegant Victoria coming toward us up Park Row, and tried to imagine myself ensconced in such luxury.

"We have much in common, you and I. A certain recklessness of spirit. A sensitivity to detail. A sense of being apart. Alone. A vague awareness that some significant portion of ourselves has been amputated. This, I believe, because we have been forced to grow up without fathers. To fend for ourselves. These are a few of the burdens we share.

"But what I am proposing, Augie, is that despite these burdens, perhaps because of them, you yet may prosper. If you are willing to do what is necessary."

I finally found my tongue. "Meaning what?"

"Meaning divesting yourself of the past. Separating yourself from all the corrupting and demeaning influences that surround you."

He paused for a moment, then continued. "The Old Brewery, Augie. It will sooner or later engulf you."

And so I told him. "I already decided. I'm quits of that place."

He studied me for a moment, he stroked his chin. "And what of your mother?"

He did not hurry my response, but waited until I could string together the words. "I don't see no reason to think about that."

"This is not a decision to be quickly made. A mother, even a less than perfect one . . ."

"Shit," I said.

He blinked at that, but waited.

"Shit piss fuck."

I do not know what made me say it. What putrefying emotion made me retch up those words. But the tears that streaked my face brought a new sting to the old welt on my cheek.

He looked at the ground then. It was awhile before he spoke. "I have found a comfortable place for you to live," he said.

I admit that my heart fell at the remark. I had spent the past few nights in a comfortable place and wanted only to continue spending my nights there.

He seemed to read my thoughts. Or had anticipated them. "In some ways your prospects there will be even more secure than my own now are. My current home, as you know, is very small, and if I do not secure a more permanent position we shall no doubt have to relocate once again. And Virginia . . ." He could not bring himself to finish the thought, to give words to her illness.

"We would of course accommodate you if possible. But I am confident that these other arrangements will in the long run prove superior."

I wiped my nose with finger and thumb. "What kind of arrangements are they?"

"You will have a bed of your own in a room you share with several other boys. You will be fed and clothed as needed. You will be schooled in the merits of a regular, disciplined life. And in a few months' time a position will be found for you on a farm in the Midwest. Where you will have all the same and more. Hard work, fresh air, and the opportunity to mold your life as you see fit. The choice, of course, is yours and yours alone. I merely lay before you the expedience."

I did not know what to say to this. It was too much. With one hand he seemed to be offering me the world, and with the other hand pushing me out of his. I wanted to turn to him, fold myself in his arms, weep like a child. But I had not been such a child for a good many years. I sat as still and cold as a stone.

I only said, "I don't need no dollar for that story of yours."

"It is as much your story as mine. You, as it were, discovered it."

We sat a while longer, but I knew already that the decision had been made. A better life, that was what it boiled down to. He saw in me his own nature, his own failed potential, and he did not want me to grow up in the same miasma of want and misery. It was no less than any father—most fathers, at least—would desire for his son.

Of course he did not mention that I would spend five years as little better than an indentured slave, that I would be worked until I dropped, pushed like a field nigger, housed in a shack, treated like chattel. He did not suspect such a fate for me any more than he suspected his own awaiting him in Baltimore, else he would never have pointed me in that direction. For despite the black pool of despair in which Poe often floundered, he maintained at other times a resolve to force life toward the better, to wrestle from it some concession of goodness much as Jacob wrestled the penurious Angel of God. And one does not usually engage in such a wrestling match with the foreknowledge of utter defeat.

20

THE NEWSBOYS' Lodging House at the corner of Nassau and Fulton was as solemn a place as a cemetery. Such was my first impression of the stolid brownstone, whose rooms, I would discover, were as dark as its facade. The entrance hall through which I walked with Poe was empty of furnishings, with not even a small rug to enliven the hardwood floor. The side rooms were very nearly as spartan, each housing perhaps a pair of straight-back chairs, a sideboard or armoire, a body-worn sofa.

At the end of the long hall, positioned as if to block entry to the dining room and kitchen, were a desk and a chair in which sat, like a combination concierge and traffic cop, a pinch of a man, bald and bent, so wasted of body that his bones seemed about to come poking through his clothes.

This was MacGregor, whom I would eventually learn was not as frightening as he appeared. Like those of us half a century younger he had been taken in by the founders of the House and given a position. His duty, which he upheld miserably, was to protect the cupboards from juvenile raiders.

Nor was the building the mausoleum I first assessed it to be. Half of the sixty or so boys who at any one time called it home were scattered out across the city, earning their daily dues by hawking papers. At this time of day these were the older boys, aged nine through eleven or twelve. An unwritten code among newsboys allowed that the regular editions were reserved for these lads, while the extras were the purview of arabs younger than nine. In every case the newsboy would purchase from the printer as many newspapers as he could carry, then sell them individually for a meager profit. Of this profit, five pennies a day were contributed toward his board and lodging.

Poe had explained all this to me on our way to the lodging house. Residents of all ages, I learned, were expected to return to the house by nightfall, at which hour the massive front doors were barred. All boys were required to participate as well in the building's housekeeping duties, plus a few hours of regulated activities each week. Otherwise all were free to pursue individual interests.

It was not a jail, Poe explained, but, like any home, a house with certain rules and standards of behavior. A life without discipline, he said, was like a cup with no bottom—it could never be filled.

We arrived in the midst of one of the mandated activities, which explained why a houseful of boys could be so still. We were directed by MacGregor to a large common room on the second floor, and there came upon a scene of such burlesque that it might have run for several weeks at the Bowery Theater.

Picture a battalion of small boys, all in ill-fitting if clean kit, engaged in military-style calisthenics, rhythmically jumping with legs spread while flailing outstretched arms back and forth, nearly three dozen such boys all in the same room and therefore slapping and knocking one another about, deliberately or not, falling and righting themselves and falling again, but doing all this as mutely as possible, suppressing giggles and curses and yelps, their enthusiasm held just short of hysteria by the humorless gaze of a ramrod of a man who stood apart from them against a side wall, and by the booming voice of their exercise leader, a sinewy barefoot fellow clothed neck to ankle in flowing white linen, gray-haired and muttonchopped.

"Vegetables, fruit, water, and bread," he shouted to the beat of his lunges, "fresh air and hard work stand a man in good stead."

I looked up at Poe, ready to laugh out loud, surprised as I was to hear the man's words echoing Poe's advice to me from thirty minutes earlier. But Poe's somber countenance held me in check, and I merely snorted once or twice.

Again and again the drill instructor barked out the same message or some amplification of it. (In a week's time it would become as natural to me as a pulse beat, which is no doubt precisely what was intended.) His name was Sylvester Graham. He was in his mid-forties and had but a decade left to his life when I first beheld him. From nose down, his face seemed squeezed together, the thin lips and slightly hooked proboscis pinched toward a receding chin. A former Presbyterian minister turned vegetarian fanatic, he preached a revolutionary theory to all who cared to listen—and often, as he strolled through town in bathrobe and swim trunks on his way to a daily swim in the river, to those who would rather not listen.

He had small beady eyes that flared when he spoke, eyes as wild as I have ever seen, wilder even than Poe's. If at times Poe's eyes were smoldering coals of passion and bitterness, Sylvester Graham's were firecrackers in a constant state of fulmination.

In his white shirt and trousers and starched white collar he jumped about in the front of the room, barking his mantra. It was easy to see why much of the city—indeed, much of the eastern seaboard—regarded him as, at best, vaudevillian, and at worst a dangerous crank. Even seventy years later his philosophy of healthful living has not been fully vindicated. His sweetened bran crackers might become a favorite of children and piecrust makers, but most adults even now consider beer and wine and fatty beef the staples of a nutritious diet.

Poe and I watched these exercises until most of the boys lay panting on the floor. Sylvester Graham, who showed no signs of fatigue other than the flaming splotches on his cheeks, finally relented and yielded the floor to the somber man who had been standing against the wall. This transaction was the equivalent of fire giving way to ice.

In contrast to Graham, Jacob Van Rensselaer appeared glacial in his movements. At first glance I had recognized him as the man Poe spoke with briefly in editor Neely's outer office. A large man, broad of chest and shoulders and with a shaggy white head, top heavy, thick handed, with not a hint of merriment in his arctic blue eyes, he moved to the front of the room and stood before the group and fixed his gaze like a bayonet about to cleave the room down its center. He kept himself as far from the nearest boys as possible considering the confines of the room, and kept his hands, gloved in bleached doeskin, laid one atop the other on his sternum.

His voice was deep and slow and resonant; it rattled the unsheathed soul. In any case it rattled mine. He did not mince words nor did he flinch from suggesting that every boy present was a base creature at his core, a vile animal, who, unless subdued by the higher faculties of reason and discipline, could without a moment's notice succumb to his natural tendency toward gluttony, avarice, excess of every kind and color.

His voice was half as loud as Graham's, and nearly as monotonous, but all the more hypnotizing for it, all the more chilling. "If meats, alcohol, and tobacco will lead as Mr. Graham predicted to digestive misery and a sullenness of spirit, and they will, they surely will, such degradation is trivial when held against what awaits your eternal souls, boys, do you not forswear not only the above-mentioned pleasures but also the gross indecency of onanism and the defilement of fornication."

(So penetrating was this promise that even years later, each time my hand in the darkness of my bed slipped netherward, the imp of my conscience would take up a chant, a Graham/Van Rensselaer duet of prescription and prohibition, *masturbation mastication, mastication masturbation,* an auger in my conscience until the horrors of Antietam finally cleansed me of any guilt over indulging in whatever small pleasures we might be able to lay hold of along this twisted road of life.)

But to the point, the story, my tenure at the newsboys' refuge house, whose founders stood before me. (My future radiated out from this hub in so many directions, like myriad spokes on the wheel, that every small incident reminds me of a connection, an after-effect, so that I feel compelled, like an old man reminiscing—which is exactly what I am—to bring it forth. But my larger goal is a narrower one, a more linear story with not myself but Poe at the forefront, and this I will henceforth attempt to limit myself to, and save the remembrances for the private hours, of which I have no shortage.)

Van Rensselaer's sermon left the room mute. It's true that some of the boys were asleep, others numbed by boredom, but a few of the more impressionable ones, myself included, were paralyzed by guilt and fear and a resolve to ascribe at least some portion of the admonitions to their own lives. What had been suggested to me by the end of the hour was just what Poe had suggested earlier—the concept of choice. I could, to some degree at least, mold Augie Dubbins, the guttersnipe, into whatever kind of man I desired.

With a hand on my sleeve Poe held me behind until the large room emptied, with first Van Rensselaer and then Graham and then the herd of boys tromping out. He then looked down at me with eyebrows raised. I understood his question.

I asked, "Just how often would I have to put up with what we seen here?"

"My understanding is that Mr. Van Rensselaer, the second gentleman, comes by twice a week. It was he whose approval I sought concerning your residency here. Mr. Graham, when he is not lecturing elsewhere, speaks to the boys as many as four times a week. But there is in every case an exercise session daily, conducted when necessary by one of the older boys. Besides Mr. MacGregor there are two matrons responsible for meals and decorum. You will be expected to keep your bed, your personal belongings, and yourself organized and clean. You will be schooled regularly in reading and ciphering."

The longer he talked, the more my face screwed up.

"It is no more, Augie, than is expected of every merchant's child. No more than was expected of me by my foster parents. No more than I would expect from a child of my own."

I gazed deep into the gray of his eyes. "You're telling me I can leave anytime I want to?"

"You will be as free as you ever were. The discipline here is intended to be self-imposed."

"But I'm expected to get a regular job."

"Not immediately. I have pledged to pay in advance for two months' room and board, as soon as my funds from Mr. Neely are forthcoming, which might be as early as tomorrow. You will also have the silver eagle I will pay you for your assistance thus far. But it seems to me that selling newspapers is not all that different from your other employment along the waterfront. You might even sell your newspapers to passengers of ships and barges as they arrive in port."

I pretended for a while longer to be mulling it over. As if this were a difficult decision. As if deliberation were required before a boy could choose between squalor and cleanliness, between unpredictable violence and routine if sometimes didactic security.

I finally shrugged. "I'll try it out awhile, I guess."

"A mature and responsible decision."

"What about your story though? Don't we need to keep at it?"

"The work is all but finished. You saw as well as I the furtiveness in Mr. Andrews's eyes, the manner in which he gave himself away. All that remains is for me to expose the culprit in the *Mirror*. This afternoon and evening I shall organize and compose the findings of our investigation. By tomorrow's late edition, you shall be famous."

"Not me," I said. "I don't want to be mentioned in none of this."

"No?" said Poe.

The truth is that I feared my mother yet, feared that she or one of her stinking companions might be spurred by the prospect of coinage to come looking for me, leather strop in hand.

"I ain't the writer," I told him. "I'm just the *fido akees* something or other."

"Fidus Achates," he said. He clamped a hand on my shoulder. "And yes, my young friend. You are that indeed."

21

IT WAS an awkward day and uneasy night that followed. Though the residents of the Newsboys' Lodging House were ostensibly learning a degree of civilized behavior, their circumspection of strangers remained untamed. At every opportunity I was bullied and threatened and otherwise made to know my place at the bottom of the pecking order.

Somehow we were all more wary of one another for being boxed together within those brownstone walls, less willing than we might have been in the open to view each other as brothers in misfortune. The longer the tenure at the boardinghouse, the more one accumulated: an extra shirt or pair of boots, the advancement to next in line for a coveted job or a coveted bunk space. In most of the boys, a subtle meanness grew. As scavenging rats we had shared what little we had with all other rats and had found a certain comfort among the community of rodents, but one by one through the civilizing generosity of Messrs. Graham and Van Rensselaer, many of us were learning greed and ambition.

Presiding as schoolmaster of these qualities in the room I shared with eleven other boys was a bulbous-headed whelp named Moonie Weaver. He was not only the largest boy in the room but the loudest and rudest. The others swirled around him like soiled water down a drain.

I knew him as a former resident of the Old Brewery. He had moved out six months earlier, much to my and every other child's relief. We imagined him (not without some glee) dead and buried in the building's basement, having cursed at one adult too many. Yet here he was again, a full three inches taller than I remembered him, and with an even more ogreish grin.

He and a half-dozen others came to my bed that first night and formed a wall across the edge of it. One of the boys lit a candle and held it close to my face. "Come to show you somethin'," Moonie said. He had grinned at me all through dinner; I had been expecting a welcoming ceremony. Still, I clutched at my thin blanket and tried not to draw my knees up to my chest.

"Brought you a picture of your mother," he said. He then drew from behind his back a painted playing card and held the illustrated face of it close to the sputtering candle, which itself was near enough to warm the tip of my nose.

At my first reaction to the picture on the card—I whimpered a little, I think, and jerked my head back—the entire pack of whelps broke into guffaws. The picture showed an obese and naked woman sitting with legs spread, one hand cupped beneath each mountainous breast.

I looked up at Moonie but said nothing.

"Tell me that ain't your mother," he said. There was no mistaking the challenge of his words. Rebuke him and I would soon suffer more than humiliation.

I held my tongue.

"It's his mother all right," he announced to the room. "And this here's your sister, ain't it?" He produced another card and held it to the candle. "Don't know who the dog belongs to, though—do you?"

"I don't have no sister," I said.

He whacked a fist against the side of my head. "You ain't callin' me a liar, are ya?"

I turned my eyes to the candle. I found that by staring at the base of the flame, at the small pool of melted wax accumulated on the candle's caldera, I could blank out the remainder of the room but for a wall of looming shadows.

"Here's another one of your mother," he said. "It shows how she keeps the leatherheads happy—two at a time!"

He baited me for ten more minutes, even rubbing one of the cards in my face. "Kiss your mommy's quim," he ordered. "Kiss it good night."

I could smell his body on the card, the stink of his pocket.

It seemed an eternity before he finally tired of me. With a parting thump to the crown of my head he left me to my share of darkness. He and his disciples retreated to a far corner to slaver over the playing cards awhile longer.

In time a smallish boy whose name I do not recall crept up to my bed and tapped me on the shoulder. "You awake?" he whispered.

I chose not to answer.

"I just wanted to tell ya that he does that to all of us," the boy said.

I finally mumbled a response. "I figured."

"We all know it ain't your mother. We figure it must be his own."

"He never had no mother," I said. "He was shit out by a crow."

The boy giggled, but softly. "Anyway he'll get his before too long."

"From who? Ain't nobody in the house big as him but MacGregor. And MacGregor can't hardly even wipe his own nose."

"You heared about Death, ain't ya?"

"I know what death is, I ain't stupid."

"I'm talking about Death hisself. People down in the Bowery say they see him walking around there most every night now. Looks just like you'd think Death would. They say he walks all around like he's down there looking for somebody special."

"That ain't Death. There's no such person. Death don't have to go looking."

"You don't know," the boy said.

"Even if he was, what makes you think he's looking for Moonie?"

" 'Cause of what we been feeding him. We been putting cat piss in his mush."

"Who has?"

"Some of us."

I tried not to laugh out loud. "What good you think that'll do?"

"It's better than nothin', ain't it?"

"I don't see why. How do you get the cat piss in the first place?"

"There's this place a coupla blocks from here where a bunch of cats hang out. We put down some rag and leave it and the cats piss all over it and the next day we let the rag soak in Moonie's mush for a while. He don't even notice the difference!"

Sometimes I wondered how people my own age could be so childish. (I still do.) "You think this Death fella likes the smell of cat piss, do ya?"

"Don't see how he can help hisself, being who he is and all."

"Well . . . good luck to you. That's all I can say."

"We'll get the rag to you when it's your turn to serve the mush."

"Sure thing," I said.

Surreal as the evening had been thus far, it was not this conversation or even Moonie's bullying that most unsettled me my first night there. Not the tiresome prayer before and after supper. Not even the mandated wash of hands and face before turning into our bunks. It was instead the sense of apartness, of being turned out through my own efforts from my real family and then turned out from my surrogate family. Here I was housed with no fewer than five dozen of my peers, and never had I felt more alone.

I kept thinking of Poe at home, composing at his kitchen table. He did not value journalistic writing as he did poetry and criticism but neither would he give it less than full attention. I lay abed in the quiet hours of that first night and in my own mind composed along with him, laid out the facts of Miss Rogers's bogus illnesses, her confederation with Lieutenant Andrews, a confederation concealed even from her own mother. I then constructed the scenario of how the seaman, in a fit of rage no doubt, perhaps told by the lady that she would not break off her engagement with Mr. Payne, a duller but more reliable exemplar of what she looked for in a mate, had lashed out at her, struck her down, and then, moved by tenderness, remorse, his sudden anger spent, had replaced her bonnet upon her head and secured it with the knot that came most naturally to him.

Many days later, her body discovered, he had found it necessary to bribe the medical examiner, to create a scenario that, though besmirching the young lady's character, would draw attention away from the way she had actually died.

It seemed all of a piece, with but one exception. Again and again I stumbled over the single small bump in my logic. If Miss Rogers was sufficiently enamored of Lieutenant Andrews to continue a two-year liaison with him, why perpetrate the charade of romance with Mr. Payne? The latter was employed as a bank's clerk, a respected but hardly lofty position. The former, it could be assumed, hailed from a family of some affluence and note, as did all the naval officers in those days.

Was Miss Rogers's relationship with the lieutenant one of mere carnal convenience? I knew enough of fornication to know the kind of beasts it turns both male and female into, beasts who growl and flail for a few minutes only to shiver and yelp and then show their backs to each other, so this was the only conclusion I could achieve, and then with but the vague understanding of a nonparticipant and theorist.

The next morning found me awake and ready for the door before breakfast was laid on the table. The moment it was set before us and we had muttered our amens I attacked my bread and mush and baked apple (all the while with a twitching smile as Moonie did the same) and flushed it all down with a mug of tepid water.

It was the job of us mid-age boys to carry the dishes into the kitchen afterward, where half a dozen older lads, those few not turned out early to hawk the morning editions, scrubbed and dried and put the dishes away. The dining room chairs then had to be lined up like soldiers, the floor swept clean of every crumb, the tables set with bowls and spoons and glasses for the first supper shift to arrive some ten hours later.

By the time I hit the street the city was already abuzz. The day's edition of the *Mirror* had sold out. Copies of the broadsheet were passed from hand to hand. I was able eventually to get my own copy only when it rose, in a bizarre defiance of gravity, up and out of the pocket of a gentleman's waistcoat and into my palm, which just happened to be in a proximity to catch it.

Apparently Poe had composed his piece with alacrity, for there it was on the left half of the front page. Poe's scenario read exactly like my own, if more voluminously and with larger words. As did Poe's conclusion that Miss Rogers and Lieutenant Andrews had been engaged in a relationship "of mere carnal convenience" (it was from him I took the phrase).

You cannot imagine the atmosphere of scandal that was generated by this article, the shock to the sensibilities of Park Row, the nods and winks from lower Broadway to the Battery. Poe did not explicitly accuse the lieutenant of the young lady's murder but his delineation of the facts afforded no other assumption.

I wondered for a time if Mr. Andrews had had the time to put to sea or otherwise absquatulate, but by 10 A.M. the word was out: he had been arrested. Only then did the city's agitation transform itself, bifurcated, if you will, into a scornful certainty by one half the populace that Mr. Andrews would never be brought to justice, and indignation by the other half that one of their own should be treated so roughly over the demise of a wanton shopgirl.

I wondered too what Poe was making of this hullabaloo. Up and down the streets I trudged, imagining how he and his family must be celebrating up there in the country. Somehow, by late morning, I found myself standing behind an elm near the end of their lane, staring at Poe's cottage.

Several times I saw Mrs. Clemm move to or fro past a window. Once, Virginia came to the doorway and gazed out. But Poe never showed himself. Still sleeping, I told myself, exhausted from his long hours of ratiocination. And so I waited, standing for as long as I could, then sitting against the elm, and finally dozing off in its shade.

It was in this latter position that he discovered me. His hand on my knee woke me. I opened my eyes and saw him kneeling there and I waited to hear how he would upbraid me.

He held out a bright moon of silver. "Your payment, sir."

When I did not reach for it, he pressed it into my hand.

"I went looking for you at the lodging house," he said.

"They turn us out not long after breakfast."

"In any case, I have found you. And none too soon. A celebration is in the offing, and you, of course, must attend."

"I knew you'd be all chirky about this. The whole city's read what you wrote."

"It is the beginning of a great change for us all. Mr. Neely has proposed a less tenuous position for me with the *Mirror*."

Though the word *tenuous* was not one I yet claimed to understand, despite its application to my own existence, I answered, "Ain't that something?"

"It is indeed." A moment later he pushed himself erect. "I have informed Mr. MacGregor that you will be lodging with us this evening. Provided you are amenable."

"I'm staying here tonight?"

"We cannot have you strolling the streets after dark with your belly full of pandowdy and sweet potato pie, can we?"

"Mrs. Clemm's making pies?"

"That and more," Poe said. Moments later I was at his side as before and striding down the lane and feeling very nearly weightless just to step foot in his dooryard once again.

22

We spent a pleasant enough lunch together, except that it was hurried a bit by Poe's gleeful restlessness. One moment he was reciting to us a new poem, the next he was whisking away the sausage to drag me outside to the woodpile. He split maybe four logs for the cookstove, with me fetching and stacking, before deciding that it was more important to clear the weeds from around the springhouse. In short he was too happy to sit still, and his happiness was exhausting me.

It must have been around two in the afternoon when Mrs. Clemm called for him to return to the house. We were both standing knee-deep in the springhouse at the time, barefoot, with our trousers rolled to the knees; Poe had, a few minutes earlier, been inspired by the dank and earthy coolness to imagine the springhouse as the scene of a fictional murder, a place where bodies could be kept fresh until diabolically reanimated by a school of electric eels. It was some such scenario, in any case, and he had insisted that we experience the chill firsthand, all the better to describe it, he said.

And so we were standing knee-deep in sweet coolness, trying to imagine our legs and ankles being stung by a thousand slithering eels, when Mrs. Clemm's voice reached our ears. Poe stepped outside, and a moment later mumbled something and hurried toward the house. I meant to peek out only long enough to see what he was up to and then retreat to the springhouse again, but when I saw the hackney at the gate, and the frock-coated man standing beside it looking our way, with a very anxious Mrs. Clemm wringing her hands on the porch, I changed my mind and trotted barefoot after Poe.

On the breast of the man's blue frock coat, cloth letters had been sewn: BNYP. The Bank of New York Police was but one of many small police forces in the city, each privately endowed and with its own patrol area (frequently disputed), its own claim to absolute authority. Most were little more than hired thugs who enforced their claim with nightsticks. All but Hays's troop of leatherheads were privately financed.

Poe had not yet bothered to roll down his trousers, and so cut a rather comic figure standing next to the officer. The man had a face chiseled from rock—though from a cragged and porous block of limestone. His eyes seemed deep hollows, his mouth a scratch. He had come, he said, to talk to Poe's witness, the unnamed individual who, according to Poe's article in the *Mirror,* had fingered Lieutenant Andrews as Miss Rogers's escort on the day of her disappearance.

"I have no idea where the man resides," Poe said.

"You found him once before, didn't you?"

"In point of fact, no. He found me."

"We need to talk to him," the officer said.

"In regards to . . . ?"

"In regards to whether he's telling the truth or not."

"Do you have reason to believe that he lied?"

"We'll go find him, you and me. It won't take long."

"How would you know that, not knowing where the place might be?"

"Come along now."

Poe stood completely motionless for the next ten seconds, eyes fixed on the officer's as if he hoped to see through to the workings of the man's brain. Water trickled down my legs and made me want to scratch, but I dared not move.

"Augie," Mrs. Clemm finally said, and softly broke the silence. "Run and get Mr. Poe's shoes for him."

Poe looked at her and smiled. It was all the acquiescence I needed; I raced to the springhouse and gathered up our shoes and stockings. Poe and I then sat on the front porch and reshod ourselves.

"The boy don't need to go," the officer said.

"Master Dubbins is my assistant."

"You won't need no assistant for this."

"Again I wonder," Poe said with a strange smile, "how you would know that in advance?"

In answer the officer went to the hackney and climbed into the driver's seat and took up the reins. The moment Poe and I had settled in ourselves, the officer snapped the reins and set us moving.

I noticed as we neared the end of the lane that he showed no sign of slowing down, and I leaned very close to Poe and whispered in his ear. "How does he know where to take us?"

Poe raised one finger and whispered, "Shh."

At the end of the lane the officer pulled his horse to the right and turned us toward the city. Only after another half minute of travel did he look over his shoulder—it seemed a kind of afterthought—and ask, "Where to?"

Poe said, "You seem to know without my telling."

"Somewhere in the city, right?"

"Is it necessarily so? Could the man not just as well live north?"

The officer drew hard on the reins and stopped us so short that I nearly slid off my seat. This time he did not so much as lean toward Poe as lean into him, putting his weight onto Poe's left shoulder, his mouth so close to Poe's cheek that he almost seemed ready to kiss him.

What came from the man's lips was not a kiss but a snarl. "Where to?"

I saw Poe's jawline harden, his teeth clench.

"Velsor Club," I quickly said. "Down on Cross Street."

Poe would not look at me throughout the remainder of the ride.

THE WITNESS was not to be found inside the club. The constable made a show of walking from table to table, scrutinizing each patron in turn. From the hooded glances with which he was answered, the quick cold looks, from the way he swaggered, the chill wave he pushed before him, I knew in a moment that he was not new to this place.

Poe noticed only that the informant was nowhere to be seen. "Alas," he said, barely able to suppress his satisfaction, "I fear we have run into a cul-de-sac."

But the officer's charade was only just beginning. He went to the barman and with a hand conspicuously on his nightstick he asked several questions we were not privy to overhear, all the while nodding toward Poe. The barman nodded in return and mumbled his answers with head bowed.

Eventually the officer returned to grasp Poe by the sleeve. "He's got a crib around the corner. Let's go."

"How could you ascertain as much when you don't even know the man's name?"

"Barman remembered you. Remembered the man you was with."

"How wonderfully convenient," Poe said.

The room was on the second floor of an adjacent building, a warren of hovels only slightly less odoriferous than those of the Brewery. It was the kind of place wherein people did not so much live as cower, in hiding not only from the laws of society but from each other, and so it seemed odd to me that nearly every door we passed stood open, every doorway occupied with two or three individuals peering out like rats inside their rat holes, safe themselves from the marauding cat but eager to watch a fellow rodent being torn to shreds. How they knew to anticipate our arrival is another question, but they knew.

The officer led us up a set of creaking stairs. The banister rail was missing, so we hugged the oily wall. Several of the rodents crept up furtively behind us. Others stepped out into the hallway to better hear what might be heard.

The second floor hallway was even more crowded than the first, more thick with smoke and anticipation. The constable did not pause to peer inside any of the rooms we passed, made no inquiries of the tenants. He led us directly to a closed door three-quarters down the hall. Outside this door a small huddle of bystanders had gathered. One oil lamp hanging from a nail in the wall threw their shadows toward us long and gnarled. Again I noticed that as we came close, they looked upon the officer only fleetingly, with darting glances, but at Poe and me they smiled the kind of smiles that might send a shudder up an undertaker's spine.

The constable went without hesitation to the closed door and without even reaching for the handle he placed his foot along the door's edge and shoved it open. But he did not enter. He stood back from the wash of crackery air and jerked his head at Poe.

Poe stood for a moment outside the cubicle. He knew from the silence within, he knew from the smell of the place, he knew from the gathering of onlookers and the smug demeanor of the constable that he was an actor in a show now. He turned only his head so as to fix the constable with a look as cold as lead. He then turned to me and with a gentler look, a nudge on the arm, signaled that I was to remain in the hallway.

He then strode forward, three long strides. I followed half a stride behind him.

I was struck initially by the emptiness of the place, the single crate and saucered candle in the middle of the room, an old coat tossed into a corner. Nothing remained of the candle but an inch-long nub, sputtering erratically, the pool of liquid wax dripping over the saucer's edge. The only thing revealing about the room was a black stain on the floor, an adumbration made from what first appeared to be a shallow pool of oil but which all of us knew immediately was not.

And then the constable stepped in behind us, carrying the lamp. Now the color of the stain on the floor changed from black to black-red, carmine. Emanating out from one side of the pool was a tail, a wide smear, and our eyes followed this tail to the corner behind the door. There sat Poe's informant, his head lolling forward, chin on his chest, his chest and legs soaked black from the blood that had poured from his riven throat.

The officer held the lamp close to the man's right ear. "This your witness?"

Poe spoke with a hand over his mouth. "He bears a small resemblance."

A smile flickered on the officer's mouth. Then he grunted something and turned away, taking the light out of the room. We followed like moths.

The three of us then rode back toward Poe's cottage in silence, at least until we came to the southern end of Union Square, where the officer pulled his rig to a halt. "This is as far as I can take you," he said.

Poe put both hands on his knees and leaned forward, but did not rise from his seat. He sat with his head cocked, his gaze on the inside of the carriage. "I don't suppose there will be an investigation," he said.

The constable asked, "Of what?"

"The murder of my witness."

"Who said anything about murder? Looked like a suicide to me."

"Of course. The man slit his throat in the middle of the room, then dragged himself behind the door. And in the meantime disposed of the razor or whatever implement it was that he had employed."

The officer smiled. "Sounds right to me."

After a moment's thought Poe climbed down one side, I climbed out the other. He put a hand on the forward wheel. "Am I correct in assuming that the lieutenant will now be released?" he asked.

"You got any other witnesses?"

Poe studied the flank of the horse for a moment. Then, without another word, he turned his back to the carriage and stepped away. The officer snapped his reins and drove off.

I fell into step beside Poe. We walked several yards in silence, until I was rattled by a shiver and spoke in hopes of generating some heat. "I ain't never seen anything like that before," I said. "Have you?"

"And hope to never again."

Despite the midday warmth I felt more chilled than I had in the springhouse, a full-body chill as if my spine were formed of ice. Poe saw me hugging myself and laid a hand on the back of my neck. "We should be able to smell Muddy's pandowdy soon," he said.

"You mean we're still having that celebration?"

"Muddy and Sissie have been cooking all day. We mustn't disappoint them."

"But when you tell them about that man . . ."

He shook his head. "There are some things we do not share with the people we love. There are some things that, as responsible men, we must keep to ourselves."

It was fine with me. I had been keeping most things to myself for most of my life. I only hoped that I could enjoy pandowdy and sweet potato pie without seeing with every swallow the obscene gape of a man's split throat.

23

As it turned out I had no problem devouring my share of dinner and a double share of treats afterward. The women were obviously tired but pleased by the fuss both Poe and I made over their lavish spread, and they did not remark upon his subdued mood except to ask, upon our arrival, if all had gone well. To which he answered, "Yes, my dears. For we are home again and with our beloveds—what could be better than this?"

After dinner, in the still of a rose-streaked evening, Poe smoked his pipe and rocked and held General Tom on his lap as the twilight wrapped around us. Virginia sang "Sweet William's Ghost" and "Rowan Tree." Had her voice not faded into a breathless whisper I would have pleaded for a dozen encores. She and Poe talked of Saratoga again, of moving there soon, of the fresher air and stillness, the healing springs, the sunlight uncluttered by dust and smoke.

"We do not want to be here in the winter," Poe said, "when every inhalation is a furnace of wood and coal smoke, and when the Canadian winds sweep like banshees across the choked Hudson."

"Don't they have winter in Saratoga?" I asked.

"We will be safe in our snuggery then," said Virginia.

"We will indeed," said Poe. "Where the cacophonation of this city cannot reach us."

"We will have a piano as well, won't we, beloved?"

"A piano and a harp," said Poe. "And two maids to do the bidding of our own sweet Muddy. It will provide me no end of joy, dear Mother, when I am able to give those great strong hands of yours a rest."

"Don't you worry about my hands," she told him. "They wouldn't know what to do without some work to fill them. They would only get into some trouble, I'm sure."

"Yet how I would love to provide them with the opportunity for such trouble."

Mrs. Clemm merely smiled at this and continued her knitting of an afghan blanket. I thought at the time that her silence was a way of savoring the dreams, but in retrospect I think it was perhaps the silence of indulgence. Although but a few years older than Poe she had long outgrown all romantic naïveté, had probably reconciled herself to the cards she had been dealt, the nine of Toil, the six of Fatigue, the four of Poverty, the king and a queen of Tragedy—a hand that would win her nothing.

But she had these lovely hours at least, and then the chores that brought her truest joy, a larder full of food, a house suddenly too small for all her goodness. Even the last light of the day seemed a kind of lavender benediction on us, and not, as it would soon turn out, a further diminution of fortune's glow.

The brougham came down the road in dusky light, a shiny black box on high wheels, its door and windows gilded in deepest purple. It came moving at full chisel until it reached the mouth of the lane, then ground to a dirge so as to make the turn and come lugubriously to the gate. The single roan mare tossed its head once, snorted, and the coachman set the brake. He then climbed down from his seat and straightened his doeskin breeches, then opened the coach's side door and offered his hand to the passenger.

A young lady climbed out and stepped down, and with a rush of petticoats and the swish of fine cloth she took my breath away.

In stature she was tall and somewhat slender. With a singular lightness of footfall she moved toward the gate. The color of her face and neck rivaled that of the purest ivory, was nearly as radiant as the thin white gloves she wore. Her hair was a radiant auburn, her eyes incandescent emeralds. She seemed to me enveloped in a soft and succulent glow, an aura not itself observable but in the sheen and liveliness of the very air around her. The delicate contours of her nostrils, the harmonious and generous mouth—in an instant poor Virginia was rendered a dim and dowdy thing. Mrs. Clemm put out a hand as if to prevent me from falling off the kitchen chair I had dragged outside.

Poe laid his pipe on the porch rail and rose to stand on the uppermost step. The young lady paused just outside the gate.

"Mr. Poe?" she asked.

Her voice, a dulciana, nearly unhinged my knees completely, but did most of its damage to my ears, and the way they thereafter perceived sweet Virginia's feeble voice as a bit too shrill, and most other women's words as tuneless squawk.

"I am," he answered.

"My name is Felicia Hobbs, sir. I wonder if I might intrude upon a moment of your time?"

The name Hobbs, I am sure, sent a quiver through us all. It was a name that, were the twin gongs of Power and Wealth struck in any part of Gotham, would have been among the first resonation, sounding up and down the length of the island along with Pierrepont, Vanderbilt, and Astor. Renowned for its philanthropy, the Hobbs family supported innumerable events of a musical, artistic, literary, and scientific nature. Nestor Hobbs, the family patriarch and influential Whig paladin, had been a member of the Erie Canal Commission as well as the Manhattan Streets Commission, and had been instrumental in imbuing both projects with the republican values of balance, order, and convenience.

The name of Nestor's oldest son, Johnston Hobbs, was in 1840 synonymous with another project intended to transform the look (and smell) of Manhattan Island. Hobbs had kept alive the Croton Water Project through years of Democratic opposition, had pushed the project financially as well as politically, and, aided by epidemics of cholera and fire, had steered it around every obstacle the Tammanyites and Loco Focos could throw in its path. The plebeian dandy Walter Whitman had attempted in his newspaper columns to harpoon Johnston Hobbs as the epitome of a soulless aristocracy, but Whitman's denunciation of banks and paper money and public works projects fell on too few ears in a city greedy for progress. (Whitman, who failed to make a name for himself as a fop, would later don a slouch hat and coveralls and peddle himself as Walt, the workingman's poet.)

By that summer of 1840, a masonry conduit, most of it underground, had been completed from the Croton River in upper Westchester County to the very edge of the city. This aqueduct was expected to begin operation in another two years, conveying clean, fresh water into Manhattan's homes, flushing out antiquated sewage systems, showering the city with a wealth of fountains and hydrants. In the bargain, Johnston Hobbs stood to be crowned grand potentate as the shepherd of the era's most magnificent engineering achievement.

And here before us stood his daughter Felicia, begging to intrude upon our evening.

"Far more a pleasure than an intrusion," Poe told her. "Will you join us here?"

With a dramatic sweep of his hand he made it clear who among us was expected to relinquish his seat for the lady. I wobbled to my feet and retreated to the corner of the porch. The young lady settled herself beside Mrs. Clemm.

Only Poe retained a hint of composure in the lady's presence. During Poe's introductions Virginia went even paler and lowered her eyes in a grimace of shyness. Mrs. Clemm blushed and stammered, "Pleased to meet you, miss," and played a nervous pat-a-cake with the heels of her hands.

I was no better. At the mention of my name my ears went red hot, while some invisible force dragged my gaze to my dirty boot tops.

"Might we offer you a refreshment after your journey?" Poe asked, still standing at attention beside his chair.

"Thank you, sir, but no. It is a most pleasant ride into the country, and therefore no journey at all."

"I trust the traffic did not impede you."

"At this hour, no, the traffic was not a hindrance. But please, Mr. Poe, please sit if you will. I have a matter I would like very much to discuss with you, and I have no wish to interrupt your evening a moment longer than is necessary."

He sat, I thought, with an overly dramatic flourish, his right hand moving as a maestro's as if to conduct his buttocks to the cane seat, then left knee lifted and draped over the right, right elbow resting on right thigh, right palm to the side of his face, body inclining forward in what struck me as a burlesque of rapt attention. I cut a glance at Virginia; she was watching Poe sidelong with hooded eyes, and on her mouth the thin smile of a woman who has smelled a scent too sweet.

Felicia Hobbs turned to her. "I was in attendance last month for your husband's presentation at the Moravian Young Lady's Society. I am very much taken with his work, Mrs. Poe. When I hear, for example, such lines as he read to us—'On desperate seas long wont to roam / Thy hyacinth hair, thy classic face / Thy Naiad airs have brought me home'— I cannot help but think I am in the presence of an aesthetic very nearly divine."

Poe gave a tiny bow of his head but kept one ear cocked so as to miss not a word of praise.

"Without the inspiration of your own beauty, of course, he would no doubt find himself bereft of such sentiments."

"A poet without his Muse," Poe told her, "is but a cup without its bottom."

Virginia offered only another wan smile. Some time would pass, many years, before I learned the reason for her lack of enthusiasm; the lines Felicia Hobbs had quoted were from a poem Poe had written for his first infatuation, the mother of a friend when he was but a boy, and therefore composed long before he might have roamed any desperate seas other than those of imagination.

Now Felicia Hobbs turned in her chair to face Poe. "And that is why, sir, your most recent composition has affected me so grievously."

His brow furrowed. I could almost hear him rifling through the sheaves of poems in his mind, trying to isolate the one most recently in print.

"Because of your assertions," she continued, "which in this one regard are so far off the mark as to constitute slander, an innocent man has been made to suffer the humiliation of arrest and incarceration."

"Ahh, you speak of Lieutenant Andrews. An acquaintance of yours?"

"My betrothed," she said. "We are to be married in September."

It was a good thing I was no longer sitting in a chair, because I would have fallen out of it.

Poe too was taken aback. His eyes dilated and the vein in his temple began to pulse. He pushed a limp strand of hair behind one ear.

"I can only assure you, Miss Hobbs, that my research was exhaustive. The facts as I have assembled them allow no other conclusion."

"Your facts, sir, are incomplete. Therefore your conclusion is made spurious."

Had anyone else spoken so critically of his work Poe would no doubt have lashed out, given tongue to the scathing sarcasm of his Imp. But the young woman's hands, though clasped and gloved, were visibly trembling, and her eyes were damp with tears.

He drew a slow breath, released it, and spoke softly. "If you might edify me as to where I have erred . . ."

"Mr. Andrews's interest in Miss Rogers was fraternal and nothing more. To suggest otherwise is an offense to both his family and mine."

"I have no wish to offend either of your fine families."

"And yet you have done so. The mere fact of your accusation has done irreparable harm to my fiancé's career, not to mention the security of our own future together."

"In light of your father's influence in Gotham . . . ," Poe said, suggesting that Andrews's freedom required no more than a nod and a wink from her father, a few gold eagles passed from hand to hand.

"Mr. Andrews will be released to my father's house by the time I am returned there," she said. "But that hardly rectifies the matter. The charges against him must be withdrawn and an apology tendered."

"I have not levied any charges. I have no power to do so. In any case, the witness upon whom I relied . . . he has become, in a word . . . unavailable."

"He will not testify?"

"Not now nor ever."

"You see?" she all but shouted, jubilant, but immediately laid a hand to her breast to quiet herself. "Forgive me; this news is music to my heart." She breathed shallowly for a moment, then calmed herself enough to continue. "Howsoever, Mr. Poe. You continue to believe in his guilt, do you not?"

"What I believe is of small consequence. As I said, I have no power—"

"I think you undervalue your power, sir. Was it not the power of your words that caused my fiancé to be arrested?"

"The power of truth, Miss Hobbs."

"Half-truths. Half-truths and speculation."

"Again, if you could provide me with exculpatory evidence . . ."

"I have the word of my betrothed, sworn to me this very day. It is all the evidence I require."

"I understand. Unfortunately it is insufficient to my own needs."

"In that case I am prepared to offer you the opportunity to gather additional evidence sufficient to your needs."

"How so?" Poe asked.

"I have been authorized by my father, Johnston Hobbs, to engage your services," she said. "We desire to employ you to continue your investigation until you have gathered the factual evidence requisite to Lieutenant Andrews's full and complete exoneration. We cannot allow a single doubt as to his innocence, either in your mind or in any other."

Poe said nothing for a moment. Then, "I have just this day been made an offer of permanent employment by the editor of the New York *Mirror*."

"At what salary, if I might ask?"

It was not her bluntness that gave Poe pause, but, I am certain, this startling opportunity so unexpectedly proffered. In any case it was Muddy who, having uttered not a sound to this point, suddenly answered the young lady's query.

"Ten dollars a week," she said.

"My father will pay you twenty-five dollars per week," said Miss Hobbs. "With a one-hundred-dollar bonus upon completion of your duties." She reached for a small gold purse attached to her belt. She opened it and withdrew a gold eagle, a brilliant ten-dollar sun in the white cloud of her hand.

She leaned forward then and with her left hand grasped Poe's and turned it palm up. She laid the coin in his hand and closed his fingers over it.

"I ask you to accept this as a token of my trust in you as an honest man. A man who, I continue to believe, has been touched by the spark of divinity. And who therefore cannot be satisfied until Truth itself, which along with Love and Beauty are the threads that bind us to God, is satisfied as well."

Poe continued to look down upon his fist, enveloped as it was in Miss Hobbs's gloved hands. Virginia and Mrs. Clemm and I dared not breathe.

"Miss Hobbs," he finally said.

At that she stood. Her coachman came down off the brougham to attend her at the gate.

"My father would be grateful to receive you at our home at two in the afternoon," she said. "At which time he will learn of your decision to accept or reject his offer of employment."

She turned to the rest of us. "Mrs. Poe. Mrs. Clemm. Mr. Dubbins. I apologize for what has surely been a disturbing visit for all of you. May we soon meet again under happier circumstances."

Poe was rising unsteadily from his chair, but Felicia Hobbs did not linger for an escort. She was soon climbing into the brougham and setting off up the lane.

After what seemed a very long while Poe ceased staring after her and turned to regard first Mrs. Clemm and then Virginia. His eyes were dark and pleading, asking for something, though I knew not what.

"One hundred dollars," Mrs. Clemm said in a whisper. "It almost seems a sin just to say it out loud."

It was all I could do to keep from leaping onto Poe and prying open his fist, exposing there that wondrous thing I myself had never held or even seen up close. It made the silver dollar in my pocket as light as paper, as modest as a Bungtown copper. I was suddenly hollow with greed and could only hope that Poe in his silence was feeling the same.

24

EITHER THE midday air was atremble, or my knees were. We stood outside the heavy wooden door of Johnston Hobbs's Fifth Avenue gothic castle, Poe squarely facing the door with me slightly to his rear, not quite cowering but neither standing upright. This was the first time I had sought admittance through the front entrance of a home whose gold-plated door knockers were as large as my noggin. They, the knockers, were distended like gargoyle heads, terrifying harpy faces with gluttonous grins and ears like horns. The look they levied down on me did nothing to quiet the flutterings of my stomach, where Mrs. Clemm's scrumptious beef dodgers now sat like twin lumps of clay.

I was worried, I suppose, that the inhabitants of this castle would take one look at me and send me reeling into the gutter. I was freshly scrubbed and slicked down, true, my long hair greased back behind each ear with a smear of soap, but a part of me suspected Augie Dubbins of being filthy and reeking, a part of me always would, still does, and stands ever at the ready to scrunch up its nose at myself.

On this afternoon, rather than try to hide myself in the shadows, I opted for blending in with Poe's pant leg. He had insisted I accompany him; I was, he said, his protégé, which I took to mean some kind of an assistant.

I have no doubts now that he was as nervous as I, and that he drew some composure from my quaking presence, much as a man suffering from any malady will find comfort in those more miserable.

He had but to drop the knocker twice before the huge door swung open. There stood a portly butler with a tousled and patchy mane of silver hair.

"Mr. E. A. Poe to see Mr. Johnston Hobbs," Poe said.

The butler nodded and stood to the side. Poe strode inside as if he meant to plant his flag in the tessellated marble floor. I clumped along behind him.

The butler closed the door, then set off at a scurry into the far dark reaches of the foyer. "This way, sir."

He led us to a set of French doors and drew them open and with a slight movement of his hand indicated that Poe should step inside. Poe moved to the threshold and there faltered, a slight sagging as if all the breath had rushed out of him, a weakness of desire.

The fullness of that room, the splendor. Though it was not the ornate luxury of the furnishings that stole Poe's air, not the gilded mirrors or yellow satin wall hangings, not the gold gaslight sconces on the wall or the deep and heavy chairs, the marble fireplace as wide as Poe's bedroom, the rug with colors as rich and serene as a maharaja's sunset. It was instead, I think, the very spaciousness of the room, the great wide sweep of freedom. Poe's own existence in comparison to the one suggested here must have struck him as inexpressibly small and tight, a realization that squeezed him at the joints and stiffened his movements.

A life in a room like this—it is what I heard him thinking as his gaze roamed from one distant corner to the other—a life in a series of rooms like this, here was a life in which a man could fling wide his arms and stretch out his thoughts in every direction, the imagination unconfined; such was the life he desired. Not having to be grubbing about in the muck for a fip here, a short bit there, knocking door-to-door with hat in hand. Not living a life so pinched and mean, struggling against one's very nature to ingratiate oneself to intellectual and creative inferiors. Here before him stood a room sunny and high and festooned with fine things, in full representation of the existence he most longed to achieve—the space in which to turn himself free.

You wonder, no doubt, how a boy from the Old Brewery could ascertain such longing in the sag of a man's posture and the wistfulness of his gaze. Perhaps I did not at the time. Perhaps the recognition only grew in me over the years, grew in proportion to my own suppressed rages and bitterness, my own failure to shuck the various fetters clamped around my ankles, so that now, looking back, no less fettered but too old to kick against the restraints, I can finally put it into words. But on that morning in 1840 I sensed Poe's desire, I assure you of that. I sensed it because I shared it.

And then he was standing at our back, Johnston Hobbs himself. He clamped a hand on Poe's shoulder. "Good afternoon, sir, good afternoon. You are as punctual as you are astute."

Before Poe could do much more than blink, Hobbs turned to the waiting butler. "Bring Mr. Poe and myself a carafe of the amontillado to enjoy with our coffee, Conroy. And on your way show his valet here to the kitchen for some tea and jam. Do you like gooseberry jam, boy? I have never known a boy who didn't."

"No sir," I said. "Yes sir, I do."

But he scarcely heard my answer, if at all. Still with a hand on Poe's shoulder—Poe seemed even more stunned than I by the boom of Hobbs's voice and his manner of quick familiarity—he ushered Poe into the sitting room and left the butler to turn me toward the kitchen.

If Johnston Hobbs's glow was not as incandescent as his daughter's, there was still about the man a certain radiance of presence, an effulgence that, when considered against his otherwise plain appearance, left no doubt in my mind that the family's luminosity could be attributed at least in part to the mountains of shiners they kept stacked and piled in various banks. He was a man of only average height, probably once as lean as Poe but now going flaccid from jowls to toes. He wore wire spectacles on a nose that was not quite bulbous, and pockmarked like his cheeks with a hundred gaping pores. His pate was all but bald at the summit; a wispy thatch of reddish hair still grew from a point three inches above his forehead, and this he wore parted in the middle and smoothed over his skull like a few threads of downy mohair yarn. But it was the way he stood, the lift of his narrow chin and the emerald-hard glint of his eyes—it was this aristocratic bearing that suppressed any resistance I might have voiced to being shuffled off to the kitchen.

It was a kitchen of princely proportions, which is to say like none other in which I had ever been offered a chair. I sat at the corner of a long narrow table where two plumpish women were preparing what must have been the evening meal: a cold ham being sliced, trays of rolls sliding into the oven, cider drained from a demijohn into a pitcher, wine bottles wiped clean of their cellar dust, a kettle of pungent soup simmering on the stove, the mold scraped and rind peeled from two small wheels of cheese, mutton shivering in a green aspic, two small fowls of some kind smeared with butter and waiting naked for the oven. . . . In short there was more food visible than I could inventory or imagine.

A girl of fifteen or so cleared a corner of the table for me, pointed to a chair, and said, "Have yourself a seat."

She then set before me a tall and thick-walled mug filled with tea. The mug was made of a dull gray metal which I mistook for unpolished silver. I slipped one hand inside the handle and the other around the base and I don't know which intoxicated me more, the tannic steam or the erroneous notion that I was holding in my hands a mug worth more than a half dozen of my lives. I knew in that instant that I must steal the mug if given a chance.

"Don't you want to sweeten that up?" the girl asked as I gulped the tea. She set a silver spoon and a bowl of jam before me, then watched, grinning, as I ladled three heavy spoonfuls into my mug.

"Whyn't you do it the other way round," she said, "and drip a little tea into the jam?"

I grinned and blushed and tried to think of something witty to say.

It was then that a narrow doorway opened in the opposite corner of the room, the door adjacent to a smaller open room used as a pantry. A man leaned out, visible only from the shoulders up, and close to the floor, suggesting that he was standing a few steps lower than the kitchen floor, no doubt on the stairs into the cellar. He was a strangely countenanced man, his face as long and thin as a post, and just as stiff, the skin stretched taut, pallid, mouth pulled into a slit.

He held a dark and dusty bottle out to one of the portly women. "The amontillado," he said. "For Mr. Hobbs." His face remained motionless when he spoke, his lips barely moved. His fingers were long and thin, skeletal, and his long nails yellow.

The woman took the bottle from him without a word and wiped it with a rag. The cadaverous man ducked away and closed the door and I heard his steps retreating down into the basement.

Had I had but the slightest idea what amontillado is I would have leapt to my feet and tackled the woman as she carried the bottle to the sitting room. But I was still staring at the closed basement door, awed by the notion that a man could look so like a corpse and still move about of his own volition.

Moments later the smell of my tea brought me back to life. I spooned out another dollop of jam and stirred it into the mug. "Looks like you're having a party here tonight," I said to the girl.

"Here?" she said. "No, just the usual mess."

"All this food every day?"

"Two and sometimes three times a day," she said.

She plucked a pair of warm biscuits from a pan and set them in front of me. A moment later she dropped a tray of silverware onto the table and pulled up a chair and with polishing cloth in hand sat opposite me.

As she worked on the soup spoons she watched me shove half a biscuit mounded with jam into my mouth. "Don't your Mr. Poe feed you where you live?"

I had no wish to get into the particulars of my relationship with Poe, especially since they were none too clear to me. "He feeds me fine," I answered. "That is, Mrs. Clemm does."

"The mistress?" she said.

"His wife, you mean? No, they ain't married. Seems like it sometimes though, the way they look at each other. The way they carry on whispering and such. But no, his wife's name's Virginia."

I noticed how one of the plumpish women looked to the other one and winked. The girl said, "You mean he carries on with this Mrs. Clemm right there in front of his wife?"

I snorted so loudly that a clump of biscuit popped out of the corner of my mouth. "Mrs. Clemm is his wife's mother."

"So she's old then."

"Not much older than him. Because Virginia ain't much older than you."

The girl went stock-still for a moment, as did the other two women. And I thrilled to my sudden power to silence a room with mere words.

"Truth is I've seen him with his arms around Mrs. Clemm more often than around his wife. His wife's more like his little pet, that one. He sleeps in a chair pulled up to her bed."

"Gawd," said the girl. "And where does Mrs. Clemm sleep?"

I did not want to say that she slept on the floor, because it would suggest that I too made my bed in such a humble place. But all three women were looking at me directly now, all three had eyes wide, mouths slightly open, ears waiting for my next utterance, and I felt huge with an authority I had never before known.

"She's got her own bed," I told them. "Not that Poe sleeps much in that chair of his. He spends most every night in the same room as Mrs. Clemm."

"And his little wife don't mind all this going on?"

"She's sweet about every old thing, she don't mind nothing. Plus she's sick, that's the other thing," I continued. "Virginia, I mean. The white plague. He won't talk about it but I'm more'n more certain that's what it is. I've seen it before, of course. I've seen most everything there is to see."

They stared at me awhile longer, then the older women shook their heads and went back to their work. The girl gave me a sly grin and raised her eyebrows twice, then she blushed and turned away and concentrated on the cutlery.

As for me, I cupped both hands around my mug and drank down the tea. Afterward I sat there staring into the empty mug and wondering how to get it into my shirt unseen, and a bitterness came into my mouth as I thought about the things I had said. If imprecise in my understanding of what wrongs I might have perpetrated with loose talk, I felt shamed nonetheless and knew that I had somehow denigrated Poe and Mrs. Clemm and Virginia in the eyes of these strangers. My remorse grew stronger with every second I remained at that table, and I began to despise the three servants whose look and attentiveness had caused my tongue to flap, and when I hated them enough to want myself punished for my words I slid the mug off the table and between my legs and then I slipped it down into my waistband and fluffed my shirt over it.

But it had all gone unnoticed and I was not to be caught. I was not to be cleansed. And so I sat there and scowled at myself, but I could not scowl away the taste of metal in my mouth, the loathing I felt from having opened my mouth at all, having made public to strangers the privacies and family intimacies shared with me in Poe's cottage, the secrets that he, by taking me in, by treating me so kindly, had implicitly entrusted into my care.

To this day, the faintest whiff of gooseberry still makes me want to retch.

25

I CHOSE to wait for Poe out in the street. An hour passed before the great heavy doors heaved open behind me. Poe and Hobbs stood framed in the wide square of charcoal light, saying their good-byes. How slight and dazed Poe seemed as he offered Hobbs his hand. How confidently Hobbs gripped it, his other hand to Poe's shoulder.

Poe turned away then and came down the steps and onto the sidewalk, squinting at me, smiling curiously, regarding me, I thought, as something he could not quite identify.

"It's me," I told him. "Augie Dubbins."

He chuckled. "Do you think I've lost my senses?"

"You look a little confused is all."

"I am a bit nonplussed, to say the least."

"Is that good or bad?"

He turned northward and set to walking at a halting pace, as if his very thoughts were interfering with the power of locomotion.

I asked, "So are you taking the spondulicks or not? What the lady offered you yesterday. Are you taking it?"

"A ham," he said. "What we need is a juicy fat ham for this evening's supper. Did I or did I not detect the fragrance of a ham in that house?"

"There was one in the kitchen."

"We will visit the butcher on our way home," he said. "A special treat for Mrs. Clemm." With a nod to himself his stride then lengthened, became the long purposeful gait I had grown used to.

"I guess you took the job," I said as I hurried along at his side.

"I shall recount the afternoon's events for one and all when we return home."

"Looks to me like you took it. So I guess you're satisfied it weren't the lieutenant done in that witness of yours?"

"Of that I feel certain."

"Thing is, who else would want him quiet?"

But Poe was in no mood to discuss dead men. Even his fingers were unusually alive, tapping out a patter on his thighs.

And so we walked awhile. Minutes later he suddenly asked, "And of your own visit? How was your tea and jam?"

My stomach fluttered. I swallowed a belch. "Nothing special."

"I thought as much. Else you would not have retired to the street."

"The way they live though. That house. Can you imagine having to live like that?"

"I can indeed," said Poe.

WE HUDDLED around him like starving cats awaiting a scrap of meat. Mrs. Clemm was so nervous that she could not bear to sit but stood braced against the wall, one hand patting her bosom as if working a bellows. Virginia sat with head bowed and hands clasped; for all I knew she was muttering a prayer to St. Jude.

As for me, I believed I already knew what the news would be. I had after all helped to lug home a great pink ham, a box of pralines, a peppermint cake, and especially for Virginia a small bucket of the local lager. We had made too another stop along the way especially for Virginia, an impromptu side trip necessitated by Poe's whim. At a small emporium below Gramercy Place I had stood outside the door, minding the packages, while Poe conferred with the shop owner over the individual merits of various models of pianos. There was only one piano in the store, and this used for lessons, and so Poe leafed through an oversized book whose pages were filled with sketches and descriptions.

He lingered longest over one illustration in particular, but upon receipt of a bit of information from the shop owner Poe's eyebrows arched high and he gave the merchant an incredulous look. Finally the merchant directed him to a page near the very back of the book, and at this illustration Poe eventually nodded in the affirmative, and it was then Poe withdrew his purse and from it a coin, and then the two men shook hands and Poe soon rejoined me on the street.

"You must swear to breathe not a word of this transaction to a soul," Poe told me.

"How could I when I don't even know what went on?"

'Sissie shall finally have her piano," he said.

"No!"

He grinned at me. "A modest little upright, but how sweetly it will sing beneath her hands."

"You bought her a piano?"

"I have made a small payment in good faith. The remainder will come due when the piano arrives from Albany and is delivered to our door a few days hence."

"She's going to go wild," I said.

"As is a young lady's right."

At home the women gawked at the table piled high and made such a fuss over Poe's largesse that I felt jealous and unnecessary and wanted some of the attention for myself. I stepped back from them momentarily and removed the stolen mug from beneath my shirt and gave its insides a quick wipe.

"I bought something too," I announced. They turned to look at me and I held aloft the purloined mug. "It's for drinking tea and such," I said. "And it ain't going to get chipped or dented neither, feel it, it's as heavy as a log."

Mrs. Clemm was the one to rescue it from my hand. "Augie, it's lovely. A lovely pewter mug. And so finely made."

"Pewter?" I said. "You mean it ain't silver?"

"Is that what you were told? That it is made of silver?"

"No, no, I wasn't told nothing, I just thought—"

"Dear child, it's lovely, but it isn't silver. If you were tricked into paying a high price for it, then either Mr. Poe or I will have to speak with the merchant who misled you."

My face burned. "It hardly cost a thing at all."

"You're sure?"

"I just seen it and thought you'd like to have it is all. You can use it for any number of things."

She leaned forward and put a hand to the back of my head and pulled me forward and laid a kiss upon my cheek. I felt my ears glowing red hot, the very follicles of my hair atingle.

"You are a lovely sweet boy," she told me, "and I will cherish your gift forever."

I no doubt would have soon incinerated myself with embarrassment had Poe not rescued me. "This transaction," he said. "How could I have failed to notice it?"

"It was when you was with the p—." I stopped myself in the nick of time, having nearly uttered *piano broker*. "The butcher."

"Of course," he said, "of course," and let the matter drop.

Minutes later he gathered us around him in the center of the cottage's sitting room, his fingertips pressed together as around a small but invisible globe, the tips of his index fingers to his lips, which appeared for a change to be smiling with not the least hint of melancholy.

"We began our vis-à-vis," he said, "with a carafe of the finest coffee I have ever enjoyed. Though I had barely begun to savor its aroma when Mr. Hobbs poured for each of us an accompaniment of the finest amontillado."

At this Mrs. Clemm's head snapped up, and an instant later her eyes snapped my way, as pointed and fierce as daggers.

"The latter of which," Poe continued, "I politely declined."

Had Virginia and Mrs. Clemm actually voiced their sighs upon hearing this remark, they would surely have sounded with the sweetest of harmonies.

"A touch to my lips was all I permitted myself," he said. "So as not to offend my host I explained my peculiar sensitivity to even the noblest of drink, as this surely was. He responded with such a profusion of apologies that I was quite embarrassed by it all and begged him to stop.

"He soon directed my attention to a number of savories placed like flowers on a silver tray. These, I deduced, were being offered to me as a gauge of my avidity. He watched to see if I would shovel them in like a commoner—as was, I assure you, my first inclination, so seductive were they in sight and scent.

"But I sampled not a one," he said. "Not the foie gras. Not the salmon. Not even the caviar."

"Oh Eddie," said Mrs. Clemm. "Not even the caviar?"

"I set one of the savories on its tiny lace doily on the point of my knee. As if I intended to have it. But not once did I then look at it or raise it to my lips."

"Did you not want it after you took it?" Virginia asked.

"More than anything I wanted it. As with the amontillado. But it was a game, you see. Mr. Hobbs brought forth all these *accoutrements* of his affluence, then waited to see how eagerly I would snatch at them. By this he would know how best to inveigle me. I, of course, refused to provide him with a single point of leverage."

"You should of seen the house," I blurted out. "Tell them about the house."

"Was it magnificent?" Virginia asked. "As lavish as I imagine?"

"Whatever you can imagine, beloved, you will have to double it. But the house . . . the house was inconsequential to me. In any case it became so from that moment when his offer to me was tendered."

Mrs. Clemm drew in a breath and pressed her palms together.

At last Poe told the story of his afternoon in the Hobbs mansion.

"Mr. Poe," Hobbs had said in his resonant baritone, "my daughter is among the many who hold you in the highest regard. Her admiration of you, or so it appears to me, is very nearly religious in its nature. She feels—and I must tell you, sir, that I am not yet of the same opinion, considering the way you have bowdlerized the facts to this point—but she is adamant that you alone possess the integrity and mental prowess to make right the wrong done to her fiancé. Done, I might add, by your own hand."

To which Poe replied, "If I have perpetrated an injustice, I will see it righted, Mr. Hobbs. But I am not convinced that my conclusions are unjust."

"Which is why I am prepared to offer you the opportunity to further pursue those conclusions. My daughter has relayed to you my offer?"

"She has."

"Do you accept?"

"I am not disinclined to consider the offer, sir. Or any offer that will propel us closer to a final truth. Yet I have my concerns."

"Then you should trot them out, Edgar. May I call you Edgar?"

"Of course."

"We are colleagues, after all. United in a single goal. Better to dispense with the formalities, don't you think?"

"I do."

"Then you will call me John, as my friends do. Though I suspect they call me other names as well, but only when I am out of earshot. But to your concerns, sir. Let us keep nothing concealed. As you come to know me better you will discern that there is little I esteem more in life than a forthright man."

"What I wonder, then, is what your reaction might be should a continuation of my investigation serve to confirm and solidify what I already suspect?"

"I will not flinch from the irrefutable, you may rest assured of that. Should you prove my daughter's fiancé a scoundrel, I will be no less grateful than if you exonerate him."

"You addend no restrictions, then, to the terms of employment?"

"Damn it, man, I want the truth. Can I be any plainer than that?"

"But you are not satisfied with the truth as it now stands."

"I myself was in the company of Lieutenant Andrews on the Sunday morning in question. He was here, in fact, in this very room. From nine in the morning until shortly after noon. Tell me, if you will, how he might simultaneously have been in the company of the unfortunate Miss Rogers."

Hearing this, a leaden sensation gripped Poe's stomach. He sat silent, suddenly nauseated. He had believed the testimony of a disreputable man, had even made the testimony public, and now that man was dead, a blade drawn across his throat.

Hobbs continued. "For those three hours Lieutenant Andrews and I discussed, in a very friendly manner, for I am quite fond of the young man, the path of his future endeavors once he and my beloved daughter are married. We discussed his naval career; where he and Felicia will live; what business interests he might pursue; even where and how my future grandchildren will be educated."

Hobbs stood then and went to the fireplace. He lifted his eyes to the wall above the mantel. "Take a look at this coat of arms, Edgar. Consider its principal elements. A demi-unicorn of sable on a field of silver, reared so as to crush beneath its sinister foot a serpent poised to strike. And around the head of the unicorn a subtle nimbus, do you see it here? A symbol of sanctification, Mr. Poe. Of purity and righteousness that will not—no, cannot—hold still against injustice. Hence the dueling swords, crossed to indicate a desire for peace, but unsheathed as a promise of our readiness to fight.

"I do not claim to be divinely instilled, as my ancestors did, but I can tell you this, sir. I am guided by the same principles as were those who devised my family's shield. And it is these same qualities that I long ago detected in Lieutenant Andrews and that distinguish him in my eyes as such a singular individual. A man I will be proud to bring into my family as the husband of my only child. A man whose fine character and fine history will keep the Hobbs lineage alive, though it be by another name."

Ten seconds of silence passed. Poe sat mute, paralyzed by the realization that not only had he accused an innocent man of a heinous act, but that having done so publicly the accuser himself must soon be denounced as a public fool.

Hobbs, no doubt, had apparently anticipated this realization, for he stood ready with the remedy. "You would not be the first man in this town to credit the spurious, Edgar. But I for one will guarantee that you suffer no consequences for what, in my estimation, was an honest mistake. You might be surprised to know, sir, that I hold sway over a good many opinions in this town."

"I'm sure I would not be surprised at all, John."

Hobbs laughed at this and crossed to a divan and sat down, flinging both arms across its back. It was such a gesture of openness, the way he exposed, if you will, his very heart to Poe. It went a long way toward abolishing the guilt that until that simple gesture was threatening to engulf Poe.

"You will discover the thugs and lowlifes responsible for the poor girl's death, Edgar, I know you will. In so doing you will exonerate Lieutenant Andrews and you will vindicate yourself. You will be fairly compensated for your endeavors. As for afterward, let me say only this: my friends remain friends forever. As I rise, they rise with me."

Again Poe kept silent. He allowed the magnitude of this statement to sink in, allowed himself the indulgence of imagining that vast room his own.

Hobbs then presented him with a list of six names gracefully penned on a sheet of parchment, all individuals with whom Poe might speak in regard to the lieutenant's habits and nature, any confidences he might have shared with them concerning his friendship with Miss Rogers.

"All this information you will then publish in the newspapers and thus put an end to the besmirchment of my future son-in-law's good name. We will begin with my own statement. You will find paper, pen, and ink in the drawer at your right hand."

Before Poe finally exited Hobbs's mansion, the paladin had one last bit of dictation. "Write this name down as well. Josiah Tarr. I am told he is a waterman who operates a skiff off the New Jersey shore. In the vicinity of Weehawken, if I am not mistaken. I have been led to believe that this man, if you can find him, might provide significant information concerning the activities of local ruffians."

Here Poe's story ended. Mrs. Clemm, Virginia, and I sat waiting for something more but he did not provide it; he sat blinking, dazed, still incredulous of this turn of events.

"Weehawken," I said to myself. It lay across the Hudson and therefore was to my mind a foreign place, a whole other country. How many thousands of gazes I had flung in the direction of its shores! "I always wanted to see what's there," I said.

"And so you shall," Poe told me. "Bright and early on the morrow we begin."

"And for now?" Virginia asked, her eyes bright with the disbelief of hopefulness.

"For now, m'lady," Poe said, as he crossed to her and held out a hand, "if you will do me the honor of a dance, it will be my delight to serenade you."

Virginia giggled and put a hand to her mouth. "Oh, sir," she said, and gave full license to a Southern drawl, "I am not at all certain that I recognize you. And my mother has countenanced me that I must never dance with strange and beautiful men."

"Allow me to introduce myself," he said. With a look over his shoulder he flashed me a wink. "I am the Chevalier C. Auguste Dupin, late of Paris, France, and a man of whom, no doubt, you have heard wondrous things."

"Oh my, yes, many things indeed. But none of them wondrous."

"Then you must permit me the remainder of my life to augment my reputation."

She took his hand then and rose and moved into his arms and they glided about the small room in a minuet measured to her weakness. Poe sang to her alone, his voice a whisper in her ear, and she when she could find the breath sang along with him. Mrs. Clemm patted her hands together and wept without noise and for a while that small cottage seemed aglow with pure joy, a strange and giddifying air.

Poe's exuberance was so total and Virginia's devotion to him so real that their happiness flushed all the regret right out of me and made me feel as if I had done my friend no damage, had betrayed no confidences, had uttered not a single ill-considered word back in that Fifth Avenue kitchen.

Such was our half day of illusion, our delirious slide before the bottom fell out.

26

WE AWOKE still drunk with optimism. Then, after a breakfast we scarcely needed, still sated from the night before, Poe stuffed his pockets with paper and pencil and off we set to speak with the individuals whose names Mr. Hobbs had provided.

"I will listen to their words," Poe told me as we strolled toward town, "and record them verbatim. But you, Augie, must listen to everything else and record it in your memory."

"What everything else?" I asked.

"The look in their eyes when they are speaking. If the gaze is steady or evasive. The turn of the mouth. The hands, especially the hands—do they tap and twist against one another, do they wave about as if chasing away a lie. The body will either betray or confirm the words, Augie, and I am relying on you to see and hear and remember it all."

Of the interviews that followed, two observations suffice: first, that the subjects confirmed, to a man, Johnston Hobbs's opinion of the young lieutenant's character, and second, that a snipe only recently salvaged from the gutter was hardly the judge to sit in appraisal of the physical chicanery of the island's most powerful men.

All, when first informed that a man named Poe awaited an audience in the lobby or anteroom, rushed from their boardrooms and offices as if he were a long-lost brother. All appeared not only unsurprised by his visit but even impatient for it. All greeted him with a hearty handshake, asked for no references or credentials, made no inquiry as to why he had come, and began the brief conversation, one-sided as it might have been, with something like, "You wish to know my estimation of Lieutenant Andrews, am I correct? Very well, sir. This is what I can tell you."

Then followed a litany of the lieutenant's virtues, of which the most repeated were honesty, integrity, devotion to God, family, and country. Running a close second to these were steadfastness and reliability. They all but enshrined him as a saint. When Poe attempted to inquire of specifics, namely of the young man's relationship with Mary Rogers, each response echoed the one previous.

"I can only say this, sir. Mr. Andrews is a born teacher and counselor. Add to this his great well of compassion for his fellow human beings and you will see quite clearly the nature of his relationship with the unfortunate young woman. They were brother and sister, nothing more. You must trust me on this, for I know whereof I speak."

"You and the lieutenant discussed this relationship?"

"Nothing so unseemly as that, no. I inferred as much from my knowledge of his character."

"You know him well, then. You enjoy his company regularly."

"How many times do you need to experience rain to know that it is wet? Virtue is pellucid, Mr. Poe, and therefore easy to identify. Only evil is complex. And there is nothing complex about Lieutenant Andrews, I assure you."

"So you have met him only once."

"Once or twice, perhaps as many as three times. Always at the home of Johnston Hobbs, which alone tells you all you need to know about the man. Hobbs has been introducing him around, bringing him into the circle, so to speak. Hobbs has great plans for the boy. He will sire strong and handsome children. And now, sir, I apologize for having to return to my labors. . . ."

"One final question, if I might. And this concerns the lieutenant's whereabouts on that unfortunate Sunday morning when—"

"Whatever Hobbs told you, you can take it as gospel. I hardly remember where I was yesterday; how could I remember another man's whereabouts two weeks past?"

Afterward, when Poe had scribbled his notes and we were ambling in the direction of the next individual on the list, Poe would ask me, "And how did you find him?"

My usual response was, "He seemed all right to me."

"Nothing anomalous jumped out at you?"

In truth I stood in each of those rooms blinded by the authority and confidence of the men who strode forward to grasp Poe's hand. Each and every one of them was a captain of commerce, a paladin who commanded the flow of money in and out of banks and across nations' borders; men who plotted the shipping lines and steered the exchange of goods and who in so doing determined the balance of the world's economy; men who whispered in the ear of the governor and the president; men who over a cigar or glass of brandy were molding the world between their very hands. And here they stood before me (ignoring me, it's true, but before me all the same), men whose brushed and tailored suits made Poe look downright shabby and whose presence in turn reduced me again to an alley mongrel.

I was cowed by them, made blind and deaf. I observed only what they wanted me to observe.

After the final of the six interviews, Poe finally put the question to me.

"Throughout the entire morning," he asked, "you detected no falsities? The men did not fidget or cast about for convincing words? No, of course they did not. Considering who those men are, it is no doubt an unsound assumption on my part that they might have behaved in such a manner. Let us then study the situation from another angle. Did they not strike you as a bit too confident in their responses?"

"How so?" I asked.

"A bit too ready with praise for a man they each admitted to knowing hardly at all? A bit too, shall we say, redundant in the effusion they bestowed on him?"

I cocked an eyebrow.

"What information have we been given?" he asked. "Opinion, nothing more. An opinion of Lieutenant Andrews that has been fed through a conduit emanating direct from Johnston Hobbs."

"You lost me."

"One more name on the list," he said. "And not, I am relieved to say, a character reference for our fine young lieutenant. The waterman across the Hudson."

He folded his notes and shoved them into his coat pocket. He pushed a strand of lank hair off his forehead and turned northwest and sent a long, squinting gaze up the river and across to New Jersey. Then, with what struck me as an angry stride, he flung himself forward and set a brisk pace along Wall Street toward Broadway.

Thinking to save himself the fare and the probable soaking of a river crossing, Poe led us north to Forty-second Street, thence to the waterfront directly opposite the shoreline of Weehawken. Here he hoped that the waterman Josiah Tarr would sooner or later appear to discharge or pick up passengers. The problem with this was that watermen in their small boats did not keep to regular schedules or routes, but rowed whenever and wherever the fare dictated.

We passed a full two hours waiting for Josiah Tarr to manifest himself. In that time four oarsmen and their eight passengers, in other words two of the long, low-bulwarked rowboats, ground ashore onto Manhattan gravel, but none of the people questioned by Poe recognized the name of the man he had been assigned by Hobbs to interview.

In the end Poe's mounting curiosity bested his thrift. We climbed aboard a low craft recently emptied and thusly engaged the pair of burly watermen to convey us to New Jersey. The river was not rough that day but the Hudson is seldom a mirror, and so we bucked and lurched and were doused with splash and spray.

In the interim Poe ascertained that these two watermen—by name the Burach brothers, men whose only dissimilarity, as far as I could discern, was in their volubility—had been crossing the Hudson five or six times a day for more than three years, and neither had ever heard the name Josiah Tarr.

The man in the stern rowed facing New Jersey, correcting with a turn or twist of his oar when the bow veered off its straight line. The man forward rowed with his back to New Jersey and, facing Poe, acted as our tour guide and information officer.

"There's a Josiah Lehnort you can find at the roadhouse there off the highway," he said, and jerked his head toward an opening in the trees some twenty yards back from the shore. Through the trees I could see a glimmer of dull white clapboard with a slate roof painted red.

"It's his mother runs the place," the oarsman said. "Then there's two more Josiahs I know of back into the town there. Josiah Schiffhauer, he's eighty if he's a day, couldn't row you across a washtub so I doubt as he's your man. The other's a schoolteacher, spindly and cross-eyed. I can't recall his Christian name except to know it ain't Tarr. Them's the only Josiahs you're going to find 'round here, mister."

I swear I could see the hackles rising on Poe's neck. He turned to look at the rear oarsman for confirmation, and the man nodded grimly.

If it can be said that darkness shines, Poe's eyes became luminous with an ebony glow, a luster I recognized by then as comprised of equal parts anger and the intractable resolve to undo whatever rogue had angered him.

"Right up there in them woods is where Burr shot Hamilton," the forward oarsman said. "Died from it, Hamilton did, as of course you know.

A duel was the only thing could put an end to twenty years of squabbling between them two. Burr was the better lawyer, Hamilton the better politician. All of which had them at each other's throats time and time again. Till the General fixed it so's Burr couldn't be governor, and that was the last straw. Hamilton's boy died the same way, did you know that? Now what was that boy's name? Philip, that's what it was. The general's eldest. Him that got himself shot dead the very same way just three years earlier. Both father and son, now ain't that peculiar."

Poe was less thrilled by this recapitulation of violence than was I. He sat seething, hands clenched atop his lap, shoulders hunched forward. When we finally ground ashore he thanked our ferrymen and without a word to me hopped out and strode up the footpath. He did not wait for me to catch up until he stood atop the low bank. There he surveyed the shoreline from north to south, slowly turning until he once again faced Manhattan.

"Someone is attempting to mislead us," he said.

"Which someone would that be?"

"Which someone," he said, "is precisely what I mean to soon discover."

27

WE FOLLOWED the carriage path south along the New Jersey shore for a quarter mile or so, and there, some thirty yards in front of the clapboard roadhouse set back in the trees, we came upon, dragged to the edge of the grassy riverbank, an overturned skiff much like the one in which we had recently crossed but smaller and noticeably less seaworthy, its hull stained here and there with rot and, upon closer inspection, over the rot a fine gray fungus.

Beside the skiff was an empty chair, a scarred straight-back of sturdy if indelicate construction. At the foot of the chair, a small area of trampled ground.

"Could this be the station of our Mr. Tarr?" Poe wondered.

"If it is he ain't been doing much rowing. Not in that tub anyway."

"Have a look underneath for the oars."

There was nothing beneath the skiff but for shaded ground and a cricket.

Poe turned toward the roadhouse. Above its front door a shingle hung bearing the establishment's name: the Red Onion. "If we are to find the owner of this skiff," Poe said, "we will likely find him there."

Unlike the saloons and doggeries I had had occasion to enter on the island, where usually a pianist or harpist plinked background music to the rumble of gambling and thieving and general skulduggery, this one bore a quiet and even respectable air.

At a table near the fieldstone hearth sat a family of six enjoying a midday repast of lamb and potatoes. At two other tables sat men alone, peaceably nursing their grog. At the final occupied table, the one nearest the back wall, were a well-dressed burgher with a girl who might or might not have been his daughter. (Considering the proximity at which they sat to one another, and the way he averted his face from view upon our entrance, and the place on his person where she tended to rest at least one hand at most times, I would hazard a speculation that they bore no blood relation to one another.)

Behind the counter stood a large man of middle age, a sallow round-faced man who looked us over as we entered but did not welcome us with a smile. Poe greeted this man with a nod but did not yet approach him. Instead he went straight to the lunching family and, after apologizing for the intrusion, asked, in a voice low enough not to be overheard, if the gentleman was acquainted with a local waterman by the name of Josiah Tarr.

Not only was the gentleman unfamiliar with the name but he directed Poe, if he wished to engage the services of a waterman, to the Burach brothers a quarter mile up the carriage path.

Poe thanked this gentleman and moved to the next table, where he conducted the same inquiry. At each of the four tables, the answer was the same.

Finally he advanced on the counterman, who all this time had stood with both hands braced on the counter's rounded edge. Poe's mouth by now held a firm line that could only be called a sneer.

"I am endeavoring to locate the waterman Mr. Josiah Tarr," Poe said. "I was told he might be found in this locale."

"Told by who?" the counterman asked.

"By a gentleman in the city. One whose fine name is beyond reproach."

He stared at Poe for a full ten seconds. Then, before he spoke, he looked away. "That's his boat out front there on the bank."

"And yet no sign of Mr. Tarr."

The counterman shrugged. "Maybe he's in the privy out back."

"You would not mind were we to wait here for him, would you?"

"He don't come in except to get his pint at the end of the day. You'd do better to wait for him down by his boat."

"Thank you, sir," Poe said. "We shall do just that."

We were barely out the door before Poe whispered that I should race around back to ascertain if the privy was occupied or not. I did so, then caught up with Poe again as he was crossing the carriage path.

"Not," I told him.

He nodded and continued toward the rotting skiff. There he turned and looked back on the Red Onion.

"Your impressions?" he asked.

This time I was ready for the tutorial. "Why is it that nobody else but the counterman ever heard of this Tarr?"

"Why indeed."

"And like I said before, this boat ain't seen water since at least last summer. A man sits on one of those boards he's like to go right through."

"Did you notice as well that the counterman knew without benefit of a glance out the window that the boat lies here on the bank?"

"And he didn't much want us hanging around inside there neither, did he?"

"Nor was he the least curious to pursue my deliberately elliptical reference to Mr. Hobbs. Why would that be so, Augie?"

"Because he knew already who you was referring to."

Poe smiled. He jerked his chin toward the Red Onion. "And now approaches the elusive Mr. Tarr."

Hurrying around the side of the roadhouse came a man stuffing his shirt into his trousers. He too was a large man but one whose physiognomy in no way resembled that of the Burach brothers, those broad-shouldered and barrel-chested men whose profession was inscribed in the musculature of their torsos. All of this man's muscles had settled in a pouch about his middle.

"He looks like he's been in the water about as often as his boat," I whispered.

Poe put a hand on my shoulder to quiet me.

The man came waddling toward us, swiping a hand across his mouth. "Somebody been asking after me?" he said.

"Mr. Josiah Tarr?"

"At your service, sir. Sorry about the delay. I was answering the call of nature in the Lehnorts' privy back there."

"We apologize for the interruption."

"No interruption, none whatever. No, sirs—now what can I do for the two of you?"

"We would like to engage your services to return us to the island," Poe said.

Both the waterman and I turned wide eyes on Poe. I, for one, had no intention of climbing into Tarr's skiff. Nor, it appeared, did Tarr.

"You mean . . ."

"I am needed in Manhattan and would like to return there at once. You are a waterman, are you not?"

"Well I am, yes, to be sure; it's my job as you can see for yourself. And in the normal course of things I would be right happy to oblige . . ."

"Things are not now normal?" Poe asked.

"Well they ain't, that's my point exactly." He laid a hand over his kidney and screwed up his face. "I've had this terrible pain here for going on a week now. Don't even want to think about putting my hands to an oar."

"Were there any, in fact, to lay hands to."

"Sir?"

It was all I could do to keep from giggling out loud.

"Besides," the waterman went on, "it was the Burach boys brought you over, wasn't it? I mean, they're the ones working this stretch now that I'm laid up for a while."

"Ah," Poe said. "Well then. Back to the Burach boys we go, Augie. And to you, good sir, my apologies. We should not have disturbed your convalescence." Poe gave the man a nod and turned away and started for the road.

"Surely, surely," Tarr said. He followed Poe for a step or two. "Excepting which . . ."

Poe turned. "Sir?"

"It was my understanding," Tarr said.

"Yes?"

"My understanding was that you was come for some information."

"How, sir, was that understanding reached?"

"What's that?"

"Did you, Augie, express a desire for information?"

"Wasn't me," I said.

"Nor I," said Poe.

The waterman scrubbed the palm of a hand back and forth across his cheek. "Well they told me you was asking, you know. Back there at the Onion."

"Were you not in the privy *outside* the Red Onion?"

"Well yes, surely, excepting that Merlin in there, he come out and let me know."

"And how fortunate for us that he did," Poe said. "Else I might well have walked away without the very information I seek."

The sarcasm escaped Tarr completely. He relaxed now, relieved to assume his role as amicus curiae. "You wanted to know about them ruffians," he said.

Poe continued to smile.

"There was a pack of them out in the woods there most of that week," Tarr said. "The week that girl got done in. There was eight, ten, it's hard to say how many there was in all. Had a big campfire going most every night, whooping and hollering, doing who knows what all. Then early Sunday morning we seen them heading across to the island in a couple of boats."

"We did?" Poe said.

"I did, is what I mean. Wasn't nobody else up that early from the looks of it. Wasn't much after first light, lots of fog still laying on the river."

"And what, if I might ask, would require you to rise so early, especially now that you are convalescing from an ailment?"

"Well I, you know, I'm used to it, being up and around at first light. And this pain I got in my side now, it don't let me get much sleep. So I was just out walking, you know, trying to walk off some of this stiffness."

Poe said nothing. He waited.

"Besides which, there's the river and all. It's been my life for so long now, I never stray too far from it. Lots of days I come up from my place and just sit here in my chair like I'm still good for something, you know?"

"And where is it you live, sir?"

"What's that?"

"Your place of residence. Your home."

"Well, you know, it's back there into Weehawken some. Back off the road apiece. It's fairly hard to find unless you know where you're going."

Poe nodded and stroked his chin and held his gaze on the waterman.

"And then that same night it was, Sunday night, when I heard them again out there in the woods. Them ruffians, I'm talking about."

"They had returned."

"Yes, sir, they had. And it was later that same night I heard somebody screaming. A young girl's screams, you know. There's no mistaking a sound like that."

"And you were able to hear this unmistakable sound because you were out walking again, is that it? Or were you sitting here in your chair in the dark?"

Tarr blinked a couple of times before answering. "I had come up here for my supper at the Onion. It was on my way back home that I heard the screaming and ruckus out in the trees."

"You are quite certain they were the cries of a female."

"Clear as a bell they were."

"You summoned the police, of course."

"The constable's back there in Weehawken, you see. And me here without a horse. And the screaming, you know, well it didn't last long at all. A minute at the most, if even half that. So at the time, you know . . . I mean looking back on it now, now that I know better what was going on and all . . ."

"Of course," Poe said. "And the gang of ruffians? They no doubt vacated the premises the very next day."

"They did just that, yes, sir. Up this road the whole gang of them went, kit and caboodle."

"Carrying their boats on their shoulders."

"Sir?"

"Had they not employed boats to cross to the island on the previous morning? And, I assume, to return here?"

"Well yes, of course they did. And some of them, that's my guess, some of them must of skipped out with the boats in the middle of the night. That's the only thing I can figure. 'Cause there weren't more than half of them headed out of here up that road, and them without boats of any kind."

Tarr stood there blinking awhile longer, licking viciously at his lips. His broad forehead was speckled with a greasy perspiration.

Finally Poe unlocked his gaze. His eyes turned toward the roadhouse now. "You have made my journey worthwhile, sir. I am most grateful for your candor."

"Nothing of it," Tarr said. The muscles in his forehead relaxed. He smiled. "Glad to have been of some service to you."

Poe held out his hand to him. "Perhaps we will meet again, Mr. Lehnort."

"To be sure," he said, and eagerly seized Poe's hand. Then his grin broadened, and he pulled Poe toward him and whispered, "Excepting that my name is Tarr, you remember?"

"My apologies, sir. I have never had a good head for names."

"Nothing of it," the man answered, and massaged his huge belly. He leaned even closer. "We're on the same side after all, now, ain't we?"

A muscle twitched in Poe's jaw, and for an instant his dark eyes flared. Just as quickly he subdued his surprise and grinned slyly. "We draw our water from the same well," he whispered.

"That we do, that we do. You got everything you need then?"

"More than enough, I would say."

They smiled at one another. I had no idea what was going on between them and was getting ready to ask when Poe scratched his chin. "One last item," he said, his voice again as low as a whisper. "The lieutenant's pocket watch. He fears he might have left it here."

"Left it here?"

"He hasn't seen it since that Sunday. Might he have left it behind somewhere?"

"I ain't seen it if he did."

"Could he have left it inside?" With this last word Poe inclined his head toward the roadhouse.

"Would've turned up if he did. More likely one of them had it with them when they left."

"The girl perhaps."

Tarr did not reply for a moment, and his eyes showed fear, as if he suddenly realized that he had said too much. Finally he answered, looking away, "If it wasn't him, had to of been her."

Now Poe paused as well, sensing probably that he had pushed the game as far as it would go. "My friend will be pleased to know," he said, "that nothing here can incriminate him."

Tarr scratched at the back of his head and opened his mouth as if he might speak, then stopped himself before uttering a sound. He cocked his head, thinking, and his gaze fell on me. I saw only confusion in his eyes. Uncertainty.

Whatever he was thinking, he must have warned himself to say no more, for without another word he turned away from us and, walking in a kind of zigzag pattern, scratching his head all the way, waddled back toward the roadhouse.

28

I CANNOT say with any authority what Poe should have done at this stage of his investigation. I only know that it should not have been what next he did. Attribute the error to his Imp of the Perverse, or to his obsessive obsequiousness to candor, or to his hope of flushing out the truth, or, perhaps, to his zealous desire to elevate himself by bringing down those more elevated. Whatever his motivation, his tree shaking bore a wormy fruit.

In short, and to employ a different metaphor, he believed himself in possession of a winning hand, and he showed his hand too soon.

We returned to the Hobbs mansion shortly before the dinner hour, where Poe announced to Conroy that, his interviews completed, he would now like to relate the results to the master of the house. We were whisked into Hobbs's library, soon to be joined there by the big bug himself. Hobbs and Poe sat facing one another while I, as usual, was left to stand against the wall and be ignored.

"Lieutenant Andrews will be down shortly for dinner," Hobbs said before even seating himself. "Shall I send for him to join us?"

"I think you should not," Poe said.

Hobbs brushed at the knees of his trousers. "You must tender him an apology sooner or later, sir."

"The six men whose names you gave me—" Poe began, only to be cut short.

"Corroborated, did they not, my own high opinion of the lieutenant?"

"They did," Poe said.

And now Hobbs launched into an animated recapitulation of the myriad and sundry virtues of Lieutenant Andrews, punctuated with a lot of finger shaking in Poe's direction, plus several references to the obtuseness of any individual too blind to see the evidence before his very eyes, the fatal flaw of hubris, the sin of obstinacy. It struck me as a bit over the top; his words echoed with a counterfeit tone in that vast room. Throughout it all Poe sat with hands folded atop one another on his lap, giving him the appearance of a humble parishioner suffering his weekly chastisement. This time he took no notes. He remained altogether motionless but for the iambic clench of his jaw and the subtle tension of his musculature.

Even after the litany, Poe remained silent. Finally Hobbs placed both hands on his knees and, leaning forward, made ready to stand. "And that, sir, should be sufficient for any reasonable mind."

"Indeed," Poe said, "indeed." But now he raised a hand to stroke his chin. "Though perhaps I am not reasonable enough to ignore the one small fly that has landed in this soup."

"If you have reservations on some particular, make them clear to me."

"On the particular of Josiah Tarr."

"The name is familiar, but . . ."

"The waterman. You sent me to Weehawken to speak with him."

"Of course, the waterman. With information concerning the ruffians thereabout."

"The very same." Poe paused. His smile was crooked—and as calculated as Hobbs's diatribe had been just a minute earlier.

"Yes? And did he have any useful information?"

"He surely did. But what I wonder, sir, is this: how did you, here on Fifth Avenue, come to learn that a waterman in Weehawken—a faux waterman, as it turns out—was in possession of such information?"

"Faux?" said Hobbs. "What do you mean by that?"

"I mean that the man revealed himself to be a fraud."

Hobbs leaned back in his chair, eyes wide.

"As you yourself knew him to be," said Poe.

At first this roused no reaction in Hobbs other than a furrowing of his brow. I could almost hear him thinking to himself, *I should look angry now,* and a moment later he assumed a mask of outrage, a squint of his eyes, a scowl, a seeming rage in escalation.

"Mr. Hobbs," Poe said, and now leaned forward himself, and spoke in a tone that bore no accusation, no challenge, only empathy. "I understand completely—I understand with every bone and nerve and atom of my being—your desire to protect the people you love. But, as we now discover, one man does not warrant your protection. Nor does he deserve your loyalty. And that man, Mr. Hobbs, is Lieutenant Andrews."

Had Poe not charged me earlier with the task of meticulous observation I might well have missed the subtle signs of Hobbs's changing expression. I might not have said to myself, when Hobbs's hard squint relaxed into a melancholy gaze and his scowl softened to a sorrowful frown, I might not then have said to myself, *The man is acting even yet.*

"Your one mistake," Poe told him, "was to send me to Weehawken. Had you not I would never have known of Josiah Tarr, né Lehnort, nor inferred from his charade that the Red Onion was in fact a place of rendezvous for the lieutenant and Miss Rogers."

"Lehnort told you as much?" Hobbs asked. He seemed on the verge of whimpering; I, on the verge of laughing out loud.

"I employed a subterfuge," Poe said. "Having tricked the man into revealing his true identity I then deceived him into thinking that we were confederates in the same sham. That he, you, the lieutenant, and myself were colleagues in the same stratagem. Thusly reassured, he let it be known that the lieutenant and Miss Rogers were in company at the road-house. They left the establishment together on Sunday last. And she was not seen alive again."

Hobbs closed his eyes and slowly rocked his head back and forth. "The man is a dolt," he muttered. "I trusted my daughter's future to a dolt."

"I cannot fault your motives, sir."

At this Hobbs opened his eyes and once again leaned forward. He sat with hands clasped between his knees, as if he were now the penitent and Poe the judger of sins. "You have to understand that my faith in the lieutenant was still firm. He admitted to the one liaison but only one. After which he delivered her to the home of her aunt. He swore this to me, Mr. Poe, just as he swore repentance. Else I would not have attempted to shield him. In fact even now there is little evidence that he is responsible for the girl's death."

"She was not delivered to the home of her aunt," Poe said. "And yet the lieutenant returned to his home that very night. The young lady was last seen alive not far from the western shore of the Hudson River. Her body was discovered downstream of the very same river. With the marks of a hand still evident about her neck. And the strings of her bonnet secured with a sailor's knot."

Hobbs propped both elbows on his knees and hid his face in his hands.

And just to my right, a thud. There in the doorway Felicia Hobbs had been listening, and when she had heard too much to bear she swooned and fell to her knees. I caught her by the arm just as she was about to tumble forward. A moment later Poe was at her side, rubbing her hands in his while I held her upright. Then Hobbs was there as well, dropping onto his knees to embrace his daughter, holding her as she wept, crowding Poe away to murmur, "Leecie. My Leecie," as he pressed her tightly to his bosom.

"It cannot be true," was all she said, but over and over again. "It cannot be true."

For my part I wanted only to escape from this discomfort, this effusion of emotion. A beautiful woman grievously weeping, her father stroking her hair with one hand, his other hand moving in small circles over her back, his voice murmuring. I wanted to cry myself, though the reason was unclear to me. My chest ached, my eyes stung.

Poe, I thought, intruded too closely upon this grief. At one point it seemed he was about to jut his own head between father and daughter's, so near did he lean to them. But he only put a fingertip to her collar, held it there for a moment, stared hawklike at her throat, and then withdrew. It struck me as such an oafish thing for a man to do, too insensitive for even a writer, for it seemed to me that in that moment he was more interested in studying her grief than in assuaging it.

In any case I was none too relieved when Poe stood and nodded toward the front door. We slipped away quietly, without another word. We were but two yards outside the door when it heaved open behind us and Johnston Hobbs came rushing out. He seized Poe by the sleeve. "One thing, sir. One request, between honorable men. I ask only that you do nothing. For now, for the moment. Allow us some time to . . . adjust to these circumstances."

I imagined that Poe was thinking the same thoughts as I, that what Hobbs really wanted was a chance to get Lieutenant Andrews out of the city. Which is why Poe's response so startled me.

"Granted," he said. "On the condition that I be allowed just a moment of your daughter's time."

"Sir?"

"I am no foreigner to grief, Mr. Hobbs. Perhaps I can find a few words of comfort for her."

Hobbs thought it over for fifteen seconds or so, then nodded. "I will leave the decision to her." He turned and went inside, leaving the heavy door ajar.

Two minutes later Felicia Hobbs came out onto the porch. She looked none too steady on her feet. She now despised Poe, that much was clear in the set of her jaw, the heat from her eyes.

Poe wasted no time in getting to the point. He moved to within a hand span of her and spoke so softly that had I not inched forward myself I would have been unable to hear.

"Your brooch," he said. "Might I ask where you obtained it?"

Her hand went to her collar and fingered what I had earlier failed to notice, a golden angel brooch pinned at the neck. "You called me here to ask about a brooch?" she said.

"It is not irrelevant, please. In fact it might yet save your young lieutenant."

"A brooch? But how could—"

"Did Lieutenant Andrews give that brooch to you?"

"My father gave it to me. He had it made in Bruges for my twentieth birthday."

"And how many such brooches did he have made?"

"Only one, of course."

"If I told you," said Poe, "that I have seen another just like it, another identical to this one . . ."

"I suppose it would not be impossible. Someone saw mine, perhaps, admired it, and had another fashioned just like it."

"And if I said that the one identical to yours belonged to Mary Rogers?"

She drew in a sharp breath. "Then I would say that you are mistaken."

"I assure you, I am not."

"In that case I would like very much to hear your explanation."

Hobbs stood behind the front window, holding the curtain aside.

"The most logical assumption is that both brooches were given by the same man."

"Logical? I think you mean ludicrous, Mr. Poe."

"Is it possible, then, that he might have given one to Lieutenant Andrews, to be presented to his mother, or a sister, or—"

"To a shop girl? How dare you, Mr. Poe? How dare you!" With that she slapped him so hard that my own ears rang from the sting of it. "I took you for a gentleman. And here you stand on my own father's doorstep making these vile accusations. You are hardly a gentleman, Mr. Poe. You are the lowest of beasts!"

"Being a man," he said, "I cannot disagree."

She glared at him a moment longer, then turned away and stomped inside. The door slammed shut. The city shook.

29

SOME MEN, I think, are the kind who wish to be alone with misery, are solitary brooders, though when good fortune comes they gather around them those they cherish and in this manner redistribute the merriment. These are men who spend much of their time on the edge of the abyss, peering so hard into the darkness that they imagine an intimacy with its depths, so that it becomes the source of their most enduring comfort.

When in good spirits, fresh from a triumph, Poe wanted nothing more than to stride about with a disciple or devotee in tow, his weak chin thrust high. At moments like these he had sufficient confidence to bridge the gap to arrogance. Yes, he could be imperious. He knew himself to be a brilliant man and knew also that few others grasped the extent of his genius, and at certain infrequent moments he could not keep himself from striding through the world like a Moses parting the Red Sea, commanding his followers to trust him. The waters of ignorance could not dampen his shoes at such times. Nor, unfortunately, could the mist of reason, which might have dampened his mania enough to save him.

But the arrogance would not appear for a while yet. For now he wished to be alone with darker, roiled thoughts. He sent me back to the Newsboys' Lodging House.

"I have many things to puzzle out concerning Messrs. Hobbs and Andrews," he said. "If the solution to the puzzle occurs to me, you should look for it on the *Mirror*'s front page in a day or so. I regret the effect such news will have on the young Miss Hobbs, but perhaps in the end I shall be doing her a greater service than she can now appreciate."

I mustered the nerve to caution him against tilting his lance at a windmill so impregnable as Hobbs.

"There is no man so powerful as the written word," he told me. "If you forget all else, remember that at least."

He promised to call for me two or at the most three days hence. By then he would be ensconced, he said, in his permanent position at the *Mirror*—a sinecure he now considered inevitable—and would be ideally situated then to arrange for my employment as a printer's devil. Better yet, he would demand that I be hired as a copyboy. And when in a few months' time he was in a position to begin his own journal—destined, of course, to be the city's, no, the nation's literary and cultural clarion—he would move me with him, taking his fidus Achates into the rarefied air of Olympus.

"As I rise," he told me, "my friends rise with me."

(Did he ever realize, I often wonder, that this was the moment when we both, he with his eyes on Olympus and me with no idea what the name implied, began our Hadean slide?)

And so I returned to the Newsboys' House to await my promotion from gutterslink to gallinipper to, in time, a big bug myself. Perhaps I even bragged a bit to the other boys that I would soon be leaving them behind for a splendid house on Fifth Avenue, where I would eat eggs and rashers off fine china instead of scraping mush from a cracked bowl. And that is why I attended Jacob Van Rensselaer's lecture the following evening with a clot of dried blood in my nose, compliments of Moonie Weaver.

I had made no friends at the House who, whether in opposition to Moonie or other forces, would have sprung to my aid. Nor did I cultivate any friendships. I had Poe; no other chums need apply.

That evening as Van Rensselaer droned on in his monotonic rumble, I sat apart from the other boys and picked flecks of blood from a nostril. I sat there despising all of them, projecting my self-loathing onto boys whose names I had not bothered to learn. Instead of hating myself for behaving like a field mouse in the face of Moonie's fist, I oozed contempt for every other boy in the room, their crude and vulgar ways, their inevitable destinies of violence and crime.

Van Rensselaer seemed as ridiculous as the rest of them, as complete a fool. Throughout his harangue about the need to be vigilant over turpitude of mind and body, the other boys attempted to torture him with rude sounds. Instead of silencing the perpetrator with a whack to the head, or better yet a thrashing with his belt, Van Rensselaer reacted with a passivity that smacked, I thought, of cowardice.

Sin lies crouched at our doorsteps, he told us, waiting to pounce upon us as it had pounced upon Cain . . . and a boy off to his left shrilly barked. Van Rensselaer flinched, looked about for the culprit, but all faces were deadpan.

Van Rensselaer then admonished us to avoid highly spiced foods, for they would engender an inflammation of the bowels, which in turn would cause an irritation of certain nether parts, a heat too often interpreted by older boys as an animalistic urge in need of venting. At this, one of the boys vented a fart.

Not only did the ragged percussion startle Van Rensselaer even more than the bark had, but the rank effluvium threatened to lay him out flat. I have never since seen a man so paled by a fart as he was. His face went snow white and his eyes watered and his lips, what I could see of them behind his hand, began to quiver.

He spoke a while longer but, unwilling to risk an inhalation that might well prove fatal, he finished up chastising us all as low beasts and sent his charges tittering out the door.

In time I would discover that the ailments of Van Rensselaer were well known throughout the House, just as they were known throughout the upper echelons of Gotham society. He suffered principally from an acuteness of the senses. Any strong scent, whether sweet or rancid, set his stomach to heaving. Sounds louder than a low conversation, with the one exception of softly played violins, made him want to plug his ears and grit his teeth. Spiced foods, if ever a morsel found its way past his tongue, would have him perched in the privy for the next forty-eight hours.

He wore only silks and fine linens and, unable to abide the weight of even a down coverlet atop his body as he slept, was forced to keep a fire going in his hearth on cooler summer nights. Lastly, any sight visually loud was offensive to him, even noxious: bright colors, sudden movement, unfiltered sunlight, the dizzying spectacle of a milling crowd.

It was said that he had once tried to escape the throb and jostle of Manhattan with an excursion to Sagaponack. There he embarked upon a solitary stroll through the birch woods on a splendidly overcast and monochromatic day. And for a while, an hour or so, he found the gray stillness conducive to bliss. But when the clouds parted suddenly and sunlight flooded down through the canopy of slender trees, where it was then broken into irregular golden shafts that seemed to dart and dance all around him, he was dropped to his knees by a fit of vertigo. Unable to scream for help because his own voice would have driven him completely insane, he had no choice but to cower there until sundown, when, after the strobing illumination had ceased its giddy dance, he was able to crawl back to civilization.

Despite these infirmities, Van Rensselaer exerted tremendous influence inside Gotham and beyond. Because of his pedigree—his family had worked alongside Minuit and Stuyvesant in wrestling a city from wilderness and swamp—and because of his inherited wealth, both liquid and in real estate, his eccentricities were not only tolerated but coddled.

Unable to abide a woman's touch or scent, he was the evolutionary dead end of the Van Rensselaer aristocracy. But it was his goal, before he departed this veil of sensory irritation, to temper the city's cancerous growth with his own moral exactitude. In short, he intended to leave the island a cleaner and quieter and duller place, the barks and farts of newsboys notwithstanding.

Of course none of this would matter to me for a while. I was merely marking time until Poe came for me again. Little did I realize that our roles were about to be reversed.

At the end of Van Rensselaer's lecture that night the other boys were quick to exit the room, eager to return to unsupervised devilments. In no hurry to be at the mercy of Moonie Weaver again, I lingered. In so doing I became the target of Van Rennselaer's attention.

"Mister Dubbins," he said, without bridging the ten feet of empty room between us, "how do you find your new lodgings these days?"

I studied a fleck of blood on my thumbnail. "It's like paradise," I said. "Just like the Garden of Eden."

My sarcasm went unnoticed. He nodded and pursed his thin lips. "And your mentor, Mr. Poe. How is his work progressing?"

"Writing up a storm," I said.

"In regards to . . . ?"

"Some kind of poetry, I don't know. Stories. Things like that."

"And his newspaper work?"

"Fine, I guess."

"It is bearing fruit?"

"Huh?"

He dabbed a gloved fingertip at the corners of his mouth. "Tell him, if you will, that I send my regards. That I wish him well."

He stared at me for a moment or two, possibly because I was staring at him as well. Something about his manner of feigned nonchalance, his curiosity of Poe, struck me as odd. On the other hand, he was a very odd bird all told.

In any event that exchange, as I now recall it, was the moment when my evening's uneasiness began, a kind of nervous agitation. I grew *all-overish,* as we said back then, as if there were ants wriggling through my veins.

No doubt some of the discomfort was in anticipation of returning to my bedroom, which was also the bedroom of two dozen other boys, including Moonie Weaver. So when Van Rensselaer departed and left me alone in the lecture hall, I did not rush to my bed but remained huddled in a corner of the empty room.

In time the building grew quiet; all noises faded to an infrequent whisper, an occasional creak. Yet my restlessness would not subside. My muscles seemed to know what my senses could not confirm, that this night sat teetering on the edge of some greater darkness. I could not at first identify that darkness as evil, but merely as prelude, and waited nervously as you might wait for a knock on the door, or the first lightning crack of a blackening sky.

I was not well trained in inactivity. I sat hugging my knees for as long as I could stand it. Perhaps an hour, though it seemed much more. There was no question of sleep; sleep was for the foolish, for those not attuned like Poe and me to the tremblings of the night.

But though attuned to these tremblings I had not yet learned to interpret them, and identified the flutter in my stomach as hunger. In the morning I would be forced to sit down to another serving of bran bread, mush, and water. Mrs. Clemm on the other hand would have stuffed me with chunks of ham, fried potatoes, johnnycake, and tea. I think it was her I missed most of all that night, not merely her meals but her gentle and loving solidity. Even in poverty she was far more generous than all the benefactors of this parsimonious place.

I doubted I might find any ham in the kitchen downstairs, but with luck a biscuit or two. Maybe a jar of fruit preserves. So I gave in to my urge for a bit of petty thievery. I had tried my best to remain upright and honest but I had no knack for it. Besides, to just think of Mrs. Clemm shone a small light in the darkness I felt gathering all around me, squeezing me in. This then became the equation: a bit of food would make me feel closer to Mrs. Clemm, this sense of closeness would light a candle in my gloom, and with luck this one small candle might hold the snarling beasts of night at bay.

30

EVERY SNEAKING step down the stairs sent a slow creak throughout the house. Once or twice I thought my creak answered by one in another part of the building, and I froze in place until I could bring my breathing under sufficient control that I could again hear the silence of the building. By the time I reached the first floor my hands were slick with perspiration, the pulse pounding in my temples. There was a hollowness in my stomach that I mistook for deepening hunger. Again, my body already knew what my mind did not.

I felt my way through the darkened foyer, past MacGregor's empty desk. A smudge of weak moonlight filtered in through the windows, but only enough to make me long for more.

I was just inside the kitchen, my hand reaching for the first cupboard door, when a floorboard squeaked above my head. One of the matrons? I wondered. On her way to check the beds? If she found mine empty I was sure to be punished for this violation, and punishment here was of the type I could least abide, a kind of house arrest that imprisoned the culprit inside for an entire day, washing floors and scrubbing down walls. I stood there paralyzed, wondering if there was any chance at all I might sneak to bed before being discovered.

Then came the second squeak. But this one different, not a floorboard but the squeak of a hinge. And not above my head but at my back, twenty feet away in the pantry.

The hackles were as stiff as splinters on my neck. For now the footsteps above my head were continuing, one slow creak after another. By their sound I could trace the creeper's movements across the upstairs hallway, moving toward the stairs. Made not, I knew clearly now, by one of our heavy-footed waddling matrons. Too stealthy and deliberate. Too circumspect.

I felt I had no choice but to retreat in the direction of the other squeak, which in contrast had seemed not ominous but accidental. On tiptoe I crept to the pantry threshold and there saw, in its sliver of moonlight, the source of the noise. The back door stood open by six inches. Even as I stood there staring at it, dumbfounded, another small breeze blew it open a half inch farther and squeaked the hinge once more.

The door could not have been MacGregor's fault, this much I knew. His routine of locking up was so ingrained in him by now that he would sooner forget to take off his boots before climbing into bed. The conclusion was inescapable: whoever had picked that lock was now creeping down the upstairs hallway.

What I should have done was to throw open that pantry door and fling myself out into the night. I almost did so. But two steps from freedom I was seized by a sudden fear: what if someone else waited just outside?

When the heart begins to hammer as loudly as mine did then, when the mouth goes dry and the blood begins to splash and roar behind your eyes, it does no good to try to think. The only thing to do is to move.

I could not force myself out the pantry door and there was no safety in my bed. Only one path lay open to me—through the front door. I hurried out of the pantry and kitchen, turned the corner, and, still on tiptoe, all but sprinted for the foyer. Bang into MacGregor's table, a quick screech of its legs, the shock of impact stabbing into my hip. I froze for just a moment, long enough to hear that the footsteps above my head had paused as well, but only for an instant, and then had increased in pace, one quick creak after another, now nearly to the stairs.

I grabbed the glass knob of the front door and twisted it with both hands and pulled with all my might. But here MacGregor had not been undone. And the key, I knew, the massive iron key on a leather thong, would be on his bed table now, or still in his trousers pocket.

In any case the door would not budge. And suddenly all those earlier murmurs of the night congealed in solid form, all those vague premonitions materialized. The stairway creaked at my back, but my legs would not run. My hands kept twisting at the knob though my mind screamed to release it. Another stair step creaked. And a third.

I broke free of my paralysis and turned just in time to see a black boot descending into view, black boot and flapping black trouser cuff.

When its mate came down to join it on the stair I fled. Three steps back toward MacGregor's desk and I then dove to my left, plunged breathless into the wide deep parlor, the room we boys were forbidden to enter, its soft chairs and divan reserved for those more genteel than we, for Mr. Graham's lectures to the General Society and the Sunday School Union.

A pitch-black room it was, on the wrong side for moonlight. But I had glanced inside it often enough to know its basic layout, and I made it to the far side of the room without knocking anything over. There I crouched behind the side of the divan, and peered over the brocaded armrest, and tried not to blink as I watched the wide rectangle of gray that was the parlor's door.

He came down the stairs and paused. I could not yet see him but his wariness was tangible. His eyes searched the foyer. He sniffed for my scent. Then the footsteps began again, a slow scrape. Step by step they grew louder. And then his figure filled the parlor door.

It was little more than adumbration, a shadow slightly darker than the doorway, yet I recognized him immediately. He was Death. The one who prowled the Bowery. The one whose existence I had denied. And now he was here, peering into this room, probing its darkness.

I saw him as a stiff scarecrow of a man, a kind of Ichabod Crane, but sinister rather than ineffectual, a corpse himself, emaciated by a hunger that could never be sated. When I heard myself whimpering with fear I dropped down below the armrest and cowered, hugging myself.

There was no question that he was looking for me. Why else would I feel the chill of his heart in my own bones?

I should have screamed out, should have raised an alarm.But I was mute.Did I imagine he could not hear me there, quivering like a mouse? I don't know what I imagined.

But I felt him coming nearer, I felt his presence fill the room. He smelled of tobacco smoke and musty earth, an odor of dry dead leaves. But if this perception was accurate, my auditory sense was not, was clouded by a fog of fear as I lowered myself onto all fours and began to crawl—away from him, I thought.

His hand was suddenly on the back of my neck, five fingernails seizing, a pinching grip. Hauled up onto my feet, I was pushed before him like a dangling puppet, thrust toward the door. He was grunting with every breath now, every exhalation a small moan of effort, and this was all that saved me, all that kept me from hanging there forever like a limp gaffed fish—the recognition that Death was subject to fatigue, not indefatigable, not inescapable, that he was, perhaps, more human than demon after all.

I swept my feet back, I dropped to my knees. The extra weight pulled him forward, off balance. As my knees hit the floor I twisted in his grasp, felt his fingernails raking skin from my neck, streaks as hot as fire.But his grip broke and I was rolling away even as he put out his left hand to break his fall, even as he lunged after me, and now the fear in me turned to joy, energy, and his claws snatching at my shirt came back empty, for I was on my feet and running now, flying through the kitchen, through the pantry, and out the unlocked door, free for the moment at least, delicious freedom, though my neck burned with fresh blood, and I knew not what or who might be out here awaiting my emergence into the night.

31

Across Nassau Street I flew full chisel. Up empty Broadway and to the guttering gaslights below City Hall. A half-dozen glances over my left shoulder, over my right, and the realization began to sink in finally that I was safely away. I stood in the middle of Broadway, hands on my knees, gasping, vigilant for any small movement in the layers of night. Sweat that was cold on my scalp ran into the scratches on my neck and seared the scratches deeper.

But I was free. Slipped through the Grim One's fingers. I felt like laughing out loud, like sending a victory whoop high into the sky.

The first thing I heard was the flutter descending on me, the loud flap like a luffing sail. Instantly then his footsteps registered on my ears, boom boom boom as he came in from the west, swooping black and huge down a narrow sidestreet with the tails of his frockcoat fanned out behind him, flapping like wings. I shot away from him with more speed than I knew I had, but also blindly, my field of vision reduced by terror to a peephole, my only other functioning sense, auditory, attuned to nothing but the wild gallop of my hysterical heart.

I had never before thought of the Old Brewery as a sanctuary but in that moment it presented itself to me as one, only two minutes away, a labyrinth of darkness in which to hide. It was the only thought I could hold in my head. These were after all the streets I knew best. I made for Five Points on a zigzag course, through garbage-strewn alleys and scraggly lots and deep-rutted lanes. Except for holding in my mind the image of the Old Brewery I did not pause to think and scarcely to breathe until the rambling hulk itself loomed before me.

Never had decay and squalor looked so inviting. Yet I would allow no diminishment of fear, not the slightest whisper of relief, until I bolted through its front door and slammed the door shut behind me and dropped into place the rusted latch that no resident ever employed.

For three, four, a half-dozen minutes I leaned against that door, my ear to the crack. It took me half that time to attune my senses to the external. And then . . . nothing. Only silence without. Had silence ever sung so beautifully? A few minutes more and I even began to entertain the notion that I had escaped outright, that I had outwitted Death.

Suddenly, then, on the floor above me, so startling through the rotten wood as to sound only inches from my head, a loud thud, as of a chair falling over. In my heightened state I imagined that the sound, every sound, pertained to me, that Death had managed somehow to climb in through a window but had knocked over an object (a body?) in the process.

And if Death was inside, I wanted to be out. With an excuciating slowness I lifted the latch. Breathlessly, I eased open the door. The street before me, seen through the two-inch opening, lay empty. I eased the door open a bit wider, all the while keeping one ear attuned to the floor above, stingy with every movement lest the sound of it might drown out the creep or scuffle of Death's approach.

Ever wider I lay open the door, ever broader my view. None of the building's noises distinguished itself as particularly invidious; no lank shadow stood before me. I blinked the stinging sweat from my eyes and leaned forward, half out the doorway, needing only a last look to my left before I could break into a run.

I stretched out my foot, took one step across the threshold. A claw swiped at my face, bones cracked across my cheek. But I was still mostly inside the building and only had to jerk in my head and again throw shut the door, not stopping this time to fumble with the latch but diving for the nearest egress, the open doorway into the basement, half-tumbling half-sliding down to the bottom of the steps, to the soft moldy corner of pitch blackness where I crammed myself into the dirt.

The front door opened with a drawn-out squeak; he was in no hurry. My only hope was that I was in a basement so dark, so redolent already with the scent of death, with the myriad diseased and slashed bodies already buried there in shallow graves beneath the earthen floor, that I would be all but invisible even to night-keen eyes. At worst he would descend and in his attempt to zero in on me give me room to flash past him, up the stairs and out onto the streets again. I would run all night if need be. I would run to the Mississippi and beyond.

But no. His footsteps thudded up the narrow stairway—*up*. After the first flight of stairs I could hear him no more. At first I told myself that he had given up on me and would take somebody else this night. But even as I unwound this thought I knew it was not true. He was hunting for me and me alone. And would go to the most logical place to find me—my old room.

I would like to claim now that I acted without a moment's hesitation, that what happened next was in no way due to a failure of courage on my part. I would like to make this claim, but cannot. I cowered in the basement for ten full minutes, striving to discern in the dull symphony of groans and curses and all the usual muted thuds of the place some indication that my mother, too mean for death, had tossed the fiend out. But such salvation was not possible, no easy end to this dilemma, and I knew it. She was a drunkard whose most animated act was to swing the strop at me. Her only power had been my own passivity.

I ascended the stairs with as much stealth as I could muster. I was chilled to the core, quivering like a rabbit. But I made it finally to within a yard of our door, close enough to hear the question in its final utterance, the croaking voice as deep as Hell itself, "Where's the boy, damn you!"

My mother spat at him, I knew the sound well. But the one that followed it, the liquid hiss, and then my mother's startled, "Ah—you bastard you," and then the hiss again, again, sloppy and thick, a sharp knife cleaving soft flesh, and I burst through the open door and saw him straddled atop her from behind, she on her hands and knees and wanting to fall prostrate but held half aloft by her hair clutched in his left hand, pulling her chin high, the dirk in his right, striking, plunging, and then his hand yanking the dagger from her side and driving it into her neck, dragging it sideways, a sound like nothing I have ever heard coming out of my mother then, a sound no human should ever have to hear.

I must have screamed, must have cried out, I don't recall. I only know that he looked up at me and grinned. I recognized his face then, his bony hand. I knew this man.

He let go my mother's hair and she fell facedown to the floor. I heard her teeth break when her chin struck the wood.

I ran.

32

FEAR HAS a way of crowding all reason from the brain, of filling those wrinkles and creases with a thick sludge impermeable to light. I had but one thought as I ran, the thought of every terrified rodent: to find a small tight space too narrow for any body but my own, too deep for a long bony arm to plumb. I ran with my vision still reduced to a tunnel view of the world and this time blurry with hot tears, so that I had to swing my head as I ran in order to see more than a constricted path before me.

Across Canal I ran, through lots and dooryards, veering one direction and then the other, zigzagging north as if drawn there magnetically. It did not occur to me that I surely had outdistanced my pursuer after a block or so; I imagined him relentless and knew I could beat him only by being more of the same.

Not far past the Bowery Theater I understood suddenly where I was headed, where I must go—to the open pipework of the Croton Aqueduct, those narrow masonry tubes in their ditches. From the Thirteenth Street holding tank on down into the city these sections of three-foot pipe were being laid willy-nilly, all sections to be connected one day but for now seemingly random, the handiwork of a mad architect. A section sixty yards long or so traversed Grand Street, and it was to this one I found myself racing.

Down into the ditch I leapt without a moment's thought of what lay beneath me. Shin-deep into rancid stinking water. Sloshing forward like a heart about to burst, then onto hands and knees in the slimy mud, slithering into the pipe, slipping and sliding and clawing my way through the darkness. I banged my head so many times and scraped my elbows so frequently that the pain alone was what slowed me down, what finally brought me to a halt somewhere near the center of the section.

Beyond me lay a gray pinpoint, the eastern aperture. By lying on my side I could look down the length of my body and see another pinpoint to the west. If he attempted to enter from either end I would see him coming, could slither out the other way. But a pistol ball, that was a different matter. I could not sink low enough in the mud to hide from a pistol ball. I spent the next quarter hour looking frantically from one aperture to the other.

The mud on my neck dried and stiffened, cracking each time I swung my head to the right or left. The air was foul and sticky; any breath deep enough to fill my lungs made me want to vomit. But as long as both apertures remained clear, this pipe would remain my home. I resolved that I would sooner expire there of hunger or pistol ball than by a knife drawn across my throat.

I grew chilled. My body ached. I sobbed and whimpered. Eventually I slept, exhausted. Haunted by dreams, my sleep was broken and fitful. When I awoke from time to time I was hardly better than asleep, no more sentient or less prone to the phantoms of fear. I dreamed I was awake and when awake assured myself that I was only dreaming.

In this manner the night somehow passed. Daybreak came, the apertures grew brighter. Warmer. The air thickened into its own invisible mud. The light at the western opening flickered with the shadows of workmen. Voices echoed down the pipe to me, but none with a tone sufficiently reassuring to coax me into the uncertainty of the outer world. Nobody knew I was there. I was utterly and irretrievably alone.

The heat, the stink, the fear—what a narcotic it was. I must have slept ten minutes out of every fifteen. Often I awoke writhing in the mud, spitting and gagging. I despised myself for the coward I was and always had been. All my fears, whether personified by Moonie Weaver, or by the man who had murdered my mother, or by the seething world at large, whatever form my fear assumed I had proven myself too craven to stand and face it. I had latched onto Poe for the same reason, to be my protector, to assume the duties I was too spineless to assume myself.

My only comfort was the boyish notion that I could simply lie there in my pipe and fade away into oblivion. But even this idea brought no lasting peace. I dreamed that I was comfortably dead when the pipes were finished, buried, and connected and the water was released to flow beneath the city. The sudden gush dislodged my body and sent me speeding down the tube, spinning and wobbling like a badly fletched arrow, caroming from one wall to the other. I awoke flailing and dizzy, deafened by my own echoing screams.

When finally I came sufficiently awake to realize I had been dreaming, another voice penetrated the cotton of my thoughts. Someone was shouting down the pipe, someone at the western opening. A workman alerted by my shrill cries.

His concern was all I needed to drive me out in the other direction. Like an inchworm I made my way toward the eastern light. The nearer the opening came, the fresher the air. With it, my desire for life returned. I all but dove out the open end of the pipe.

Then scrambled to my feet in the pool of stagnant water. A furtive glance over my shoulder revealed a workman walking toward me down the pipe. Up out of the ditch I scurried. Waterlogged and stiff with mud. I was covered head to foot in slippery ochre clay, stinking like an outhouse. And yet . . .

How to explain the way the city looked to me then? Despite its usual bustle, its clop and clamor of routine, despite the almost musical buzz of the sudden brightness of a summer day, despite the slosh of my boots and the sticky whoosh of plastered limbs, despite all this, there seemed a calmness all around me, the same tranquillity I had imagined must be found in death, a serenity of silence inside my brain.

I knew with a knowledge that had seeped into me with the mud that I was an orphan now, whether my father lived or not. Yes, I was saddened by my mother's death, saddened in a remote and guilty way, but it was a peculiarly peaceful kind of sadness. I felt as if I had taken the worst life has to offer. The worst fear and shock and there I stood whole in the sunlight. I was made of mud and slime but so are we all.

At my filthiest, hungriest, and most perilous moment, I felt good about myself. I had outrun Death. I knew Death's name, I knew his employer. Off I trotted for a quick bath in the Hudson, then to share my triumph and revelations with the only man in the world whom I knew I could trust.

33

THE SCENE at Poe's cottage dispatched my serenity the way a hatchet dispatches a chicken's head. Mrs. Clemm sat on a porch step, huddled up in a clot of fidgets and worry. When she saw me coming down the lane she leapt to her feet and came thundering out to meet me. The look on her face made me think she was about to throttle me, or at least bowl me over and stomp on my bones.

But no, she pulled up short, she seized me by an arm. "They took him!" she cried. "My lord in heaven they got him and are keeping him somewhere, Augie!"

Her words ran past me in such a rush that I could make neither heads nor tails of them. I stood there blinking at her, still damp from my dunking in the river. All I knew was that she had been weeping for more than a little while; her eyes were red rimmed and her cheeks puffy. I had her repeat herself again and again, which only served to make her more agitated and confusing. In this manner we returned to the house.

Inside I went to Poe's bedroom and peeked into the dimness, and there in Poe's chair sat Virginia wrapped in Poe's shawl. She looked at me with the blankest, most bottomless stare I have ever witnessed on a living body. I would get no information from her, she was all but catatonic with dread.

It took me the better part of thirty minutes to coax a coherent story out of Mrs. Clemm. She told the tale in disconnected bits and pieces that I, aided by a large measure of hand patting and gentle questioning, was finally able to puzzle together.

Early that morning a man had called on Poe. Mrs. Clemm described him as exceedingly tall and as thin as a stick. "He looked for all the world like the Grim One himself. I fear now he was the angel Azrael, the one who comes to separate a person's body from his soul."

But on that day I knew him to be the very same man who had sent me scurrying into the water pipe, Hobbs's cadaverous servant. Mrs. Clemm of course had no knowledge that he worked for Hobbs, or any knowledge then or ever that he was my mother's murderer. She only knew that an odd-looking man who called himself Careys had arrived by phaeton while Poe was still in his morning gown. The man had introduced himself as a messenger for one Horace Greeley, who was desirous of a meeting with Poe to discuss the poet's participation in the inaugural issue of a new literary journal.

"I did not like the man from the start," Mrs. Clemm told me. "He had such a horrible smile, Augie, you would've flinched to've seen it. More like a knife cut than a smile, though I'm sure you can't imagine what I mean."

I surely could.

In any case Poe was not so unnerved by the man and hurried to dress and ride off into town with him. For the next three hours Mrs. Clemm busied herself with broomery and other household chores and tried not to fantasize about any monies Poe's latest opportunity might produce.

Around noon a scowling leatherhead arrived by foot with the disastrous news. Poe had been found insentient outside the Sportsman's Hall on Water Street, reeking of rum. (The things I might have told her about the notorious clip joint, but did not: that rat fights were held in the basement while soiled doves performed their own acrobatics in the third-floor bedrooms, with every other kind of liquored debauchery welcome on the two floors in between; that while a pianist and female singer entertained in the main barroom, a spider monkey in a red suit scampered from table to table, delighting the customers with his antics while surreptitiously relieving them of their slag and super, their money and pocket watches; that a favorite cabal of the establishment was to dope a sailor's grog with laudanum, then carry the unconscious man outside, clean out his pockets, and summon a constable—though usually scarce in that part of town, one could always be conveniently found just around the corner—who would slap the gob into a state of semi-wakefulness, drag him back to his ship, and there demand from his captain a good portion of the man's advance wages in exchange for not locking him up until his ship left port.)

"This constable who brought you the news," I said. "Was he wearing the initials of the Bank of New York?"

"No, the blue frock coat," she said, meaning that he was an HP, a member of Hays's Police. "He had a face like a long box."

"We seen that one in the Tombs when we went to check on Mr. Payne."

"That's not the half of it," she went on. "They're going to hold Eddie on a charge of public drunkenness. They say he was talking wild about that girl they took from the river—that he even claimed to have put her there himself!"

I recognized in a flash what Mrs. Clemm did not, the sinuated path of black intentions. Hobbs had sent his manservant to shanghai Poe and discredit him as a drunk, and now had enlisted at least one leatherhead in an effort to have Poe swing in the place of Lieutenant Andrews for the murder of the shop girl.

"He had evil on his mind, that constable did," she continued. "Looked straight at Virginia and told me I'd best keep a close eye on her lest she turned up missing too. 'That goes for yourself as well,' he told me."

I knew Hobbs's methods now, the impunity of the powerful. "You've got to get her away from here. The both of you have to get away."

"I wouldn't know where to go," she said.

"You can't stay another night where they know where you are."

"I don't understand any of this, Augie. Who's responsible for this?"

I looked into the trees, studied the shadows. "Promise me you'll get away from here."

"I'll have to think," she said.

I sat motionless for a while, holding her hand, feeling the spring of my resolve wind ever tighter. Finally I pulled away. "I'm going to the Tombs," was all I said.

She did not utter a word or put out a hand to deter me. How do you call back your only hope, small as he might be? I raced out the lane and into the softened light of a yellowing afternoon.

34

IF MY thoughts when I arrived at the cottage had been clean and bap-
tismal, they now on the egress were charnel. I understood with a sudden
clarity why Poe so detested this city. It was a cursed tongue of land upon
whose lower end festered all the more conspicuous boils of mankind, the
thieving and drunkenness and turpitudes of the flesh, and whose rest
nurtured the remaining perfidies not so obvious to the naked eye, the
deceits and subterfuges and the Machiavellian disregard for people's lives.
Over the length of the island the swine ran wild, one breed distinguish-
able from the other only by the number of legs on which it ran, with the
fattest of the boars holding sway with filigreed tusks used to pierce and
push and prod the police and the newspapers and the government and
the trade. It could not be long, I knew, I hoped, before the entire island
sank beneath the weight of its own fetid corruption.

No wonder Poe wanted to pack up his family and move out. To
Saratoga, Richmond, Baltimore—in any case to a gentler society. Where
at the least a superficial civility prevailed. A milieu of serenity and balm
compared to this open privy called Manhattan.

I ran most of the way back into that privy, then slowed to a walk a
block from the Tombs so as to catch my breath and collect my thoughts.
Poe and I had once been able to enter that granite fortress easily enough,
but could I do so alone? And then what? What was I going to do inside?
I had no idea. My stratagems could not progress around that corner,
could not see around that turn. Find Poe: that was as detailed as my plans
would grow.

For thirty minutes or more I circled the block, discarding one
grandiose plan after another, always returning to gaze up at the ominous
door with but one objective intact: to get inside. Once there, could I

maybe affect an accent of some kind, an educated boy, claim perhaps to be a messenger from the *Mirror*, Neely's emissary sent to check on the welfare of his star reporter?

My clothes were torn and, though rinsed in the river, still stained here and there with wide shadows of mud. My face and neck were marked by fresh scratches. No sober man was going to accept me for more than I was, a liar and a sneak.

So there was no way around it, no alternate course of action. If sneaking was my forte, I would sneak.

To the corner of the building then and sidelong up the wide steps. Across the front of the building to the heavy door. Ease open the door and sneak inside. Stand small and invisible against the near wall. No one paid any attention to me; I was a harmless mouse. Like a mouse then I crept along that wall, pausing beside each doorway to first cock an ear for any telling bit of conversation, then glancing quickly into the room, moving past, slinking along the wall to the next room in line.

I made it as far as the doorway to the courtyard without being accosted. I was noticed, yes; more than one pair of eyes cut a glance my way. But apparently I was too inconsequential for concern. This thought emboldened me. I now reversed my course, and, less surreptitiously than before, I checked out each of the offices and interview rooms along the opposite wall, working my way back toward the front door.

In the end I gleaned no sign of Poe. Was he in a cell already? On one hand it seemed unthinkable to me; I could not imagine my hero so demeaned. On the other hand he had been picked up for public drunkenness a full day ago—it was only logical to assume that they had thrown him in a cell until he could be trotted out for his ten minutes in the Police Court.

So he would be in the men's prison, beyond the courtyard. *Sonsabitches,* I thought, working up my anger for it, *those dirty sonsabitches.* When sufficiently incensed I marched down the main hall and out into the courtyard, across the smooth bare earth trampled and baked as hard as brick. I counted three guards standing nonchalantly at their stations around the courtyard, saw them watching me and grinning, four feet of insolence tramping sharply to the right, to an arched doorway beneath the Bridge of Sighs, to a gate of iron bars and the guard seated there behind it.

"I've come to see a man named Poe," I announced to the guard. He did not bother to get up off his chair, but only leaned forward a bit and peered at me through the bars.

"Who has?" he said.

"Master Dubbins."

This brought a chuckle from him. "Not *the* Master Dubbins himself?"

"I'm Mister Poe's assistant," I said, though my bravado was rapidly dissolving. "Editor Neely sent me here to check on him."

"He did, did he?"

"So you'd better let me do so. Else somebody's fur is going to fly."

He grinned at me awhile longer. Then something happened to his gaze, it moved just to my right, went over my shoulder, back across the courtyard, and toward the main building. At the time I imagined that he was thinking over my demand. His eyes narrowed into a squint, and after fifteen seconds or so he gave a slight nod, then looked me in the eye once more.

"Lemme see your pass," he said.

I almost started to pat my pockets, then gave it up. "Where do I get that?"

"Back where you come from. Third door on the left."

"Be right back," I told him.

This time my step was lighter, more optimistic as I returned to the main building. It was going to be easy after all. Nothing to it. Ask and ye shall receive.

Out of the sunshine of the courtyard and back inside the main building at a trot. One stride later and suddenly the floor fell out from under me—I was hauled up by the hair, another hand twisting my shirt at the scruff of my neck, cinching my throat. Hobbs's constable turned me in midair and held me up eye level with him and pulled my face within three inches of his own. His breath stank of garlic and meat fat.

"And now we catch the smaller rat," he said.

My throat felt strangled tight, yet I managed to squeak. "Where's Poe?"

"You come to rescue him, did you?"

"You better tell me where he is."

He laughed at that. His voice became a rancid whisper. "Oh you'll join him soon enough. Come nightfall you can share the bottom of the river with him."

He looked around then to see if he was being watched, and of course he was but without much interest. I was just another gutter rat being dragged in by the scruff of the neck. He grinned to himself, and holding me at arm's length like a squirming bag of manure, he carried me halfway back toward the front door. For a moment I thought he was going to take me outside but instead he stepped into an open room and I knew instantly that he was going to toss me into a corner and close the door and do whatever he wished to me, and I was not agreeable to that.

I could not reach his face with my hands, but my legs were slightly longer. I kicked with my right one as hard as I could. I swear I felt his balls squish against my boot top. His breath exploded in my face, a shower of stink. But all the tension went out of his hands and I dropped to the floor and ducked and skimmed across the dark stones of the floor more cat now than mouse, long graceful strides so that I felt I was flying, then banging hard against the heavy door and twisting out through the opening and down off the steps and away.

35

IF THERE had been any breath in my lungs when I went racing between the Corinthian columns and into the massive Merchants' Exchange Building, it would have vanished in a gasp with my first glance at the place. The central hall was all granite and mahogany, every cavernous inch of it ablaze with gaslight, dozens upon dozens of gaslights in crystal sconces. I went inside and skidded across the granite floor and found myself suddenly reduced to a miniature size, dwarfed by the high domed ceiling and flamboyant proportions that, were it not for the buzz and drone of human voices, might have silenced me with religious awe.

This lobby was a beehive of bankers, brokers, sellers, and buyers, financial opportunists of every ilk. I grabbed the sleeve of a young clerk hurrying past. "Jacob Van Rensselaer," I said. "Where's his office at?"

The clerk shook me off with scarcely a look.

I had no better luck with the next four queries. In fact the last gentleman offered a swift kick back to the gutter if I did not vacate the premises posthaste.

In answer I strode to the center of the rotunda and raised my eyes to the tiers of offices and meeting rooms and screamed as if to God Himself. "Jacob Van Rensselaer! I need to talk to you *right now!*"

All movement in the beehive stopped, all voices silent. My own shrill voice echoed off the granite. In a moment someone would take the initiative to seize me by the scruff of the neck and send me sliding out the door, but for the next five seconds I stood breathless, panting, eyes watering, dizzy, summoning the breath to scream again.

And then a sound from somewhere above and to my right, a finger snap. I turned my head, looked up. There on the mezzanine he stood at the rail but sideways to me, as if not acknowledging me at all, not even aware of my presence as he tugged a white glove back onto his fingers. Without a glance in my direction he pivoted away then, his back to the lobby, and returned to his office.

I looked about for the stairwell, found it before anyone could lay a hand on me, raced to the stairwell and up the flight of steps, found the door to Van Rensselaer's suite left open, hurried inside to the empty anteroom, counted three more doors, only one of them ajar, strode up to it and shoved it open and there behind his desk he sat, hands clasped atop the ink blotter.

"Close the door please," he said.

In a gush I told him everything, everything I knew or believed to know, how Poe had been tricked by Hobbs's cadaverous servant, led away somewhere, then allegedly arrested, and how I had been threatened by the constable in the Tombs, promised a death by drowning to match the one that awaited Poe.

Van Rensselaer listened without a word, without so much as a cocked eyebrow. I challenged his statement of concern for Poe, the one he had made to me in the Newsboys' House. I questioned his integrity. When I finally ran out of breath and words he sat as still as a stone. He looked down at his hands. They never moved.

"Please wait in the anteroom," he said. "Close the door behind you please."

"So are you going to do anything or not?"

"Please wait," he said.

I retreated to the anteroom and stood in its center for three long minutes, sat on the edge of a brocaded chair for three more. Stood again and began to pace. I was on the verge of hammering on Van Rensselaer's door when a second door in the anteroom opened and out stepped Glendinning.

"Come with me," he said.

I had no time to marvel at this coincidence, of Glendinning as employee of Van Rensselaer; no time to recognize it as hardly a coincidence at all. He led me down a rear stairway and out onto the street. "Hurry," he said. "It will soon be six."

"What happens at six?"

"It's the end of the watchmen's shift."

I understood now that we were returning to the Tombs. But instead of storming inside as I hoped and pummeling the brutish constable,

Glendinning had me wait around a street corner a half block from the Tombs' front door. He waited in a doorway not far away.

At six, the day's constables, eight or nine of them in all, emerged from the Tombs and wandered off singly or in pairs. Hobbs's constable was the last to emerge. He stood near the door and waited until all his colleagues were well away. I signaled to Glendinning that this was our man. He nodded and held up a hand, telling me to remain in my place.

Only when Hobbs's man came down off the steps and headed due south down Centre did Glendinning wave me forward. (I noticed with more than a little pleasure how stiffly the constable walked.) We followed him all the way to Wall Street, then east as far as Front, then south again. Now the constable looked over his shoulder more and more frequently, checked often to his left and right. Glendinning made sure to keep us in the shadows.

East to the waterfront then. The constable slowed his pace, tried for a saunter of nonchalance. He was not easy to follow through the anarchy of the waterfront, wending his way through the clog of coal carts and stone haulers, the passengers coming or going on their way to the clippers and packets waiting at the piers, the carriages and wagons, the vendors and grifters, all the usual soaplocks and butt-enders, the mudsills and banditti.

The street literally rumbled beneath our feet. The air smelled of fish and coal dust, of sewage and horse shit and oft-fingered money.

The constable slowed to a crawl in front of a row of squat warehouses. He paused before one door in particular, stood there for a moment as if thinking, then spun quickly to look back up the street. I, of course, was too low in the boodle of people to be noticed, and Glendinning had turned to stand in profile, ostensibly gazing upriver.

"He's moving again," I said a moment later. We moved with him. Down nearly as far as the Whitehall Slip before he made a sharp about-face and came back in our direction. Glendinning spun me around and pushed me forward.

"He'll go back to the warehouse where he paused a few minutes ago," Glendinning told me.

"And how do you know that?"

"He thinks he's being clever."

We passed the warehouse and continued on for twenty yards. There Glendinning slipped sideways into a narrow space between two ramshackle structures. He pulled me up close to his legs and admonished me to watch what I could from my low perspective.

It was like trying to see through a pair of venetian blinds that keep opening and closing, but I managed to keep my eye on the constable. He approached the warehouse door, just as Glendinning had predicted. He put his hand on the padlock. Looked to his right, looked to his left. Lifted a key from his pocket, fitted it into the lock. Turned the key, lifted the lock off its latch. Opened the door cautiously, a few inches at first. Peered inside. Then he leaned away from the door and glanced up the street and down one last time. Then he yanked open the door, slipped inside, and yanked the door shut.

"You think he's got Poe in there?" I whispered.

"He's got something in there."

"The bastard."

And Glendinning said, "Quickly now."

36

How to get inside, that was the problem. The entrance door was locked on the interior, as was a larger double door that could be swung open to load and unload merchandise from the pier. There were no windows out front. The building butted up against other warehouses on both sides.

"Perhaps the solution is to have the constable come out," Glendinning mused.

"He said that by nightfall Poe would be at the bottom of the river."

"Then we must not wait until nightfall."

"What if he's done something to Poe already?"

"I know the man," Glendinning said. "He would take more pleasure in sending Poe alive to the bottom than already dead."

"So what are we going to do?"

We went halfway around the block and sneaked down a dirt alleyway crammed with carts and empty crates. In the warehouse's rear wall, six feet off the ground, was a pair of small windows, shuttered. Glendinning went to one of the windows and stood there looking at its wooden face. Then he looked down at me, then back at the window.

"What are you thinking?" I asked.

"If I were to pry this shutter open, could you fit through it?"

"Maybe so. But then what?"

"You make your way to the front door and unlatch it."

"And what if I don't make it that far?"

He looked down over his nose at me. "And what if you don't even try?"

I could not tell him then that my legs had suddenly gone numb, that my spine felt as brittle as ice. I could still smell the constable's breath in my face, and that alone was enough to paralyze me. It was all I could do to give Glendinning the slightest of nods.

He stepped close to the shutter and slipped eight fingers under the bottom edge. He pulled the shutter toward him, gingerly at first. The bottom hinge began to creak. He stuck his right foot against the wall and leaned backward and used his weight for leverage. Just when I thought the effort futile, I saw the wood around the hinge begin to split, a nail head protruding.

"It's coming!" I whispered.

He paused for a moment, sucked in a breath, and then finished it off with a mighty heave. The hinge popped free of the wood and Glendinning let go of the shutter. He put a finger to his lips and stood very still. We listened for movement within. Nothing.

Satisfied that his actions had gone undetected, Glendinning proceeded to pry the hinge out of the wood. He laid the hinge on the ground. By lifting up on the bottom of the shutter he was able then to loosen and finally remove the top hinge as well. The shutter fell free into his hands. We now had our entrance, a rectangular hole perhaps sixteen inches wide and twenty-four high.

Glendinning peered inside. Half a minute later he ducked down below the window and whispered to me. "There's a light on the left side near the front. You'll need to stay away from it."

"What's between here and there?" I asked.

"Boxes of some sort, crates; it's hard to tell. You'll have to find your own way, I'm afraid. Are you up to it?"

"There ain't no way you could fit through that window, is there?"

His smile was sardonic, his answer clear.

I said, "What about a knife or some sort of weapon? You got anything on you?"

"Knives are for cowards," he said. "Are you a coward?"

"I ain't no coward but I ain't no fool either."

He leaned away from me then and blinked. I had a strange feeling that I had insulted him somehow. He said, as if to himself, "I thought you better than this."

Now I was the one insulted. "Goddamn you. Gimme a boost."

He seized my shirt at the back of the neck, my trousers at the waistband, and before I had time to gasp I was halfway through the opening. Headfirst I crawled in farther while he, holding to my ankles, lowered me to the floor.

On my feet again, I waved a hand past the window to let him know that I was safely inside.

He whispered, "Go to it, lad."

It was a large room with bales of tobacco stacked against the side walls, leaving an alley perhaps ten feet wide down the middle. A dark and redolent place, it smelled of burlap and cigar leaf. The air was dry, dusty, it scratched at my throat. My eyes itched, my skin felt prickly.

I kept close to the bales on my right, my hand sliding across them as I crept forward inch by inch. A pigeon purled in the darkness above. I wanted more than anything to cry out to Poe, wanted his voice and presence to save me from the terror I was feeling. The dry heat of the warehouse scaled my skin but below that I was chilled, shivering in my bones. I had to piss, I wanted to whimper, I wanted to run back to the window and dive upward through the opening.

But there was a dim light glowing up ahead, the flickering light of a candle. Five more yards and I could see that the light came from a kind of side alley in the bales of tobacco. Another few yards and I could look down that alley; I saw it empty, saw the way it opened again to its right, to where a kind of cave had been formed between the warehouse wall and the stacked bales. The candle was inside that cave. As was, I told myself, Poe. And no doubt the constable.

But the door—the front door could be no more than a dozen truncated steps ahead. I tiptoed toward it, but always with my head turned to the left, my eyes on the candlelit alleyway.

I was sneaking forward with my head turned to the rear nearly as far as it would go when I smelled the stink of garlic and fried meat. With that breath my stomach heaved, I wanted to vomit, I knew I was doomed. He chuckled then, a sound like wet gravel. I turned my head toward the door. The constable struck a sulphur match and held it up to his grinning face.

"Come to join the party, did you?"

Something about the flame from that burning match hypnotized me, something about that hideous grin. I could not run, could not call out. He came toward me with the match held before him and like a timorous child all I could do was to squeeze shut my eyes.

He grabbed me by an arm and flung me so hard against a bale of tobacco that all the breath went out of me in a whoosh. All I could see as I crumpled to the floor was the match lying there at his feet, a red ember. And I remember thinking, as if they were the last thoughts I would ever have, *What made Glendinning imagine I could do this?* And answered with the thought, *He never did.*

I was, of course, correct. Glendinning knew I would fail. But even in my failure I would provide him with the distraction he required. For suddenly there was a crack as loud as thunder, a flare of light which though softer than lightning was no less startling, and here came Glendinning through the kicked-in door, Glendinning striding forward and dragging a tide of soft light in behind him.

The constable turned and squared himself and pulled out his nightstick, but that was the last deliberate movement he was to make. I had never before nor since seen fists so quick as Glendinning's, so graceful and relentless as they hammered at the constable's broad face, as they followed with their shattering music as the constable staggered backward, already too dazed from the first blows to defend himself, as they hammered him up against the wall of tobacco and did not stop hammering, not even when the nightstick clattered to the floor and the constable's arms hung limp at his sides, fat hands fluttering with every blow, the blood pouring from the constable's nose and mouth in thin streams of shadow, the black ooze of his soul.

On my hands and knees I crawled away from this carnage, crawled into the alleyway of candlelight. I stood then and made ready to turn toward the cave to look for Mr. Poe.

But I could not resist a last glance at Glendinning. I saw him standing sideways to the constable now, standing with his chin lifted, mouth slightly open, catching his breath. The constable, though still on his feet, was beginning to slide toward the floor, knees slowly folding.

Glendinning stuck his left hand against the constable's chest, fingers splayed, and pinned him in place against the bales of tobacco. Then, reaching behind himself with his right hand, Glendinning twisted at the waist and bent low as if to pick something off the floor.

For another two seconds he maintained this posture, tensing, increasing the torque. As quick as a rifle shot, then, he unwound. His fist came up in a sweeping arc, so vicious a blow upon the constable's jaw that had the baled tobacco not acted as a restraint, I swear the constable's head would have swung the whole way around.

The sickening crack alone was enough to make me flinch and jerk away. I staggered forward to find Mr. Poe.

He was bound hand and foot and mouth, wedged into a tiny opening behind a bale of tobacco that had been pulled away from the wall. It took me a quarter of an hour to free the knots. The first thing he said when I took the gag from his mouth was, "Muddy and Sissie? Have you seen them?"

"They're fine," I said. "Just fine."

He wanted to know how I had located him, how I had overpowered the constable. "I had some help. Glendinning."

"The same gentleman we encountered on the street?"

"The same. He's out there now. Finishing up."

But when I led him out of the cave and into the center of the warehouse, there was no one else in sight. A wide smear of blood led to the doorway, and from there to the end of the pier. Poe and I stood on the edge of the pier in a dusky light and watched the constable's nightstick floating off toward Brooklyn.

37

HE WOULD listen to no reason but, concerned for the welfare of his wife and Mrs. Clemm, insisted upon returning to his home at once. No hackneys were about at that hour and so again I trotted at his side. (The miles I piled up in Poe's company!) I attempted once or twice to shorten the journey with conversation, but he was strung too tightly for talk, his only speech in the form of grunts and quick mumbles. All of his energy was invested in his stride, in whittling away the miles to those he loved. And so I followed his example, I strode on, hoarding my darkest thoughts to myself.

Under a sky charcoal gray we arrived at the mouth of his lane. And there it seemed our darkest thoughts were made tangible. The cottage sat as silent as a shadow, as unlit. No movement inside or out.

He trembled, tightened, and would have bolted forward but that I caught him by the sleeve. "It might be a trap of some kind. There might be somebody in there waiting for you."

He drew his arm out of my grasp, but not brusquely, with measured deliberation. "Wait here," he said.

"No, sir, I won't."

"Then walk directly behind me. We'll approach from the side, shielded by the trees."

In this manner, moving from one tree to the next, from the trees to the lilac bush, we made our way to the side of the house. Poe peered in the nearest window. Then along the house to its rear, where he did the same. And on around to the front of the house again. "It's completely empty," he said.

"Unless there's somebody hiding inside."

"Then damn their cowardly souls," he announced, and with that he marched onto the porch and threw open the door.

The cottage was empty, as gray inside as the night. While he went from room to room, calling for his wife and mother-in-law, I found the oil lamp and matches and gave us some light. Only after he had returned from the basement would he admit to himself that they were gone.

"I need to know where they are," he said. "I cannot rest until I find them."

"Just because they're gone don't necessarily mean that somebody took them. In fact last I seen Mrs. Clemm, she was trying to think of someplace safe to go."

"She was? She told you that?"

"Yes, she did. And there ain't no signs of fighting here, are there? Ain't nobody could of got Mrs. Clemm out of here without a fight."

He nodded, and allowed himself a tentative smile. "She would've left me a sign of some kind. We'll just have to find it, that's all."

But the sign was not immediately found, and his apprehension returned twofold. "Even the cats are gone," he cried. His voice was broken and shrill.

"But that's a good thing, ain't it? It means they took them along too. It means they left in their own good time."

An inventory of the house did little to settle his emotions. Mrs. Clemm's broom was missing, as was her favorite skillet, her keepsake box made of curly ash. But very few articles of their clothing—perhaps no more than what they had had on. Poe's shawl was gone, and Virginia's songbook, and one whale-oil lamp.

"I cannot think straight," he said. "I cannot tell what's gone and what remains."

"Seems to me they grabbed a couple things and set off. They didn't stop to plan it, just did it. Took whatever meant the most to them, that's all."

"But where have they gone?" he moaned. "Where are my beloveds?"

Finally, then, in his trunkful of manuscripts, he found Mrs. Clemm's semaphore. "Augie, look, look!" he cried, calling me out of the kitchen. "Here is where they have gone!"

I carried my candle to him and saw that he was holding a piece of parchment, and on the parchment the pencil sketch of a farmhouse that looked vaguely familiar.

"It is Mrs. Curran's farm," he said. "In Fordham. Where we lived previous to this place."

"I thought I'd seen that house before."

"I made this sketch for Muddy when we had to leave. She kept it in her keepsake box." He looked at the sketch for a moment with wet eyes. Then, almost violently, buried it beneath his manuscripts. "We must go to them at once."

"And lead Hobbs right to them?" I said.

He turned and looked at me, glared, his eyes black with rage, as if I were Hobbs himself.

I spoke more softly. "What we need to do now is to stay away from them. That's how to keep them safe. We need to keep at this thing until we get the goods on Hobbs and that lieutenant. Only when you put the nails to them are you gonna be safe."

He spun toward the door as if he had heard a noise. But there was only the open rectangle of night. "Even here we are not secure," he muttered.

"Least of all here."

And now the last of his strength seemed to go out of him. He sagged like a half-empty sack. I asked, "You got any friends hereabouts? Even back in town maybe?"

"Any who would be quick to take in an alleged murderer?" He shook his head. "And you?"

"Here's what I know," I told him. "I can trust you and you can trust me. Beyond that, I ain't willing to speculate."

He nodded. He looked about the small room, his face uneven in the candlelight. "Make yourself a bedroll," he finally said. Then he went into the bedroom and rolled up two blankets for himself and then we closed up the cottage and went out to the woods and lay shivering and tense through a warm summer's night.

WITHOUT A campfire, with the canopy of trees blocking the moon and most of the stars from view, we had only each other's voices to give us comfort as the hours ticked toward midnight. We talked until I, at least, was weary enough for sleep, our voices little louder than a murmuring of streams.

He told me of how he had come to be in the warehouse on the waterfront, the sequence of deception to which he had succumbed. How

Hobbs's manservant Careys had seduced him away from the cottage, then escorted him to a table at the Sportsman's Hall, where they shared a pot of tea while awaiting the appearance of Horace J. Greeley. Soon Poe became drowsy; Hobbs's man suggested a short walk in fresher air. Next thing Poe knew he was trussed up and gagged in a cave that reeked of tobacco leaf. He had no idea until Hobbs's constable told him, gloatingly, that Poe had been marked for the river.

In turn I filled him in on how Hobbs's manservant had followed me to the Old Brewery, where I had overheard him questioning my mother. I left out the part about my mother's gruesome murder, for Poe would have blamed himself, and that burden was my own, I would not share it. He worried vociferously about his wife and mother-in-law, about the mountain of anxiety his actions must be causing them.

"Yours is the only life my efforts have actually improved," he told me, and I could not disabuse him of the notion, not because his joy in that illusion was too great but because my guilt over his misery was.

I felt his misery as palpably as a winter fog. I knew that I had brought all this misfortune down on him. The way I had run off at the mouth in the Hobbs's kitchen, my tongue lubricated with tea and gooseberry jam. The intimacies I had revealed now raced through the blood of Poe's family like gangrene. If anyone was responsible for his family's upheaval it was not E. A. Poe, but Augie Dubbins.

"And this Glendinning, or Nostrand," Poe said, "whatever his name might be—he works for Van Rensselaer?"

"He does his bidding, seems to me. He's the one Van Rensselaer sent for, leastways."

"The convolutions," Poe mused. "This snakepit of power. It is not easy to keep the serpents straight."

"Van Rensselaer ain't no serpent, is he? Else why would he be helping us out? Twice now Glendinning saved your skin."

"I credit you, not him."

"Both times he led me to you."

"Very curious indeed," Poe said.

The phrase kept echoing in my head, a kind of metronome that eventually lulled me to sleep.

THE CROWS woke me. Or rather, their morning cries woke me by blending somehow with my dream, a dream in which I had been hunting on a fine bright day, hunting with bow and arrow in a clean western land of my imagination, stalking a magnificent bull elk when a crow came to roost on a nearby boulder and started cawing at me. The elk, a hundred yards out, turned at the sound and looked back, twitched its tail, cocked an ear. The crow kept cawing. I shooed it away lest it make my position clear. The crow then began to fly in circles above my head, scolding me with its raucous cries. I notched an arrow and pulled back the string and took aim on the crow. It ascended in a tight helix above my head, rising higher and higher and growing smaller and smaller though its caws did not diminish in volume. When the crow was but a black pin dot I let the arrow fly. I watched it up, up, until it disappeared from sight. And then the pin dot crow stopped flying as if stuck to the firmament. A moment later it began to fall. All the while it kept cawing at me. It fell spinning, growing ever larger, wings splayed out wide. At length I recognized it as Poe himself, black frock coat flapping as he fell, black eyes raging, arrow in his chest, his jagged caws diving down to engulf me.

I sat bolt upright, drenched in perspiration, and saw that it was morning; I was not out west but in the woods above New York. Poe sat wide awake against a nearby tree, watching me, softly smiling.

"You are a lively sleeper," he said.

I brushed the dew from my face. Glanced furtively at his chest. No arrow there. I rubbed both eyes with the heels of my hands. "You been awake long?" I asked.

"Some time," was all he said.

38

HAVING WITNESSED no evidence of a visitor to the cottage during the night, we returned to it briefly in the morning. After a hasty breakfast and a quick wash at the pump Poe announced that we had no choice but to return to town, there to gather as many facts as were needed to lay this matter to rest. He spoke with resolve if not confidence, a kind of resigned determination. The man was not without his flaws, but the absence of grit was not one of them.

Circuitously, then, keeping to the east side of the island and the narrower, less trafficked streets, we made our way into Gotham. Poe's first order of business was to obtain a copy of the morning edition of the *Mirror;* I spied one unattended in a newsboy's stack (he was a good two steps away and with his back to me) and gave it a home in Poe's hands. We found a shaded doorway of an empty garage on lower Pearl and concealed ourselves there.

He did not appear surprised by what he read in the *Mirror*. I watched his finger moving down the lines of an article, watched his face for a sign of his mood but saw no change of expression, no tightening of features. He read the article, tapped it once with his finger as if placing a period at the end of the final sentence, then handed the paper to me and gazed east toward the river.

This is what I read:

A certain poet-critic, lately from Richmond but well-known throughout Manhattan for his vitriolic attacks upon the works of more esteemed writers who are themselves beloved institutions of American belles-lettres, was discovered on Wednesday to be in a state of insentient repose in an area not far from a Water Street doggery. The unmistakable air of John Barleycorn accompanying the poet's breathing, the constabulary was left with no uncertainty as to the nature of his repose. Two watchmen attempted, in their compassion, to return the poet by hackney cab to his modest home north of the city, there to be consigned into the care of his mother-in-law, a strong and able woman, and to Mrs. Poe, who is yet but a child and by all descriptions unable to grasp the gravity of her husband's recurrent condition. Before this could be accomplished, however, the poet's somnambulance wore off, and by degrees he became more and more agitated. According to the single watchman who accompanied Mr. Poe on his journey home, this agitation manifested itself in a flailing of limbs and "wild talk" concerning the demise of one Mary Rogers, whose unfortunate story is already well known by readers of these pages. The watchman further noted that the poet's tone and attitude in this regard intimated a degree of collusion in the young woman's dilemma, the specifics of which the watchman was reluctant to reveal to the general public. Suffice it to say that the constable thought it wise to return Mr. Poe to the city for continued interrogation, but upon signaling to the driver to turn his hackney about, the constable was surprised by a sudden escalation of the poet's erratic behavior, and was consequently unable to restrain him from vacating their conveyance and taking to the streets. A thorough search ensued, but Mr. Poe's whereabouts have yet to be discovered. It is only hoped by those many who know Mr. Poe and admire his talents that he will return herewith to the able care of his mother-in-law, who, we are confident, will minister to him with the tenderness of a wife. Such attention, unusual though these connubial circumstances might be, will not only speed the poet's recovery but cause him in the interim to at last forswear those profligacies that have laid him so low.

I wanted to crumple that paper into a ball as tight as a rock, into a bomb I would hurl at the heart of the island. But Poe was strangely calm. The tiniest of smiles graced his lips.

I blinked back the sting from my eyes. My cheeks felt aflame. There on that page, laid out for all of Manhattan to read, was spewage from my own mouth, all my loose talk in Hobbs's kitchen. Someone from Hobbs's house had fed my vomitus to Neely.

I was too ashamed and frightened to confess. Poe was all I had left in the world. I could not endure to be orphaned from him as well.

And so I asked, blinking, "Why would that Neely fella print such a thing? I thought you and him was friends."

"Friends?" he said, and smiled again. "Mr. Neely is a journalist. His only friend is misfortune."

"So what do we do about this then?"

"We refute his delineation of the facts."

"And how do we do that?"

"We put our ear to the ground."

"Huh?"

"Did you not tell me once that within your circle of acquaintances—among your former acquaintances, that is—braggadocio is the norm?" He saw the wrinkles in my forehead and continued. "Misdeeds are bragged about, are they not? Within the circle at least?"

"Sure," I said. "It's how you get to be important."

"So then. We have a dishonest constable, now deceased but whose past affiliations must yet remain. We have Hobbs's manservant, an individual of rather distinct physiognomy, who is knowledgeable, it would appear, of the less savory institutions in town. We have a roadhouse in Weehawken employed as a rendezvous for Lieutenant Andrews and Miss Rogers. Information concerning any one of these principals, information no matter how trivial, might lead us in turn to more revelatory material."

"So what you're saying is we got to start asking questions of anybody who might know anything."

"But carefully. I for one must remain especially circumspect. And you, Augie—I will not allow you to place yourself in any danger."

"Don't you worry about me," I told him. "You think we should split up then?"

"The less conspicuous, the better."

"We need a place where we can meet up later on."

"The woods again. Beyond the cottage."

"Okay, yeah. But listen, we can be hiking back and forth the rest of our lives if that's what you want. Point is, I don't see no point in it. They'll be looking for you out there sooner or later anyway. Don't you think it's better if we find some other place?"

"What other place?" he asked.

"Someplace where even the leatherheads won't go."

He thought for a moment. "Five Points," he said.

"Tell you what. You meet me back here, right here in this same doorway, about three this afternoon. I'll have us a place to stay by then."

"We could meet at the Velsor Club," he said.

"You just stay out of the Velsor Club. You don't belong in that place any more than I do."

"We might happen upon an informant there."

"The only thing you'll happen upon is more of what got you in trouble the first time. I think you liked that place too much."

"I only thought—" he said.

"Yeah, I know. Just meet me back here, all right?"

Something had shifted in our roles with each other, some subtle reversal at the mention of Five Points. I confess that I reveled in it.

"Promise me," I said.

His smile this time was wistful. "You have my word."

And so we parted. I had no idea where Poe was headed and did not ask. As for me, I strolled the lower end of the island without specific goal in mind, keeping a sharp eye out for leatherheads, the other eye in search of a friendlier face.

Near the corners of Broadway and Wall Street I spotted a corn-girl I knew only as Princess. She was called this because of her most prominent possession, a cheap tiara rescued from a trash heap or picked up on the street the morning after a Fifth Avenue costume ball. A half-crown constructed of soft wood and gold paint, it sat always atop her head, at least when she was plying her barefoot trade, pushing up and down the street a battered perambulator in which sloshed a kettle of boiled corn.

She was twelve or thirteen years of age, her skinny legs getting longer every year, long ago outgrowing her threadbare dress. All of which was no doubt good advertisement for the other facet of her trade, for it was not only ears of boiled corn being hawked when she and the other corn-girls sang out, "Fresh and hot, fresh and hot, sweet and tender from the steaming pot!"

She broke into a wide smile when she saw me coming. She picked up her corn fork as she always did at my approach, ready to dip into the kettle for my free lunch. But this time she paused.

"I hear you been moving up in the world. Maybe I should start making you pay."

"Give it," I said, and held out a hand. My mouth was already watering.

"Not so fast. All you muckety-mucks gotta pay double."

"I don't know who you been talking to about me, but he's a liar."

"Jakey Mott," she said. "You want me to tell him you said so?"

"Can't say I ever heard of him."

"They call him Jakey Swipes. Or sometimes just Swipes. 'Cause he's got such quick hands, or used to anyway, seeing as how he don't do that anymore. Hardly ever. Except when he gets the chance."

"There's a fella named Swipes at the place I'm staying."

"That's him. He's a boyfriend of mine. Told me all about you."

"I never even talked to the guy."

"He's seen you coming and going. Says some muckety-muck got you in. You don't have to sell the papers or nothing. He says everybody's wondering what kinda deal you got going with this fella. 'Cause he's got a peculiar look in his eyes, Jakey says."

"I'm his valet," I told her.

"Which means what?"

"I sorta take care of him."

"That's what Jakey thought."

"Not that way I don't. He's a writer, and I kind of like keep track of things for him."

"Why don't he just write them down for hisself if he's a writer?"

"Some things ain't so easy to put into words."

She thought about this for a moment, then finally shrugged and lifted the lid off the kettle and speared a fat yellow ear of corn and held it out to me. It was still hot, so I held it by one tip and then the other, passing it from hand to hand as I gnawed on it.

Between bites I managed to keep the conversation going. "How's things been at your end?"

She became very still all of a sudden. "There was a fire in the building," she said.

I paused, my teeth on the cob.

"You didn't hear?" she asked.

How to feign innocence when you are painted black with guilt? "Hear what?"

"It was at your place, Augie."

I lowered the corn from my mouth. "It was?"

She nodded. Her eyes were wet. She was feeling something for me I could not feel myself, and I knew why: fire, the great concealer. Defiler of the truth.

I turned the corn in my hand, looked at the gnawed kernels. "Was she in it?"

Princess nodded again.

"She get out?"

This time her head moved from side to side, just as I had known it would. "She was on her bed and must've been drinking and smoking, must've passed out they think and spilled the rum all over herself. And that pile of rags she was sleeping on, they didn't help matters much."

And so, I thought, this is the way life will be from now on. One horror piled on top of another. My stairway to Hell. First I see my mother's throat spilled open, and now, next picture, an image of her body roasting.

"I'm sorry, Augie. I really am."

I shrugged, though stiffly. "Wasn't your fault, was it?"

"Wasn't nobody's but her own, I guess."

"That's right."

"Even so."

I lifted my head away from the corn, stood as straight as my fluttering stomach would allow.

Princess put her hand on my arm. "Truth is, Augie, if you want to be honest about it, it's no less than what she had coming to her. She didn't have to be as mean as she was."

"So what'd they do with her?" I asked.

"Same as with everybody else."

So she was buried in the basement. Buried under two feet of damp earth. Strangely, it was a comforting thought. The basement was cool, the darkness a blessing.

Princess squeezed my arm. "Good riddance," she said.

I nodded and swallowed hard. "They got the fire out though, huh? Before it spread?"

"Pissed on it, spit at it, threw their slop buckets on it, whatever. Musta worked, I guess."

"Thank God for small favors."

She nodded. Fifteen seconds passed. "Anyway," she said.

"Anyway."

"You and this muckety-muck. He don't need another valet, does he? I could take care of him too. We could take turns with him. Give each other a day off now and then."

"He ain't no big bug; he's a writer for the newspaper. He's the one wrote the piece about that girl got washed up out of the river."

"I heard about that. He's the one, huh?"

"I'm the one found her."

"Get out."

"I did."

"What I heard was a couple of oarsmen found her. Over across the river."

"Yeah but before that she was stuck under the dock over here. I showed her to this writer, and he worked her loose. And then she floated on over to New Jersey all by herself."

Princess laughed so hard that she bounced on the balls of her feet. "You're gonna make me pee myself."

"Believe it or not."

"Stranger things have happened," she said.

"He's still trying to figure out who it was done her in. Been running into some fairly suspicious types."

"Anybody I know?"

"A fella named Hobbs," I said. The name elicited no response from her, so I continued. "Another fella works for him, looks like death warmed over. Big, spooky-looking fella, goes by Careys." Again, no more than a lift of one eyebrow, no sign of recognition. "Plus a lieutenant in the navy, name of Andrews." Nothing. "Plus a fella supposed to be an oarsman over near Weehawken."

"Not one of the Burachs," she said.

"Says his name's Tarr. Poe, this writer I'm working for, he thinks it's Lehnort."

At the mention of Lehnort her eyes widened momentarily and she quickly averted her gaze.

"That's a name you know," I said.

"I've heard it maybe, that's all."

"Over in Weehawken."

"That's what you said already."

"So what do you know about it?"

"Nothing you need to know."

"Something about the Red Onion, I'll bet."

"Never you mind. Just finish your corn and move along now."

"Corn's cold," I said.

"Whose fault is that?"

"Tell me about the Red Onion, Princess."

"You're way too young to know that kinda stuff."

"I grew up in the Brewery same as you. I ain't too young for nothing. So come on; what's going on over at that place?"

"Nothing you need to worry about. Not for a few more years anyway. And maybe not even then if you watch what you're doing."

"Is that supposed to make sense?" I asked.

"It's a woman's problem, all right? That's all you need to know."

"I need to know a lot more than that, Princess."

"I gotta get busy," she told me, "or else all the corn's gonna be cold. I'll see you around, Augie." She wheeled her perambulator upstreet and, turning away, gave me a playful bump with her hip.

"Fresh and hot!" she cried out. "Sweet and tender from the steaming pot!"

I headed up toward Five Points then, taking my time because of a piece of corn or something that seemed stuck halfway down to my stomach. I kept trying to swallow it, working up gobs of spit to wash it down with, but it wouldn't go. In fact it got bigger and bigger, it started swelling inside of me. Burning my chest. It hurt so much that I finally came to a stop and closed my eyes, but that was a mistake, because then all I could see was my mother with her head pulled up by the hair and a long gash like a grinning mouth opening up along the side of her neck, and when I squeezed my eyes tighter I saw an orange curtain of flames with my mother still there inside them, still grinning at me while the skin curled brown and bubbled on her face. I scarcely had enough time to duck behind a low hedge before I doubled over, retching.

Five minutes later I was on my way again, wobbly and blurry-eyed. *That corn,* I kept telling myself, a chant to squeeze off all nauseating thoughts, *that damn corn Princess gave me was bad.*

39

WE MET at the agreed-upon time in the Pearl Street doorway. There was no sign of Poe's former calmness now; he constantly fidgeted or fussed with his collar, stroked his chin, leaned out the doorway, and peeked up and down the street as we exchanged our stories. He was not animated by fear but by a restless energy to keep moving, keep building upon what we had learned.

I told him about Princess's recognition of the name Lehnort and her refusal to discuss specifics; he found the news intriguing. He told me of how his first call of the day had been on Van Rensselaer, to thank him for Glendinning's assistance the day before and to request additional support. But Poe had made it no closer to Van Rensselaer's office than the opposite street corner.

"Positioned outside the building," Poe told me, "was the very same Bank of New York watchman I had dealt with earlier. The moment he spotted me across the street he hastened to intercept me. I could not make up my mind whether to run or wait. I waited. It soon became clear to me that he had been positioned there in anticipation of just such an encounter, for he warned me in very measured tones that I must under no circumstances call on Van Rensselaer in public. I asked to see Glendinning and this too was refused. He then pressed two gold eagles into my hand, but with the implication that if I failed to abide by this dictum, my fate would not be a pleasant one."

"He gives you twenty dollars and threatens you at the same time?" I said. "What do you make of that?"

"It was he who accompanied us—more accurately, led us—in our discovery that my witness from the Velsor Club had been silenced. I suspected then and even more so now that the watchman himself was responsible for the murder. I learned today that this watchman is in the employ of Van Rensselaer. In other words, he does Van Rensselaer's bidding."

"But that witness of yours was the one person who could put the lieutenant with Mary Rogers on the day she disappeared. Why would Van Rensselaer want to shut him up?"

"My question precisely," Poe said. He leaned out the doorway, looked up the street and down, then ducked back inside. "Next I made my way to Mrs. Rogers's boardinghouse," he told me. "She being engaged with her kitchen chores, and the house being otherwise empty, I chose not to disturb her as I availed myself of another investigation of the girl's room."

I almost squealed with delight. "You sneaked inside?"

He hushed me with an upraised finger. "The girl's room was exactly as before, with but one exception."

"Let me guess," I said.

He smiled and waited.

"That angel pin was gone."

"The brooch and the statuette both," he said.

"You think her mother maybe put them away somewhere?"

He shook his head. "Mrs. Rogers would want nothing there disturbed, want nothing changed from the way her daughter left it. No, Augie, those items were purloined by someone who came and left as secretly as did I."

"The lieutenant."

"The logical assumption. But one not substantiated by a search of his own quarters. A rather hasty search perhaps, but thorough nonetheless."

"Did you check out Payne's room too?"

"I did."

"And?"

"Nothing."

"So where to now?"

He rubbed his chin. "You found us quarters for the night?"

"I have a place in mind, it's on Rivington Street. It's a free Presbyterian church is what it is, but they take people in at night who don't have nowhere else to go and let them sleep down in the basement."

"Fine," Poe said. He took one of the gold eagles from his pocket and handed it to me. "Take this and have yourself a good supper somewhere. I will look for you come nightfall in the basement of the church."

"And where are you off to in the meantime?"

"I believe another visit to Weehawken would not be unwarranted. There are more layers to the Red Onion than are immediately visible."

"Then I'm going with you."

"I think it is best if—"

"I'm going with you. So here, take your money back."

"Keep it," he said. "Better not to put all our resources in one pocket."

"So I can come with you then?"

"Perhaps you should," he said. "Perhaps you should."

The truth is that I needed his company as much as he, for his own safety, needed mine. There were layers of intrigue at work here that even Poe did not suspect, those concerning my mother's death and the cover-up by fire, both perpetrated no doubt by Hobbs's ghoulish manservant. This was my secret knowledge and while the hoarding of it imparted to me a sense of authority and privilege, it also blew a dank breath across the hackles of my neck.

IT WAS not yet five when we arrived on the New Jersey shore, the sun still white above the trees. We disembarked from the Burachs' boat and I could hear songbirds in the woods, the scolding chitter of a squirrel. It struck me as an odd but somehow beautiful dichotomy, the discernible music and the inaudible agonies concealed in those woods; the trees so tenuously green, as temporarily lush as are we all, as marked for decay; while at my back the mercurial river, its mud and weed-choked bottom; the symmetry of shadows and light; the balance, not always fair, of evil and good.

In front of the roadhouse we found that the rotting skiff had not been moved, though the bogus oarsman and his chair were nowhere to be seen. Poe peeked into the Red Onion's front window and saw the same scowling barman behind the counter, but no sign of Tarr/Lehnort.

Around the back there was a wooden staircase leading to a doorway on the second floor. Poe stood staring up at the blank face of that door for half a minute. As he did so I watched the anger in him rising closer to the surface, his thirty years of rage. "Stay here," he finally said. Then he climbed to the door and knocked.

It was not long before the door swung open. And there stood the oarsman, smiling for just a moment, long enough only to recognize Poe. At the same moment he moved to fling shut the door, Poe lunged inside and seized him by the wrist.

"Mr. Lehnort," Poe said, and used his own body to prevent the door from closing, "you will not hide from me. I will have my answers, sir, or you will answer to the police."

Lehnort attempted to jerk free but Poe held fast. "My name's Tarr, I told you that. Now let me loose or you'll be the one'll be sorry."

Poe gave the man's wrist a turn so that the palm faced upward. "From the looks of your hands you have done very little rowing in your life. How do you account for that?"

There was a brief tug-of-war then, with Lehnort jerking to free himself while Poe, one foot braced to the door frame, looked for all the world like he was attempting to yank the man out and over the railing.

Then suddenly Poe's hand flew into the air, back toward his own shoulder. A moment later I saw why. A long knife, its wide flat blade at least nine inches long, was thrust within an inch of his throat. And the individual wielding it, the person who now backed Poe out of the doorway, was a small plump woman in a blue gingham dress. She was white-haired and stout as a barrel. She had a face like a fighting pug from one of the pits back in town.

"You had your warning," she growled at him. "You won't get another."

Poe backed to the rail but did not descend the stairway. "You are protecting a murderer," he said.

She jerked her head toward the interior of the room, where the bogus oarsman had retreated. "He never hurt a soul in his life. Never would."

"I refer to Lieutenant Andrews, Mrs. Lehnort."

Her pause was a beat too long. "I don't know any such person."

"Your son does; of that I am sure."

"What my son knows or don't know is none of your business. Now get down off my steps. You're not welcome here."

"I advise you not to compound your involvement in this crime."

"And I advise you," she said, and moved closer, and spoke to him in a hiss that struck me as all too gleeful, "you back away from this here and now. Or else your little boy there is going to find you dead in the street one of these fine days."

Poe's movement was so quick I could not follow it. I blinked, and there stood Poe with his fingers clamped around the woman's fist, the knife tip turned away from his own throat and pointed toward the bridge of her nose.

"If that be the case," he told her, "I intend to have some company."

I have never seen such eyes as theirs burn into one another. I was frightened by both pairs of them.

Poe used his free hand to pluck the knife free. He carried it with him halfway down the stairway, and there, with a sidelong thrust, left it stuck vibrating in a clapboard.

He did not look back at her, as I did, as we crossed to the corner of the building and turned toward the road. Her door slammed shut, and I jumped a bit. Just as I did when, as we breasted the front corner of the roadhouse, the barman, who had been waiting outside his door, his back pressed hard to the wall, clicked his tongue at us.

Poe stopped in his tracks and turned. I stood on heel and toe, ready to run.

"Adelia Blaine," the barman whispered.

Poe studied him for a moment, cut a glance toward the upstairs window, then moved closer to the barman. "Sir?"

"You talk to a woman named Adelia Blaine. Worked at the Sportsman's Hall over there." He jerked his chin toward the river and the city beyond.

"And why," Poe whispered, "would I be talking with her?"

"She'll tell you what you want to know."

"But you will not?"

He gave Poe a look, indistinguishable, it could have been either grief or derision. Then he turned and went back inside the building and softly closed the door.

40

"I MUST create a disguise," Poe said. "Else some nefarious character might remember me from my previous visit and suspect what I am up to."

"You don't need to go inside. You can get her to come out to you."

"How so?"

We were heading east from the waterfront, closing in on the Bowery and the Sportsman's Hall.

"There's a boy I know works as a kind of scout for them," I said.

"A scout for whom?"

"Whoever's willing to pay him for it. He helps sporting men find what they're after."

"This is a service he provides? A boy?"

"The way it works is, he's got these little picture cards he sells. You buy one, see? And then maybe you work around to the subject of the real thing. You slip him a couple of bits and he'll direct you to what you're looking for. Even get things all set up if you want him to. He knows all the girls from the Sportsman's and some of the other clubs. Plus a bunch of girls who don't have a regular place of their own."

"You are telling me that this boy you know is a procurer."

"All I know is what he does. If that's the word for it, then that's what he is."

"And how does it happen that the two of you are so well acquainted?"

"Not as well as all that, but I know him to see him. He cribs at the Newsboys' House."

"And you will provide the introductions?"

"Better you just talk to him yourself. Maybe like a customer, right? The two of us don't really get along."

I did not care to tell Poe how much I feared Moonie Weaver, that big moon-faced slob of a boy with a zeal for making smaller boys cry and bleed.

"And where will I find this young entrepreneur?" Poe asked.

"This time of day he won't be far from Five Points. Probably somewhere along Anthony Street."

"Then that is where we must go."

It did not take long to find Moonie Weaver. I recognized the hulk of his profile from thirty yards away. Despite his thick back and shoulders, his head sat ponderously atop but a stub of grimy neck, and he was longer in the torso than in the legs, an oddly shaped and top-heavy boy who half a lifetime later was destined to be shot through the larynx (with an exit wound through the back of his skull) for pummeling an unfaithful sweetheart at the Haymarket Dance Hall.

On some days, and this was one of them, he earned a few extra cents and concealed his principal trade by handing out flyers for legitimate entertainments. But even in this endeavor he kept one eye on his more lucrative craft and approached only those gentlemen who, identifiable by a glint of circumspection in their gaze or by the lopsided lift of a knowing smile, might be sold a second or even third diversion.

"That's him down there," I told Poe while I hid myself behind the corner of a building.

"How best do I approach him?"

"Just go on down there and take whatever it is he's handing out. Then maybe, if he don't say something first, you might ask if there's anything else he's got to offer. He'll be suspicious of you, not having done business with you yet—do *not* tell him your name or mention mine—but if you look like you know what you're up to, he'll bring a deck of cards out of his pocket for you to look at. You'll need to buy at least one of them."

"For not an insignificant amount, I presume."

"He'll say the cards are a dollar each, but you can jew him down to a couple of shillings. After that you can ask him to go fetch Adelia Blaine and have her meet you somewhere. You'll have to slip him at least another fip for that."

Poe was patting his pockets, checking his resources. "Why don't I simply offer to send the boy to Harvard?"

"And one last thing. About those picture cards."

He looked down at me with a kind of fatherly amusement. "I have already formed my assumptions as to what is depicted thereon," he said.

"I just don't want you looking shocked is all."

He patted my shoulder. "Thank you, Uncle August."

And then he strode off down the street.

I clung to the corner of the building, my cheek to the wood, and watched the transaction from a safe distance. Poe dipped into his change purse but twice, and when he returned up the street three minutes later he came with a picture card palmed in his right hand, a flyer rolled in his left, and a brow so furrowed that it could have been used as a washboard.

"I knew those pictures was going to take you by surprise," I said.

He handed me the flyer. "It was not the pictures but the news concerning Miss Blaine."

"Won't he set up a meeting?"

"He would no doubt be happy to do so were she in the vicinity."

"She's not at the Sportsman's no more?"

"She is not."

"So where's she working now? I can get you in to most any place in town."

"She is no longer employed," he said.

"She ain't dead is she?"

"She is a resident of Blackwell's Island."

"TB?" I asked without thinking, and saw the way he flinched.

"Master Weaver was very thrifty with his details. I do not know the nature of her residency. Nor whether it is voluntary or not."

"Looks like we take another ferry ride," I said, my own enthusiasm at the prospect more than balanced out by his look of trepidation.

"It would seem I have no choice. But tomorrow. I do not wish to navigate the Bowery in full dark."

And so we headed for the Rivington Street Presbyterian Church. Along the way Poe handed me the rolled-up flyer, which I barely glanced at before folding it in half three times and storing it in a pocket for future review. I waited eagerly for him to hand me the other treasure as well, but Poe soon closed his hand over the picture card and then dropped it into a refuse barrel outside a grogshop.

From that point on, my mind, I admit, was turned to nothing else. I had glimpsed a few of those cards before but a few is never sufficient to a growing boy. At the first opportunity I excused myself from Poe's company so as to attend the call of nature, circled the block, and a few minutes later caught up with him again, but this time with the pleated card now safely tucked into my boot.

A few minutes before nightfall we joined a dozen other itinerant souls already stretched out in the basement of the church. We were given a blanket and a piece of molasses cake and a folded broadsheet with which to read ourselves to sleep by the greasy light of three oil lamps dangling from the ceiling. Poe, an avaricious reader, took to his tract like a stray dog to a pound of sausage, but after ten minutes of reading sighed aloud, overstuffed, and laid the paper aside.

For my part the tract had the opposite of its desired effect. Already inflamed with a desire to gaze long and hard upon the illustrated playing card still wedged into my boot, I found the tract's admonitions more inflammatory than deflating. Like Graham's and Van Rensselaer's proselytizing, the tract cautioned against a reckless spending of one's energies, especially those that might result in pleasure. Drinking, flesh eating, impure thoughts—all would lead to dissipation, insanity, ruin. The release of sperm was particularly destructive and was to be avoided except in marriage, and even then achieved sparingly and, it seemed, grudgingly.

I dreamed that night that my soul was leaking out of me to dribble on the floor.

Morning came none too soon, though I awoke to see Poe already sitting upright against the wall, the thin blanket drawn tight around his shoulders. I rubbed the crust from my eyes and asked, "Don't you ever sleep? How long you been up?"

"Long enough to know that the chorus of a dozen men's snores is in no way soporific."

"You should of heard the Old Brewery at night. This ain't nothing compared to that."

He gave me a small smile and patted my head.

In those days I awoke fully alert and ready for adventure. Half a minute later I was on my feet. "There's a little yard out back," I told him. "Meet me there in fifteen minutes and I'll have some breakfast for you."

"Which you will purchase legally," he said.

"But—"

"We are not beasts, Augie. Even if we appear to be beasts and are beginning to smell like beasts, we must never allow ourselves to behave like beasts."

"Mooooo!" I answered, and was halfway to the door before I looked back at him, and saw him grinning, and was warmed by the notion that I was capable of engendering happiness, however destructive the Presbyterians thought it to be.

We breakfasted on apples and a small loaf of pumpkin bread. The morning was still, the air cool, the churchyard veiled in a vaporous mist. "No other hour is like this one," Poe mused. "At this time of day the city is almost tolerable."

He was reluctant to get on with the day's business. "Once this is over with," I told him, "you'll be able to skedaddle for good."

I don't think he believed it anymore. He strove constantly for better fortune, but never in the deepest parts of himself fully countenanced it as his due. The truth is that he could be soothed but not comforted. Sissie's tender small voice could soothe him, her hand on his arm. Muddy's solidity and unwavering faith. Even I on occasion could soothe him with a joke, the eager look on my face. But nothing could comfort him. Nothing could extinguish forever his darkness.

Sometimes the fear would swirl in him; I would see it in his eyes. It would rise in him like a swirling tide, the fear that failure was about to engulf him, drag him under and into its maelstrom. He expected failure and feared it most at the height of his brief successes. There was a sense in him always that the ground he walked on was slippery, wet; it might drop from beneath him at any moment; he would fall and fall forever.

By eight o'clock we were on the march again, this time northward to Turtle Bay. We followed the horsecar tracks up Fourth Avenue as far as Forty-second Street, and there Poe informed me that I was not to accompany him to Blackwell's Island. "It is a place not fit for a healthy child," he said. "Not if he wishes to remain healthy."

"Ain't there lots of children there already?"

"None of their own volition," he said.

Had I not been burning to examine in detail the painted playing card in my boot, as well as the flyer announcing an exhibition of oddities, I might have argued against him, but I did not. At Turtle Bay Poe was fortunate enough to catch one of the boats used by the Department of Charities and Corrections to ferry goods and personnel to that long splinter of misery in the East River. The boat was manned by a crew of four, all sporting the black and tan stripes of the penitentiary.

The bosun, one of the prison guards, made room for Poe among the various crates and three other passengers. I stood near the water's edge long enough to watch the boat pushed off on its slow pull toward the penitentiary docks, then found for myself a grassy spot to sit and pass the time in the consideration of the artistic pursuits of New York City.

On the garish card, the visual arts: a buxom cancan girl so bent and twisted at the waist that both her posterior *and* anterior endowments appeared in full display. And on the flyer, the lively arts: the announcement of an exhibit at the Vauxhall Gardens, where a man named Barnum was charging five cents admission to a world of exotic wonders including but not limited to a tattooed marvel—"Ninety thousand stabs! And for every stab, a tear!"—a kangaroo, a reptile girl, a living skeleton, a two-brained baby in a bell jar.

And to think that Tocqueville had had the nerve to suggest that New Yorkers are indifferent to the arts.

41

ABOUT HIS two-hour visit to Blackwell's Island, Poe needed no invitation to speak. He was paled and shaken by what he had experienced there, and upon setting foot on the bigger island once more required only the arch of my eyebrows to let loose his narrative.

"Hell is not so well ordered as Dante would have us believe," he said. "So I do not know which of the nine circles Blackwell's inhabits. But I doubt I shall ever forget the sound of that place. It rings in my ears even yet."

We walked southward, but slowly. I did not inquire of our destination; the destination was his story.

The first sound to resonate from Blackwell's Island, he told me, was the terrible silence of fear. An eerie silence signaled from the onset by the boats' crewmen, who were not permitted to utter a word lest they be assailed with the cat-o'-nine-tails. And from the massive stone edifice of the penitentiary itself came even more of the chilling stillness, for the thousand men and women imprisoned there suffered under the same rule of silence.

To the south of the penitentiary, near the tip of the island, sat the main hospital complex, two fine granite buildings with mansard roofs, plus a number of smaller wooden structures. Here the city's charity cases were brought, as well as those being treated for typhus, smallpox, ship's fever, and other communicable diseases.

Here too the day's visitors were registered by name and directed according to their mission to one of the island's several facilities. Poe, who had no idea in which of these purgatories Miss Adelia Blaine resided, was forced to perpetrate a subterfuge.

He registered as the Chevalier C. Auguste Dupin and affected for the benefit of the registrar—a soft-voiced mole of a man, Poe said, who blinked and sniffed, blinked and sniffed—a subtle accent to suggest the vineyards of Burgundy.

"I have been informed that my niece is recently arrived here," he told the registrar. "I have arrived of late myself, though from much farther afield than she. I do not know to which facility she has been assigned. I know only that she is my niece, and I bring her news of her *grand-père*. If you would be so kind as to point me in the proper direction. *Merci*."

After long study of the patient list, Poe eventually ascertained the information he needed. The clerk offered to have Poe rowed to the northern end of the island in another jail boat, but, the island being less than two miles long, Poe decided in favor of a stroll along the wagon path that ran the western shore.

"I was none too reluctant to quit that building," Poe told me. "Despite the magnificence of its exterior, the interior, of which I could view but a portion from the anteroom, offered small comfort.

"The entire place," he said, "could benefit mightily from Muddy's mop and broom. And from a few more windows, or candles at the least, for the air is rancid and heavy there and the atmosphere overall is pervaded by a rankness of odor. The hallways are crowded with patients who either shuffle about aimlessly or stand stock-still as if frozen in place, and from all of these, who do not or perhaps cannot be made to endure the prison's rule of silence, emanates a continuing moan and babble. It is a veritable symphony of wretchedness, I tell you. A dreadful, dreadful place."

Outside again he thought of abandoning his mission and turning for home. If the hospital, where individuals were presumed on the road to better health, could be so dreadful, what of the island's other facilities where no such hope pertained?

He was emboldened finally by the knowledge that he could at any moment call off his journey and return to the bosom of his family, if not back to his rocking chair and his home impeccably clean, at least to an atmosphere sweetened by the presence of his beloveds. And so he set forth on the wagon path, again past the penitentiary, on whose grounds no person was allowed to set foot without authorization.

Guards were stationed here and there adjacent to the path. Other guards patrolled the river in small boats. Between the hospital to the south and the almshouse north, the penitentiary stood as an island unto itself, grim and mute.

Poe thought the almshouse bore a kind of Protestant handsomeness to its facade. In its two large stone buildings, one for men and the other for women, were housed the city's triply cursed: the aged, destitute, and infirm. A goodly number of them were seated about the grounds on hard chairs and stools and benches, enjoying the sunlight. A few who were able raised their hands to Poe as he passed.

"Because it was such a pleasant day," he said, "there was a salutary air to this scene. But imagine it in winter, when the window panes are sealed and frosted shut, and the heat from the furnaces can scarcely ascend to the third floor, and the entire island becomes like a stick of wood frozen in the river's slush and ice. The place must seem then like nothing so much as a grave."

And he had not yet reached the worst of it.

Next came the workhouse. At this point in the narrative he turned to me and said with a wry smile, "If ever you find it necessary to take up residence on Blackwell's Island, this is the place to do so."

Here some fifteen thousand souls found themselves living each year, albeit briefly, the usual stay being about ten days long. Drunkenness, vagrancy, disorderly behavior—these were the offenses to prompt incarceration. But here the imprisonment was an active one, with every prisoner obliged to work, for there was no end to the island's maintenance: the sewing and cooking and washing and cleaning, the carpentry and masonry, the cultivation of gardens and the construction of seawalls and buildings and the grading of the wagon paths. Here too the rule of silence prevailed, but not so rigidly enforced as at the penitentiary, or so Poe speculated, having witnessed no guards patrolling while armed with the dreaded cat.

Then came the lunatic asylum. "If the hospitable farther south could be known by its groans and sighs and all manner of miserable articulations," Poe said, "you need only amplify these sounds a hundredfold to appreciate the aurality of the asylum." Even from behind the great heavy walls the inmates could be heard. "A choir of a thousand," he said, "in their ceaseless dissonance and gloom."

And finally, his objective. It stood alone at the island's northernmost end, outcast, the hospital for incurables. Here lived those whom society thought it best to remove from their midst, those who required no treatment other than the erosion of time. The wards of this hospital were distinct and various. Visitors were rare here, and those who braved contagion were cautioned against physical contact with all persons and objects therein.

Poe, after registering again at the main office and reiterating, disingenuously, the purpose of his visit, was directed to a small gallery outside the venereal disease ward. Here were two chairs separated by a bare wooden table. A mutton tallow candle in a sconce on the wall gave the room its only illumination, a gray and greasy light. Poe seated himself in the chair facing the door, and there awaited the arrival of Miss Adelia Blaine.

"When finally she appeared," he said, "and came to sit before me, she seemed less a human being than the personification of the single human emotion of abject despair. There was a terrible lethargy to her every movement, even to the gaze with which she considered me. No doubt she was once a comely woman, once fulsome and gay, with hair and eyes as sleek and brown as chestnut hulls. There was this suggestion to her appearance, at least, the hint of it but now veiled, enshrouded, if you will, by a cloud of doom, a cloud that cast her smallest gesture in somber shadow.

"I could not look upon her," he said, "at this specter she had become, emaciated not so much by her disease, which was only recently discovered, as by her knowledge of the disease, the presentiment of how certainly she was damned—I could not look upon her without envisioning the Adelia Blaine of an earlier day, of a Saturday in June, perhaps, and how her laughter must have rung as sweet and clear as that of my own dear Sissie, and shone in eyes that her suitors must have seen as incandescent. And then to juxtapose this joyful ghost upon the woman seated before me, a woman in wait for the madness and agonies to come."

He said nothing for half a minute. Then only, "There is no end to the misery of this world."

I steered him back to his narrative. "It was the French pox then?"

He nodded grimly.

Next he recounted how he had leaned close to Adelia Blaine and revealed in a whisper that he was not who he had presented himself to be, not Auguste Dupin nor any long-lost relative but merely a man in search of a sepulchred truth. Her eyes, he said, registered neither surprise nor indignation.

"I cannot tell you much about myself," he explained to her, "for my life too now hangs in the balance. But it has been suggested to me that you alone might shed some light on the mystery I now pursue. The mystery of the death of Mary Rogers."

At the mention of this name, a light shot through the dark clouds of Miss Blaine's eyes.

"You knew Mary Rogers," he said.

"She was my friend." Her voice was flat, her mouth without expression.

"You know how she died?"

To this she gave no answer.

"You were very good friends then? You and Mary?"

"Since childhood," said Miss Blaine.

"And you maintained that friendship all these years."

"We did."

"Were you with her on the Sunday of her disappearance?"

Again, the silence of a stone.

And now Poe had little idea what line of questioning to pursue. There was but one thing he wished to hear—the name of Mary Rogers's murderer. A confirmation of what he already knew. Perhaps, as well, a motive.

"Her fiancé, Mr. Payne," Poe said. "I have met with him but briefly, twice, and on both occasions he struck me as a man laid low by genuine grief."

"As well he should be."

There was something in her tone that seemed amiss to Poe, some faint hint of animus.

"You did not approve of their betrothal?"

"He is an ignorant man."

"How so?"

She blinked, a cold, reptilian gesture. "He saw only what he chose to see."

"And this was?"

"A pretty young woman to become his wife. To provide him with children. To round out the life he envisioned."

"He treated her badly? Is this what you imply?"

"Not badly, no. But he was indifferent to her as a woman."

Poe thought he knew what she meant by this, yet struggled then, as he did now in the re-creation for my benefit, with how to clarify the matter so as to permit no misunderstanding.

"And so, for that," he said, "she sought the company of Lieutenant Andrews?"

Her answer was a vacuous stare.

"Miss Blaine," he implored, "I was led to believe that you would provide for me this information. I was told by the barman at the roadhouse in Weehawken—"

And suddenly her stoicism cracked like thin glass. At the mention of the barman her face screwed up into a mask of pure misery, and she threw herself forward and buried her face in her hands and she sobbed so hysterically that Poe was at a loss as to how to comfort her. He could not wrap her in his arms or even stroke her hair, for he had been admonished that they must not touch.

He could only murmur to her, "Miss Blaine. Miss Blaine, please." Words to no avail except to exacerbate the sobbing to the extent that she was soon gasping for air, as if she were suffocating on her own tears.

He paused in the narrative now to gaze into the distance, to scrutinize some distant notion. At length he asked, "Does life not sometimes strike you as more a dream than as the wakeful portion?"

I thought back to my days and nights at the Old Brewery, much of it blurred together already as a single nightmare.

He said, "Even when one knows in his heart that life is not poetry, that it lacks the beauty and order of poetry, still it comes as a shock to learn how thoroughly deplorable this life can be."

In years since, I have often recalled the look on Poe's face when he made this remark, and have used it as a measure from time to time of my own misery, and have, strangely, derived some solace from it. For I have come to learn that there are three kinds of individuals in this world. The first is blind to all life's corrosive and degrading forces, and goes about in blithe ignorance until struck head-on by one of them, and is thereafter irremediably broken and crippled by the fear that another blow waits lurking just around the corner. The second type is able to accept life for what it is, imperfectable. With this acceptance comes the possibility of happiness, of moments stolen where and how one can, exquisitely precious because of their very transience. The third type of individual views the world's imperfection as a personal affront to his aesthetics and logic, and can never fully immerse himself in its transitory pleasures for he is more attuned to the transience than to the pleasure, and every day of imperfection exacerbates his frustration, his need to provoke change, until either his spirit or his body is broken by an ambition that can never be fulfilled.

I consider myself fortunate to have become, in my middle years, the second kind of individual. The shit of life, if you will excuse this vulgarity, no longer clings to me as it did to Mr. Poe.

In any event, to return to Blackwell's Island. To that brown bare room with insufficient light and a stifling air of doom. A place neither Poe nor Adelia Blaine wished to be.

And so, painful as it was for him to prod her, he did so. "You tell me that the lieutenant and Mary Rogers were intimately involved," he said. "Yet Mr. Andrews denies any such relationship."

With a fingertip she wiped one eye and then the other. "I never said they were involved. Never even said I knew anything about the man."

"I recall that you did."

"Then you recall wrong. I never mentioned his name. It was you that said it."

"Is this now your claim?" Poe asked. "That you are as ignorant of him as he is of you?"

"I know a lot more about him than he would want me to."

"And where did you come by this knowledge?"

"From Mary, of course."

"It is she who told you of their love affair?"

She put a hand to the collar of her blouse, fussed with a button or pin. "I never said anything like that."

"I remember distinctly—"

"It was you who said it, not me. You only think I agreed to it because it's what you believe. But believing don't always make it so, does it?"

"Miss Blaine," he said evenly, "my patience is wearing thin. I have covered every block of Gotham already but I assure you that I will not let this matter fade. If need be I will provide the police with both your name and the name of the barman who first directed me to you."

"You let him out of it!"

Again, the chink in her armor. He thrust in his dagger.

"I assume that Madame Lehnort is unaware of her employee's disease."

She leaned across the table as if to spit on him. "And if she finds out, we'll know who told her, now, won't we?"

"I have no intention of—"

"Because if you think I don't have friends out there, you're wrong. I have friends of all sorts. And some of them you don't never want to meet."

"As I said, I have no intention of revealing your secret. He is not the man I hope to bring to justice."

She glared at him a few moments longer, then settled back in her chair and sat with arms folded over her bosom, a hand at her throat.

"How long have you two been sweethearts?" Poe asked.

She sat silent for a full minute. In the end her need to talk, to reconnect with the world of tenderer emotions, prevailed. "It would be a year this November."

"Did you first meet him at the roadhouse?"

She shook her head. "The Sportsman's." She read Poe's silence as censure. "And he wasn't like you neither. He didn't judge me ruined for it."

"Nor do I."

She gave him a searing look.

"The point I endeavor to make," Poe told her, "is this. I have no desire to involve this man unnecessarily. But if he is indeed involved in—"

"He had nothing to do with any of it! Didn't I tell you that already?"

"Then who, Miss Blaine, are you striving to protect? Not Mary Rogers certainly. Unlike the rest of us, she is well beyond retribution now."

"She is but I'm not."

He felt he had no choice but to state the obvious. "How more miserable can you be made?"

She did not move.

"And if you think your silence is protecting the barman," he told her, "you are mistaken. He is a very frightened man, Miss Blaine, I can tell you that. And with good reason. I have already seen one man whose throat was slit as protection of the lieutenant's secret."

She fingered her collar; she shook her head slowly back and forth. In the dim light he could not read her mouth as either a smile or a scowl. "You got it all so wrong," she told him. "You don't have any idea."

"I am here to learn."

"And what good will that do anybody? What good will it do for Mary's mother, answer me that. And Mr. Payne, who even though I don't like him much never treated Mary bad. And Mary's aunt. And Mr. Anderson at the tobacco shop. Just think what this would do to all of them."

"How can I think it when I know not what *this* is?"

She sat there shaking her head back and forth.

"The one you most protect with your silence," Poe said, "is the murderer himself."

She lowered her eyes, looked at the table. "I did it to her myself," she said.

He could think of no response to this.

She looked up at him and offered a horrible smile. "You want the truth or don't you?"

"I do."

She continued to smile, though her eyes shone with tears. "If you want it, you have to keep digging for it."

He attempted to piece together what he knew with what she had insinuated. "You are not personally acquainted with Lieutenant Andrews," he reiterated, "but you know that he did not murder your friend. You only know of him because Mary spoke of him to you. You know also that Mr. Payne and Mary Rogers were not well suited romantically, but that he did not treat her badly. You know that Mary, then, more romantically inclined than her fiancé, sought out other avenues of . . ."

He paused for a moment, then looked her squarely in the eye. "She worked with you at the Sportsman's Hall."

"She did not," said Adelia Blaine, and smiled more broadly, pleased with the intrigue she had created. She ran a finger over her lips, then trailed her hand down to the collar of her blouse, where she again fingered a button or pin fastened there.

Poe considered how best to proceed. Stroking his chin, he stood and paced back and forth for a quarter-minute. He asked her a few irrelevant questions about the tobacconist, and then, before returning to his chair, he lifted the candle from its sconce on the wall and carried it with him to the table. He dribbled a pool of wax onto the center of the table and stuck the candle in it.

Finally he could see her face plainly, saw that she was smiling still, enjoying the confusion she wrought with the riddle of her life. But it wasn't her face he had hoped to illuminate. He looked at her collar, no longer hidden beneath her hand, and saw the gold and sapphire brooch she wore. A winged seraph. An angel. Identical to the brooch he had first seen in Mary Rogers's room. Identical to the one worn by Felicia Hobbs.

It came to him then, as clearly as if his movement of the candle had illuminated the very heart of the mystery. It came together so snugly, all seams flush, the three angel pins dovetailing with the nimbus apparent in the Hobbs's coat-of-arms, a halo circling a unicorn's head.

"Johnston Hobbs," he said.

The utterance of the name struck her like a slap. But she strove quickly to recompose her smile. "You're only guessing," she said.

"Ratiocination. The facts conjoin."

"And what facts would that be?"

Poe ticked them off for her on his fingers, and as a means of aligning them for his own confirmation. "It was Johnston Hobbs who first sent me to the Red Onion, hoping there to mislead me with a subterfuge. Unfortunately for him, he trusted the subterfuge to the hands of a dolt. Namely Josiah Lehnort.

"Secondly, it was a servant of Johnston Hobbs who caused me to visit the Sportsman's Hall, where I was further misdirected and discredited.

"Thirdly, Johnston Hobbs's efforts appeared to be aimed at the protection of his future son-in-law, but this, I now suspect, was also calculated to misdirect.

"Fourthly, how would a man like Johnston Hobbs become sufficiently acquainted with a man like Josiah Lehnort to employ him in the perpetration of a fraud?

"Fifthly, the Hobbs family crest, which I have had the pleasure of viewing, is adorned with several interesting elements, but none so intriguing as the halo employed to suggest a life divinely guided. As does the angel on your rather expensive brooch, Miss Blaine. Which, as you know, is identical to the brooch once worn by Mary Rogers. A third I have seen on the lapel of Mr. Hobbs's daughter, his own beloved Leecie."

"Leecie?" she said. "His daughter's name is Leecie?"

"Her given name is Felicia."

"But he calls her that?"

"I have heard him do so, yes. Why does this surprise you?"

She closed her eyes to him and sat there motionless. With wrists crossed atop her chest, fists closed. Her posture struck him as at once religious and defiant.

Softly he told her, "Your silence protects only him."

"You don't know," she said in a voice grown suddenly meek. "He'll hurt anybody he has to just to get what he wants."

"Mary Rogers is dead, Miss Blaine. And you are dying. As is your lover."

"If only she hadn't brought me into it," she said, which seemed to Poe apropos of nothing. "I could blame her just as easy. Or him that got her started in it too. He's the first person to blame."

"Hobbs himself, yes. All blame comes back to him."

"Not him, the other one. The one that put her onto Hobbs in the first place."

"And that would be?"

"The one she worked for."

"Mr. Anderson?"

She shook her head. "The boss of that councilman that was murdered. The fella with the longish name."

"You have lost me completely."

"It's Dutch, I think."

He could not believe it even from his own mouth. "Van Rensselaer?"

She held up a hand. "That's all. Not another word more."

"But Miss Blaine—"

"That's all!"

"Only this, I beg of you. This one last thing."

She exhaled loudly. She waited.

"Your reaction to the name of Hobbs's daughter," he told her. "It strikes me as extreme. It is almost as if you have heard the name before. As if, perhaps, you have heard it whispered in your own ear?"

She shuddered now; he had found a nerve.

"It is what he called both of you, isn't it, Miss Blaine? Was it not Johnston Hobbs's endearment for both you and Mary Rogers? He called you Leecie, did he not?"

She stared straight across the table at him, murderously, but he could not find himself in her eyes. He could hear her breathing.

"With you here," Poe told her then, and leaned forward across the table, and spoke in a whisper, "and with Mary Rogers dead, do you think Felicia Hobbs will remain safe for long from her father's desires?"

With that she slapped her hands onto the table, she shoved back her chair, she raised a hand and swung it out and sent the candle flying against a wall, she stood and turned and like a midnight storm she fled the pitch-black room.

42

"WHAT NOW?" It was all I could think to say at the conclusion of Poe's narrative.

"Firstly," he said, "I must go to Lieutenant Andrews with this information, the knowledge I now possess."

"What about the constables? Should you tell them too?"

"The constabulary is owned by Hobbs."

"Van Rensselaer's watchmen?"

"It was one of the same, was it not, who showed us the murdered witness?"

"It was, wasn't it? Now why in the world . . ."

"Because it was he who had murdered the witness. Because Mr. Van Rensselaer somehow knew that the man, the witness, was provided to me courtesy of Mr. Hobbs. Who contrary to all appearances actually wanted his future son-in-law to be indicted for the death of Miss Rogers. Van Rensselaer's man acted preemptively, then, to silence the bogus witness."

My head was spinning. "I can't tell who's in the right here. Has everybody been playing us for fools?"

"To a man."

"So again I ask, what now?"

"Now," he said, "now we do what little we can. We attempt to save the young Miss Hobbs from her own descent into her father's Hell."

Because Poe had nearly been a navy man himself, briefly a cadet at West Point, and knew well the rigors of military discipline, he suspected that Lieutenant Andrews would have been relieved of his teaching duties aboard the *Somers* pending the outcome of the murder investigation, and so would be passing the time in private quarters. In other words he would be keeping a low profile either at his usual residence, Mrs. Rogers's boardinghouse, or in the mansion of his future father-in-law. Poe hoped to locate Andrews in the former, for he had no desire as yet to beg entrance to the lion's den.

In either case he could not show himself in public lest he be apprehended and jailed, or, worse yet, shanghaied again by Hobbs's thugs. Even the lieutenant might fly into a fit of temper at the sight of him. So at the boardinghouse Poe concealed himself around the corner of the building while I knocked at the door. The door was answered by one of the boarders, a man I did not recognize.

"Is Lieutenant Andrews about?" I asked.

The man gave me a disapproving once-over while he picked his teeth with a thumbnail. "What's your business with him?"

"I have a message for him from a friend."

"Let's have it," he said, "and I'll see that he gets it."

"It's a private message," I answered.

He scowled at me a few moments longer, then turned away. I went to the corner of the porch and peeked around the wall and held out my hands and shrugged.

"Is he here or not?" Poe asked in a whisper.

"He wouldn't tell me."

Just then the door opened again and out stepped the lieutenant. He put only one foot over the threshold, held open the door but did not yet step fully onto the porch. He was dressed in civilian clothes now, blue pantaloons with a white blouse and matching vest. To say that he seemed a different man than the one I had first met says little to convey the change in him. It was almost as if he had become smaller in the interim. Or had been shrunken by some savage illness. The pallor of his skin, the dark shadows of his eyes, the slope of his shoulders. I knew immediately that Poe need fear no attack from this man. This man was already beaten.

He did not smile to see me there. He said, "I was told the message was from a friend."

I pointed toward the side of the porch. "Your friend is over here."

He no doubt reasoned by the time he reached the corner of the house that the person waiting for him was Poe. In any case he showed no surprise, though he squinted like a man unused to sunlight. "Mr. Poe," he said. "I am glad to see that you have recovered from your recent illness."

"Are you, sir? Are you glad indeed?"

"I wish you no harm, Mr. Poe."

"Then I ask that you might join me here. If you would not mind, sir."

The lieutenant had no energy for jousting. "What is it you want from me? I can tell you nothing I have not already told the police."

"Have you told them about Adelia Blaine?"

"I know no such person."

"And yet she knows you quite well. Well enough, at least, to speak of your relationship with Miss Rogers."

At this the lieutenant lifted his chin and hardened his eyes. There was life in him yet, it seemed. "You have made many statements about me that are not true," the lieutenant said. "And no doubt will make even more. But the one thing I will not allow, Mr. Poe, the one assertion I will never abide, not from you or from anyone else, is that my affections for Felicia Hobbs have ever strayed. Tell what other lies you will, but I warn you: Do not voice this implication ever again."

"For that," Poe said, "I wish to apologize. I was mistaken. And I beg your pardon, sir."

The lieutenant did not know whether to trust him or not.

Poe smiled. "What a maze a man's life is," he said. "Would you not agree, Lieutenant?"

"Of whose life do you speak?"

"Please, if you would join me here. I have a great deal to tell you about."

Andrews considered the invitation for a moment, then smiled as if in resignation, in surrender to whatever might come, and went down off the porch and around the corner of the building. Poe stood as close to the building as was comfortable and made certain to conceal himself from the street behind the lieutenant.

"I wish to begin," Poe told him, "with a more complete apology. I know now that I have accused you unjustly. I ask for your forgiveness."

I would have thought that such an admission would bring a smile to a man's face, but not so the lieutenant's. At first his eyes widened unnaturally, as in witness to a horrible accident. Then his eyes drooped shut, and he looked to be a man asleep standing up, at any moment to topple forward.

He spoke even before he opened his eyes again. "You have uncovered the truth, then?"

"I have."

Lieutenant Andrews nodded. Half a minute later he opened his eyes. His face appeared calmer now, less drawn. He had all but consigned his fate to the inevitable.

"And what will you do now?" he asked.

"I will make it right, sir. To you and all concerned."

"You will not be persuaded to do otherwise?"

"I cannot."

Again the lieutenant nodded. "Thank you for coming." And he moved to turn away.

Poe touched him lightly on the sleeve. "About Miss Blaine," he said. "Miss Blaine and Miss Rogers. There are still a few particulars . . ."

"Which you will not get from me," said Andrews.

"As you wish. But there is one thing I must make known to you."

The lieutenant stood there and waited, slouched, lax, exhausted enough to fall over.

"The man you protect, sir, has been attempting, quite ingeniously I might add, to cast you as the young lady's murderer."

"Now I see that you cannot be trusted."

"I am the only man you can trust," Poe told him. "And you, I think, are the only one I can."

Andrews blinked once, hard, a long hard squeeze of his eyelids. Then, "Continue."

"Johnston Hobbs has provided for me two witnesses to the fact that you were Miss Rogers's escort on the day of her disappearance."

Something tightened in Andrews; he stood an inch taller, stiffer, but one shoulder higher than the other, still crooked.

"Two, sir. So as to lead me to the assumption that you and you alone are responsible for her death."

"These witnesses . . . ," Andrews said.

"Have since been proven spurious. Not that I now believe you were not in the young lady's company. But that you were delivering her to a third party. The man with whom she and Adelia Blaine were engaged in their ménage à trois."

The lieutenant blew out a breath. He sagged again.

"But on this day, at the Red Onion, there was no such liaison intended, was there, sir?"

The lieutenant stared at the ground.

"She was taken there for an abortion, was she not? Performed by Madame Lehnort?"

It seemed to my eyes that the lieutenant began to tremble. His fingers, a hand pressed to a trouser leg, tapped against the cloth.

Poe moved a step closer; he laid a hand on the younger man's shoulder. "I only want to add," Poe said, "that I understand your actions. You were placed in the untenable position of having to implicate yourself in protection of your future father-in-law."

Andrews shook his head for a moment, settling into the truth, allowing it, giving up. "My concerns were not for him alone," he finally said. "How could I not consider Mrs. Hobbs? She is as kind and generous a woman as any you would meet, and has been unstinting in her affection for me. But principally . . . principally my thoughts were of Felicia. Of how the news of her father's . . . dalliances? No, the word is insufficiently appalling. How the news of his turpitudes might have affected her."

"And so you resolved to do his bidding."

"Had I not, he would have found a way to turn her feelings for me aside."

"You felt you could not reveal to her what you knew of him?"

"She would have despised me for it and labeled me a liar."

"As I said: an untenable position."

"Well . . . ," said the lieutenant.

"It was Adelia Blaine who exonerated you."

The lieutenant thought on this a moment. "I never knew her name," he said. "I was aware that he had enlisted the services of a second young woman awhile back, but Mary was always careful not to reveal her friend's identity. I doubt that even Hobbs knows her real name."

"When did you come to know that he was employing two mistresses instead of Mary alone?"

"In the early autumn of last year he began providing two silver eagles for me to pass on to Mary, rather than the usual one. This continued until a fortnight ago, when Mary returned one of them to me and asked that I return it to its owner. But Hobbs pressed it back into my hand with the admonition that I instruct Mary to do what she could to find it a grateful home."

"He had grown used to the arrangement."

"Mary claimed to have no knowledge of where her friend had gone. And she was equally reluctant to enter into a similar arrangement with anyone other than the friend she held so dear."

"Might I ask how Miss Rogers and Mr. Hobbs first became acquainted?"

"He stopped regularly at the tobacco shop. He had known her for several months, I believe, when one day, when the opportunity arose, she suggested to him that they . . . that he might. . . ."

"Would it surprise you to learn that Mary was probably instructed by another man to begin this affair?"

"By Jacob Van Rensselaer. No, it would not surprise me now."

"Is that why Hobbs had her killed? Because she was a spy for his rival?"

"*Had* her killed?" Andrews said.

"Are you insinuating that he did so himself?"

Now that the truth was out, there was no holding it back. "When we were informed of Mary's subterfuge . . . ," Andrews began.

"Informed by whom? The Red Onion's barman?"

"How would you know that?"

"He was the lover of Adelia Blaine. Blaine insinuated to me that she had betrayed her friend. For gold, no doubt."

"Of course," Andrews said.

And now Poe kept silent.

"When we were informed of Mary's subterfuge, that she had given Van Rensselaer some kind of damning information that might do Hobbs in, or at least wrench control of the water project from his hands—"

"What kind of information?"

"He would not say. But something he had revealed to her in private. He sometimes met with her alone and not with the other girl. They enjoyed, I think, a special kind of intimacy."

"This information," Poe said. "Might it bear upon the disappearance earlier of the councilman?"

"That was my suspicion, yes. Councilman Fordyce was an outspoken opponent of Hobbs's leadership of the water project."

"A mouthpiece for Van Rensselaer."

"No doubt." He paused to withdraw a handkerchief from his pocket and wipe his forehead. He then refolded the cloth and returned it to his pocket.

"In any case, Hobbs immediately began looking for an opportunity to silence Mary. My assumption, and this is what he promised me, was that he would purchase her fidelity as he did everyone else's. Yet, when he looked in on her in that room at the roadhouse, after the abortion . . . He came downstairs and whispered to me that something had gone wrong. That she had died from the procedure. He left me there to . . ."

He could not finish the sentence. He swallowed hard. Then started again. "I went to her. Alone. There was no one else in the room; the woman and her son were downstairs as well. I went to Mary and . . ."

"Hobbs's explanation did not ring true."

"I was puzzled by the absence of evidence to suggest that she had hemorrhaged to death."

"There was no blood?"

"Almost none. She was fully clothed, and there was no blood apparent on her clothing. But there was something else."

"The mark of fingers about her neck."

Andrews flinched. "What he does not know is how regularly I counseled Mary to end the relationship. To find more fitting company, if not with Mr. Payne, then another man."

"Would that she had heeded your counsel. In any case," Poe said, "you need no longer concern yourself with the prospect of prison."

"A different kind of prison perhaps." He was silent for a moment, then turned at the waist to look at the ground behind his feet, as if there it might be somehow greener, fresher, a different landscape, a different life.

Poe said, "This was not Mary's first abortion, was it? Her disappearance from home two years previous. It was for the same reason, was it not?"

"It was," the lieutenant said.

"And that time as well as the last—you were obliged by him to accompany her?"

"This last time, however, he joined us there."

"Permit me, if you will, one last question," Poe said. "You are a man who understands currents and tides. Why would you place her body, unweighted, in a river that flows past the shores of your very home?"

"Can you think I would not have given her a decent place to rest? She was as much a friend to me, a sister, as any I have had."

"You left her, then, to be disposed of by the Lehnorts."

The lieutenant's answer was a prolonged grimace of anguish.

"You tied the straps of her bonnet around her chin. You bade her farewell. And you left her to be disposed of by a dolt."

"My instructions to him were explicit. He was to convey her by wagon to a place deep inside the trees where she would never be disturbed. There she was to be interred with all the dignity he could muster. He swore to me that he would comply with all this, and for his word and labor he was well rewarded."

"But he was not true to his word, was he?"

Lieutenant Andrews put out a hand to the wall of the boardinghouse and steadied himself.

Poe moved even closer to him. "And now, sir, what might in fact be the worst of it."

The lieutenant barely had the strength to look up at him, his eyes, heavy with a desire to sleep, clouded with torture.

"Have you ever heard Mr. Hobbs refer to his daughter as Leecie?"

"Many times. It is his pet name for her. The man's single redeeming trait is that he adores his daughter."

"It is what he called Mary Rogers and Miss Blaine as well. During their most intimate moments together."

The lieutenant was suddenly breathless. "Do you mean to suggest—?"

"He gave each of the three an angel brooch."

Andrews slouched against the building, his forehead to the wood. "This is too much to believe . . ."

"And he was trying his best to have his future son-in-law incarcerated for murder."

The lieutenant's fists slowly drew shut.

Poe put a hand between Andrews's shoulders; only the fingertips touched. "If I may offer a suggestion, sir."

The lieutenant made no response.

"You must go to your beloved," Poe told him. "This very day. This very hour. You must convince her by whatever means avail to leave this sink of pollution behind. To leave it immediately. Return with her to Boston, sir. Or Saratoga. Albany. To any town or city where you can make her comfortable. In any case you must not be here—she must not be here—when the truth of this matter explodes."

"We cannot run far enough to escape it."

"No. But you can perhaps avoid the worst of it."

Fifteen seconds later the lieutenant met Poe's gaze. "Will you allow us until morning?"

"I will wait until the noon hour."

"And then?"

"Then I shall do what I must."

The lieutenant nodded. A few moments later he held out his hand to Poe. They clasped hands and exchanged a solemn look. Then the lieutenant turned and trudged onto the porch and disappeared back inside the house.

I admit to a warm swell of pride, even arrogance, as Poe and I then made our retreat as stealthily as we had come. We had done this, he and I. We had brought this thing to pass. And all the long way back to the

Bowery I luxuriated in a haughty and gleeful sense that the mighty were about to tumble at our feet. Poe's own bearing, though less buoyant than my own, suggested that he felt likewise.

We could have used Mrs. Clemm's good company at that moment, her heavy hand of restraint, and her whisper in our ears, *Pride goeth before a fall*.

43

WE SPENT the remainder of the day strolling here and there, sitting in doorways, slouched against buildings, until dusk finally came and we made our way to Rivington Street. There we passed another night in the basement of the Presbyterian church along with another dozen of more or less sober yet indigent itinerants. Poe's constant refrain, muttered to himself but like a gnat in my ear, annoying because I could do nothing to assuage the buzz, either for myself or the gnat, was, "I wonder how Sissie is faring today. She and Muddy must be consumed with worry for me." Several times it took all the forensic skill I possessed to keep him from marching us those thirteen miles into Fordham, despite his understanding that his presence there would be more dangerous to his loved ones than salutary.

His restlessness the night before was as nothing compared to this night's. Once inside the church he paced constantly, stepping over sleeping bodies, waking quite a few of them until one man, a very old gentleman in a shabby gray suit, raised himself up on an elbow to whisper wearily, "If you please, sir. A few hours sleep is the only peace this world allows me."

Poe apologized and offered the man his hand, having detected in the old fellow's speech some familiar nuance of the South. And soon they were huddled together in a corner, whispering and chuckling, even quoting verse to one another. When I awoke a little after dawn they were still at it.

The morning hours, then, after we were turned out of the church, ticked by like sludge dripping from a pipe. Poe was both anxious and reluctant to keep the appointment he had set for himself at noon, both fearful and eager. By eleven-thirty he had brought us to within sight of Hobbs's mansion, and there we toured the same row of buildings for the next twenty minutes, Poe muttering to himself and rubbing his cheek all the while, so agitated that to anyone who did not know what was going on inside his head, that cerebral wrestling match, he must have appeared to be a skin full of cockroaches, all twitches and mumbles.

Shortly before noon he could wait no longer and strode brusquely to the front door and pounded on it with the heel of a fist. The door was opened by Conroy, the butler, who in the face of Poe's disquiet calmly informed him that at this hour Mr. Hobbs could be found lunching at a businessman's club on Wall Street. And again we marched.

In the anteroom of the businessman's club Poe sent the maître d'hôtel to Hobbs's table with a request for a few minutes of the man's time. We were then shown to a small side room furnished with five leather wing chairs, silver spittoons, and crystal ashtrays on marble pedestals.

Soon Hobbs joined us there with wine glass in hand. He stepped inside unsmiling and closed the door. I stood in the corner and stared at the floor.

The pleasantries were brief and pointed, but Poe wasted little time on either courtesy or sarcasm. Instead he offered Hobbs a summary of the facts as he had pieced them together, all of which led to Mary Rogers's demise on the abortionist's table. The ultimate cause of her death was left unstated, though there was no mistaking his conclusion.

Hobbs had not taken a seat upon entering nor did he throughout most of Poe's soliloquy. He stood facing the room's only window, his back to Poe, who was seated just inside the door. When Poe finished his remarks, Hobbs remained quiet for a minute or so. Then, strangely, he chuckled softly, and spoke as if to his own pale reflection in the glass.

"I have heard it said that you are mad. And now you yourself bring me proof of it."

"If such is my reputation, it is as a result of your own efforts."

Hobbs sipped his wine. "Are you claiming that I have driven you to madness?"

"I refer to your attack upon my person and good name, sir. Which shall not go unrequited."

"Is that so?"

"No one attacks me with impunity."

"Interesting motto for a writer whose renown, small though it be, is founded upon his attacks of writers far more successful."

"We can perhaps discuss literary criticism at another time. For now I offer you a gift. I offer you the opportunity to do the manly and honorable thing."

Hearing this, Hobbs turned to face him. With his back to the window he stood in his own shadow, face dark, eyes unknowable. He aimed a finger in Poe's direction. "I have but one question before I call for your ejection from this gentleman's club. Where is my daughter?"

At this Poe smiled. "I can only assume that she is where she best needs be. Where dissembling is not the order of the day."

"A single word from me and you will find yourself in the Bloomingdale Asylum."

"I am a native of the madhouse, sir, remember? And therefore well familiar with its many rooms."

"I daresay I know of a room or two in which you will not feel yourself at home."

"Perhaps you have not yet recognized the advantage of my situation over yours. When one has nothing to lose, one has nothing to fear."

If Hobbs intended to wither him with a look, he was unsuccessful. Finally Hobbs crossed the room to him. He raised one foot to the cushion of the chair nearest Poe, rested an elbow on his knee, and assumed a position of amused insouciance.

"What I wonder is this," Hobbs said. "Precisely what do you propose to do with this theory of yours?"

"It is no theory, sir."

Hobbs waved his wine glass through the air as if shooing a mosquito toward the door. "Look closely, Mr. Poe. Where is the evidence of these crimes? Where are the witnesses to corroborate your claim?"

"I can produce one of them," Poe said.

"You cannot."

"Her name is Adelia Blaine."

"A name like any other to me. A figment of your imagination, Poe?"

"I failed to inquire what name you knew her by. When next we meet, I shall not be so remiss."

"When next you meet. Be careful lest you weave a tale so tangled you find yourself stumbling over it."

"She still wears the angel brooch you gave her, sir. Identical to the one you gave Mary Rogers. In addition to the five dollars paid each girl for their liaisons. At which time your endearments for them were murmured to the name of Leecie."

Hobbs drew a slow deep breath through his nostrils. He exhaled just as deliberately, lips puckered. His face, animated only by a repetitious blink, bore the rigidity of a chess master who has returned to the board to find his king exposed, with naught to defend him but a puny pawn four moves away.

It was not long before Hobbs's features softened. It was merely a game after all. He seemed almost happy to concede defeat.

"You say you came here looking for candor," Hobbs finally said. "Very well, sir. We will speak man to man. As one admirer of feminine youth to another."

"I am faithful to my marriage vows, sir."

"Yes yes, of course you are. In any case. As to Mary Rogers. Our relationship, as you have rightly ascertained, was one of mutual consent. And it was she, sir—*she*, not I—who suggested the addition of a third party. A friend of hers, of whom she was exceedingly fond. I knew her only as Amanda. And that arrangement, Edgar, was not long-lived. The girl intuited, I suppose, that I, at least, was not a devotee of *poly-eros* and preferred a simpler and more conventional arrangement. And so, she disappeared. Neither Miss Rogers nor I ever saw or heard from her again."

"You misunderstand my motives, Mr. Hobbs. I did not call on you here to take your confession. I came to rectify the harm done to the good name of your future son-in-law, a man over whom you exerted undue influence."

"Mr. Andrews has been and will be well compensated for his loyalty."

"The situation requires a more public assumption of responsibility."

"You truly are mad, Edgar." He laughed for a moment. Then, "And how would you have this assumption made public? There is not a newspaper in the state that would print such a story. Not only because of the indelicacies involved, but because you attach to them the name of Johnston Hobbs. So tell me this: what is it you hope to befall me? And for what crime? A crime of which no one has accused me except for you, a known drunkard, and your alleged confederate, a whore. Can you believe for a single moment that any reasonable person will credit such a claim?"

"I think you overestimate the readiness of the populace to approve of your behavior."

"The populace will approve of whatever is in their best interests. The Croton Water Project is in their best interests, sir, and Johnston Hobbs *is* the Croton Water Project. A few years hence, this city will be transformed by the flow of Croton water. And from that day forward, every time a fire is extinguished, every time a fountain glitters in the summer sun, every time a mother hands a glass of sweet clear water to her child, it is my name, sir, *my* name, that will be remembered. Do you think the name of Mary Rogers will be uttered with such reverence? Or the name of a bitter and insignificant writer who cannot afford even a pair of decent shoes?"

To this Poe had no argument. He had long ago come to the opinion that if indeed man was the highest of the animals, he had risen to that state by virtue of being the lowest and most vile creature.

Hobbs seized upon the silence. "I see by your expression that my point is well taken." His voice was calmer now, almost placatory. He swished the remaining drops of wine around the bottom of his glass, then raised the glass to his lips and drained it. He looked at the crystal facets for a moment, turned them in the light until a tiny arc of rainbow colors formed and was cast atop Poe's hand.

He nodded toward the rainbow, and Poe looked down and saw it there. When he looked up again, Hobbs was smiling.

"You say that you have come here to offer me an opportunity, Edgar. And now, I shall return the favor." He laid the glass on its side in an ashtray.

"You are a moral man, that much is clear. Unfortunately there is small room for a stringent morality in the economic matters that govern this island. What passes for moral and right behavior in my circles is recognized as a rather arbitrary stricture. Necessary for the control of the general populace, but narrow and confining for those whose kismet requires greater freedom of movement. As does your own. This is not to suggest that I am a wholly one-sided individual. My interests in art and philosophy are kept distinct from my business interests, it's true, but they are no less real. I am as intrigued by the numinous as you are. And so, a proposition.

"I propose, sir, to appoint you the guardian of my soul."

Poe's response was the cocking of an eyebrow.

Hobbs laughed as if they were old chums, and even leaned forward to slap him on the knee. "A magazine of your own!" Hobbs whispered. "Think of it, man. To be *the* arbiter of literary tastes on an island destined to become the very center of the world! To sculpt with your own fingers, your own words, the artistic and intellectual and moral heart of a nation."

Poe held Hobbs's fevered gaze for a long ten seconds, then averted his eyes to me, then down at last to his own hands. They had been empty for so long. They were empty still. But with a word from Johnston Hobbs, a nod, they could be filled to overflowing, and not with the ephemera of a rainbow shimmer, but with real gold. Gold to put an end once and for all to the myriad hungers that had so long assailed himself and his beloveds.

To fill his hands he needed to make but one small concession. Agree to forget about Mary Rogers. Agree to erase from his mind the image of her corpse, which, freed by his touch, had finally found its resting place ashore.

Did I doubt how Poe would respond? I did. In a short time I had come to know him well. I knew his vanity, his susceptibility to flattery, his need for retribution, his tendency to bear a grudge. I knew his craving for acceptance and respect. I knew his hatred of the city. I knew his moral outrage. I knew his greatness and his desperate desire to have it recognized. I knew his meanness and its desperate desire to have its way.

He inhaled deeply, but with a grimace that suggested the acrid sting of the air he breathed. He placed his hands on his knees, leaned forward as if to stand, and looked Hobbs square in the eye. "The authorities may not believe me, it's true. Nor will the confessional stutterings of your Josiah Tarr sway many opinions. But perhaps the word of Jacob Van Rensselaer will carry some weight among—"

"Van Rensselaer is a lickspittle and a sodomite! Is that whose side you choose?"

"This has nothing to do with sides—"

"Balls, you say!" Hobbs's face was bright with blood. When he spoke again, all but hissing, he had to lick his lips to grease the words. "I have heard a great deal about this contrary nature of yours, Poe. Have you no idea what you will bring down upon yourself?"

Poe stood. He straightened his trousers. "Is it contrariness to want what is right?"

"Right? There is no right, man. Right is the crutch of a crippled mind. There is no right, there is only progress or the lack of it. There is only growth or stagnation. Choose the latter and I warn you. . . . Choose the latter and you do so at your own peril."

"Good day, Mr. Hobbs." Poe started for the door.

"Don't be a damn fool, man!"

I had my hand on the crystal doorknob an instant before Poe reached out for it. I gave the knob a twist, and that was when the wine glass shattered against the wall just inches from Poe's head. Poe flinched. A moment later he plucked a fragment of glass off his cheek, but he did not turn around.

Hobbs's last words were like something seeping up from dark soil. "No one can beat me," he hissed.

Poe placed his hand atop mine and turned the knob and guided me out the door.

44

The walk from Hobbs's club to Van Rensselaer's office was not a long one, but Poe seemed in no hurry to get there. He must have viewed Van Rensselaer in a different light now, as I did, a man just as capable of murder as Hobbs, just as ready to destroy others in pursuit of his own needs. To enlist the help of one in bringing down the other . . . it was like using a porcupine to beat a cobra to death, or vice versa. In either case you were not likely to stroll away unscathed.

"What is it you miss from your old life?" Poe asked me as we walked. He was constantly surprising me with these non sequiturs, these notions out of nowhere. "Is there anything you miss?"

"A couple of friends, I guess. Boys my age. Not really friends but . . . fellas I knew."

Poe nodded. "I miss my manuscripts. I miss the paper and pen. The quietude of my own thoughts. I miss that life as if it were taken from me ten years ago, and not but one week past."

He laughed softly then. "The peculiar thing is, they are of small value to anyone else. One dollar . . . three dollars . . . at the most they might garner four dollars each. Four dollars for a full month's work." He shook his head. "All that work. More chaff than wheat. To labor half one's life and produce only that—barely enough wheat for a small and bitter loaf."

It is thoughts like these that destroy men. Unless they are blessed with a perversity of spirit, as was Poe. A writer of Poe's ilk sees in his toil not the grain of wheat itself but the spirit of the wheat, a spirit that dwells inside the chaff as well. To a true writer, and Poe was nothing if not the truest of the true, principle will always be more nourishing than bread, no matter how much butter and meat you pile on. It is a kind of perversity, yes, a disdain of or even contempt for what most of the world knows as real. Thank heaven for men and women so flawed.

THIS TIME there was no guard stationed outside the Merchants' Exchange building. We strode into the central hall, and there amidst the echoing footsteps and the hollow reverberations of a hundred voices I pointed up to the mezzanine and singled out the door to Van Rensselaer's office. Without hesitation but with a dogged resolve Poe went to the stairs and climbed and I followed silently behind.

The door to the anteroom was open but the room was unoccupied. Poe went straight to the door I pointed out as Van Rensselaer's and tried the knob but the door was locked. He rapped on the door with his knuckles, rapped a second time, and having received no response whatsoever he put his mouth close to the wood, to the crack between door and frame, and spoke clearly.

"The matter is finished," Poe said through the door.

There was no answer from inside the room, no sound at all, yet I felt Van Rensselaer's presence as surely as Poe felt it, a holding of breath, a damming back.

Poe pounded on the door with his fist. "Would you rather I go elsewhere?" he demanded. "Would you rather I take my information, all of it, to the Boston press?"

Almost immediately there was a scuffling sound from the other side of the door, agitation, hurry, a chair being moved. This was followed by ten seconds more of silence. Then the lock clicked and the knob turned and the door came slowly open. Glendinning stood there on the threshold, his face a blank wall, as expressionless as granite. (I could not help but look to his fists, those wondrous fists, quiet now, open, such miracles of destruction.)

He gazed steadily at Poe, then looked at me by his side, looked to see that the anteroom was otherwise empty. He then strode past Poe to the anteroom door and pulled it shut and turned the lock. He came back to stand to the side of the door to Van Rensselaer's office, and there held out his hand, then turned it palm up as a signal that we should enter. He followed us inside and closed that door as well.

The man himself sat in a windowless corner behind a plain wooden desk, looking for all the world like a pious deacon in a black suit and calfskin gloves. Other than the desk, a brass floor lamp, and an extra chair positioned to face Van Rensselaer from some six feet away, the room was bare. It gave off an odor of lye so strong that it stung my eyes and burned my nostrils.

Van Rensselaer nodded toward the empty chair. "Have a seat, Mr. Poe. Make yourself comfortable."

Poe remained standing behind the chair. "Comfort is precluded by the subject of my visit."

"Life itself is uncomfortable. Sit, sir. If you will."

And so Poe sat and wove his tale. To my ears he spoke with too much concision and with insufficient oratory, providing for Van Rensselaer what amounted to a bloodless summation of our work, the conclusions we had reached, conclusions we thought irrefutable.

I could almost feel Van Rensselaer's heartbeat quicken as his imagination filled in those details that Poe, in his sense of delicacy, had glossed over; I could certainly see the excitement in Van Rensselaer's eyes. "It was at his own hands then?" he said. "You are sure of this—she died at his own hands?"

"Lieutenant Andrews is convinced of it."

"Very good, very good." He sat there tapping his fingers against the edge of the desk, a repetitious thud muted by the gloves he wore, a stingy and effeminate gesture. "Very very very good, sir."

He thought to himself for a while. Then said, "This barman, however. I am concerned about this barman. Why would he direct you to Miss Blaine. What would he gain by the betrayal of his sweetheart?"

"Miss Blaine is . . . in hiding. She has disappeared from all she knew, including him, without word of her current whereabouts. I suspect that he believes, though erroneously, that Hobbs is behind her disappearance."

"And yet you managed to find her."

"I did."

"I would like very much to speak with her. To send Glendinning—"

"It isn't possible."

"You protect a whore, Mr. Poe?"

"From a murderer? Yes."

"I can provide better protection from Hobbs than you, sir."

"And who will protect her from the protector?"

The blood that rose in Van Rensselaer's cheeks looked unnatural there, nothing so common as a blush, but venomous, unhealthy for all concerned. "Are you making an accusation against me as well?"

Poe said nothing for a moment, then turned to face Glendinning.

"The watchman I will allow as an accidental death. Or necessary. In any case he needed to be subdued. In any case, for that, I thank you for your intervention."

Van Rensselaer said, "As well you should. In fact you have more for which to thank Glendinning than you might know."

Poe turned to him again. "I know enough, sir. I know, for example, that the man I met at the Velsor Club, Hobbs's witness, the man who might have testified as to the lieutenant's relationship with Mary Rogers, I know that man ended up with his throat split open."

"I have no knowledge of his individual."

"Or of the Bank of New York watchman who killed him?"

Van Rensselaer said nothing. His hands were still, eight fingertips perched on the edge of the desk, his thumb tips touching.

Poe continued. "The very same watchman who was stationed outside this very same building the last time I attempted entry here."

Van Rensselaer did not even blink. Nor did Poe. Half a minute passed. Finally Van Rensselaer drew his hands away from the desk, slowly, almost morbidly slowly, and rested both hands atop his thighs. Without moving his head he looked to Glendinnning.

Glendinning came forward then and stood beside Poe's chair. He removed a wallet from inside his suit coat and opened the wallet and lifted out a two-inch stack of banknotes and placed them on the arm of the chair.

Now it was Poe's turn to remain motionless. If he moved at all it was only to look sideways down at the money, to glance at it as something foul or dangerous, something one dare not look at directly.

Van Rensselaer said, "The paper is good, Mr. Poe. If you wish, you can exchange it for gold downstairs."

Poe leaned forward with a slowness to match Van Rensselaer's and put his hands on the arms of the chair so as to push himself forward even more. In doing so his elbow knocked the banknotes to the floor. He did not watch them fall but said, "You are a panel thief, sir. You hid beneath the bed of Mary Rogers, you employed her as a prostitute to procure the information—"

Glendinning dropped a hand onto Poe's shoulder. I flinched.

Van Rensselaer held up a gloved hand to Glendinning.

And Glendinning lifted his hand away.

Van Rensselaer tried a smile then, but it did not seem to fit his face.

Very softly he said, "You were rescued twice from imminent danger, Mr. Poe. Have you forgotten that?"

"I forget nothing," Poe said. Whether it had been the money, or Glendinning's touch, or the insult of not being treated with absolute candor, he was angry now, he was shaking with anger. He pushed himself to his feet. *"Nothing."*

Van Rensselaer held fast to his fraudulent smile. "Nor do I."

Poe turned on his heels and strode to the door and seized the knob, then yanked open the door and marched into the anteroom.He must have sensed my movements in Van Rensselaer's office, however, for my hand had not yet touched the banknotes when he turned and barked at me, "Augie! You will *not.*"

And so I backed away empty-handed; I crept backward toward the office door, momentarily unable to lift my eyes from those banknotes scattered over the floor like leaves shaken from the money tree. When I did look up, just before stepping into the anteroom, it was to take one last glance at Van Rensselaer in the far corner, rigid in his chair, calfskin gloves gripping the desk, his smile as sharp as a dagger.

45

NOTHING COULD keep Poe from Fordham now. I kept pace with his gallop for the first quarter-mile, but all the way the gold eagle in my pocket kept slapping against my leg, begging, *Spend me! Spend me!* Perhaps it had something to do with all that money I had been unable to grab in Van Rensselaer's office, but whatever the reason, my earlier inclination to hoard was being expelled with every huff and puff. *Money does not last, enjoy me while you can!* I finally halted to listen more closely to the eagle's song.

Poe looked back at me and I waved him on. "I'll catch up! Don't wait for me!" It was all the assurance he needed to leave me behind.

The next few hours were the best of my life, and the best for a good many years afterward. Poe was not yet as far north as Bleecker when the cab I had hired pulled alongside him. "Care to ride awhile?" I asked, like a smug little potentate. On my lap sat a cake box. More packages were stuffed beneath my legs.

Poe, red-faced and breathless, perspiring like a fat man in a Turkish bath, began, almost, to giggle. He climbed up beside me and slapped me on the knee and we both set to giggling in earnest. It was a rare and delicious feeling we shared, to be so stupid with relief.

The joy of our homecoming (of Poe's homecoming; I was but an addendum) gilded the remainder of that day and night like a page from an illuminated book. I was passed from one set of feminine arms to another and even spent several jarring minutes bouncing on the knees of Mrs. Curran. I was petted and hugged and stroked so frequently that by nightfall I felt my skin glowing from all the polish.

We feasted on the delicacies I had brought and on others from Mrs.

Curran's cupboards, and we feasted on each other's smiles and scents. The women, able at last to let go of their anxieties, to admit their exhaustion, retired to their beds not long after nightfall. But Poe and I found ourselves too enlivened for sleep. We sat together on the side porch where we could watch the sliver of moon make its way up the sky. He held Asmodaios and Aristotle, I cradled General Tom. The profound sense of fraternity I experienced in his company that night, as soldiers who had weathered a terrible battle side by side—I have not before nor since felt such comfort in being a creature of this earth.

I did not at the time understand the attraction that drew me to Poe, did not understand it for the longest of times. In the years since, however, I have watched his reputation as a writer grow large and have seen his ratio of admirers to detractors reverse itself from those bleak days, and I think I have a better notion now of the quality in Poe that speaks to us. We are drawn by his darkness. Because darkness is beguiling, it whispers and beckons to our most primitive selves. By which I mean not the base or animalistic but the ancient, primordial—the elemental. Such darkness is exciting, it enlivens the mundane and suggests exotic possibilities. And only in darkness, only in darkness complete and total to all the senses, a darkness impermeable, only in anticipation of this finality can we derive our surest hope for peace.

I asked quietly, "What's going to happen to Hobbs over this?"

He watched the moon and smoked his pipe. Then, "Nothing ostentatious, to be sure."

"He won't be arrested?"

"He owns City Hall," Poe said, "he and his cronies."

"You mean he'll be allowed to get away with what he done? Won't nothing happen to him at all?"

"Something will," he said. "Something will. In time."

He knew a fact that had not yet occurred to me, and he was drawing his comfort from it, his vindication. I on the other hand had to content myself with the purr of General Tom, the sibilance of smoke being sucked through Poe's pipe, the long deep darkness, and the tiny slice of moon.

For that night, at least, it was sufficient.

WE REMAINED at Mrs. Curran's farm for two more days. Each morning after breakfast Poe asked if I would care to join him in a stroll, and we walked as far as the East River, leisurely, as if that were not in fact Poe's goal all along. Once there we stood about pretending to be purposeless until a ferry arrived and on it a boy hawking the city's papers.

"As long as we're here," Poe then said, "I might as well see what's happening in town."

And finally, on the second morning, the news he had been waiting for was delivered. The first article appeared on page four, the second on page ten.

Gotham is saddened this day to be bidding adieu to one of the most favored of its favorite families. Mr. and Mrs. Johnston Hobbs have announced that they have taken a cabin on the SS *Josephine*, which will be departing for the French port of Bayonne at the stroke of midnight this Friday evening.

According to Mrs. Hobbs the couple expects to travel by coach throughout southern France during the remainder of the summer and fall, enjoying at this most pleasant time of year the splendors of Marseilles and Nice, to name just two stops along their itinerary, before taking up residence in Tuscany for a Mediterranean winter.

As to Mr. Hobbs's many civic interests, most notably the Croton Water Project, he has with a mixture of emotions turned over all authority to the Common Council, who will be aided in their decision-making by Jacob Van Rensselaer, named yesterday by Hobbs as the new chairman of the Croton Aqueduct Commission. Mr. Hobbs further wishes it be known that he has complete and total confidence that these two entities will continue to see the project through to the betterment of us all.

Mrs. Hobbs could not say with any specificity when she and her husband might return to our environs, but suggested that a change of climate was what both she and her husband now crave, each being depleted of energies from their many years of unstinting social and civic service. To this we can only say Bravo and Bon Voyage, and wish them both Godspeed and an expeditious return to the bosom of a grateful city.

The second article was far less wistful in its prose. It did not mention Poe's name but it was about him all the same.

High Constable Hays reported yesterday that all investigations into the death of the cigar-girl Mary Rogers have been concluded. The constabulary is now quite satisfied that the young lady's demise was brought about by accidental means, namely that while walking alone along the banks of the Hudson River she slipped into the water and was drowned.

This, then, was Van Rensselaer's solution. Hobbs would be banished to the splendors of Europe. As for Poe, all intimation that he had had a hand in Mary Rogers's death was wiped away.

"Looks like Van Ren ain't such a bad sort after all," I observed.

Poe lowered his chin nearly to his chest and looked at me askance. "If he has done me any good, it was not out of goodness. He wants no more attention paid to the girl's death, that's all. My vindication is a necessary adjunct."

The next morning was a slow one, subdued, gray, not threatening rain but not allowing much sunshine either. We lingered over breakfast, took our time cleaning up, took our time packing. I was sent to a neighboring farm to hire a man with a wagon to take us where nobody wished to go, back to the cottage off Bloomingdale Road, closer to the city in which Poe would still have to make his living.

And the sooner the better. On the previous afternoon I had voiced an opinion that we might be better advised to stay with Mrs. Curran awhile longer. She was eager to have us, and Mrs. Clemm and Sissie were eager to abide. But Poe insisted that the family move at once. He was in a hurry, I think, to validate himself in their eyes as a capable provider. And in his own eyes as a man who would not run and hide.

That is why his behavior once we were back at the cottage struck me as so odd, so contradictory. He came to the door carrying some small package, opened the door and looked inside, and then released the mightiest of sighs and turned and slouched onto his wicker chair on the porch. There he remained while the rest of us unloaded the wagon and dismissed the driver.

His behavior angered me, this sudden loss of all initiative. When I spoke to him he merely grunted in reply.

"What's made you so worthless all of a sudden?" I asked.

He would not even turn his head to look at me.

I reasoned as a child then that he was upset with me for some reason, because I would again be taking up precious space in his cramped cottage, or because I had somehow usurped his manhood by arriving at Mrs. Curran's loaded down with packages when he had none. In any case I blamed myself, thought him fed up with my presence, and after the few belongings were returned to the cottage I said to Mrs. Clemm, as blithely as I knew how, "Well, that's done. Time for me to be heading back to the Newsboys', I guess."

Because we were in the kitchen at the time, not far from the front door, she drew me closer to the opposite wall and leaned close to me when she spoke. "Would you consider staying for a while?" she asked in a voice not much above a whisper. "Another day or so?"

She had looked once or twice at the open door when she spoke. I now did the same. "I think he's gotten tired of having me around."

"That's not it at all," she said. She stroked the back of my head, and seemed, to my eyes, on the verge of tears.

"It's just the way he gets at times. I can see it coming on him now. And I think it might do him some good to have you here. It might do us all some good."

"What is it you see?"

"It comes over him from time to time. A shadowy kind of thing. An eclipse of his spirit. Because he tries so hard, you see, and never seems to get anywhere. His father had it too, his real father, the one who disappeared on him. It's not his fault, Augie, so you must not think ill of him for it. He cannot help its approach. It comes over him sometimes like a great black bird and there seems little he can do to hold it at bay."

"A sadness?" I asked.

"More than that, deeper than that. He gets, sometimes, so that the thing he wants most in life is to cease all thought and being."

"He wants to be dead?"

"More, more than that. He wants to have never been."

46

FOR TWO days afterward he wore his darkness like a woolen cloak but-
toned tight around his shoulders. No word or gesture could bring him
out of it. His gaze remained unfocused, weary of seeing, and drifted past
each one of us with small glimmer of recognition.

I could not fathom his disposition. Had he not accomplished what he
had set out to do? Should he not instead be exultant?

Mrs. Clemm explained it to me. "It is because we are back to nothing," she said. "Yes, he has a few dollars in his pocket now, but in fact we
are worse off than ever. Because his reputation has been stained with lies.
But that, Augie, is just the outer reason. There must be inner reasons too,
which none of us can know. We can only take care of him until the better
part of this cloud passes over."

She made it known that I was not to disturb him in his brooding.
Leave him to his darkened bedroom at whatever hour he retreated there.
Leave him to his mornings huddled on the porch, his short walks down
to the mouth of the lane. Leave him to stand there alone for the better part
of an hour, glaring, seething, his heart boiling over with a rage even he did
not understand. And when the rage grew cold, reducing him once again
to an emptiness, leave him to his exhausted sleep, his brief annihilation.

I was not to speak to him unless he asked something of me. My job
was simply to keep an eye on him. Follow discreetly when he wandered
away from the cottage.

Be there as he courted madness, this was what she implied. So that I
might pull him back, if necessary, from the brink of the abyss into which
he gazed so longingly. As if I would know how to do so. As if any of us
would.

In the meantime Virginia took up the broom and dust cloth as best she could. She tired easily and often lost herself in the middle of a task, drifting off into the ether of her own troubled thoughts. From time to time she sang something to him in their bedroom. Other times they sat side by side and held hands and quietly wept.

In the mornings, soon after her usual chores of breakfast and cleaning, Mrs. Clemm left the house for several hours. She had dragged a battered portmanteau up from the basement and filled it with Poe's manuscripts. Poe, watching from his rocker, did nothing to arrest her, but said only, "There's a new one in the bedroom."

The manuscripts of his poems and tales and essays were carried by her into town and peddled from door to door. Equipped with a list of names and addresses from one of his notebooks, she called on every editor in Gotham who might be inclined to purchase his work. It was a remarkable sight to watch her marching out the cottage door with suitcase in hand, and to know what she was up to, this woman as big as a man, homely, work roughened, but magisterial in her determination, off to importune the nation's leading editors and publishers to exchange a few dollars for her son-in-law's words.

Had she been successful at this even once, had she managed to place a single poem, Poe's mood would no doubt have brightened immediately. A picayune for a couplet would have been like a strong rope tossed into his miasma, and he would have scurried, I am sure of it, to pull himself from the muck.

A writer, you see, is fashioned less of flesh and bone than he is of faith—faith in himself, in his own ability to create something of worth. But faith by its nature is a slippery thing, slick and insubstantial, and each time it slides away, it is harder to regrasp; it separates like mercury and rolls off in all directions. And if it slides away often enough, then someday, no matter how desperately he reaches out, his hands will come back empty. In that instance there is no writer left. There is only the empty container, hollow and brittle as an empty glass, a vessel now so fragile that it can be shattered by as little as a high-pitched sound.

Come Friday, midmorning, he walked as usual to the end of the lane. But this time instead of standing there with hands stuffed in his pockets, as slack as a scarecrow, he stretched his arms out at the shoulders, rolled his arms, and stretched his spine. Instead of staring at the ground, he looked into the sky, a perfect summer's sky so smooth and robin's-egg blue. He was coming out of his ennui, crawling up from the pit.

It was such an agreeable sight to behold that while he performed those few minutes of exercise I closed the distance between us, did not hang back my thirty yards but went to his side and, infused with hero worship once more, emulated his movements. He looked at me and grinned.

"Vegetables, fruit, water, and bread," he began, quoting Sylvester Graham's recipe for fitness.

I finished the quote. "Fresh air and hard work stand a man in good stead."

We exercised a while longer. "Good," he finally said. "Good enough for now."

It was not long after that when we heard Mrs. Clemm trudging up behind us with the portmanteau. Poe reached out and took the suitcase from her hand. "Not today, dearest," he told her. "Come Monday I will take up the lance anew."

Her eyes lit up, her broad face beamed. "I won't say no," she told him. "Who would ever have thought a stack of words could be so heavy?"

"Think of the ones I carry in here!" he teased, and tapped the side of his head.

Before she returned to the cottage, there came the cloppity rumble of a conveyance approaching, and we all turned to watch it coming up Bloomingdale Road, heading north, a Dearborn pulled by a chestnut bay. Poe raised his hand as the vehicle passed to wave at the driver, a stout little bearded man who answered with a curt nod.

"I watched that same wagon go past last evening," Poe said.

Mrs. Clemm mused, "Wouldn't it be lovely to ride about in one of them all day?"

The Dearborn was a mere box of a wagon, nothing fancy, a covered shell with curtains enclosing the sides. But for Mrs. Clemm it must have represented the highest luxury she might aspire to.

"And someday you shall," he told her. Arm in arm they returned to the cottage.

The rest of the day was passed in, if not high spirits, at least the hope of higher spirits to come. Poe retired to his bedroom but not to brood; he sat with a tablet of paper on his lap and made notes for himself, laid plans. His ambition was returning, a low fire yet but warming. By Monday he would once again be ablaze with it.

After our five o'clock supper he was his old self again. "Fried bananas," he said out of the blue.

Virginia clapped her hands together. "Oh yes!" she cried.

To me Poe said, "Master Dubbins? Shall we have fried bananas or shall we not?"

"It's okay with me if we do."

He rose from his chair, went to a cupboard, and took out the small pail used for carrying beer from the local grogshop. He came back to hand me a shilling, a dime, and some pennies.

"There's a greengrocer on Bloomingdale Road at Sixtieth," he said. "I would be pleased if you would go there for me, take the horsecar if you can find one, and bring us back a bunch of bananas. As many as you can buy. They must be ripe but not overly soft. In the meantime I will fetch a drink for my songbird, who perhaps will serenade us later as we feast."

I took the coins but cut a glance at Mrs. Clemm. She smiled and told me with a small nod that he was all right now, this was not some odd brachiation in an unpredictable temperament.

And so down the lane we went once more, Poe swinging the beer bucket at his side. At the mouth of the lane, where I would turn right and he left, we saw again the same Dearborn that had passed us earlier, but this time stationary, pulled to the side of the road some forty yards north.

"In all likelihood a broken axle," Poe said. "Those damnable cobblestones in town, and out here nothing but ruts and bottomless pits. They'll break a man's bones if he doesn't tread carefully."

"You'd think whoever owns that rig would unharness the horse," I said. "Why walk for help when you can ride?"

Poe replied that he would survey the animal for signs of distress before returning home, and we parted company. In half an hour I was back at the cottage, out of breath from having trotted most of the way with a bunch of bananas under my arm.

Mrs. Clemm had a good fire going on the stove and had set out the skillet and sugar and fetched the butter from the springhouse. I laid the bananas on the table and then produced from my pocket a small paper sack. "Look what else the grocer gave me," I said.

She opened the bag and peered inside. "Cinnamon!" she exclaimed.

"He told me I had to have it, wouldn't take no for an answer. Said you couldn't make fried bananas without it."

Mrs. Clemm's eyes were dancing. "Won't Eddie be pleased!" she said. "Have you ever tried fried bananas, Augie?"

"No, ma'am, I haven't."

"Eddie makes them with so much caramel sauce you'd think we were as rich as maharajas."

I nearly swooned at the thought of so much sweetness, coming, as it would, hard on the heels of such bitterness.

Virginia now joined us in the kitchen. "On Thanksgiving he likes to have it over bread pudding. That's heaven too."

"I never tasted bread pudding neither," I said.

"Then you shall," said Mrs. Clemm. "By Sunday at the latest."

We were all three of us so anxious for the treat that we peeled and sliced the bananas and for a good while sat there staring at them as we awaited Poe's return.

Finally the wood in the stove had burned down and the bananas were turning brown on the plate. Mrs. Clemm by this time had gone to stand at the door. Virginia had moved to the sofa and was sitting with her head laid back, eyes closed. She, finally, was the one to break our silence. She turned to me and smiled sweetly.

"Will you run out the lane for me, Augie? And remind Mr. Poe that we are waiting here at home for him?"

I knew full well what sometimes happens to men when they visit a grogshop. "What if he ain't ready to come back with me yet?"

"Then you will do whatever you must, won't you? Whatever you must to bring him home to us."

I nodded and stood and headed for the door, slow of movement at first, uncertain, afraid of how Poe might react when he turned from his glass to see me standing there beside him. Afraid too of the way Poe might look at me then, a black look I had imagined gone with my mother, the curl of her mouth, the way her hand would come up, almost indifferently, to knock me aside.

But Virginia had asked this of me, and I would not fail her. Out into the dooryard I went, the summer night in full dusk. At the end of the yard I broke into a trot. Then at the end of the lane I turned toward the grogshop and immediately sensed some inconsistency in the air, something amiss in the balance of this crepuscular night, and I came to a standstill, stood motionless for a moment, then made a quarter turn, looked north, and understood.

The Dearborn was gone. I walked slowly toward where it should have been. Until finally I recognized the two dark objects lying on the ground. The first, innocuous, a bushelful of horse dung. But a few feet beyond it, the thing that gripped my heart—a small tin pail, overturned, and an ebony sheen of beer-soaked earth.

47

"IT HAD to've been Hobbs's doing," I argued. "Who else could it've been?"

Virginia said, "A man like Hobbs would not ride in a Dearborn. Was it not a Victoria that brought his daughter here?"

"I'm not saying he was in there himself. He don't get his own hands dirty. Besides, if he wanted to cart somebody off without being suspected, he wouldn't use his own wagon, now, would he?"

She could not bring herself to imagine that her husband had been abducted. "You're certain he is not in the grogshop yet?"

"The barman said he came in, he bought his beer, he left. Never even had a glass for himself. And now there's the empty pail, still wet. Right there before your eyes."

Still she shook her head. "An admirer, then. Who prevailed upon him for a ride in the country and a bit of conversation. Surely it cannot be—"

Mrs. Clemm interrupted. "Surely he would not toss away a brimming pail."

"He will return home any minute now," Virginia said. "He would not worry us like this."

And so we sat. The fire in the stove died out. The bananas blackened and drew a speckling of tiny black fruit flies. Virginia fell asleep in Poe's rocker with his favorite shawl drawn around her. A half hour later she awoke coughing, a racking, glutinous, wrenching cough that was calmed finally by Mrs. Clemm's pounding on her back.

Virginia was exhausted by this, of course, and was soon tucked into bed.

Later her mother returned to stand awhile longer at the front door, gazing out into the darkness. "I wish you would eat those bananas," she told me. "I can't bear to have to throw them out."

"I'm not hungry now," I answered, though my belly was hollow with an old familiar ache.

We went out onto the porch and sat side by side on the deacon's bench. General Tom came and walked from one end of the porch to the other, looking for Poe. I patted my lap and the General leaped onto it and curled beneath my hand.

The night sky had clouded over, had gone from lavender to charcoal to a dull and uniform black. The moon was but a small and fuzzy slice of gray. We could see not a single star.

In time Mrs. Clemm admitted to herself what I already knew. "Something's happened to him."

It was the acknowledgment I had been waiting for. I leapt to my feet. "I'm going to town."

She sat motionless, hands clenched. "Where would you search?"

"Hobbs has got him somewhere."

"Where?"

"All I know is where to start looking. Where the shit begins."

Instead of admonishing me she stood and went into the house and checked on Virginia and a minute later came back onto the porch and eased shut the door. "Take me there," she said.

WE MADE decent time on the final leg of the trip by catching a ride in a drummer's wagon; of course I had to empty out my pockets before the driver would agree to take us aboard. But by all appearances we nevertheless arrived too late. The Hobbs mansion stood as black as a sealed tomb. We studied it from the street, disbelieving, as if we had fully expected to see Poe standing calmly behind a well-lit window, awaiting his rescue.

"Closed up tight," said Mrs. Clemm. "There's not a soul inside."

"Some animals prefer the darkness."

"Augie, the house is closed up. Their ship leaves for Europe at midnight tonight; isn't that what the newspaper said? Which means the Mr. and Mrs. are in their staterooms already."

"A man like Hobbs wouldn't just walk away without trying to even the score."

"No one is inside that house. We have come all this way for nothing."

I wasn't convinced. More accurately, I *was* convinced—convinced of the reliability of my suspicions. The house still felt alive to me, it gave off an emanation of inhabitancy, as peculiar as that might sound. I felt somebody still inside, left behind. The hackles of my neck had not lain down since first we spotted the building's hulking silhouette.

"I'm going to check around back," I said.

I left her standing there on Fifth Avenue, doing her best to appear inconspicuous as she paced beneath the gaslights. I ran quickly through the large side yard, as light on my feet as only a child can be. And there in the rear stood the carriage house, the same stonework and gabling as the mansion, a one-sixth version of the house.

It too was dark but as I crept closer I heard a horse nickering, and I followed that sound until I determined that the stables comprised the southern half of the carriage house. On a night like this there was bound to be a window open for ventilation, and I scoured the wall for evidence of one, discerned only a blank sameness, then crept to the eastern wall and found there the off-colored square, shutters folded open, the window eight feet off the ground.

From out the open window came a horsey scent and the smell of hay and the snuffling nickering sound that horses make. I raced back to the front corner of the mansion and kept close to the wall and went *Sssst! Sssst!* until Mrs. Clemm nervously joined me there.

"I need a boost," was all I told her, and was off again to the carriage house. I flinched with every heavy footfall that came thumping behind me.

When she stood beside me finally I pointed up to the stable window and whispered, "I need to have a look inside. If there's a chestnut bay in there, we'll at least know if we're on the right track or not."

I bent over then to unbuckle my brogans, because I did not want to leave filthy heel marks on Mrs. Clemm's shoulders. But she, for once in her life, was not meticulous. She seized me under the arms and with one swift movement raised me over her head and set me whomp atop her shoulders.

It was easy enough from that perch to haul myself inside. I dangled from the inside ledge as long as my arms would take it, getting my eyes accustomed to this even deeper darkness, then let go and dropped softly to a bare wooden floor.

I landed less than three feet from the Victoria that had brought Felicia Hobbs to Poe's door. Beside it sat a phaeton, a smaller carriage with a folding top. But no Dearborn.

Then to the stalls. Two horses, this much I could see at once. It took awhile longer to distinguish them. A roan mare. Another mare, black.

I felt my way along the wall until I came to a side door and unlatched it and tiptoed back to Mrs. Clemm; she was standing yet beneath the open window, staring up at it. She gasped when I tapped her on the arm.

"It's not there," I whispered. "Neither the wagon nor the horse."

"Then . . ." She turned to gaze at the house, that huge blank edifice, as if its only door had been forever closed to us now.

"I never expected to find that wagon here anyway," I said. "He hired somebody to do his dirty work. You know as well as me that he ain't—"

She put a finger to her lips and with her other hand turned me to face the mansion. Then she raised her arm and pointed a finger.

"I don't see nothing," I said.

"Close to the ground. There was a light passing by. It's gone now but I'm sure I saw it."

"Somebody in the cellar," I said.

We moved like a Siamese shadow to the rear of the house and found the window well and the small rectangular glass. I lay on my belly and put my face close to the glass and cupped my hands around my eyes. A minute later I sat back on my knees.

"Nothing," I said. "It's black as Hades in there."

"There was a light," she said.

I stood and walked a few feet back from the house and looked it over. The rear wall was a sheer face but the left side sported a small covered porch from whose roof I could easily scramble over the many dormers and gables. I had no doubt that I could find a way inside.

But first I scuffed my foot over the ground and kicked at any protuberances I felt.

Mrs. Clemm came and put a hand on my shoulder and whispered in my ear. "What in the world are you doing?"

"I need a rock or something hard. I'm probably going to have to break a window so as to get inside."

"Augie, no. That is more than I am willing—"

"You want to just sit here and wait until they find *him* in the Hudson?"

She reached into one of the deep pockets of her dress and brought forth an object and held it out to me. "Will this do?"

It was the pewter mug I had stolen from Hobbs's kitchen, the very one from which I had been plied with tea and gooseberry jam.

"What are you doing carrying this thing around?" I asked.

"I just grabbed it on my way out the door. In case we needed to defend ourselves."

At first I thought it a curious choice for a weapon, until I slipped my hand inside the curved handle and felt again the mug's solidity and heft. "Good for you," I said.

She hoisted me onto the porch roof and I scampered up onto the slates and then pulled myself to the narrow ledge outside a second-floor dormer. It was not at the rear of the house as I would have preferred, but neither did it face the street directly, and as long as I kept close to the building I would appear, even to someone as close as Mrs. Clemm, but a bump of darkness.

The window was latched. I peered through one of its twelve square panes of glass and saw only a cavern of pitch. Then pulled the pewter mug from beneath my blouse and knocked the base of the mug hard against the bottom corner pane and flinched at the brief chime of broken glass and held my breath and did not move until a long quarter-minute passed and there were no other sounds.

My arm snaked through the jagged opening then, feeling for the latch. While all the while I had to chuckle to myself, considering the irony of the situation. How many hundreds of times had I fantasized about breaking into a house like this one, of filling a sack with enough swag to keep me in tea and biscuits all the rest of my days. And now here I was doing precisely that, but not to steal a single shilling. I almost semed to be playing a joke on myself.

Finally my thumb found the window latch. Fingers straining, I tried to wiggle it loose. A splinter of glass stabbed the underside of my forearm. Then the latch broke free and with the heels of both hands I pushed hard on the casement and drove the window up.

The scent of the room washed out to me, the dry caged heat of the place. Then inside I went, crawling like a snake. Slithering headfirst to the floor. And then with a smile I climbed to my feet and stood there smiling. I wanted to turn to the window and shout down to Mrs. Clemm that I had made it inside, to exult in it, thumb my nose at Hobbs, but of course any celebration would be premature, might even jinx what remained to be done.

I wanted as well to move deliberately about this bedroom, wanted to whisk away the linen sheets that had been laid over all the furnishings, wanted to sprawl atop the gigantic four-poster bed, wriggle down deep into the feather mattress, run my hands up and down the damask draperies. I wanted to touch everything and leave my presence everywhere. I wanted to do less innocent things as well, wanted to wipe my shoes on the carpet and break things and steal and do the kinds of despicable acts so routine to the place where I used to live. I wanted to own this place, and because I could not, I wanted to defile it.

But I turned my mind again to Poe. Toward Poe and away from that small guttural voice of destruction. The open doorway. Out into the corridor. Creeping. Trying to glide from the ball of one foot to the other but flinching with every slow creak of a floorboard.

By the time I reached the bottom of the staircase I could see well enough to make out most every obstacle that might trip me up. Here too every piece of furniture had been draped with a linen sheet, and each stood out in a lighter shade of darkness, so that I seemed to be wending my way through a field of gray mounds, each of them larger and more sinister in the darkness than they would have been in daylight.

Because of this it took me several minutes to navigate through the foyer and into the kitchen without knocking anything over. The kitchen, though, was not enshrouded; no sheets had been laid here. I caught the scent of cold meat, congealed fat. The biting scent of snuff tobacco.

From the kitchen I crept to the pantry. There I unlocked the door and eased it open and stuck my head out beneath the porch roof.

"Sssst! Sssst! Sssst!"

Mrs. Clemm was there almost instantly, pushing past me like a moose cow through swamp grass, searching for her calf. "Where?" she whispered. "Which way now?"

I took her hand and led the way to the cellar door. It seemed to take us a lifetime to descend those narrow steps, down into the cool and musty basement. We had no matches or candle, no illumination of any kind, and so we felt our way along three-quarters blind, my left hand riding one wall, right hand riding the other, Mrs. Clemm's breath warm and close on the top of my head.

The hallway at the bottom of the stairs was long and not very wide; the floor was paved in brick. The doors to each of the rooms along the hallway were closed, the laundry room and pickling room, the curing room and servants' kitchen, the many other rooms we could not identify.

All told, we passed a dozen rooms before attaining the end wall, and for a moment thought ourselves tricked, stymied, until I leaned against that wall and felt it give a little. I bent at the knees and ran my hand along the wall until I felt the knot of rope that served as a door latch. I motioned Mrs. Clemm back a few steps and eased open the door.

A cool wet whoosh of deeper air, the scent of earth and mold. I put out a foot and felt for the first step and found not a step but an earthen floor that sloped away down a short narrow corridor. This tunnel was barely large enough for Mrs. Clemm, whose body was hot against my back, her hand gripping the waistband of my trousers.

Waiting at the bottom of the tunnel, as if too weak to ascend any farther, was a soft yellow glow. I felt for the pewter mug beneath my shirt and pulled it forth and gripped it like a club handle. I heard blood drumming in my temples and the shallow rasp of Mrs. Clemm's breath. I felt the collusion of every muscle and bone employed as I tried to set myself in motion.

And then a faint clanging sound. I froze in my tracks. Mrs. Clemm thudded into me. I put up a hand and hoped that she could see it. I cocked my head and listened. Another faint clang. A scraping sound. A sputtering of lamp light.

It was all we needed, it was everything. From that point on we both must have felt the same force seize and pull on us, a hand as strong as terror, as hot as rage, for without a word we were soon into that tunnel and moving along it and heading heedlessly down to its terminus.

48

THE TUNNEL was no more than thirty feet long. We had progressed barely a sixth of the way before Mrs. Clemm took me by the arm and held me in place while she squeezed to the front. She walked with her head bent low so as not to scrape the dirt ceiling. So fully did she fill the tunnel that I could see nothing before me but her backside. An oil lamp hanging from a hook driven into the end wall threw a weak yellow light over her shoulders.

Because of this I saw everything a few moments after she did, each of the small caves carved into the side walls, the first one on the right holding baskets of potatoes, yams, parsnips, and turnips, the first one on the left all manner of squash and pumpkins, onions and cabbages. The second on the right held only apples; the next, hams wrapped in waxed burlap and hanging from a rod above barrels filled, probably, with salted meats; the next cave lined with racks of bottled wine; the next, filled with demijohns and small casks. The rounded opening to each cave was no more than five feet high and four wide and another four deep. From each cave came a scent of bare earth, the cloying scent of dirt and rock.

It was the last pair of caves, though, dug not at right angles to the end wall, as were the previous ones, but on a sixty-degree slant on opposite sides of the oil lamp, it was these two caves, when we came close enough to glimpse a portion of their apertures, that brought Mrs. Clemm to a sudden halt. I bumped into her backside, then quickly poked my head under her arm so as to see what had brought her up short. I could glimpse approximately half the opening of each of the remaining caves.

The one on the left was partially sealed with brick, the first ten or twelve courses already in place, a pile of bricks remaining to be laid. More accurately, I suppose, sections of the top courses of a previously intact wall had been removed, for old mortar still clung to the bricks that lay in a pile.

And the person responsible for this endeavor, for dismantling and now reassembling the wall, was at this moment resting from his labors, taking a bit of snuff while sitting atop a stone inside the opposite cave. All but his huge feet and bony knees remained invisible behind the cave until he shifted forward and bent low to pick up the snuff pouch that had fallen off one knee. It was then his long face came into view, yellowed even more by the waxy light of the oil lamp, the gaunt cheeks and wolfish chin, the cadaverous tautness of his skin. He looked every bit as necrophagous in that position as he had while bending over my mother.

Mrs. Clemm cocked her head around to look at me, eyebrows raised in silent question. She knew nothing of this man but I knew everything, knew with a single glimpse of him that the cave he was resealing contained not hams or wines or turnips.

I jammed my finger at the partially sealed cave, jabbed it repeatedly and violently, and mouthed the word *Poe!* The truth of the situation dawned on Mrs. Clemm in a flash, a flash that all but exploded in her eyes. She covered the remaining distance in a bull-like charge, heedlessly forward straight to the cave on the left, where she thrust head and shoulders over the courses of brick and cried out, shrieked, and then spun on the man who was awkwardly scooting clear of the other cave in an effort to stand.

It was then I saw the dark stains all up and down his clothes, the splatter of dried blood on his hands, blackened further with dirt. A moment later Mrs. Clemm was on him, her hands flying at his face, her rage like a roar inside that tunnel.

The man's great height and long limbs did him no good here. Nor do I think he could have bested Mrs. Clemm inside a boxing ring, not even were she less provoked, for the man's movements were as stiff as his features and it was all he could do finally to shove her away from him, propel her backward and over the the built-up bricks and inside the cave with Poe.

With the wall demolished I could see him now; he lay on his side bound head to foot with rope, a rag tied over his mouth, a wide stain of black beneath his nose and covering his chin. Nor was he alone in the tomb; his intended decay would have increased by no more than a fourth the population of gray bones and rotted ropes already there. Including one poor soul who, judging from his bloated and gray appearance, had been entombed just weeks prior to Poe.

Without a glance in my direction Hobbs's man moved in on Mrs. Clemm. He picked up a brick in his right hand and raised it nearly to the ceiling and moved toward her. He had but a moment to turn toward the scuffling sound of my approach before I swung the pewter mug with all my might and caught him squarely on his wolfish chin. The effort not only spun me off my feet but dropped Hobbs's man to his knees, eyes vacant. He dropped the brick and lurched onto his hands.

I rolled over and crawled into the cave beside Mrs. Clemm, who was already pulling at Poe's ropes, crying "Eddie! Eddie, my Eddie!" as he lay there mumbling and rolling his head. She was too frantic to understand his message, so it was left to me to pull the rag out of his mouth so that he could speak.

"You mustn't pull, Muddy, please," he said, his voice weak but so surprisingly gentle, almost dreamy. "You will have to untie them, dearest."

She asked me to bring her the lamp and I rose to do so, only to be swung at by Hobbs's man. He was unsteady and unfocused and I had no trouble dodging his blow. I picked up the brick nearest me and heaved it at him but it missed his head and bounced off a shoulder. He howled and fell away from me, but would have come at me again had Mrs. Clemm not pulled me back and risen to take my place.

At the sight of her he turned and fled, hobbling, lurching up the tunnel.

I handed the lamp down to Mrs. Clemm and together we set to work on Poe's ropes, she at his wrists and me at his ankles. At one point I paused, my gaze seized by the swollen corpse not two feet away. His stench was sharp and ripe; I could see maggots in his ear.

"Fordyce," Poe said. "The missing councilman."

Mrs. Clemm put a hand to my cheek and turned me away.

Finally Poe was able to sit upright. He massaged his wrists, then rubbed the cobwebs and dirt off his face. Mrs. Clemm leaned close to brush the caked blood from beneath his nose and to scrutinize his face for other injuries.

It was then we heard the awful thud of a door slammed shut, a black and final sound I felt like a blow in the pit of my stomach.

As quickly as we could we crawled out of the cave and made our way in single file up the narrow dirt path of the tunnel. At the mouth of the tunnel we were all of us surprised when the door swung open after first Poe, then I, then Mrs. Clemm threw our weight against it. The door, which had no lock, had been propped shut with a small chest, but it was no match for Mrs. Clemm's broad shoulders.

We emerged into the larger hallway of the basement as if into freedom itself. I for one felt like dancing. And then came the second thud, clearer and even louder than the first. We realized in an instant that we were yet far from freedom. Hobbs's man had ascended the stairs into the kitchen. Our prison had been widened but we were no less trapped.

I raced through the basement and up the stairs ahead of the others. The door to the kitchen would not yield. I could tell from its solidity that, whether locked or barricaded, this one would not give way no matter how hard Mrs. Clemm pushed. And even if it did, would we open it to see Careys filling the doorway, this time with sword or even pistol in hand?

Poe, at the bottom of the stairs, called me away from the door. "He might be arming himself for an attack," Poe said. "We must find a better way out."

I hurried down to them. To Mrs. Clemm I said, "Maybe I can crawl out through that little window we saw."

"It's too small for even you. Look for the coal chute instead."

We found the coal bin after a few minutes of searching. It was filled to four feet high with shiny lumps of anthracite. Another few feet above this pile was a small square door, hinged at the top to swing inside, latched at the bottom. I undid the latch but still the door would not open.

"It must be latched on the outside as well," Poe said.

Mrs. Clemm seized the largest lump of coal she could hold in both hands and with a great heaving swing she crashed it squarely against the coal chute's door. Again and again she swung, until finally the hinge gave way. Now she slipped her fingers into the opening and pulled at the top of the door. She yanked at it until her hands were bloody. Then Poe put out a hand and moved her aside and, battered as he was, finished the job.

I climbed up and into the opening and managed to squirm outside without leaving too much skin behind. I wanted nothing at that moment but to lie there on the grass and breathe in the scent of the night, the sweet green wondrous fragrance of liberation. But Mrs. Clemm and Poe remained inside.

I ran to the side porch and crept onto it and peered in through the pantry door. The kitchen was well lit now, an oil lamp in the center of the table. Standing bent and vigilant to the side of the cellar door, his ear cocked for the sound of footsteps on the stairs, was Hobbs's man, a meat cleaver at the ready in his huge right hand.

I had no idea what to do. I knew that Mrs. Clemm and I had left the pantry door unlocked, but I was not so foolish as to believe that I could simply stroll inside and confront Hobbs's man face-to-face. He was not swift of movement, but apparently strong enough to have shanghaied Poe. Armed as he now was with a kitchen broadax, what could he do to a boy barely half his size?

My only choice was to outwit the man. Draw him outside somehow, set him in pursuit of me around the block, then circle back and turn the prisoners free before he could catch up. At the time it seemed a wonderful plan. Even foolproof. I was ten years old.

I hurried back to the coal chute and stuck my head inside and asked Mrs. Clemm to pass me up a couple of good-sized lumps of coal. As she did so she asked, "What are you up to?" but I did not answer; I merely grinned and arched my eyebrows.

Back to the side porch then, the coal cradled in my arms. I eased both lumps to the floor, then picked them up one at a time to heave through the pane of glass in the top half of the pantry door. The first lump shattered the pane completely; the second sailed through to bounce off crockery inside and set it ringing.

In answer to the noise I was making a dog not far away launched into a chorus of barking. Another dog joined in. By now I was off the porch and waiting in the yard for Hobbs's man to come flying out after me. But he did not appear.

I waited another quarter-minute, then approached the pantry door. By degrees I moved close enough to peer inside. The kitchen was empty. Had I frightened him away? Apparently so. I swung the door open and let it bang back against the wall. Still no sign of Careys. I entered with more confidence than caution. Into the kitchen, a quick glance to see that the way was clear, then straight for the cellar door.

I twisted the knob but the door would not open. The door was locked and the key had been removed. I turned away so as to scour the kitchen for the key and it was then I saw him, his great gangly form emerging to fill the open doorway on the far side of the kitchen, cleaver dangling at his side.

His mouth was stretched tight in a hard and grotesque smile. "You're about to lose that hand of yours," he said. He raised the cleaver to his shoulder and came toward me. With one long stride he cut the distance between us in half.

Nothing but the table kept him from reaching for me. And so I seized the only thing there available, the oil lamp, and holding it by the wire handle I swung it out wide and let go and sent it flying at his face. He twisted aside and the lamp smashed into the wall and the glass and oil exploded out in all directions. He stood there blinking for a moment, the right side of his face in flames, his right hand a torch.

An instant later he made a sound like a dying animal, an animal panicked by the scent of its own death, and staggering forward, he lurched into the table, driving it into me. I, so as not to be pinned against a wall, lifted it by the corner and shoved it with all my might, slamming it against him. Careys dropped the cleaver but continued lurching forward, half-blinded by pain, beating both hands against his face. I slipped to the inside of him, toward the other rooms, while he staggered headlong into the pantry. He was still aflame when he disappeared from view and went banging out the back door.

I retrieved the cleaver and hacked away at the basement door. By the time I had it open and called to Poe and Mrs. Clemm, by the time they decided to trust my voice and had ascended the stairs, the entire corner of the kitchen was in flames. A fog of gray smoke two feet thick blanketed the ceiling.

"This way quick," I said, and stepped into the pantry, and, on the verge of warning the others to keep an eye out for Careys, there met him creeping in, advancing in a stiff crouch. Never before had he so resembled Death himself. His face seemed half melted, blackened, and hairless. In his seared right hand he clutched a dagger. In his left, a short cudgel of stove wood. I smelled the reek of his burned flesh and saw his twisted grin and all I could think was that he had used that same dagger on my mother.

"You stinking rat bastard!" I screamed, and lunged toward him with the cleaver.

Poe jerked me back so violently that the cleaver flew from my hand and clattered to the floor. He then dragged me back into the kitchen and shoved me past the flaming wall and in a moment all three of us were racing for the front door.

But that door was locked as well, as we should have known it would be. And far too solid to ever yield to a battering from Mrs. Clemm's shoulder.

"You'll want this key," Careys said from behind us, croaking out of the corner of his mouth as he came lurching through the flames. The heavy key dangled from his left hand. Cocked in his right was the cleaver.

"The window upstairs!" I told them, and set off up the steps, leading the way. We thundered up the staircase with Careys lurching up behind us.

Down the hall we raced. "This way!" I cried, and led them into the darkened bedroom, Mrs. Clemm's breath as heavy now as the footsteps like hammer blows that were mounting the steps.

I slammed shut the bedroom door and took Mrs. Clemm by the arm and pulled her to the open window. "Climb out. And watch yourself on the broken glass."

As her legs were disappearing into the darkness I turned to Poe. "You'll have to help her down and off the roof."

"Go," Poe told me.

I pushed him toward the window. "I ain't tall enough to help her. I'll be right behind you."

"Go!" he shouted, and with that he shoved me ahead of him. Even as I ducked into the opening he kept his hand on the small of my back, urging me forward. Mrs. Clemm was by then inching her way down the sloping roof, scooting toward its edge, scraping forward on her heels and backside.

With my head out the window I did not hear Careys's heavy stride pounding down the hallway, but I heard the thunderous crack at the door as his foot kicked it open, and I felt Poe's hand fly off my back as he turned.

Had I at that instant dived headfirst out onto the pantry roof, there might have been time for Poe to follow. But I did not. Something compelled me to stop halfway out the window, to twist my body around and look back into the room.

Poe had turned to stand with his back to me, a shadow, a shield. Twelve feet beyond him, but closing that distance quickly, came Careys. Behind him the doorway was filled with a rose-colored light, smoke gray, flickering and alive. He looked huge, as did the kitchen cleaver still in his fist.

Poe put a hand out behind himself, probably feeling for the window ledge. Instead he felt me still blocking the only escape. He knew in that moment that he no longer had time to crawl out the window, knew that I, apparently paralyzed, was in danger myself. And so he charged. He lunged forward, head tucked into his neck, shoulders hunched, and rammed Careys in the midsection, wrapped his arms about the man's waist, and strove to drive him backward against the wall.

Careys was thin and stiff but as hard as forged steel. Even as he stumbled back, he raised his right hand, and in an awkward sideways chop slammed the flat side of the cleaver against Poe's skull. Poe dropped to the floor in a heap.

Careys looked up at me now and grinned. It was all I needed to break the paralysis. I leaped forward and pulled my legs out behind me and scrambled on my hands and toes down over the slates.

But I did not jump to the ground, did not join Mrs. Clemm already on the grass, standing there looking up at me with her arms outstretched. At the edge of the porch roof I looked back over a shoulder; somehow I knew he would not follow. He stood framed in the window for just a moment, smiling and nodding his head at me, acknowledging, I thought, my cowardice. Then he ducked back inside.

All of the air went out of the night. Something inside me collapsed. I felt deflated, an empty skin. Because now Poe was doomed. I had abandoned him. I and I alone had brought him to this impasse, I with my encouragement, my greed, my loose talk in Hobbs's kitchen. From the moment I had met Poe I had been angling him toward this fate, just as surely as I had directed Careys's knife into my mother.

Mrs. Clemm was calling to me from below, but how could I go to her now? How could I ever look into her eyes again, or bless myself with Virginia's smile? Even their forgiveness would be too painful to bear.

You might as well be dead yourself, that was the refrain that echoed inside my head. And I knew it was true, the truest thought I had ever had.

So I crawled back up toward the window. Sneaking like a mouse, I crept up to it and peeked in through the haze of smoke and saw Careys dragging Poe by the ankles, out to the hallway and into the carnation-colored light.

The window seemed smaller as I eased one leg inside, straddling the sill, then ducked and brought in the upper half of my body. The room itself seemed smaller, the ceiling two feet closer to my head now, a ceiling of gray smoke, oppressive and acrid. My eyes stung, my chest burned, but more than that my soul ached with emptiness, with the hollow red throb of futility.

Into the bedroom I crept, and toward the door. The thin fog of smoke rendered the sheeted furnishings all the more eerie, but I was resigned to their foreboding now. I heard Careys's first heavy footfalls on the stairway, the thump of Poe's body being dragged behind.

Out into the hallway then, out into the fluttering light. It was there I saw the source of the illumination, and the reason Careys's footfalls had abruptly ceased. He stood one-quarter of the way down the stairs, facing downward but still holding one of Poe's ankles in each hand, holding them like yokes atop his hips while Poe, on his back, lay unconscious. Five steps below Careys the fire had burned through the stairway, the flames were reaching up, fluttering pennants of blue and orange and golden flame. I thought how strangely beautiful they looked, how strangely sad. Everything at that moment struck me as beautiful and sad, the entire world, and certainly the way I was now walking toward the top of the stairs, heedlessly, without caution, as doomed as everyone and everything else in this sad and beautiful universe.

Just as I reached the top of the stairs Careys heard me and looked back, but I did not pause to let him grin, I threw myself forward, I sailed off the top landing, swooped down on him, flung myself at his head. He could not raise his hands fast enough to catch me. I crashed into him and together we were catapulted into the flames, into and suddenly through their heat to land in a tumble at the bottom.

He was more dazed than I, having fallen on his back with me atop him. In a second I was on my feet again. My one objective was to draw Careys away from Poe.

I vaulted out of his reach, then looked up the staircase to where Poe still lay. The flames were not far from his feet but he was beginning to stir now; his head went to one side and a hand came up to rub his cheek. I knew that if he saw me down there he would come after me, and I did not want his intervention. I did not want to be saved, but to be the savior.

And so I hurried away, out of Poe's sight. I stepped behind the door-jamb of the nearest room.

I heard Careys rising to his knees and pulling himself up, the way he grunted now with every movement. The wheeze of his angry breath enraged me. And those scratches where his claws had once raked my neck, they began to throb anew. Their heat became a liquid flame that trickled down my spine. There was no room in my mind for logic, no space in my heart for anything but black fury.

But this room was without opportunity, it was a room too small to hide in, and windowless, too dark to see my own hand before my face. Realizing this, a wave of panic rushed through me, that I had made a fatal error, I would die without revenge.

I went to the threshold and peeked out. Poe was crawling on his hands and knees, nearly to the top of the steps. Below him, at the bottom of the staircase, Careys watched, seething but impotent to follow, too stiff to ever leap upward through the thickening wall of flames.

At the top of the stairs Poe seized the banister and pulled himself to his feet. He glanced back just once, though not at me standing in the darkened threshold, and, seeing Careys unable to pursue him, thinking no doubt that I was safe outside, he hobbled toward the bedroom, coughing softly into his hand, and soon disappeared into the smoke.

Careys came down off the landing and stood there for a moment as if confused. Then he dug into a coat pocket and pulled out the thick key and lurched toward the front door.

The moment I realized what he was up to, that he was still, though circuitously, in pursuit of Poe, I stepped into the hallway again. An idea had only half formed in my mind, but there was no time left to let it take shape fully. I stepped out behind him as the key scraped into place.

"Rat bastard," I said.

He swung around at the sound of my voice. He saw me and grinned. His hand came away from the key then, leaving the key fitted to the lock. He started toward me, his hand free now to slip into another pocket, free to ease out his dagger.

I pivoted to my left and ran. But not far, another ten feet, and then with both hands stretched out before me, palms flat to strike the wooden frame of a pair of French doors. The doors flew open and I raced into Johnston Hobbs's library, his den, that vast luxurious room where he had first entertained and deluded Mr. Poe.

I had no doubts that Careys had seen me enter this room. No doubts that by virtue of the streetlight bleeding in through the windows, he would find me there. I raced to the far side of the room, to the fireplace, the fieldstone hearth. Ten seconds later I saw Careys's lank shadow passing in front of the French doors, and I hurried to position myself behind Hobbs's wing chair, shielding myself behind its high, brocaded back.

Careys came to the threshold, paused, and studied the room. A moment later he saw me huddled close behind the chair, my thin chest and shoulders, my smoke-stained face. He gave me an exhausted smile, half a twisted grin. Then stepped inside, turned, and closed the doors behind him. He faced me once again and said, "He got away for now, I'll give ya that. But don't ya worry, boy. He'll be following ya inta the grave soon enough."

He showed me the dagger then and took his time coming toward me. "Let's see if it cuts you open as easy as it did your mum, eh boy?"

I said nothing, had nothing to say. All of my energy, all of my animus, I directed into my fists.

Outside that room the house was snapping and crackling, pouring forth smoke, creaking and dying. The reflection of flames danced across the beveled glass of the broad French doors. Every breath stank of smoke, every blink burned my eyes. Yet I stood motionless, a paralyzed mouse.

I was a mouse, yes, but with the heart of a rat. For when he came around the side of the chair, when he came crabbing sideways toward me, an arm's length away, his dagger held cocked, I did not flee in the opposite direction, did not run for a mouse hole; I stepped toward him, I raised up my fists, showed him the dueling swords I clutched there—the swords yanked down off Hobbs's coat of arms above the fireplace, his shield of nobility, divine lineage—and the moment Careys's eyes widened at the sight of them, I lunged into him, I charged headlong with my wrists cocked at my waist and then thrusting outward.

Into the softness of his belly I plunged both swords, and not only that but my hatred as well, every moment of hatred in my ten hard years, rammed it all into his gut, twisting and pushing, the end of my impotence. The rattling shock of vibration rippled all the way up into my shoulders, the violence of the act lifted me up off my feet, carrying me into him as he fell. I tumbled against him, into his arms, and we crashed to the floor together.

His body writhed beneath me, his hands fluttered. My own hands, their grip finally broken, lay against his hard chest, felt the throbbing engine therein, felt the dark hot slippery flow of his blood.

I don't know how long I lay atop him, staring into his face. Long enough to watch his eyes, so darkly bright, begin to cloud. Long enough to see the bubbles of blood come out of his nostrils with every snorting breath. For a few moments his scent filled and narcotized me.

By slow degrees, my other senses returned. I tasted the slick salt of blood in my mouth, either my own from biting my lip, or Careys's, splashed upon my face. I saw what seemed a dark cloud gathering outside the French doors, hovering against the ceiling but growing thicker by the minute, and I smelled its choking scent.

All the rest is like a dream to me. I pulled away, I found my feet. I went out through the French doors and into the hallway and past the searing staircase of flames. I recall standing at the front door, working the heavy key, and feeling the fire singeing my back. I recall how the lock finally clicked, how very difficult it was to drag the door open, how weak my knees suddenly felt, how distant my feet, how cool and fresh the night as I then walked down off the porch and through the yard and around to the side.

Mrs. Clemm was standing as last I had seen her, gazing fervently up at the pantry roof, but this time with both hands pressed to the side of her head as she swayed anxiously from one heel to the other. She heard my boots scraping across the grass and she turned and saw me and cried out, "He's here! He's here! Come down quickly, oh please Eddie please hurry!"

Poe had been climbing back up the porch roof, on his way back in through the window, no doubt. Now he scrambled down to the edge and, lying on his belly, eased himself over, then dropped onto the ground.

He came to me and seized me by both shoulders, gave me one long searching look, then said, "Let's go!"

Dragging me by a sleeve he hauled me away from the house, around to the rear. Halfway to the carriage house he released my arm and immediately I turned to face the mansion; I had to look back. The house by now was a huge granite box from whose windows poured an obscene and florid light. I had started to shiver.

A window exploded, yet I did not move. "Augie!" Poe said.

I turned away from the mansion to look at him, but instead I saw the carriage house illuminated by the mansion's flames, and suddenly I cared again, I cared about living, about life itself. I sprinted toward the carriage house.

"Augie, please!" Mrs. Clemm cried out.

"There are horses in there! Two of them!"

Poe came running up behind and siezed me by the arm. "I'll turn the horses out. Take Mrs. Clemm and go."

"The side door is unlocked," I told him.

"Go!" he said.

Mrs. Clemm grasped my hand and dragged me into the darkness. We were not forty yards from the house before a whinnying was heard, and soon the harried clop of hooves on earth, a kind of countermelody to the snap and flutter of flames that had begun to tumble and roll in an echo down the street, the mansion's windows blowing out one by one, each dull explosion thumping in the soreness of my heart.

Mrs. Clemm and I were within sight of the Croton Aqueduct's reservoir on Forty-second Street when Poe caught up with us. In silence then and three abreast we hurried past that massive Egyptian edifice, that monument to a banished pharaoh, and at nearly a trot we headed north and toward that small, clean house in which Virginia lay sleeping.

49

WE WERE not far past the reservoir when Poe asked us to stop for a moment. "You go on ahead with Muddy," he told me. "I have one last bit of business for the evening."

Mrs. Clemm sighed and tapped her chest. "My goodness, Eddie. Is it never enough?"

"To the South Point docks, no farther."

"No. You come home now and rest. What good will it do to walk yourself to death?"

"I have never felt more fully charged with energy than I do this night."

"You need to attend to yourself. Look at the both of you—you're bloody, and burned, and all blackened up with soot. . . . I don't even want to know what went on inside that house."

"Do I look the ghoul?" he asked.

"You and the boy both."

"All the better." He gave me a wink.

To Mrs. Clemm he said, "There will be no more brawling, I vow."

"I know too well what you are up to," she told him. "And I know the kind of trouble it will produce."

"The trouble sets sail within the hour, Muddy. I merely hope to wish it bon voyage."

"Why can you not let matters be? Come home and be with your wife and family."

Poe flinched and was silent for a moment. Then, but gently, he told her, "There remains yet time enough for that, dear Muddy. But at the stroke of midnight the *Josephine* will depart, and my opportunity shall have been missed."

"It is not an opportunity I would have you meet."

He gave her that crooked smile of his, the one that somehow suggested both merriment and pain. "I shan't be long."

He turned and headed south, striding briskly. We watched him for a minute and then Muddy said in a very tired voice, "Go with him, son."

"But he told me—"

"He'll be needing an attendant more than I will."

"What if he sends me away?"

"Then go. But never so far that you lose sight of him."

I was eager to join him and did not argue any further. Three minutes later I sprinted up to his side. He had heard me coming and was not surprised.

"She made me," I told him.

"I thought as much."

"Is she going to be safe walking home alone?"

"Safer than we," he said.

We headed southeast together then, with me taking two strides to every one of Poe's. He would not, for another several days, ask what had happened to me inside Hobbs's mansion, and I did not that night volunteer any information. A strange kind of calm had descended on me, a feeling difficult to describe. Call it confidence and humility mixed, with a small thin streak of bittersweet regret.

In any case, we walked for several minutes before I asked, "Are you going to knock his block off when we get there?"

"I am," Poe said. "But I shall do so without laying a finger on him."

"How do you intend to do that?"

"The gentleman's way," was as much as he would tell me.

To do so we did not have to walk as far as the docks after all. Just south of Union Square we spotted an entourage advancing on foot, marching in our direction up the center of Broadway. Behind us Hobbs's mansion was lighting up the night sky with whirling plumes of glowing smoke, a million swirling embers.

Poe slowed just a bit, squinting ahead; he put out a hand to hold me back. Beneath the sputtering gaslights it soon became apparent that Hobbs himself was leading the approaching group, hurrying along as briskly as he could without sacrificing his aristocratic bearing, accompanied by eight or nine other men, all in tuxedos, many still holding the champagne flutes from which they had been sipping when news reached the ship's salon of the conflagration on Fifth Avenue.

Thirty yards or so behind this group came the females, their gowns and petticoats rustling like a dry hot wind.

Poe positioned himself in the middle of the street and crossed his arms over his chest. I stood at his side. My first instinct was to reach for his hand, but I squashed the urge and doubled up my fists instead.

Hobbs started shouting as soon as he recognized us. "By God, Poe! By God, man!"

He was quivering by the time he came face-to-face with Poe; he was trembling with so much rage that he could find no words to express it.

"Allow me to speak quickly before the ladies arrive," Poe told him. His voice was not loud or dramatic but neither was it uncertain, and so was, therefore, all the more compelling. The men in Hobbs's entourage made not a sound.

"I come only to wish you Godspeed, sir. And to pass along the same from your young mistress. I refer not to the one who died on the abortionist's table, not Mary Rogers but the second girl, the one you knew as Amanda. She sends to you her regards, as well as her hopes that in Europe you might discover a cure." And here he paused for just a second, just long enough for the final word to prick the men's curiosity.

"A cure," Poe said, "for the French pox from which she will surely die. But you? Perhaps in Europe there exists a remedy for syphilis we have not heard of here. If so, you might yet spare yourself her fate."

He now reached out a hand to clap Hobbs's shoulder. Hobbs recoiled at the touch as if Poe's hand itself were transferring to him the horror of the disease. "A lie," was all he could mutter.

"You know me too well for that."

At this Hobbs pulled away with a jerk, staggered backward. The men in his entourage did not grasp and brace him up as they would have just half a minute earlier, they drew apart from him, his tight circle of friends expanding outward as on the ripple of something repugnant tossed down from high above.

Poe too took a step away. He bowed slightly from the waist, then straightened, turned, and with his hand resting firmly atop my soot-blackened shoulder, his weight leaning into me, he set us in motion once more, northward to home and away from the lights.

50

IN THE wake of a triumph there is often a dead calm, the emptiness of an end that has come and passed and left nothing in its place. Such was the ambiance we in Poe's cottage awoke to next day.

If the morning following Poe's rescue was gray, the afternoon was pitched in black. Shortly after noon a wagon came rolling down the lane. I was at that moment on the porch steps, playing with Aristotle and a piece of dirty string. I saw the wagon and the two robust men and the shiny black piano rising from the wagon's bed to stand high above their shoulders, and I did not know whether to announce the delivery or to wave it away as if from a plague house.

By the time the wagon rolled to a stop out front, Virginia stood in the doorway. I watched the transition of emotions in her expression. Her eyes lit up so brightly at the sight of the piano, a child's eyes, gleeful, but soon her sense of thrill collapsed, as did her smile, and she said to me, "Is it paid for, Augie?"

I had no time to answer, for here came Poe pushing past her, dressed only in his banyan and slippers. He had in one hand his pocket watch and chain and in the other three volumes of his published poems. He stopped beside me long enough to whisper, "Your money. Have you any left?"

"Not a fip," I answered. "Where's yours?"

"Stolen from me in Hobbs's house."

"That bastard."

He hurried out to the wagon's driver then and attempted to strike a bargain. The pocket watch and chain, the three published volumes. The driver produced an invoice and pointed to the figure at the bottom of the paper, the balance due upon receipt, as per Poe's agreement with the piano broker. Poe insisted that they take the watch and chain and the slender books of poetry not in barter but as a small initial payment in good faith, the rest to be submitted regularly, one dollar per week. And here, wait, there were valuables inside the house as well, sketches, more writings. . . .

They argued for a full five minutes. The voices of the delivery men grew progressively harsher, Poe's weaker and more desperate. It was Virginia finally who came to the wagon and asked in a voice so sweet as to turn all anger aside if they would please extend her sincerest apologies to the piano's owner; she begged forgiveness for this inconvenience but they simply could not pay, there was no money to pay. If the good gentlemen would please be so kind as to return the piano with her profoundest regrets, if they would please be so kind, if they would please, please, please be so kind.

And we watched the wagon turn, and the delivery men go off scowling, and the piano like polished darkness throwing the dirty sunlight back into our eyes.

For the next hour or so Poe remained deaf to his wife's pleas that he come inside. Instead he paced up and down the lane in his banyan and slippers, scuffing away at the tracks in the dirt left by the wagon.

Only when the tracks had been obliterated did Poe abandon this exercise in self-negation and return inside. There he stood at the window for another half hour, looking out at we knew not what. Finally he retreated to his rocking chair, and there he remained for another hour, not rocking. He either stared at his hands folded in his lap or, if he looked up, at the blank face of the door.

Mrs. Clemm stood by the window for a while herself. When she turned away it was to announce that a nor'easter was coming. There was no suggestion from any of them that I return to the Newsboys' Lodging House just yet. Mrs. Clemm asked if I would cut some wood for the stove.

I went out back to the woodpile to chop a bucketful of kindling. I could smell and taste the rising storm now. The sky looked as hard as gunmetal, as gray as a bruise, a long dark cloud like a puckered welt approaching from the horizon.

As I split and chopped the logs I tried to think of what I could do for those people inside. I made up my mind that I would get into another mansion in a day or so, not Hobbs's unfortunately but in another just like his, because to me these men were all the same, thugs in silk and diamonds. I would steal all the fine silver and anything else I could carry, and maybe in the bargain I would leave a message for Hobbs and his ilk, I would piss on his carpets, I would torch that place too, I would embark on a methodical kind of rampage, destroying one mansion after another. I would reduce Fifth Avenue to ashes.

It was all fantasy, of course, a boy's angry dreaming. But my mood fit perfectly with the mood of the sky. I watched the local murder of crows making hard against the wind for the cover of trees, and their flight gave rise to an idea. I knew then that the thing to do, the only sensible thing for all of us to do, was precisely what Poe and Virginia longed to do, to clear out of New York City once and for all. But not to Saratoga or Richmond; we should head for the territories. Poe could do well there, a man with his gift for words; he could start his own newspaper, his own magazine, and I would personally peddle the copies to every farmhouse and sod hut west of the Mississippi.

By the time I carried the wood back inside I was so charged up by my plan that I couldn't keep quiet; I stacked the wood beside the stove and rattled on for several minutes about the inevitable prosperity that awaited all of us beyond St. Louis.

Mrs. Clemm and Virginia both smiled as they went about their evening business, preparing the evening's bread, setting the table, holding fast to routine and the illusion that if nothing had been gained through the events of the past few days, at least nothing had been lost. Before long Virginia needed to rest and she went to the sofa and lay back and covered herself with a shawl.

Just as she had made herself comfortable she was racked by a spell of coughing. She pressed one hand to her mouth, the other to her bosom, until the bruising episode passed. And I saw clearly now for the first time, saw in the grief of her mother's eyes and the misery in Poe's, how every breath she took was another small blow to her strength, another soreness, so that just the act of living, the deliberate effort of breathing in and breathing out, reminded her, reminded all of us, of the tenuousness of existence, the evanescent moments that remained.

It was then Mrs. Clemm answered my earlier soliloquy with a look, a look at her daughter and then a look at me, and suddenly all the wind went out of my sails because I understood as clearly as she did that Virginia could never make the trip out west. Even the constant talk of moving to Saratoga was but a fancy. A journey as brief as her walk to the piano wagon had all but ruined her for the rest of the day.

At one point Poe rose and went to Virginia and asked if she was warm enough. She said yes and asked him to read to her awhile. But all he did was to smooth the hair from her brow and smile down at her as if he hadn't heard, and then he returned to his chair and his ruminations.

After a while Mrs. Clemm spooned the soup into bowls and took a loaf of bread from the oven. She asked us all to sit and eat now, but I was the only one who came to the table. Her blessing that evening was especially protracted, especially hoarse. Then she and I ate our soup without conversation.

After a while Poe asked if he might have a glass of brandy, and to this nobody moved or replied. Mrs. Clemm looked down at her soup bowl and Virginia turned her eyes to the wall. And finally Poe nodded to himself and said nothing more.

The rain began about eight that evening. We could hear it pocking on the roof and plinking hard against the glass. The wind howled like a pack of distant dogs, and the hemlocks at the side of the cottage swept their branches back and forth across the wood, shushing us again and again, a repetitious reprimand all the more harsh for our silence.

Unexpectedly, Poe came alive. He stood sharply, straightened his jacket, and asked Mrs. Clemm if he might have use of the table. "Of course," she said. She cleared away her knitting and went to sit in the vacated rocker.

Poe went quickly to his trunk and pulled out all of his manuscripts stored there, the poems and the essays and the stories, and he spread them across the table and then laid a clean sheet of vellum over each manuscript. He took out his ink and pen and then sat at the table and pulled the first manuscript to him.

For the next hour I watched as Poe considered each piece of writing in turn and noted one by one where each manuscript had been sent or delivered and then rejected, or in a few cases where the piece had been accepted and how much he was to be paid for it. For each of those not yet sold he listed the remaining markets untried.

In the beginning he was full of energy and eagerness, thinking, I suppose, that his fortunes could yet be made by his genius if only he could figure out where to market it, the one right place where an editor's ear would be tuned to the frequency of Poe's hard-chosen words.

But as manuscript after manuscript was pushed to the side, and the evidence of his failure piled higher and higher, his spirits sagged again, a slow but ineluctable descent of hope, as graceful to my eyes as a leaf's slow fall from a high branch down to salty water.

Virginia saw it too. She had been watching him as closely as I had, of course. And now she began to weep. It was the first acknowledgment any of us had made to the mire of their situation. She made barely a sound, yet Poe heard. He lifted his head and looked to her, and a moment later he was at her side. They sat holding hands for several minutes, his head against hers.

"My Eddie," she said then, and stroked the back of his head. "I am so sorry for all the darkness I have brought into your life."

"Beloved," Poe told her, and laid a hand to her scarlet cheek, "you are light itself. You are my only illumination in this black, black world."

They fell asleep like that. And Mrs. Clemm, bent over her knitting, did likewise. And I dozed off as well, though fitfully, because each crack of lightning or quick rumble of thunder jerked me up out of my dreams. As did, sometime well into the night, a steady knocking sound, crisp and quick and brittle. I sat awake for half a minute before I identified the source, and then I rose and went into the bedroom and crossed to the window and saw there the crow perched outside on the sill, its plumage as shiny as ink, its eyes bright yellow. The bird was pecking at its own warped reflection in the rain-blurred pane, and I shooed the lank visitor away before its incessant tapping could break the glass.

Poe was awake, though not fully, when I came back into the sitting room. "Is there someone at the door?" he asked.

I told him, "It was nothing. Don't worry."

He must have heard the shudder in my voice, the chill I could not suppress, for now he gazed about the room, blinking slowly, as if he had never seen this room before, as if all were unrecognizable.

"What is it?" he asked in a hoarse whisper. "Who's come?"

I spoke softly to him then, because I did not want Virginia to hear, not even in her sleep. "Just a crow at the window is all. It's gone now, don't worry."

He looked down at his wife; he fingered a strand of her hair. "She should stop feeding those birds," he finally said.

"She's a gentle soul, all right."

He nodded, then laid his head down beside his wife's again.

I pulled my blankets into the corner, close to the stove, and I curled around myself, and I too fell asleep eventually, exhausted by the storm.

It must have been nearly 3 A.M. when I awoke to a familiar sound. I looked up to see Poe there at the table again, bent low over a manuscript, his fingers already stained with ink, his pen scratching quick across the paper. And in his eyes as he wrote there was that familiar bright fire again, not extinguished at all but only suppressed for a while, now flaring as bright as ever with the heat of a new idea. I could almost hear the throbbing rhythm of his mind as the pen unfurled his sentences. The man had a metronome for a pulse.

He paused after a while and, searching his mind for a particular word, happened to glance in my direction, and saw me watching. I wished for all the world that I could give him what he needed.

A moment later a smile came to his mouth. "Respite," he whispered as if trying it out, testing its sound, and a moment later the fire in his eyes flared once more, "respite and nepenthe," as if he had just then discovered it, something important, the answer, or maybe just the elusive phrase, and he went back to his work then, mouth set in a thin, hard smile, head bowed as in prayer, while the rain drummed and his pen scratched on and a single lock of hair as black as a raven's feather hung over one bright and restless eye.